KHAN

KHAN

Nicholas Grant

LITTLE, BROWN AND COMPANY

A *Little, Brown* Book

First published in Great Britain in 1993
by Little, Brown and Company

Copyright © Nicholas Grant 1993

The moral right of the author has been asserted.

All rights reserved.
No part of this publication may be reproduced,
stored in a retrieval system, or transmitted, in any
form or by any means, without the prior
permission in writing of the publisher, nor be
otherwise circulated in any form of binding or
cover other than that in which it is published and
without a similar condition including this
condition being imposed on the subsequent purchaser.

A CIP catalogue record for this book is
available from the British Library.

ISBN 0 316 90413 9

Typeset in Sabon by Leaper & Gard Ltd, Bristol
Printed and bound in Great Britain by
Clays Ltd, St Ives plc.

Little, Brown and Company (UK) Limited
165 Great Dover Street
London SE1 4YA

This is a novel. The characters are invented and are not intended to portray real persons, living or dead.
 The events depicted have not yet happened.

And from this chasm, with ceaseless turmoil seething,
As if this earth in fast thick pants were breathing,
A mighty fountain momently was forced.

           Samuel Taylor Coleridge, *Kubla Khan*

CONTENTS

PROLOGUE: OCTOBER 2000 — 3

THE FIRST PART: SHADOW ON THE STEPPES

The First Chronicle: London, October 2000 — 41
   CHAPTER 1: Yakutiya, Spring 1976 — 48
The Second Chronicle: Moscow, October 2000 — 61
   CHAPTER 2: Omsk, 1976–8 — 66
The Third Chronicle: Moscow, October 2000 — 89
   CHAPTER 3: Afghanistan, 1979–86 — 95
The Fourth Chronicle: Yakutiya, October 2000 — 122
   CHAPTER 4: The Steppes, Summer 1989 — 134
The Fifth Chronicle: Yakutiya, October 2000 — 144
   CHAPTER 5: Yakutiya, Spring 1996 — 149

THE SECOND PART: THE WARLORD

The Sixth Chronicle: Yakutsk, December 2000 — 169
   CHAPTER 6: Yakutsk, December 2000 — 174
The Seventh Chronicle: Yakutsk, December 2000 — 193
   CHAPTER 7: Yakutsk, Spring 2001 — 201
The Eighth Chronicle: Yakutsk, Spring 2001 — 218
   CHAPTER 8: Yakutsk, Spring 2001 — 225
The Ninth Chronicle: Yakutsk, Spring 2001 — 244
   CHAPTER 9: Yakutsk, Spring 2001 — 253

The Tenth Chronicle: Yakutsk, Spring 2001   272
   CHAPTER 10: The West, Summer 2001   279

THE THIRD PART: GENGHIS KHAN

The Eleventh Chronicle: Yakutistan, Summer 2004   299
   CHAPTER 11: Yakutsk, Summer 2004   319
The Twelfth Chronicle: Yakutsk, Summer 2004   327
   CHAPTER 12: Yakutsk, 2004–5   333
The Thirteenth Chronicle: Yakutistan, Spring 2005   346
   CHAPTER 13: New York, Summer 2005   356
The Fourteenth Chronicle: New York, Summer 2005   370
   CHAPTER 14: Kazakhstan, Summer 2005   377
The Fifteenth Chronicle: Yakutsk, Autumn 2005   402
   CHAPTER 15: Yakutsk, October 2005   420
The Sixteenth Chronicle: Yakutsk, October 2005   425
   CHAPTER 16: Yakutsk, October 2005   440

PROLOGUE

October 2000

The evening was shrouded in a steady fall of snow, driven by a freezing north-easterly wind. In the high steppes of north-central Siberia, winter was due, in mid-October. The skies were grey, in keeping with the landscape. But the River Lena, broad and powerful, continued to flow to the north, rushing down from the mountains of Central Asia, enjoying a last few weeks of freedom before even this bubbling water was seized in a frozen grip; its lower reaches would already be packed with ice.

This vast plain, dominated by the river, was nothing more than a huge forest of pine and larch, but where there was a clearing, close to the water, a group of eight people, two of them women, waited, their horses' heads drooping in the wind. Men and women wore fur-lined jackets and pants, boots and gloves, fur-lined hats. Occasionally one of them would slap their hands together. They looked along the bridle path that followed the riverbank, peering into the gloom.

It had been snowing for several days, and there were drifts. The white carpet deadened all sound save for the swish of the river; the horseman emerged from the white mist before they heard him, walking his shaggy Mongol pony, exactly like those waiting for him, along the path. He guided his horse up to the others, and drew rein.

'Is it ready, Maloun?' asked one of the waiting men.

'All is ready, Prince Batalji,' said the new arrival.

The man who had asked the question turned his head to look from face to face. 'Then it is time.'

He urged his horse forward, rode beside the new arrival. 'Tell me what has been done,' he said.

Batalji Borjigin, Prince of the Borjigin tribe of the Mongol nation – though his title, and even his nation, had long been officially abolished by the Soviets – was a big man, not very tall, but with wide, powerful shoulders, so heavily muscled they almost gave his back a hunch. His legs were long, and equally strong; they clung to the pony's ribs as if the animal and the man were one. Batalji's features were broad, Mongoloid, but handsome. And frightening. The mouth was a flat line, the chin arrogant, the nostrils flaring with surging energy. The eyes were black and never changed expression. He was armed with an AK-92 carbine slung on his shoulder and two sidearms – a conventional Browning automatic pistol, and, hardly larger, a Skorpion machine-pistol – while a long-bladed knife was thrust through his belt. Another belt, of grenade pouches, was strung round his waist, and a haversack, containing the plastic spare magazines for the AKS, was slung over his shoulder. Incongruously, also thrust through the belt was a yataghan, the long, slightly curved, razor-sharp sword of the steppes.

His companion was altogether smaller, and diffident. 'The commanders wait at the house,' he said. 'But their people are in position. Will it be tonight, Prince Batalji?'

The big man nodded. 'The blizzard is our ally.' He allowed his horse to fall back, so that he rode beside the two women, whose faces and bodies were bundled beneath the thick winter clothing. They too were heavily armed. 'You will remain outside the city, Mother, with Barone, until it is safe to enter,' Batalji said.

'No,' his mother said. 'I will accompany you. We fight and win, or die, together.'

Batalji looked at the other woman. 'You will obey me, Mortana.'

Mortana made no reply, but her mother-in-law gave a snort of laughter. 'It is right for a wife to obey her husband.'

'My fate is your fate,' Mortana said quietly.

'No,' Batalji said. 'Your fate is to be the mother of Barone, and the others waiting at home. When I die, they will take my place.'

Mortana reached from her horse to his, closing her gloved

hand on his. 'Do not die, Batalji. Not now.'

He grinned. 'I do not mean to.'

The little band rounded a bend in the river, and even through the snowflakes could make out the huge glow, still several miles away.

'Is that Yakutsk?' asked the young man who rode immediately behind the two women, his voice eager; he had never seen it before.

'It is the city,' Batalji agreed, and now rode beside his son. 'You will remain with your mother, Barone, until I send for you.'

'But, Father, am I not your strong right arm?' Like his father, and the women, and everyone else in the group, he was armed with a variety of weapons, principal amongst which was the AK-92, the latest version of the Kalashnikov.

'You are your mother's protector,' Batalji reminded him. He knew the boy would obey him. They were close enough in age to be friends, for Batalji was only thirty-eight and Barone already twenty, and for the past five years they had campaigned together, on the steppes. Now he pointed. 'Over there.'

The suburbs, a gloomy row of apartment buildings, were strung along the river to the north, and now the group was being joined by other men, who had been waiting in the shelter of the high-rises, where the bridle path ended in a metalled road.

'Greetings, Batalji,' said one of the newcomers. 'We are ready.'

Batalji nodded. 'Greetings, my father. How many men have you?' In the darkness it was difficult to be sure.

'Seventy-nine.'

'Time check.' They compared the luminous dials of their watches. 'My son and your daughter will stay with you, Khalim,' Batalji told his father-in-law. 'Remain quiet until twelve o'clock. Then put up your roadblock. No one is to leave the houses, either. Post men on the street doors, and shoot anyone who attempts to get out.'

Khalim Anhusat nodded. 'I understand.'

Batalji squeezed his shoulder, and returned to where the women waited. Mortana threw back the cowl covering her face, the better to see him. She was thirty-five, and for more than ten years had lived the life of a fugitive outlaw, at her husband's side. Yet her features were still those of a girl, even if her figure had thickened. To Batalji they remained beautiful features, however often he might have strayed to other tents, other beds – monogamy was not a Mongol trait. 'In a few hours,' he said, 'all will be avenged.' He turned his horse and rode down the street, his mother at his elbow.

Selphine was herself only fifty-four, and she also retained the looks which had once turned the heads of more than one nomad herdsman. But on her the high forehead and cheekbones, the firm mouth and pointed chin, the deep black eyes – her tawny hair was concealed beneath her fur hat – had hardened into a rigid mask of anger and hatred. Selphine was this night indeed given an almost unearthly beauty by her glowing ardour: she had waited twenty-four years for this day.

Yakutsk huddled against this first blizzard of the year; its people knew the snow would now be with them until next April. They sat in front of their television sets to watch the flickering reception; most of their programmes came all the way from Moscow, more than three thousand miles away, brought by means of a series of relay stations, all liable to be affected by the snow – only a few people had satellite dishes.

Yet they were content to be snug and warm, well fed and comfortable. Yakutsk, especially in winter, was a totally self-contained entity; it had no choice. In the summer, it was a bustling place, a seaport on the rushing River Lena, which led down to the Arctic Sea. From Yakutsk were shipped vast quantities of lignite coal; the city sat on a base of permafrost four hundred feet thick, packed with fossilised forests left behind when the first Ice Age had dawned. In the winter all external trade ceased; the only link with the outside world was by means of the airport built by the Soviets, close to the city, but few people visited Yakutsk in the winter, even when the airport was not closed for ice or fog.

For centuries after the coming of man, these inhospitable wastes had been the cradle of conquerors. Here on the steppes from time immemorial the nomads had driven their herds to and fro, south in the winter, north again in the summer. As the centuries had passed the clans had become tribes, the tribes had become hordes, the hordes had become moving nations. Vast as was the area of central Asia, it was not vast enough. As civilisation had fastened its grip on China, celestial emperors had built a huge wall to keep out the nomads and their destructive ways. Repelled and constricted in the east, the people of the steppes had wandered west, seeking space. That movement had in turn set other people moving, away from the fearsome Huns, as they had then been known. The Middle East and Europe had been subjected to wave upon wave of hungry immigrants, Goths, Avars, Vandals, until in the fifth Christian century had come the Huns themselves, to spread devastation almost to the English Channel and precipitate the Dark Ages.

The Huns had been followed, at an interval in time, by the Turks. But the Turks, readily converted to Islam, had been comparatively civilised when compared with *their* successors, the Mongols, led by Temujin Borjigin – he they had called the Great King, Genghis Khan – and *his* descendant and successor, Timur the Lame.

Around the campfires of Central Asia, only three historical names were of any importance: Alexander the Greek, the Macedonian marvel who had only scraped at the edges of Siberia; Temujin the Mongol; and Timur the Tatar.

But that had been long ago. Even Timur was all but six hundred years in the past in this October of 2000. Since his time the people of the steppes had been brutalised into submission by the onward march of Imperial Russia. Yakutsk itself had been founded as a frontier post in 1637, and had grown with each generation. Yet although the shamans had been forced to conceal their magic, and sacred ikons had replaced the gods of the thunder and the wind, and the khans had bowed their heads before the name of a man called Tzar, whom they had never seen, the life of the nomads had not greatly been interfered with, until the coming of the Commissars, only eighty years ago, sent by a new Tzar, named Lenin.

The Commissars would claim to have brought civilisation to Yakutsk, and its neighbourhood. Within the city, roads had been paved, and street lighting had appeared – powered by electricity, Lenin's panacea for all ills; there was enough rushing water in Yakutiya to provide electricity for all Asia. Natural gas had been discovered, and had proved another source of energy. Even a university had been founded, to educate the Yakuts in the ways of Marxist civilisation, and where there had never been roads, there was now one at the least, a huge motorway stretching south almost to the Chinese border, and east to the Pacific port of Magadan. That a few thousand recalcitrants had had to be shot was surely a small price to pay for such benefits.

Even the Commissars, however, with their machine-guns, their dogs and their lists, had been unable to bring Yakutiya properly and fully within the Soviet system. It was not possible to institute collective farms where there were no farms, in a country where even the Trans-Siberian Railway was six hundred miles to the south of its border, and the climate varied from plus fifteen degrees centigrade in July to minus forty in January. Nor was it possible properly to regiment a people who from time immemorial had been on the move. The Commissars had tried, had shot a few thousand more recalcitrants, but had been forced to realise they were dealing with something more primeval even than the dialectic. Thus had been formed the Yakut Autonomous Soviet Socialist Republic, a vast area, one million, two hundred thousand square miles – six times the size of France – occupying two-thirds of north-central Siberia, part of the Soviet Union, but allowed to go its own way so long as it paid lip service to Moscow, forgotten by the rest of the world behind its mounds of snow, its huge mountains, and its vast forests.

PROLOGUE

As if the land, and the climate, which had spawned Attila and Genghis and Timur could ever be truly forgotten.

Batalji Borjigin and his six companions walked their horses down the main street of Yakutsk, The Avenue, recently completed, the supreme achievement of the Taychin regime, a broad concourse cut through the very heart of the city. Illuminated by the streetlamps and the shop windows, this wintry night The Avenue, the Champs-Elyseés of Yakutsk, was all but deserted; there were few cars in Yakutsk, and only the occasional vehicle slithered by in the snow. The horses' hooves made no sound on the white carpet, and if anyone glanced from a curtained or shuttered window at the seven people, it was no more than a glance. This was a night for staying indoors.

A policeman, greatcoated and fur-hatted, stamping booted feet and slapping gloved hands together, hailed the little band from a street corner and was answered with a jest. They were from the mines, come to enjoy the fleshpots on a Saturday night. With their weapons concealed there was nothing to prove them liars. The policeman was aware that out on the steppes, it was said, there lurked the brigand Batalji Borjigin, who called himself a prince and claimed to be a direct descendant of the Genghis Khan, and who for ten years had left a trail of robbery and rebellion, mayhem and murder, through Yakutiya. Like most representatives of the government, he blamed the collapse of the old regime, the misguided attempts at reform by men like Gorbachev and Yeltsin and their successors, for the breakdown in law and order which had permitted villains like Borjigin to create legends for themselves, but he also knew that Borjigin had mounted an abortive coup four years before, which, though it had caused the death of old Andrei Taychin, had been such a disastrous failure little had been heard of the bandit since. Indeed, at the time, Borjigin himself had been reputed to have died of a bullet wound. Certainly he had disappeared, and not been heard of again. Only during this last summer had there come a whisper out of the steppes that he was actually alive. But the government, and the police force, discounted that as the sort of rumour which always followed the death of a folk hero, the sort of thing on which the Christian religion had been founded.

Anyway, the patrolman did not suppose even Batalji Borjigin, dead or alive, was going to be abroad on a night like this, and besides, judging by the last time, should Borjigin ever again come to Yakutsk, he would surely be accompanied by a horde of shrieking, yelling Mongols, not five grinning middle-aged men and one woman. He watched the little group walk round the corner, and disappear.

Batalji led his people to the house of Hilaim the wine merchant, several streets away from The Avenue. Three knocks, and they were admitted into a darkened hallway, to stamp the snow from their boots and brush it from their coats. Hilaim peered at them. 'Prince Batalji,' he said.

'Are our people ready?'

'They wish only to hear from you, great Prince. Your captains are inside. Princess.' He bowed to Selphine, recognising her as she took off her outer clothes.

'This is the day,' she said.

Hilaim licked his lips. He was nervous. To talk, to plan, to dream ... that was easy. But to put the talk, the plans, the dreams into reality was frightening. He remembered the last time. Failure meant death, and death at the hands of Boris Taychin's secret police would not be an easy business.

Batalji opened the inner door, and entered Hilaim's tasting room. Here a dozen men were gathered, still wearing their outdoor clothes. Their weapons were stacked in the corner, but most retained revolvers or automatic pistols in their belts. Selphine accompanied him into the inner room, and the man named Maloun. The other four men remained in the hallway, on guard.

On a table in the centre of the room was spread a large map of Yakutsk and its immediate environs. There was another table against the wall, and on this there was a television set.

This was switched on, but the sound had been turned down. 'Let us hear what he has to say,' Batalji commanded.

The volume was increased, and they gazed at the man seated before a desk in front of the cameras. He was a middle-aged man, with a close-cropped head of white hair and a strong face, made slightly sinister by his thin moustache.

He was just coming to the end of his telecast. 'Thus I know you will support me in this,' he said. 'Our Russian comrades need our assistance, and as always in the past, we shall give it to them. It is, it always will be, the policy of this government to support Moscow, whatever sacrifices this entails for ourselves. That way lies prosperity for us all. The new decree will take effect from midnight tonight.'

His face faded, and the announcer said, 'That was His Excellency Boris Taychin, President of Yakutiya. Now...'

Batalji waved his hand, and Hilaim switched off the set. 'What was he saying this time?' Batalji asked.

'What he says every winter: that we must ration our coal stocks because most of it is to be shipped to European Russia,' Hilaim said. 'As usual.'

'The lighters are loaded, and leave tomorrow,' said one of the other men. 'It is necessary to beat the ice.'

'Has it been paid for?' Batalji asked.

'Oh, yes. According to Taychin.'

'That is good.' Batalji bent over the map for several seconds, while his men waited, then he sat down, and from inside his coat took a sheet of paper. This he unfolded and placed before himself on the map, while he thumbed a ballpoint into readiness. 'Kalmane?'

'The last flight landed thirty minutes ago, Prince Batalji. My men are in position.'

'Tell me your orders.'

'I and my people will disarm the guards and seize the control tower and the administrative offices. We will kill all members of the secret police or known members of the Taychin clique on duty at the airport. We will prevent any news of what has happened from leaving the airport. We will await further orders.'

Batalji made a tick on his paper. 'Jagnuth.' He raised his head to look at his brother-in-law; Jagnuth Anhusat was his most faithful follower, thus he had the second most responsible assignment this night.

'I and my people will arrest General Simonoslov at his house. We will take him and his family to the army barracks, and make him neutralise his men. We will secure all radio equipment. We will tell the soldiers we will not harm them if they do not interfere. We will not execute Simonoslov or his family without further orders. We will make Simonoslov command his drivers to operate the tanks. We will man the tanks and at the appointed time take up our positions.'

Batalji ticked. 'Pirale.'

'I and my people will surround the central police barracks, disarm the men on duty, and place the remainder under arrest. Policemen on beat duty will be arrested. Anyone who resists will be shot. All secret police will be shot, whether they surrender or not.'

Batalji ticked. 'Maloun.'

'I and my people will seize the television and radio building. Anyone who resists us will be shot. As it will be late, we will simply continue the current programme; it is in any event recorded. We shall stand by to make the announcement as soon as we are ordered to do so.'

Batalji ticked. 'Carowan.'

'My people are in position, ready to seize the telephone exchange. Anyone who resists will be shot.'

Batalji ticked. 'Dalnuth?'

'My men are in position, ready to take control of the university. Any students or professors who resist will be shot.'

Batalji ticked. 'Sartine.'

'My people are waiting to throw up roadblocks at the southern exit from the city.'

Batalji nodded as he ticked. 'Khalim is already in position at the northern exit, with my son Barone.'

'What of the military aircraft?' someone asked. 'The helicopters?'

'They are grounded by the blizzard,' Batalji said. 'By tomorrow morning they will be in our hands.'

'They will be my responsibility,' Kalmane promised.

Batalji nodded. 'Now, Almani.'

'My men are waiting, Prince Batalji.'

Batalji made his last tick, and looked around the faces. 'The operation will commence at ten minutes past midnight. Check your watches against mine. The time is three minutes to eight.'

'Three minutes to eight,' they agreed.

'Then take up your positions and alert your people. Remember, go into action at ten minutes past midnight. There will be no further orders until after that. This especially applies to your tanks, Jagnuth. I want them on the main streets, I want them outside the Presidential Palace, I want them outside the International Hotel, and I want them covering the docks, at ten past midnight. But keep your radios turned to the national wavelength. Maloun, you have the announcement?'

'Yes, Prince Batalji.'

'You will read it the moment you receive a telephone call from Carowan. I will join you immediately afterwards.'

'Yes, Prince Batalji.'

'Well, then, go to your people.'

'Wait.' Selphine, hitherto only a spectator, spoke brusquely; she was the only person present who would dare contradict the Prince. 'Where is the old man?'

There was movement from the dark recess of the room, and the shaman stepped into the light. He wore a beard, and his clothes exuded a rank odour. His grey hair was scattered. 'We seek the blessings of the gods,' Selphine told him.

The shaman did a little shuffling dance, raising his foot and stamping it down again as he slowly rotated, while uttering a sound from the back of his throat, 'Hi*yum*, hi*yum*, hi*yum*.' He did this for several minutes, while the men and the woman watched. Then he stopped, panting.

'Well?' Selphine demanded.

'Pierroun will ride at your side this night,' the shaman said, his voice hoarse.

'Give him a bottle,' Selphine told Hilaim, and looked at the men. 'Now obey the Khan.'

The men looked at Batalji, whose face was expressionless. Selphine knew that Batalji did not believe in gods, even the gods of the steppes, only in himself. 'Go,' he said. 'I will see you again when this is over.'

The men filed out, each in turn bowing to Selphine. Hilaim closed and locked the door behind them. Almani had also left, although his people would be under the direct command of Batalji himself. Now only Batalji and his mother remained in the wine store, with Hilaim and the shaman, who was drinking vodka from the neck of his bottle. 'I would like a glass of vodka,' Selphine said.

'Of course, Princess.' Hilaim looked at Batalji. 'And for you, your highness?'

'No,' Batalji said. 'But fetch one for my mother.'

Hilaim hurried off. Selphine sat down, her elbows on the table. 'I have waited twenty-four years for this moment,' she said.

Batalji rested his hand on her shoulder. They had been separated for so long, between his childhood and his manhood, vital years in the formation of a man's character, in which a mother's love is so important. Lacking that had made him what he was. But for ten years she had been content to ride beside this man of steel who had once been her son, and plan for this night. Now he could feel the tension beneath his fingers. 'Then what are four hours?' he asked, quietly.

She raised her head to look at him. Hilaim brought the glass of vodka, and she waved it away; Hilaim drank it himself. 'I fear only betrayal,' Selphine muttered.

'There is no risk of that now, Mother,' Batalji said. 'It is Taychin who is being betrayed.'

'Do not forget your promise,' Selphine said. 'To give him to me.'

'I will not forget.'

'And his women,' Selphine said. She peered at her son. 'Tonight you will have the American woman.'

Batalji grinned. 'Tonight is not the night to think of women, Mother.'

'The American is the woman for you,' Selphine insisted. 'She will bear you another three fine sons. Mortana understands this.'

'We shall see,' Batalji said. 'Yakutiya is the woman for me, Mother. And I shall seize *her* this night.'

At eleven-thirty Batalji and Selphine and the four bodyguards left the wine merchant's house. Hilaim accompanied them, carefully locking the door behind them, having already locked the shaman in the wine store to drink himself insensible; Hilaim's wife and grandchildren had barricaded themselves in the cellars and would remain there until this night was decided, one way or the other – his sons and daughters, with their wives and husbands, were in Almani's strike force.

Now the snow was falling more thickly than ever, and was gathered several inches deep on the street as the last of the late-night traffic disappeared. 'There was no need to detach Kalmane to seize the airport,' Selphine remarked. 'It is closed anyway.'

The seven of them walked along the street to gain The Avenue. Here there was a policeman, tramping to and fro. 'Good evening,' Batalji said.

'Good evening, comrade,' the policeman said. 'You are out late.'

'Too late,' Batalji said. 'It is time I was in bed.' Presumably the policeman was already in the rifle-sights of one of Pirale's men.

They crossed The Avenue, treading carefully in the snow, and made their way down the street opposite, which led to the Presidential Palace, another Taychin creation, less than five years old, a huge rambling building in the worst possible taste. To their right, further down The Avenue, the International Hotel still glowed with light, but there were only a few lights in the Palace. They moved into the shadows at the side of the road and were joined by Almani and four men.

'The others are in position,' Almani said.

Batalji pushed up his sleeve to look at his watch. It was four minutes past midnight. He kept his eyes trained on the watch, feeling his wrist begin to prickle with the cold. But it was only a few minutes more. After twenty-four years, he thought. He was about to fulfil his destiny. Or die. But as one who had survived the *mujahedin* in Afghanistan, and then ten years of riding the steppes as a wanted outlaw, death held no terrors. While victory promised rewards of which he was afraid even to dream.

'I will take the gate,' Almani said. He too was looking at his watch.

'No,' Batalji said. 'I will take the gate.' Selphine and Almani looked at him in alarm. 'It is my duty, and my privilege,' Batalji told them.

He gave Hilaim his carbine and his sword, checked his hand grenades, then drew the automatic pistol and screwed a silencer into the muzzle. He put the pistol into the right-hand pocket of his coat, took a grenade from his belt and wrapped it in a loop of cloth, from which extended two strings, then placed it in his other pocket; his machine-pistol was concealed beneath his jacket. 'Wait for the explosion,' he said.

It was seven minutes past midnight. Batalji left the shadows and strolled towards the closed and locked wrought-iron gate which fronted the drive into the Presidential Palace grounds. Inside there were three armed guards, stamping about in the snow, slapping their hands together. Batalji knew there would be a fourth man inside the little sentry box, from which telephone wires led up to the palace itself. 'Good evening, comrades,' he said, standing against the outside of the bars.

'Good evening,' the guards replied.

'Have you got a light?' Batalji asked.

They exchanged glances, then one put his hand in his pocket. As he did so, Batalji drew his pistol and fired three times through the bars, once into each of the three guards in front of him. Two of the men were killed outright, and fell to the ground. The third managed to draw his own pistol, so

Batalji shot him a second time, sending him spinning away from the gate.

The door of the sentry box swung open, and Batalji shot the man inside. This range was greater, and the man was not killed; he tried to get up and draw his own weapon, so Batalji shot him three more times. Then he attached the grenade to the gate lock by its loop of cloth, tying the strings to the bars, pulled out the pin, and ran back thirty yards before falling to the ground, almost disappearing into the snow.

The explosion was surprisingly flat, but the gate sagged open. Batalji got up, now drawing his machine-pistol – there was no more reason for concealment – and pushed open the shattered gate. The dying man inside the box was reaching for the phone. Batalji shot him through the head. The phone was buzzing. Batalji picked it up. 'What was that explosion?' a voice asked.

'Someone threw a grenade at the gate,' Batalji said. 'We have shot him. You had better come down here, Captain.'

'Is everything under control?' the captain asked.

'Everything is under control,' Batalji assured him. 'But I think you should come down. I believe this man is the bandit Borjigin.'

'Borjigin? Batalji Borjigin?'

'That is correct, Captain. It would be a feather in our cap, in your cap, eh, if it is he?'

'I'm on my way,' the captain said.

Batalji replaced the phone and looked at his watch. It was nine minutes past the hour. By now Almani and Selphine and Hilaim had joined him, together with some thirty men armed with assault rifles and pistols. Several even had rocket-launching RPGs. Batalji took back his sword and carbine, thrust the sword through his belt, holstered his pistol, waved his people to left and right, and moved up the drive. As he did so there were several shots and explosions in other parts of the city, a sudden upsurge of noise; it was ten past twelve.

The guard captain ran down the drive towards the gate, followed by half a dozen men. 'Something is happening!' he shouted at the dimly visible figure of Batalji. 'There has been a telephone call from the airport, but it was cut off. Something about...'

He stopped running to peer at Batalji, and Batalji opened fire with his AK-92, as did his companions in the bushes to either side. The captain and his men died instantly. Batalji jumped over them and ran at the Palace steps. More men appeared, and were cut down in the swathe of fire. Someone slammed the huge front doors of the Palace; instantly three of the RPGs exploded. The doors burst apart. The men inside were staggering from the effects of the blast, and were immediately cut down in a hail of bullets. By now the rest of Almani's men had come up, and there were some hundred rebels inside the building. Every man had previously been issued with a plan of the Palace, and knew exactly where he had to go, and what he had to do. One squad moved for the radio room, another for the television room, a third for the guard barracks, a fourth for the roof.

Batalji ran up the main staircase, Selphine immediately behind him. A man emerged on the first landing and opened fire. His first bullet hit Batalji's shoulder, spun him round, and threw him to the floor. Selphine killed the man with a single shot, then knelt beside her son, peering at the tear in his jacket through which blood was oozing. 'It has happened again,' she gasped in sudden terror. 'We are lost!'

Batalji was back on his knees, lips twisted with pain, but with laughter as well. 'It is nothing, this time. It came out the other side. Taychin!'

He was back on his feet and running along the gallery, behind his mother, now. Selphine reached another set of double doors, these with gilt panelling over the wood. She fired a burst at the lock, and then kicked them open, Batalji and half a dozen men behind her. The room inside was in darkness, but Selphine switched on the lights. This was an ornately furnished antechamber, and was empty, but beyond were yet more doors. Selphine hurled these open. Here the lights were on, and she gazed at the huge four-poster bed, the woman sitting up in it; yellow-haired, and handsome in a dissolute manner, she held the covers to her naked breasts.

'Where is he?' Selphine demanded. The woman gasped, and pointed at the window. Selphine went to the window, looked out, at the terrace. She ran outside, stepped back as a bullet smashed into the stonework beside her head, sending concrete splinters in every direction. 'Take him alive!' she shouted.

Batalji sat on the bed, at the woman's feet; he was suddenly tired, and his sleeve was stained with blood. Two of his men helped him take off his coat; the woman stared at them with enormous eyes, slowly sliding her body beneath the covers, which were now held to her chin.

'They have him,' Selphine said, with some satisfaction. 'Bring him up here,' she shouted. 'Trying to escape, naked, in the snow!' she snorted. She came back into the bedroom. 'Where is the bitch?' she asked.

The woman licked her lips. 'In . . . the apartment.'

'Shit!' Selphine commented. 'He fucks his mistress with his wife in the same house. You!' She pointed at one of the men. 'Go and fetch Madame Taychin. Don't hurt her.' She stood beside her son, watched the bloodstained shirt being torn open to expose the bleeding flesh. 'Fetch the doctor,' she said. 'He lives on the premises.' She grinned. 'President Taychin is a hypochondriac.' She kissed Batalji. 'It is a clean wound, as you say. How do you feel?'

'I will be all right.' Batalji rolled up his shirt and held it against the wound.

'Fetch vodka,' Selphine told another of the men. She stood above the woman in the bed, used the muzzle of her rifle to lift the sheet and look at what lay beneath, then whipped it right off. The woman shivered; she had a very white, voluptuous body. 'Taychin's plaything,' Selphine remarked, contemptuously. 'Do you want her, Batalji?' Batalji shook his head. Selphine laughed. 'No, you want the American. Well, you will have her.' She looked at the door, and the people crowding in.

Four of Almani's men were dragging a fifth man between

them. He no longer fought them, and there were bruises on his naked flesh where he had been kicked, while he shivered from the cold to which he had exposed himself in his effort to escape. He was the middle-aged man from the television screen, and could now be seen to have a paunch. He panted for breath, his gasps increasing as he saw Batalji, and then Selphine.

'Well, Boris,' Selphine remarked. 'Everything comes to he who waits. Or she, eh?' Boris Taychin licked his lips and attempted to speak, but could not. 'Put him on the bed,' Selphine commanded. 'Where is the doctor?'

'Here, Princess.' The little man, wearing pyjamas and a pince-nez, was virtually thrown into the room by the men who had arrested him.

'Attend to my son,' Selphine said.

Batalji took the shirt away, and the doctor peered at the wound. 'I will need my equipment,' he said.

'Then fetch it, you asshole,' Selphine said. 'And hurry. You! Go with him.'

Someone had produced a bottle of vodka, and Batalji drank from the neck, deeply.

Some more men appeared, these headed by Hilaim. They were dragging another woman, middle-aged like her husband, but still handsome and strongly built. She wore a nightdress, but this had been torn in several places. 'Madame Taychin,' Selphine greeted her with mock ceremony, and bowed.

The President's wife looked left and right, at the men standing around her, at her husband, lying naked on the bed beside his naked mistress; both were shivering. 'They are all struck dumb,' Selphine said.

The doctor hurried back with antibiotic creams and bandages. Batalji sat in a chair while he was strapped up. 'You have lost a lot of blood, Prince Batalji,' the doctor said. 'You should go to the hospital for a transfusion.'

'Later,' Batalji said. 'Are the tanks out?'

'They are on the street, Prince,' one of the men replied.

'Then we are in control. Almani, telephone Carowan to instruct Maloun to make the announcement. Tell him I will be there in ten minutes. Bind me up, Doctor.'

The doctor bandaged the wound, then produced a hypodermic needle. 'What is that for?' Selphine asked, suspiciously.

'It is anti-tetanus.'

'Is the wound not clean?'

'It is as clean as I can make it, Princess. But if the Prince will not go to hospital . . .'

'Use it,' Batalji commanded.

'Will he be all right?' Selphine asked.

'There is no reason why not, Princess. But he will need rest. He should be in hospital.'

'Well, you stay with him and look out for him,' Selphine commanded. 'He will come to hospital as soon as he is able. Do you wish that woman?' Selphine pointed at Madam Taychin.

Batalji sighed. 'I wish no woman right now. I must appear on television, to the people. Will you come with me?'

Selphine smiled. 'I will stay here,' she said. 'I have much to do. Take the doctor.'

Batalji got up, slowly, looked at the bed, and Taychin.

'Do you wish me to keep him to show you?' Selphine asked.

Batalji shook his head. He went to the bed, looked down at the shivering man. 'You will scream as you die,' he prophesied. Then he left the room, followed by Almani and several of the men, and the doctor.

Selphine waited until he was out of earshot, then beckoned Hilaim. 'He needs stimulation,' she said. 'Go to the hotel, find the American woman, and take her to the television studio.' Hilaim nodded, and left the room. Selphine stood above the bed; there were still eight men with her, two of them holding Madame Taychin. 'Her, first,' she commanded.

The men grinned, and one of them unbuckled his pants. Two others stripped away the nightgown and forced Madame

Taychin to the floor. She made no sound, only a murmur of misery when they pulled her legs apart.

'You.' Selphine prodded Taychin with her gun muzzle. 'Sit up and watch.' Trembling, Taychin sat up and watched his wife being raped. 'Do you think I looked like that, when your men were raping me, all those years ago?' Selphine asked. 'No, I did not look like that. I was more beautiful, and I fought them until I could not fight any more. And then I prayed. I prayed to my gods, Taychin. Not yours. I prayed to Daschbog, the god of the sun, and to Stribog, the god of the storm, and I prayed to Wolos, the god of art and poetry. But most of all did I pray to Pierroun, the god of war and lightning. And this night it is Pierroun who is answering my prayer, assisted by Stribog. Where are *your* gods tonight, Boris?'

Another man was mounting Madame Taychin, then another. The woman on the bed began to weep. 'Oh, yes,' Selphine promised her. 'Your turn will come. Do not spend it all,' she told her men. 'Come and get this bitch.'

The blonde woman whimpered as she was dragged to the floor. All the men were now occupied, and Selphine stood above Taychin. 'Are you not going to try to escape?' she asked. He half turned his head at the sound of shots, too heavy to be rifles or revolvers. Selphine grinned at him. 'Yes, those are your tanks, Taychin. But they are our tanks, now. They are not coming to rescue you.'

Taychin looked as if he would have spoken, but changed his mind. Now all the eight men in the room were spent. They pulled up their pants, grinning and muttering at each other, looking from the two crumpled white bodies lying on the floor to Selphine. 'That one,' Selphine said, pointing at the blonde.

Two of the men grasped her arms and dragged her to her feet. Her body was a mass of red blotches on the white skin. She continued to shiver and to weep. 'Please,' she begged. 'Please.'

'I said please, once,' Selphine remarked. 'Taychin laughed.

They all laughed. Bend her over that settee.' The woman was dragged to the settee, and thrown across the back, so that she was facing away from Selphine. 'Open her legs,' Selphine said.

Two of the men held the woman in place, while two more pulled her legs apart. 'They buggered me,' Selphine said. 'You made them do that, didn't you Taychin? Now I am going to bugger her.' She stepped up to the woman, pushed the muzzle of her assault rifle between the buttocks, and squeezed the trigger.

Blood and flesh exploded in every direction. The woman died instantly, her body virtually ripped in two by the several bullets. Taychin scrambled from the bed with a scream. His wife sat up, and was thrown flat again by one of the men, while two more hurled Taychin across the bed, from where he stared at the bloody mess which still lay across the back of the settee. 'Now her,' Selphine said.

Still Madame Taychin did not speak, as she was pulled to her feet, the men holding her before Selphine, expectantly. 'Do you remember my begging you, once?' Selphine asked. 'To help me save my son?'

Madame Taychin bit her lip, so hard it started to bleed.

'Take her outside,' Selphine commanded. The men dragged Madame Taychin to the terrace doors, and opened them. Instantly a blast of freezing air whipped into the room. Madame Taychin gasped her terror. The men pushed and pulled her on to the terrace. 'Hang her from the balcony,' Selphine said.

Cords were taken from the drapes, and a noose was thrown around Madame Taychin's neck. Now she screamed, an agonising wail of terror. The men laughed, and carried her to the rail. 'Slowly,' Selphine reminded them.

One tied the end of the cord to one of the balustrades. Three of his companions lifted Madame Taychin from the floor and lowered her over the balcony. She screamed again, but it ended in a choke as the cord tightened on her neck. Selphine went outside to look down on her twisting body, hands clawing at her neck. 'I wonder which she will do first,' Selphine remarked. 'Strangle or freeze?'

She came back into the room, looked at the man on the bed. Boris Taychin sat up, tears rolling down his cheeks. 'I have money. Untold millions . . .'

'We will find it,' Selphine assured him. 'Tie him to the bed.'

Eager hands grasped Taychin's arms and legs and extended them, tying one limb to each of the four bedposts. Taychin shivered, but made no effort to resist them; he knew it would be futile. 'Now jack him up,' Selphine commanded.

Two of the men lifted Taychin's body from the bed while several pillows and cushions were stuffed beneath his buttocks, so that his body arched away from the bed, his penis exposed; despite everything that had happened, it was half erect.

Selphine knelt on the floor, some distance from the bed, and took careful aim. Her soldiers gathered in a group behind her, while Taychin's head twisted two and fro, desperately seeking to see what was happening. When he realised what she intended he gave a shriek of the purest terror, and strained on the cords holding him, causing his body to arch still further, and thus exposing his genitals even more. Selphine squeezed the trigger, and Boris Taychin uttered an unearthly scream as blood and flesh flew into the air.

Selphine gave a satisfied smile. 'Now bring him outside,' she said. 'And we will hang him beside his wife.'

Rosemary Leigh sat up with a start. Although she had now spent six months in this place, and slept in this bed in this hotel on most of those hundred and eighty nights, she always wondered where she was when she awoke. Yakutiya had to be the strangest place on earth. She looked at her watch; the time was twelve minutes past midnight. Then what had awakened her? No normal sound could penetrate the double-glazed hotel windows. Her room was dark, and yet, now she was awake, totally familiar. There was a line of light beneath the hall door, but there was always a line of light beneath that door.

Rosemary kicked off the covers and got out of bed. She slept naked; the hotel was warm. Sometimes she felt it was too warm, but these people seemed to have energy to burn – at least to impress overseas visitors. But Yakutsk was a place of the most remarkable contrasts. This autonomous Russian state had to be the most remote place on earth, after Antarctica, yet here she was, in a luxury bedroom in a luxury hotel in the midst of a modern city. There was even a television set mounted on the wall opposite her bed – not that she intended to start watching substandard TV at midnight. What had awakened her?

When she had first come here she had had difficulty in sleeping at all. But that had been excitement, an overwhelming sense of strangeness. And perhaps above all an exhilaration that she should have been selected for this research mission. Jim Crawford had chosen her personally. 'Well,' he had said. 'You have all the qualifications, Romy. You speak Russian, you know their history ... and you like skiing.'

She wouldn't have been human if she hadn't wondered if there might be an ulterior motive. But Jim was straight as a ruler. And so were the rest of his team. That she was the only woman in the party merely meant that she had to be protected from everything they encountered – from bewildered officials unable to comprehend why America should wish to study their country and their habits, to the copious quantities of vodka served with every meal. There were times she had felt she was in a cocoon, and she had had to resist with all the exuberance of her bubbling personality.

Especially when they had wanted to leave her behind in the safety of Yakutsk, two months ago, when they had set out in search of the legend, Batalji Borjigin. Then she had really flipped her lid. 'I'm the historian in this party, right?' she had shouted. 'And this guy is living history.'

'He's also a wanted terrorist,' Al Mather had pointed out. 'Who's officially dead.'

'So? If he's dead, what's the problem? If he's alive ...

Terrorists thrive on publicity. We're aiming to give this guy maximum publicity. He's not going to shoot us.'

She had got her way, had accompanied the small party which had ventured out on to the steppes. That expedition had had to be undertaken without either the authority or the knowledge of the regime, which had involved, in Rosemary's opinion, more of a risk than lay in encountering the Borjigin outlaws; for all the break-up of the USSR, and the liberalisation which had taken place in most of the new republics – and, most importantly, Russia itself – Yakutiya remained very much a police state. The Taychin family, which had ruled the autonomous republic now for several years, had been staunch supporters of Boris Yeltsin in the early 1990s, not because they believed in either *perestroika* or *glasnost*, but simply because they were pragmatists, who estimated that Yeltsin was the man most likely to leave them alone.

They had been right, and the status quo had been maintained, even after Yeltsin's retirement; Yakutiya remained an autonomous republic within Russia, valuable to the mother state because of its enormous lignite industry and its natural gas, and even more valuable now there were rumours of an oil strike of immense potential deep in the tundra. But, being autonomous, very little had changed since the Communist days. The Taychins still ruled through their secret police, and since the assassination of old Andrei Taychin, his son Boris, who had taken over the state, had ruled even more harshly. The idea that an American mission should research the manners and mores of the Yakut people had been foisted upon them by Moscow, and had apparently seemed harmless enough. What their reaction would be to the discovery that part of that research involved interviewing Batalji Borjigin she did not care to think. Because Batalji Borjigin was the man who had assassinated Andrei Taychin.

Borjigin had already been an outlaw, wanted for desertion from the Red Army. But he had always been a marked man, because he claimed direct descent from Temujin Borjigin, the greatest Mongol of them all, he who, eight hundred years ago, had been known as the Genghis Khan, the Great King, a savage and invincible warrior who had led his armies, or sent them under his sons, to conquer from the Danube to the Yellow Sea, and create, in square mileage, the greatest empire ever known.

The miracle was that the Borjigin clan had survived the seventy years of Soviet rule. For that they had to thank the vastness of the steppes. Now, once again, they had been driven to that ultimate refuge.

The Taychins claimed that Batalji Borjigin was dead. He had been wounded during the abortive coup of 1996, and since then nothing had been seen of him. But Jim Crawford had heard a whisper that the outlawed chieftain was actually alive, hidden in the great forests. That had been enough for him.

Rosemary had not known what to expect. The expedition had taken several weeks, as they had contacted first of all those nomadic tribes which still lived within the law, ostensibly to study their manners and mores, record their folk songs and their remembered history, learn how they lived their daily lives. Slowly they had overcome the innate Mongol suspicion of strangers to convince their hosts that they were not connected with the Taychin regime, and that they meant Batalji Borjigin, already a legend to his people because of both his name and his rebellion against the Taychins, no harm. Thus eventually a meeting had been set up, in a gloomy forest, where it had been easy to suppose blood sacrifices to the gods of the steppes still took place, and where one might expect to see a ghost.

Here Batalji Borjigin had come to them, riding a Mongol pony, armed with sword as well as rifle and revolver, accompanied by a guard of equally wild-looking men. This was as Rosemary had anticipated, a reincarnation of the past. But then she had been surprised. Batalji had dismounted and strode into the midst of the Americans, looking left and right with quick, aggressive movements of his head. He had examined their equipment with some knowledge, even of their camcorders, fingered their clothes, been obviously surprised at the absence of weapons save for a hunting rifle – that had interested him.

Then he had come to her, and he also had been surprised.

As it had been high summer she had worn an open-necked shirt with her jodhpurs – horseback was the only way they had been able to penetrate the forest. Her yellow hair had been loose and tumbling down her back, restricted only by a tortoiseshell clasp on the nape of her neck. Rosemary Leigh had never counted herself beautiful; her features were too large, and broad – sometimes she would suppose they could have indicated that she possessed Mongol blood herself. But she had a figure to match. She stood five feet ten inches in her bare feet, and all was hard muscle and flowing flesh. Rosemary Leigh, in a swimsuit or less, made heads turn; in a shirt and tight-fitting breeches she was hardly less effective.

Batalji Borjigin had actually been shorter than herself. But no one could argue the immense power of his body, either, and his face was as handsome as hers. He was also surprisingly young. She had of course already known that he was thirty-eight, to her thirty-two, but she had not expected so youthful a face.

'You sure made an impact,' Jim remarked, when the outlaws had ridden off again.

The interview itself had been a disappointment. That Batalji had agreed to see them at all had been a coup; clearly he had decided it was time to reappear, inform the world that he was actually alive. But he had refused to allow photographs to be taken, and had said little. He had come to see them, but he had still not entirely trusted them. Rosemary felt he understood less than anyone that they might be interested in him simply because of his name and his reputation. He had given little indication that he might be a born leader of men, or that he in any way resembled his famous forebear. But he had kept looking at her. Rosemary was not easily embarrassed, even by predatory eyes. Batalji's eyes had not been predatory, in the sense that the eyes of a sex-hungry New York bar acquaintance might be. But they *had* embarrassed her, because his eyes had envisaged possession, and that was not something Rosemary Leigh was prepared to grant, to anyone.

She had been more concerned by the woman, Batalji's mother, middle-aged but almost youthful in her intense virility. Her eyes too had been predatory, but her interest had been because of her son's interest. Rosemary thought they might have done better to interview Selphine Borjigin, if she would speak with them. There was beauty in that face, and sadness ... and a quality of anger which was frightening. She had been glad when the outlaws had left.

'Scared you, huh?' Al had grinned.

'Yes,' she agreed. 'He scared me.'

From that moment the mission had been complete, as far as she had been concerned. She had not really liked what she had seen of Yakutiya; police states made her skin crawl. But then, so did bandits who summoned her to submit, with their eyes.

She had been disappointed when Jim had decided to stay until December. 'We have to see what winter conditions are like up here,' he had explained, reasonably enough. 'You can't analyse people you've only seen in the summer.'

She knew he was right, and righter than ever as the days had begun to shorten and the temperatures to fall. It had been possible to see the people of Yakutsk visibly turning in on themselves, bracing themselves for the long intimacy of a winter which would continue into next May. Then, two days ago, it had started to snow, and the snow had steadily increased, even before the wind had started to blow it horizontally. For those two days they had not left the hotel. But then, Rosemary suspected that few of the hundred-and-twenty-five-thousand-odd inhabitants of Yakutsk had ventured out either.

'You know what?' Al had asked at dinner last night. 'This place is the shits in the winter.'

'Yeah,' Jim had agreed. 'Tell you what, gang, we'll leave as soon as this blizzard blows itself out.'

That had sent Rosemary to bed happy. Then what had awakened her so suddenly just after midnight?

She stood at the plate-glass window, and drew the drapes; with her bedroom in darkness, no one would be able to see her.

She looked down at the hotel drive and beyond, The Avenue, the main thoroughfare running through the city; the snow was coming from behind the building, and she could see quite clearly. There were lights in the hotel forecourt, and also on The Avenue. And on the drive there were ... Rosemary gulped, and backed away from the window. Then she dragged on her dressing gown, and ran to the door. She pulled it open and looked out, but the corridor was empty; all the rooms on this floor were occupied by the Americans.

She ran along the corridor, tried Jim's door. It was not locked, and she pushed it open, pausing to catch her breath. 'Jim?' she said into the darkness.

There was a swishing of bedclothes, and a moment later the bedside light came on. Jim Crawford had thinning grey hair, which, disturbed by sleep, stuck away from his head in a series of Dagwoods. He also had the knack of being instantly awake. And witty. 'Well, hell, honey,' he remarked. 'I thought this moment was never gonna come. What time is it?'

'Just gone midnight.' Rosemary closed the door behind her, went into the room. 'Jim, there are three tanks out there, pointing their guns at this building.'

He frowned at her, then threw back the covers and went to the window. Rosemary was not disturbed by his nudity, but she thoughtfully doused the light before he drew the drapes; someone down there might just shoot at him.

'Jesus Christ! Where are you?'

'Here.' She stood at his shoulder. 'You reckon there's a war on?'

'Nobody said anything about a war last night on TV. I'd better get down there and find out what's happening.'

'Me too. Five minutes.' She ran back to her room, threw her dressing gown on the bed, reached for her wardrobe door, and heard feet in the corridor. Heavy feet, and loud voices.

Instinctively she pulled her dressing gown back on, and went to the door to lock it. But before she got there it swung open. Rosemary backed against the bed, clutching the dressing gown against herself; she had not even had the time to tie the cord. She gazed at four men, wearing heavy coats and fur hats on which the snow was melting, carrying automatic weapons in their gloved hands. She took several deep breaths to get her breathing under control. And her nerves. 'Do you mind getting out of here,' she said in Russian, as evenly as she could.

The men looked at each other, and then over their shoulders, and she saw one of the hotel under-managers standing behind them.

'What the fuck is going on?' she demanded, trying to sound more angry than afraid.

'Is this the woman?' asked one of the men, surprisingly old.

'Yes,' the under-manager said. He was trembling; his teeth chattered as he spoke. 'That is Miss Leigh.'

Hilaim arranged his features into what he apparently considered a smile. 'You come with us, Miss Leigh.'

She gazed at his flat, Mongoloid features, then looked back at the under-manager. 'He has to be joking. Vyacheslev! Tell me he's joking.'

Vyacheslev licked his lips. 'You must go, Miss Leigh. The Prince says so.'

'Prince? What prince? Am I under arrest? You had better get Mr Crawford in here.'

'No arrest,' Hilaim said. 'You come.'

'It is Prince Batalji's wish,' said a second man.

'Prince Batalji!' My God, she thought, he's pulled a coup. And now he wants me ... to report it to the world? She did not wish to think there could be any other reason. There *could* not be any other reason. She was a citizen of the most powerful nation in the world. So ... keep calm, and reasonable. 'Okay,' she said. 'I'll come see your prince. Just step outside while I dress. I won't be long.'

Hilaim shook his head. 'You come now.'

'Like this? Are you nuts? It's freezing out there.'

'You come, now,' Hilaim snapped, suddenly impatient.

Two of his companions ran at her. Rosemary threw herself on to the bed and rolled across it to the far side. She lost her dressing gown in the process, but it didn't seem to matter if she was going to be raped anyway. She landed on her feet and one of the men leapt at her and threw his arms round her waist. She struck back at him with her elbows and another man came round in front. She kicked him in the thigh but he didn't seem to notice as he gathered her legs together and tucked them under his arm.

'You bastards!' she shouted. 'You shits! You ...'

The men grinned, and carried her towards the door and the gaping under-manager; maybe he'd never seen a naked American woman before. But if they took her outside like this ... That thought had occurred to Hilaim. 'Wait!'

The men waited. Rosemary sagged. One man had his hands in her armpits, while the other still held her legs tucked under his arms. Never had she felt so utterly exposed. Her own hands were free. She could use them to strike at the man behind her, or she could attempt to protect her breasts or genitals. Neither seemed very worthwhile, and either might bring an unpleasant reprisal.

Hilaim was rummaging through her wardrobe, and found her heavy coat. 'Wear this,' he said.

Rosemary was set on her feet, and the coat draped round her shoulders. Her hands were thrust into the armholes and pulled down. 'Listen,' she said. 'Just let me get dressed. You can watch, if you want to. Just let me get some clothes on. For God's sake, if you take me outside without shoes and stockings I'm going to get frostbite.'

'The car is warm,' Hilaim assured her, and once again she was swept from the floor.

Rosemary's nerves cracked as she was carried into the corridor. 'Jim!' she shouted. 'Al!' she shrieked. 'For God's sake, help me!'

She saw a kaleidoscope of faces, heard shouts, familiar voices, thumps and thuds and cries of pain. Oh, Jesus, she thought; them too? She was thrust into the lift, which began a rapid descent. The four men had come in with her, and it was very crowded; her head banged against the wall. 'Listen,' she said. 'Put me down. I can stand. I'm not going anywhere.'

The men set her on her feet and she hugged her coat round herself. This had to be a nightmare. She hadn't really seen those tanks and gone into Jim. She was still fast asleep and at any moment she was going to wake up, and give a sigh, and roll over and go back to sleep ... The lift came to a halt and the door opened. The lobby was crowded with people, hotel staff, other guests, and men with guns. 'Stand back!' Hilaim snapped, and Rosemary was lifted from the ground again.

'I can walk!' she shouted, but she was too busy trying to keep the coat closed to fight them.

The swing doors opened, then the glass outer door. There was a porch roof extending over the drive, and no snow was falling here. But the cold cut at her like a knife, driving her protests from her throat as it drove the breath from her lungs. A big black car waited at the foot of the steps, and she was bundled into the back, ashamed to be whimpering with the cold, curling herself into a heat-seeking ball.

But the heating inside the car was turned up to full, and slowly she regained feeling in her toes and nose. She sat up, glanced at the men who were sitting beside her and in front of her, then looked out of the windows as the car slithered quietly over the snow. For a blizzard, there were a lot of people on the streets. It was difficult to discern the sexes beneath the heavy clothing, but they were all armed. Prince Batalji! Had he really pulled off a coup? And could he possibly make it stick? To her surprise, she realised she was on his side, regardless of what was happening to her. Or what was going to happen to her.

The car slithered down a driveway and into another covered area. She saw the words Television Station and gave a sigh of relief. She was after all being summoned to do some kind of announcing. But if they thought she was going to appear before a TV camera wearing only a coat ... Once again a searing blast of cold air, then she was in the warmth of the lobby. Here there were more armed men, and she was no longer carried, merely pushed into the lift; the men came in behind her, and they ascended. Rosemary stared at the wall, discoloured with an ugly brown stain. Blood! Jesus!

The car stopped, the doors opened. More armed men, and some women, also armed. Rosemary was hurried along the corridor, her bare feet aching, her body still chilled, although the building was well heated. A door was thrust open, and she found herself in a large office, where there were several men and women, some of them technicians. On a settee against the far wall lay Batalji Borjigin.

He was draped in an undressing robe, but wore pants beneath, although no shirt; she frowned as she saw the bandaged chest. He was looking at her with hardly less surprise. 'Miss Leigh?' he asked, his expression indicating that he was realising she was naked beneath the coat.

Clearly he had not expected her. 'Your men abducted me, and brought me here,' she said, seeking any advantage possible.

Batalji looked at the kidnappers. 'Orders from Princess Selphine, great Prince,' Hilaim said. Batalji's head went back, and he gave a roar of laughter, which ended abruptly in a grunt of pain.

The little man standing beside his head bent over him. 'You must not exert yourself, great Prince,' he said. 'Nor must you excite yourself.'

'Tell that to my mother,' Batalji said. He waved his hand. 'Out!' The men and women hesitated, glancing at each other. 'Out!' Batalji said again, his voice taking on a ring of command.

They hurried for the door.

'You must rest,' the doctor begged.

'I am resting. Out!'

The doctor glanced at Rosemary, who had remained standing in the centre of the room, hugging her coat. 'He must rest,' he repeated. The door closed.

'How bad is it?' Rosemary asked.

'It is not bad at all. These stupid people think I have never been hit before. But I have lost some blood.' He smiled at her. 'I cannot fuck you, at this moment. Even if my mother thinks I should.'

'I remember your mother.'

'You will soon meet her again. Come.' Rosemary hesitated, then moved towards the couch. He certainly looked fairly weak. 'Did you see my telecast?' he asked.

'No. Will you succeed?'

'Of course. Taychin is dead. All his people are dead.'

Rosemary swallowed, as a brief idea of the carnage which must have taken place in this quiet city flitted through her mind. 'The world...'

'The world is also dead, for the next eight months. Take off your coat.'

'I do not wish to do that.' She almost smiled. 'It might excite you.'

'I wish to be excited, by you. I have won a great victory, Rosemary Leigh. I have seized the land of my forefathers. Now I wish to be rewarded.'

'Do you think you can just stretch out your hand and pluck a woman as you might pluck a berry from a bush, Prince Batalji?'

'Yes,' he said. 'Here in Yakutistan, I can do that. I can do anything I wish. Now obey me, or I will have you flogged.'

Rosemary took a sharp breath, looked left and right.

Batalji smiled. 'There are no weapons to kill me with, Rosemary. And even weak as I am, you are not strong enough to fight me. But why fight me? You are mine, as Yakutistan is mine. I have said, I cannot fuck you at this moment. That will come later. You will bear me strong sons. But for the moment,

I wish only to look at you, and hold you in my arms.'

'You are just...' She shook her head. 'Medieval.'

'I am Khan of Yakutistan,' he said, simply but proudly. 'That is a medieval concept, perhaps. But it is here and now. The world will know of it, and accept it. The world will fear it, very soon. As will you, if you do not obey me. Take off your coat, and lie with me.'

THE FIRST PART

Shadow on the Steppes

I saw Eternity the other night
Like a ring of pure and endless light,
All calm, as it was bright,
And round beneath it, Time in hours, days, years,
Driv'n by the spheres
Like a vast shadow moved; in which the world
And all her train were hurled.

Henry Vaughan, 'The World', *Silex Scintillans*

THE FIRST CHRONICLE

London, October 2000

The thin wail of Artie Shaw's clarinet drifted across the room, picking out the sensuous rhythm of his theme tune, 'Nightmare'. Sintax the marmalade cat stretched luxuriously on the settee, and rolled over. When anyone asked Clive Stanton why he had named his cat Sintax, he always replied, 'Why not?' Just as whenever anyone questioned his obsession with music which had long disappeared into history, he would answer, 'It turns me on.'

Both replies encapsulated Clive Stanton's attitude to life, an attitude which had had a great deal to do with his success. Even the great, and the nasty, enjoyed a Clive Stanton interview, because of his ability to convey a feeling of total *laissez-faire*. 'Well, President Hussein, I see the number of Kurds killed in that attack was seventy-five. It appears a regrettable number got away.'

But they also feared his sudden barbed probes, which often left them defencesless. 'I know Muslims have a different concept of life and death to Christians, President Hussein. But we both believe in an afterlife. I presume you have your defence all prepared, to offer those seventy-five shades when they cluster round your deathbed. I know my viewers would be interested to hear what you intend to say.'

That interview had been several years ago. It had, perhaps, launched Clive Stanton's career, but it had been overtaken by a great many equally famous interviews since. Nowadays, when the Anglo-French Television Network sent Clive Stanton to cover a story, that was news in itself.

The music reached a climax, and Clive stretched, very like his cat. He was a big man, tall and broad-shouldered. Now that he was thirty-seven his weight was showing a tendency to increase, as his dark hair was showing a tendency to thin. His face, in repose, was curiously soft, relaxed. But this had been cultivated over the years. The steel was there in his grey eyes, the strong chin, the occasional sudden flatness of his mouth.

His personality was illustrated by his surroundings. This den, apart from the music and the cat, was a mass of books. Most were neatly placed on their shelves, and some of the shelves were even labelled, suggesting that somewhere inside his untidy exterior there was an orderly mind trying to get out. But a considerable number of the books were scattered on the various tables, some on a chair, one large volume even leaning against his PC. There was only a smattering of novels, and these were all on the shelves. The majority of the books comprised history, biography, philosophy, and volumes of technical data, from oil production to theatre and cinema. Clive Stanton believed in being one step ahead of his possible subjects. But his job, and the research which went with it, was also his hobby: he genuinely enjoyed absorbing knowledge.

Artie Shaw was replaced on the disc by Jimmy Dorsey, and Clive looked at his watch. As he spent so much time travelling, so many nights in hotel rooms, so many days hurrying from one airport to another, these brief periods between assignments were very precious. He could do what he liked, when he liked; eat what he liked, spiced as he liked; drink what he liked, and as much as he liked. Now the first stirrings of an appetite caused him to reach out and pluck a cookbook from the nearest shelf, and idly turn the pages. He enjoyed cooking; it was simply a matter of matching up an attractive meal with what he happened to have in his fridge or deep-freeze.

As it was generally accepted by his many acquaintances – he had few close friends – that Clive Stanton had absolutely no sexual hang-ups, it was equally accepted that he had never married simply because he was so self-contained a personality he had never needed a wife. As he was both an attractive man and, nowadays, a famous one, whenever he felt the urge – and could spare the time – for a weekend somewhere in the sun, he had no difficulty in finding a travelling companion. While Mrs McNulty came in four mornings a week to keep the flat clean and attend to his laundry. Clive himself would argue that the life of an international television journalist rather precluded domesticity, except on an occasional basis, but he knew there was a lot of truth in the more popular verdict. Yet today he found himself considering how pleasant it would be, if on the far side of Sintax there was reclining a permanent blonde, or brunette, or redhead. There of course was the trouble; he had no one specific in mind – it was the *idea* that was growing on him.

He blamed boredom. Over the last couple of years the world seemed to have achieved an equilibrium it might have been seeking for a millennium. There was no real equilibrium, of course. The planet continued to seethe. But at the moment everything seemed so petty; there were no great causes any more. People had come to terms with the compromises reached to keep the planet liveable for at least the next hundred years. They might grumble that human rights were being grossly abused in Hong Kong under the new regime ... but the West had turned its back on Hong Kong. Amnesty International might continue to publicise the appalling plight of the Kurds, assailed from three sides, but since the assassination of Saddam Hussein the West had been busily mending its fences with both Iraq and Iran, and the fact that Israel, on the verge of bankruptcy as American support had dwindled, had done a deal with the PLO, had left everyone breathing a lot more freely about the Middle East. Revolutions and *coups d'état* might continue in Africa, but since black majority rule had become a fact in South Africa, the huge, powerful southern country had become the arbiter of the continent, and white interference was not welcomed, even had it been projected.

While the North Atlantic nations were basking in a return of a prosperity they had not enjoyed since the late 1950s. People were saying that perhaps the recession of the early nineties had after all been worth it, if it had inspired this surge of continuous and virtually inflation-free growth. They were saying other things as well. With the European Community moving ever closer to a true federal concept, and a European army soon to come into being, there were those advocating the winding-up of NATO. Indeed, both candidates in the US election now coming to a climax were admitting that the whole structure of the North Atlantic Alliance needed looking at; the American voters were asking why so many billions of dollars were being spent maintaining an international force when there were no enemies of any consequence, and when there was a continuing and very real trade war to be fought with Japan. Clive supposed the next really big thing to be reported was going to be the fall of the House of Windsor. Things really seemed to be moving in that direction. It was not something he wanted to think about; if, like most people, he was often totally fed up with royalist scandals, he remained a traditionalist at heart.

That had left him reporting nothing but trivia over the past few years. Eating, drinking, and perhaps marrying, had begun to occupy his mind. The telephone buzzed. He reached across Sintax to pick it up. 'Don't tell me,' he said. 'Work at last.'

'Well, I thought you'd be getting bored by now,' Threlfall said.

'I got bored several days ago.'

'Then this will cheer you up. Ever heard of Yakutiya?'

'It's an autonomous state within the Russian Republic.'

Threlfall sighed; Clive Stanton always had the correct answer to every question. 'I want you to go out there.'

'Listen, old boy,' Clive said. 'Yakutiya is in northern Siberia. Right around now it is commencing to freeze, and it is going to stay frozen until next May. So . . . you have got to be joking.'

'This could be interesting.'

'The last interesting thing that happened in Yakutiya was when Howard Hughes landed there on his round-the-world flight in 1937. No, I tell a lie. It was when some descendant of Genghis Khan bumped off President Taychin, four years ago, in an abortive *coup d'état*. And a jolly good thing, too. Taychin was a thug.'

'Well, your friend has done it again.'

'Eh?'

'It's coming across on the wire from Moscow that the outlaw Batalji Borjigin has seized power in Yakutsk, and has declared its independence from Moscow. And this time he's done Boris Taychin as well.'

'Well, hoorah. You mean this time he made it?'

'So get out there, Clive.'

'Philip, in the past eight years almost every republic in the CIS has experienced at least one *coup d'état*. Don't you have a certain sense of *déjà vu*?'

'This is the first time there has been an actual revolution, Clive. Kazakhstan, Azerbaijan, Uzbekistan, even the Ukraine, were all taken to independence by their existing local governments. Only in Azerbaijan was there any real trouble, locally, I mean, and that was a territorial business. But here we have an apparently stable government wiped out in a single night. According to the report the entire Taychin regime has been liquidated. And this is *within* the Russian Republic, no matter how autonomous Yakutiya may always have been. I think that could be news, Clive. I think a Clive Stanton interview with Batalji Borjigin would put us on top of the ratings. You're booked on the four-thirty to Paris, thence to Moscow. A camera team will be waiting for you at Charles de Gaulle.'

'Philip, do you realise that Yakutsk, the only city in that whole damned country, is on the same parallel of latitude as Anchorage, Alaska? *Nobody* goes to Anchorage, Alaska in

October unless they have to. And Anchorage at least has the sea at hand to help stabilise the temperatures.'

'You have to, Clive. Oh, by the way, Dubois has agreed to let Denise l'Auberon crank the handle.'

'Now, why didn't you say that first?' Clive asked. As well as being a brilliant camerawoman, Denise l'Auberon was one of his favourite human beings. He had even, on more than one occasion, considered placing her on the other side of Sintax. If he was going to be shacked up in some Siberian igloo he could think of no better companion.

But Siberia! Apart from the time of year, Russia as a whole had become something of a joke over the past ten years. A pretty sick joke, as government had followed government in each of the eleven republics, as mutual defence pact after mutual defence pact, and mutual aid pact after mutual aid pact, had come and gone, as teams of observers had overseen the destruction of atomic weapons only to discover there were yet more atomic weapons hidden away, as the West had raised a succession of apparent strong men on to pinnacles only to see them swept from power in the next round of discontent brought on by empty bellies.

Over the past couple of years, in fact, the Western governments had all but washed their hands of the whole mess. They had poured over a hundred billion dollars into the Russian maw . . . and people still claimed to be starving, just as Russian industry still seemed to be non-existent. Nowadays, if the Russians got aid, it came through pop concerts. Presumably Lenin and Stalin were rolling in their niches.

It was impossible to imagine how an upheaval, however bloody, in one of the most remote places on earth could be of the least interest to anyone. Even to the United Nations, which, having received such a pounding in Yugoslavia, was no longer interested in interfering with Russian internal politics, not even when, as happened at least every other year, Russia and the Ukraine all but started shooting at each other. Just about all the nukes had been found and destroyed, anyway. But he worked for this man.

'Tell me what you need,' Threlfall said.

Clive concentrated. 'Maps. Statistics. A file on Borjigin. A file on the Taychin family. That should do it.'

'They'll be waiting for you at Heathrow. Keep in touch.'

'Denise and I will send you lots of footage of snow,' Clive promised. He put down the phone, picked it up again, punched the numbers. 'Hello, Holly.'

'I'm busy tonight,' the woman's voice said.

'So am I, etc., etc.'

'Oh, no!'

'I'm afraid so. I'm off in a couple of hours. But she won't expect service before six. There are a couple of tins of cat food in the larder, and a packet of those moist biscuits she likes. I'll leave some money for you to stock up. There's also a new bag of cat litter.'

'Just how long are you going for this time?' asked the woman named Holly.

'Just as long as it takes me to find out what makes a man into an outlaw prepared to take on an entire government,' Clive told her.

CHAPTER ONE

Yakutiya, Spring 1976

Andrei Taychin sat at his desk and glared at the four men standing before him.

'So where is he?' he demanded.

'It is impossible to say, Comrade Commissar,' one of the men replied. 'He is certainly not at Kegechakh.'

'He is not anywhere near Kegechakh,' said the second man. 'My people have been the length of the Linde, and he is not to be seen.'

'It is my belief, Comarde Commissar, that Borjigin has gone west, into the high country,' said the third man.

'And when did he do this?' Andrei Taychin asked, his voice deceptively quiet. It was the beginning of May, and all Yakutiya was awakening from its long winter sleep. Birds sang, trees were green. People walked the streets of Yakutsk with a spring in their step. Factory chimneys belched smoke and huge pyramids of coal were accumulating along the waterfront, awaiting the arrival of the first ships able to break through the ice and sail up the River Lena. It was a time when every Commissar took out his lists and began to consider his quotas. But this was a more important year than usual. In two months' time there would be elections for the Supreme Soviet. No one expected any surprises or any change – Taychin glanced at the huge framed portrait of Leonid Brezhnev on the wall opposite – but no one wanted them either, apart from Baltomar Borjigin, perhaps.

'The Mongols can move even in the snow,' the first man said. 'They could have gone at some time during the winter.'

'They were told where to go, and where to stay,' Andrei Taychin snapped. 'Just as they were told which horses and which reindeer herds belong to them. Now we will find that they have absorbed another half-dozen herds. As usual. Comrade Borjigin does not disregard central directives because he needs to. He does it because he wants to. He is an undisciplined thug. Now he is trying to get out of paying his taxes. The President is furious. With us. With me! He questions the value of a Minister of the Interior who permits people like Borjigin to do as they please. I want Borjigin found! I want his taxes! And I want him returned to his proper grazing land!'

'You will need an army to do that,' said the fourth man, quietly.

Andrei Taychin turned his head, sharply. Heavy-set and moustached, himself – he had always modelled himself on Josef Stalin, whom he had met once, as a young man – he had brought up his son in his own image.

'And to what purpose?' Boris Taychin asked, also speaking quietly. He was only thirty-four, but he wore the uniform of a colonel in the Red Army, with the addition of a red commissar's star on his *schlem*. 'He will simply say he has no money, and then run off again as soon as our backs are turned, stealing more herds. He is an outlaw. He has always been an outlaw. Does he not claim a direct descent from Genghis Khan, the greatest of all outlaws?'

'You cannot expect me just to let him get away with defying the government, Boris,' Andrei protested.

'Borjigin has too much support amongst the nomads anyway,' muttered one of the other men. 'They speak of him as the Prince.'

'They believe his ancestry,' said another. 'It is part of their folklore.'

'That is exactly it,' Boris Taychin said. 'He is part of their folklore. It is time to put a stop to it, Comrade Father. Once and for all.'

Andrei Taychin regarded his son for some seconds, while the other men shifted their feet uneasily. 'It must be done legally,' he said at last.

'It will be done legally, Father. Give me the Sixteenth Airborne. We are going to find the Borjigin clan, and we are going to collect the exact amount they owe us in taxes. If Baltomar Borjigin says he has not got the money, then we will take his goods and chattels and his herds. We will also place him under arrest for leaving his appointed grazing grounds without authority.'

'Borjigin will never accept that,' said one of the other men. Boris Taychin smiled.

'Hiya, hiya, hiya!' screamed Andalji Borjigin, as his pony scattered down the hillside towards the river.

'Hiya, hiya, hiya,' shouted his brothers as they galloped behind him. The ponies were no less excited. Small and sturdy, they shared a relationship with their riders even more intimate than that of pet dogs.

'There!' Andalji shouted, changing direction with no more than a tightening of his knees as he reached the beaten earth roadway beside the rushing water. His brothers followed. In front of them was a group of girls, bathing, but now scrambling on to the bank in alarm at the sound of the hooves. The water, only recently released from the icy embrace of winter, was cold, and the naked bodies glowed with chill as the girls ran for the shelter of the bushes.

Andalji drew rein – the rein was the only furniture his mount possessed, for he rode bareback – and raised his hand, and his brothers also came to a halt, ponies panting, dust eddying. In the high land, the trees were not so thickly clustered as in the river valleys, yet there were trees a plenty, pines reaching high towards the clear blue summer sky; most of Yakutiya was a vast forest. The pines soughed in the wind, setting up a constant rustle, which often made the steppes sound like a restless sea. And now, also, as winter receded, there was colour everywhere, as grass sprouted and flowers bloomed; even the bushes behind which the girls had fled were a blaze of colour.

'Come out!' Andalji shouted.

'Go away, Andalji Borjigin,' one of the girls shouted. 'Our fathers will have you whipped.'

'We want Mortana,' Andalji said.

'Just to look at,' laughed Barone Borjigin.

'A man must look at his bride,' Tengut Borjigin shouted. 'Eh, Batalji?'

Batalji Borjigin responded with a nervous grin. Fourteen years old, he was by some years the youngest of the brothers, a tribute to his father's virility after Baltomar Borjigin had taken his fourth wife. Thus Batalji, like his chosen bride, was a virgin. He looked older than his years, his stocky body already heavily muscled; he wore only an open-necked shirt, loose pants, and soft boots, and the muscles rippled in his arms and chest. He was more handsome than his siblings, too, his Mongol features crisper and sharper. But then, all were agreed that Baltomar Borjigin had secured the greatest beauty on the steppes in Selphine Serhat, for the comfort of his declining years.

'We will not leave until Mortana has come out,' Andalji insisted, while his pony stamped to and fro.

'Perhaps we should ride in,' Barone said. 'And carry them off. All of them.'

The girls had been conferring, concerned that such an ancient custom might indeed be what the boys had in mind. They were not afraid. The two clans, the Borjigins and the Anhusats, were already linked by marriage and closely connected by both history and choice; they invariably migrated in company. It was giving best to the boys they objected to. 'You will leave, if Mortana comes out?' asked the eldest of the sisters.

'By the great god Pierroun, we swear it,' Andalji said.

The bushes rattled, and Mortana stepped through. She was thirteen years old, but she was a child of the steppes and already a woman, slender of build but with strong legs and wide thighs and well-developed breasts. Her face was crisp and pretty, her hair a tawny mass which floated down to the curve of her buttocks as she whirled before them, before checking for a moment, gazing over her shoulder at them with deliberate coquetry ... and allowing them to gaze at her as she took deep breaths, her dark eyes searching for her betrothed. When she found him, she gazed at him alone for several seconds, then she tossed her head, and disappeared back into the bushes.

'Oh, to be young again, and about to be married,' Andalji shouted. He was twenty-nine, and had been a husband for thirteen years.

'Now leave,' Mortana's sister shouted. 'You promised.'

Andalji raised his hand, wheeled his pony, and led his brothers back along the stream.

'Can you wait, brother?' Tengut asked, grinning.

'For Mortana, I can wait forever,' Batalji told him.

The sword blades clanged, and the two young men dripped sweat as they leapt to and fro, twisting their bodies, feet occasionally slipping on the turf, but hands never losing their grip on the hafts of their yataghans.

'Less haste,' Baltomar Borjigin shouted. 'More purpose.' He leaned back in his folding chair – made of reindeer skins over a wooden frame – before his huge felt yurt, and smoked his pipe, a mug of vodka in his hand. The felt of the tent was stretched over wattle rods, with an aperture at the top to let out the smoke. It was coated with white lime and ornamented with pictures. The yurt, which the Mongols had used for centuries as they had wandered the length and breadth of Asia, was in every way a serviceable home; it could be folded up and packed on to the cart, the kibitka, which waited beside it, to be drawn by a dozen reindeer to the next encampment, and while standing, its dome shape enabled it to withstand the buffeting of the hurricane-strength winds which often blew across the steppes.

It was six o'clock in the evening, the time of day, in May, that Baltomar liked best. There were still more than three hours of daylight left, but the day's work had been done, and he could relax with his family. Not that Baltomar, or any male Mongol, took part in the day's work when the clan was in camp. Rounding up the herds and driving them to their next grazing ground, that was a different matter. For three weeks in April he and his brother, their sons and sons-in-law, had spent twelve hours a day in the saddle, often up to their horses' haunches in snow, as they had moved on to the high ground. He had begun the movement early because he had wanted to be beyond the immediate reach of the Commissars before the days lengthened.

Besides, he had made a rendezvous up here with the Anhusats, for the marriage of his youngest son with Khalim Anhusat's youngest daughter. It would be one of the great years. As long as the Commissars did not catch up with him. But now that he was here, the daily business of collecting the mares' milk and turning it into kumiss – fermenting it in leather sacks – and of cleaning the interiors of the yurts and beating the carpets and cushions which acted as beds, of boiling millet or preparing any meat which might have come to hand, could be left to the women, just as fishing and hunting was left to the young men, while their elders dreamed of past and future glories.

And present problems. 'They will come, you know,' Dragone Borjigin pointed out. Like his elder brother, he sat in a comfortable chair and smoked his pipe, and drank vodka, served to him by one of his daughters. 'Even though we left early, they will find us.'

Baltomar grinned. 'By then we will have no money, eh? They will whistle for their taxes. Cut,' he bawled at the two young men. 'Do not thrust. Cut. As long as they do not find us until after the wedding, eh?' He gave a shout of laughter. 'Stop now! You are tired.'

Tengut and Batalji lowered their swords, and stood panting; stripped to the waist, their chests and shoulders glowed with sweat. 'Drink some vodka,' Baltomar said. 'It will restore your strength.'

Their sisters hurried forward with the jugs, and the boys gulped the fiery liquid, while Selphine Borjigin gave a sigh of relief. She understood that fighting, and especially with the sword, was in the Borjigin blood. But Batalji was her only child, and now that Baltomar was seventy, the boy would probably remain her only child, for all that she remained the old chieftain's favourite woman. She wrapped Batalji in his shirt – for as the evening drew in the air was chill – giving him a hug as she did so.

They were very close. Selphine had only been fifteen when Baltomar had married her, arranging the business with her father. Over the centuries the priests had done their best to civilise the Yakuts, and where they had been able to get them into Yakutsk itself they had met with a measure of success. The Commissars had tried even harder, and with even more apparent success, to eliminate the old ways, outlaw shamanism, make the people of the steppes into good Communists who obeyed the diktats of the new gods, Marx and Lenin and Stalin. But neither priests nor Commissars had evern been able to impose their ideas of civilisation on the Yakka Mongols such as the Borjigins. The Borjigins were not actually Yakuts: they were true Mongols. Once they had been the Mongol Royal Clan. Many centuries into history.

Thus they continued their Mongol ways, despite the laws. It was the Borjigin way to wander with their herds as and when they chose, regardless of the marked maps given them by the Commissars, just as it was the Borjigin way to refuse to pay taxes, because they had never paid taxes except when forced to it, and it was the Borjigin way never to vote, because voting meant going into the city, and besides, the Borjigins did not care who went to Moscow to represent them – as they did not want to be represented – or indeed who ruled in Moscow, because they were not going to obey the laws that distant power made anyway. Equally had it always been the Borjigin way for the clan chieftain to have as many wives as he chose. And as he grew older, Baltomar had sought youth, and beauty, to warm his couch. Selphine Serhat had possessed both.

Selphine had been pleased to become the wife of the old prince, even if he was old enough to be her grandfather. Born and bred on the steppes, she had known she would be married to her father's choice, and almost certainly to a man at least old enough to *be* her father. The nomad women enjoyed watching television, with its occasional glimpses of the Western world, whenever they happened to be in Yakutsk, but they knew it was not going to be during their lifetimes that women's lib would penetrate the tundra. And regardless of his age, there was no finer man in Yakutiya, perhaps in the whole world, than Baltomar Borjigin. Marriage to him gave Selphine the right to call herself Princess, even if only in Mongol circles, just as her son would be a prince, no matter that such titles had long been abolished by the government.

Batalji would never be clan chieftain, of course; he had three older brothers by Baltomar's senior wives. But he would stand at Andalji's shoulder throughout the conflicts that might lie ahead, and he would marry the girl Mortana, and give Selphine and Baltomar grandchildren, and be the comfort of her old age. She could not contemplate the thought of a careless sword cut ending that happy prospect.

'Listen!' Andalji said. All heads turned, as the drone of the piston aero-engines drifted across the afternoon.

'Glasses!' Baltomar heaved himself to his feet, as Tengut ran to fetch the binoculars and give them to his father. Baltomar levelled and focused. 'The bastards have found us,' he growled.

His menfolk clustered around him, staring at the intruder, a twin-engined plane, as it circled above the nomad encampment.

'We must move on,' Dragone said.

'We cannot move fast enough to outrun the planes,' Baltomar said. 'But they cannot put that machine down here;

there is no strip. It will take another week for them to get to us by truck.' He looked from face to face. 'We will let that fellow report our position and go away again. But starting at dawn tomorrow, we will drive the herds far away, so that no one can tell they are ours. And we will bury all our silver and money. It has been a hard winter, eh? And we have nothing with which to pay our taxes. Batalji, you will ride over to the Anhusat encampment and explain the situation to Khalim. He can mind our herds for us, eh? Now that we are to be related.' He watched the plane circling and then heading back to the east. 'Bastards,' he growled.

Batalji could not sleep. It had nothing to do with the hard work which would commence tomorrow, the confrontation that would take place with the tax collectors soon afterwards. That was a yearly occurrence and had been going on ever since he could remember. But he kept thinking of Mortana, of the glimpse of her that morning. He had met her on several occasions, of course. Long before there had been any talk of marriage. But then she had been a child, and she had in any event been totally concealed beneath the heavy clothing normally worn by the Yakut women. He had known she was pretty, had watched her growing prettier yet. When he had been told that she would be his bride he had been delighted, without perhaps understanding all that would be involved.

No doubt Andalji had realised that, and thus, having studied the Anhusat girls' habits over the past week since the two clans had been camped close to each other, had proposed today's adventure. Batalji was not the least jealous that his brothers should have seen his bride's body; rather was he pleased that they should have done so: now *they* would be jealous of *him*, of his good fortune.

But he could not get the image of her out of his mind, the beauty of her, but more important even than that, the way she had looked over her shoulder, and sought him out with her eyes, the way she had returned into the bushes, hair and hips swaying in unison. She was a girl of character, a girl who would have to be tamed ... He had said he would wait for her, forever, he meant that. But he was glad it was only a fortnight to his wedding, and happy that he was going to see her again tomorrow.

The Borjigin camp stirred at first light, which was at four o'clock. The man drank a hasty breakfast of kumiss and then mounted up to scatter the herds. Dragone would accompany them. Baltomar summoned his wives to help him bury their jewellery and his money; over the years he had accumulated a great deal of valuable silver from trading with people in the cities, as well as hardly less valuable silk cloth, essential for great occasions – he did not intend to let the Commissars get their hands on any of that. 'Ride to Khalim,' he told his youngest son.

Batalji kicked his horse, waved to his mother, cantered out of the encampment. The Anhusats were situated on the far side of the low range of hills, and Batalji knew it would be a ride of some three hours. Besides, there was no necessity to hurry; Father had said they had a week in which to make their arrangements. Thus he walked his horse once he was out of sight of the *ordu*, threading his way along the bridle path between the rocks, making for the river, watching his brothers and uncles rounding up the nearest herd. The reindeer were the source of all the Mongols' wealth, providing as they did all the essentials of life, not only meat and milk, but also the hide for the making of boots and winter clothing – while they were also used as pack animals when necessary.

The herd faded from his sight, and the shouts of the men from his hearing. He had been just an hour on his journey when he heard the growl of engines. He drew rein and looked up. The tracker plane was back, swooping low and circling. He grinned. They would be able to tell that the Borjigins were scattering their herds, but once the herds *were* scattered, there was no way any Commissar from Yakutsk was going to be able to tell who they belonged to, or if they belonged to anyone – the nomads did not brand their animals: *they* knew what belonged to whom.

He kicked his pony again, and frowned. The plane engines seemed very loud. Again he reined, looking over his shoulder. The plane had dropped down to just under a thousand feet, and was unloading parachutists. While behind it, out of the dawn sky, there came a succession of helicopters, gunships and transport planes. Batalji's heart seemed to constrict, as he watched the parachutists floating to the earth, the helicopters swooping low to unload their human cargoes. What to do? Father had sent him to the Anhusats. But if there was going to be trouble ... The Commissars had never sent troops to collect taxes before.

Batalji wheeled his horse and galloped back towards the camp, drawing rein as he approached in order not to be overseen, slipping from his pony's back amidst the last of the boulders to stay in shelter while he stared at the tents. The plane, having dropped its cargo, had turned and was flying east, already almost out of sight. The parachutists had landed, shed their chutes, and grouped, well over fifty of them, perhaps a hundred yards from the tents. The helicopters were already on the ground, and their people were also unloaded and assembled; there were more than fifty of them too, green-uniformed and helmeted men, armed with AK-47 assault rifles – the Kalashnikov; they were on the other side of the encampment.

In front of the soldiers there were several men, also wearing uniform, but with peaked caps and red tabs on their shoulders and lapels; they were accompanied by some men in civilian dress. Standing in front of them was Baltomar, but as Batalji watched, his brothers and Dragone rode up, clearly also wishing to be involved in whatever was happening. Batalji could not hear what was being said, but he could tell that the discussion was animated, for his father was waving his arms in protest. Then suddenly the morning exploded. Baltomar must have given an order, for Andalji and Tengut and Barone began running for the tents.

Now the Commissar also gave an order, shouted, waving his arms. But before anyone could respond, Baltomar had drawn the pistol he always carried in his pocket, and shot the Commissar at close range. The man fell, and for a moment there was stricken consternation. Baltomar used the time to run back to the tents, whence his sons were emerging, rifles in their hands. But the paratroopers and the soldiers were also advancing, guns levelled and now chattering. It all happened too quickly for Batalji immediately to react. Before, it seemed, he could blink, Baltomar was stretched on the ground, and so were his brothers and Dragone, limbs sprawled in the grotesque ballet of death. While the soldiers and paratroopers continued their advance, towards the women and girls, who were running to their menfolk in distraught distress.

Batalji uttered a great cry of mingled misery and defiance, leapt on to his horse, and charged at the soldiers, continuing a high-pitched scream of angry anguish. Someone fired a single shot, which smacked into the pony's forehead. The animal dropped like a stone, and Batalji, who like his brothers rode without a saddle, landed on his feet and kept on running.

'Hold your fire,' someone shouted. 'He is only a boy.'

Batalji stumbled, and fell to his hands and knees. Before he could recover, his arms were grasped and he was dragged to his feet and forward, towards the tents. His toes caught in Andalji's body, and he looked down in horror at his brother's staring eyes, the blood which had gathered on his chest. But there was more horror further on, as he came up to the tent itself. Here was pure bestiality, as he watched his mother and sisters stretched on the ground, their pantaloons torn off, while between their legs knelt the Russian soldiers. Selphine, as the youngest and prettiest of Baltomar's wives, had been taken by the commander of the soldiers, a heavy-set, thick-moustached man, who held her legs up and apart as he thrust himself into her, with violent jerks of his buttocks. Selphine's arms were held above her head by two of Taychin's men, eagerly awaiting their turn.

'Here's a tiger cub,' said a sergeant, thrusting his fingers into Batalji's hair to pull up his head.

'Batalji!' Selphine screamed.

Boris Taychin climaxed, and reared on his heels, while the woman beneath him writhed in misery. 'A tiger cub indeed.' He looked down at the woman. 'Yours?'

'Spare him,' Selphine begged. 'He is a boy. Spare him.'

Taychin grinned. 'I'll not kill a boy. He'll make a good Communist one day. But a boy should *know* his mother. Roll the bitch over, and bring the boy here.'

THE SECOND CHRONICLE

Moscow, October 2000

Denise l'Auberon was waiting in the satellite at Charles de Gaulle. 'Why, Clive,' she remarked. 'You have lost weight.'

Clive kissed her. 'But you, dearest thing, have not. Thank God!'

Denise was petite, like all the best Frenchwomen. She had, unusually for her nationality, auburn hair, which she wore short, and which was clearly genuine when one looked at her freckled pale skin; she was a throwback to an Irish grandmother. Her figure was also petite, save for her breasts, which were disproportionately large, a source of annoyance to Denise but of great attraction to an MCP like Clive.

They had liked each other from the moment of their first meeting, several years previously, when they had discovered that they shared, apart from a mutual awareness of their professional excellence, a relaxed sense of values: good food, good drink – where she put it all he had no idea – good music and good sex. And in Denise's case, couture clothes worn with the elegant arrogance that characterised her every movement. Even in ski pants and anorak she looked ready to enter a ballroom. She exuded chic, and could do so even in a sandstorm, a hurricane, up to her ears in mud, or while sheltering from mortar fire ... filming all the while. 'They say we are to go to Siberia,' she remarked.

'Our pasts have caught up with us,' Clive agreed. 'Actually, while we're on the subject, would you like to marry me?'

'When?'

'When's our flight?'

'From the next satellite in fifteen minutes. Georges and Henri are waiting.'

'Then how about Moscow?'

'I am a Roman Catholic,' she reminded him, enigmatically.

'What do we have?' Denise asked, as the jet whined into the east, ice forming on its wing edges.

'*Coup d'état*, engineered by Batalji Borjigin.'

'I thought he was dead,' Denise said.

'Apparently, like Mark Twain, that report was a trifle exaggerated.'

'Dead or alive, he's the most wanted man in Europe,' Georges said. Georges chain-smoked, alternating reefers with cigarettes. But he was the only director Denise would accept. As they shared a flat in Paris, Clive supposed he should be jealous. But somehow Denise was not the sort of woman over whom one became jealous – one merely gathered the crumbs whenever they were available.

'In Russia, anyway,' he countered. 'Presumably, now he's more wanted than ever. But it'll be interesting to discover what they intend to do about him, in their present position.'

'They can't do anything about him,' remarked Henri, Denise's sound recordist. 'Not now that winter has set in. Save maybe bomb Yakutsk.'

Clive surmised that Henri was about the only man closely connected with Denise who had not been to bed with her; on the other hand, he reckoned it might be necessary to be gay in order to work with her on a full-time basis.

'They can't do that, indiscriminately,' Georges argued.

'There are Americans in Yakutsk. Some kind of historical research project.'

'So what are the Americans doing about it?' Clive asked.

'At the moment, nothing,' Henri said. 'Like everybody else, they've been taken entirely by surprise. And anyway, like everyone else, there isn't much they *can* do.'

'So we are on an assignment where nobody knows a goddamn about anything,' Denise commented.

'We should be able to find out something in Moscow,' Georges suggested.

Denise slept with her head on Clive's shoulder, having dined well; the stewardess thoughtfully provided a blanket large enough to cover them both. 'There's sure to be a Roman Catholic priest in Moscow,' Clive whispered.

'But we are just passing through. And why do you want to marry me, all of a sudden? Have you not all of me, right now?'

'I was thinking of tomorrow.'

'I shall be here tomorrow, too,' she reminded him. 'But what about Holly? I thought you were going to marry her?'

'Only if I can't marry you,' he told her.

Norton, the station manager, was waiting when they emerged from the customs hall at Moscow International, after the Air France jet skidded to a halt on a snow-swept runway. 'When's our connection?' Denise demanded. 'Have I time for a hot bath?'

'There are problems,' Norton explained. He was a perpetually worried man, but this night he seemed to have a genuine reason. 'All flights to Yakutsk have been cancelled. Seems the rebels fired on a military plane sent in to find out what's going on.'

'So what *is* going on?' Clive asked.

'Nobody knows. There is a sizeable Russian garrison in Yakutiya, but it is in scattered posts, and these have been instructed to keep a low profile until further orders. That is in line with Russian policy throughout the past ten years, where there have been clashes during independence takeovers.'

'Well, surely these posts have reported in?'

'They don't know much more about the situation than anyone else. The garrison in Yakutsk has been blacked out.'

'You don't mean they've been eliminated? Threlfall was saying something about a bloodbath.'

'Nobody knows,' Norton said helplessly. 'But that's hard to believe. There are two thousand men in Yakutsk, fully armed and equipped with tanks.'

'It sounds like a load of shit,' Henri commented.

'Into which we are obliged to jump, if we can get there,' Denise pointed out.

'We will charter a plane,' Georges decided.

'It'll have to be a pretty sizeable plane,' Clive said. 'It's three thousand miles from Moscow to Yakutsk.'

'We will stop and fuel, when necessary.'

'That's the point,' Norton said. 'Fuel. It is very scarce. You will also need permission from the Ministry of the Interior.'

'So let's get on with it.'

'It is nine o'clock,' Denise said.

'Correction, Mademoiselle l'Auberon,' Norton said. 'It is midnight. You haven't changed your watch.'

'I never change my watch,' Denise told him. 'To me, wherever I am, it is Paris time. If you knew we could not continue, I assume you have an hotel booked for us?'

'That's right, the Berlin.'

'Then I suggest you take us there. We can do nothing tonight, and I need both a hot bath and a warm bed.'

Norton looked at Georges, who shrugged. The men trailed behind her, Henri coping with the photographic equipment. 'First thing tomorrow, Norton,' Clive said, 'we want all the big guns we can find. Rope in the Ambassador, if you have to. I want to be on my way by lunchtime.'

Clive dropped in on Denise's bath, which was always rejuvenating. 'Norton is a bloody pessimist. Says we'll be lucky to get out of here in a week.'

Denise soaped, slowly and luxuriously. 'You should ring Threlfall. Or Dubois. Or both.'

'Our best bet is the Ambassador.'

She handed him the loofah. 'Do my back.' She leaned forward, her chin on her knees. 'Anyway, what's a week? If we can't get in, nobody else can get in. And no news can get out. We'll still have the first pictures.'

He knew she was right, but he was still bothered. He discarded the loofah to knead the soft flesh. 'I keep thinking of an entire country in the hands of a bloodthirsty killer like Borjigin.'

Denise leaned back, and he started work on her front. 'Is he bloodthirsty by nature, or circumstance?' she asked.

'Circumstance certainly played a part. Seems his entire family was wiped out, oh, twenty-four years ago, for not paying taxes. He was the only male survivor. While the women were raped and beaten.'

'That would make me fairly bloodthirsty,' Denise said, closing her eyes and giving a little sigh. 'Twenty-four years ago he could only have been a boy.'

'Fourteen.'

'So what happened to him?'

'He was sent to an orphanage for the children of delinquents. Now, from what I have read about such places, that was likely to make him even more bloodthirsty. And a lot more besides.'

Denise opened her eyes. 'I think we had better move this conversation to bed, before the bath overflows.'

CHAPTER TWO

Omsk, 1976-8

By the time the train reached Omsk, there were six teenagers in the compartment, and two guards. Presumably all the other five were also orphans, Batalji reckoned; conversation was not encouraged. Two of them were girls. Thus the guards were a man and a woman. They paid little attention to their charges, save to slap them on the head when they spoke or looked as if they might be about to speak. And to mock them. 'You're going into the army,' they told the frightened children. 'That'll take the shit from your bellies.'

The compartment consisted of four double bunks, arranged in two tiers. There were no mattresses, just wooden boards. The four boys slept on the upper bunks; the two girls slept on one of the lower double bunks, the two guards on the other. Food consisted of bread and soup, and tea, which they prepared themselves in the samovar in the corridor. There were no toilet facilities, but the train stopped at least twice a day, when there was a desperate dash for the bushes beside the track.

There was a single blanket to each double bunk. This was not really necessary in June, but everyone used their blanket, and Batalji discovered that it was impossible to share a blanket with someone and not speak to him, even if their conversation had to be in whispers. 'I am Kalji,' whispered his bedmate, on the first night out of Skorovodino. 'My father wrote an article against the government. He is in prison.'

'I am Batalji,' Batalji replied. 'My father is dead.' He did not offer any more information than that.

'One of those girls is very pretty,' Kalji said. 'Do you think the guards would let me fuck her?'

'No,' Batalji said.

'I don't see why not. The two of them are fucking right now.'

Batalji had wondered at the reason for the heavy sighs and the creaking boards in the bunk beneath him.

'While they are fucking,' Kalji whispered, 'they are helpless. We could take their guns and get away. All of us. We would take the girls with us. Then we could fuck them.'

'Go to sleep,' Batalji recommended. The fellow seemed to have a one-track mind. Batalji didn't want to fuck anyone. He was not sure he would ever be able to fuck anyone again, even Mortana – supposing he was ever going to see Mortana again. But he knew that throughout his life he was never going to lose the memory of his mother, his so beautiful, passionate mother, writhing beneath him while Boris Taychin poked him in the ass with his stick and laughed and said, 'Harder, boy, drive harder. They like them harder.'

Mother had whispered in his ear as he had ejaculated: 'Remember!'

She had not been thinking of incest, but of revenge. Yet it was her he remembered. Now he needed to think. And feel. And understand. Why? *Why?* *WHY?* There had been little metaphysical reflection in the tents of the Borjigins. The gods had been *there*, urged on by the *tengri*, the spirits of the upper air who controlled the weather. Some of the gods, like Daschbog, the great glowing orb of the sun, were clearly visible for half of the year; others, such as Stribog, who rode the storm winds, and Pierroun, who hurled his lightning shafts down from the heavens, occasionally so, and the more terrifying *because* they came only occasionally. There were no feminine gods in the Mongol cosmology.

Once upon a time, according to Father – and he had merely been repeating what his parents had told him – there had been priests who had spoken of an utterly invisible god, who divided the world into good and evil, and wished men to be at peace with other men, to love them and to share with them. It was not possible to conceive of such a deity – who had clearly never had to exist on the steppes – or of such a concept. To a Borjigin good was when his belly was full, his herd was fertile, his wife was comforting, and the sun was shining. Evil was when those things were absent. Life was sacred, but only within the clan. If someone attempted to run off with Borjigin cattle, or a Borjigin woman, or, worst of all, steal a Borjigin horse, he was worth only death, and as painful a death as possible, to discourage other trespassers. A Borjigin who had been forced to rape his own mother did not bear consideration.

After the priests had come the Commissars, who had preached that there were no gods, visible or invisible. Only the State. But as the Commissars had practised all the evil ways possible, their thesis was self-defeating. Yet the Commissars had won in the end, by their sheer numbers. And the quality of their weapons. If Batalji knew he would never forget the sight of his father and brothers lying on the ground smothered in blood, their bodies cut to ribbons by the paratroopers' bullets, he knew also he would never forget the image of the AK-47s the soldiers had carried, dream weapons, as far superior to the old bolt-loading magazine rifles of the Borjigins as the aeroplane was to the horse, when it came to the speed and power of movement.

His grief had been to a certain extent alleviated by the sight of the weapons. Not his anger. He wished to possess one of those guns, to stand astride the world, and shatter anyone or everyone who stood in his way. One day.

Just as to a certain extent his horror at what had happened to his mother and sisters had been alleviated by his own experiences since that dreadful day. First had come the farewell, when their sweating bodies had been pulled apart by the laughing soldiers. Selphine had screamed his name, again and again, as he had been thrown into the cabin of the helicopter, until her screams had abruptly ended. She and his sisters and their fellow wives and daughters, having satisfied the soldiers, had been left, to bury the dead, and survive, if they could. He wondered if he would ever see her again? Or if she would wish to see him?

Then he had flown in an aeroplane, for the first time in his life, even if it had been a helicopter, and his wrists had been handcuffed behind his back. He had been taken to the city, again for the first time in his life. His father had always told him that cities were evil places, where good grazing ground was occupied by vast piles of concrete bricks and the grass was hidden beneath streams of asphalt. Where human beings lived artificial lives huddled in little boxes in front of stinking fires, and died early from the noxious fumes emanating from their factory chimneys. 'Had I my way,' Baltomar had often said, 'I would level all the cities in the world.' Then he would smile. 'That is what Genghis Khan did, many years ago.'

Yakutsk had certainly seemed an evil place, but it had only been one of so many exciting experiences thrust at him. He had never driven in a truck before, and he had never seen such a road before, stretching to the south for more than a thousand kilometres, branching away from the River Lena at Kachikattsy, rumbling through towns like Tommot and cities like Aldan – as big as Yakutsk – and climbing into the mountains of the Khrebet Synnagyn before reaching Skovorodino on the second day. On the way they had picked up his five travelling companions, but he had not been interested in them so much as the steadily increasing heat, and the luxuriant vegetation.

At Skovorodino he had seen the railway. Batalji had never even heard of a railway, had no idea what the two metal strips, too thin to walk upon, meant, until the train had come puffing into the station, the most amazing sight he had ever seen. His companions had laughed at his ignorance, and been cuffed into silence by the guards. When Batalji had realised that he was actually going to travel in this steel monster he had been afraid, for the first time in his life.

Now he felt a veteran. Now he was prepared to wait, and discover what other marvels this world held in store, marvels which he would one day use to destroy all those responsible for his father's death, and his mother's rape. This was his dream. Marvels, too, which would one day take him back to Mortana. He had said he would wait forever. So would she, he knew.

At Omsk they left the train. By then they had spent several days together, and knew each other very well, physically. People stared at them, and then backed away, from their stench and their obvious filth. They tramped through the streets and arrived at the State Orphanage, a grim foursquare multi-storeyed yellow building with small barred windows on the outside, and, after they had marched through an arched gateway beneath the building, a huge courtyard. Here there waited several uniformed men and women. The six orphans were lined up, and one of the women came forward, stood before them, hands on hips.

'I am Vera Shackinarsky,' she announced. 'I am the Commandant of this orphanage. You will address me as Madame Comrade.' She looked from face to face, and the orphans looked back. Batalji thought she might once have been a handsome woman; there were still traces of an erstwhile beauty in her strong face and deep eyes, and her dark hair, worn in a tight bun beneath her green sidecap, was clearly long. But the features were cold, the mouth cruel, and her figure was heavy, made heavier by the green skirt and thick blouse – he had never seen a woman in uniform before. Now he became aware that she was staring back at him, more than any of the others. 'You stink,' she said. 'All of you stink. To the baths.'

Two of the men pointed. 'At the double!' The orphans ran for the designated doorway. 'Drop that rubbish!' shouted the guard, and the small bundles the others had brought with them

– Batalji had nothing – were thrown on the ground, to burst open and scatter their contents. Other guards moved forward to pick through them, and one of the boys stopped to look over his shoulder.

'On the double!' shouted the guard, hitting him across the shoulders with his stick. The boy gasped, and ran. They tumbled through the doorway into a large, bare room, where showerheads jutted from the walls. 'Strip!' the guard commanded.

They obeyed, the two girls hesitating only a moment; after the five days on the train they no longer possessed any modesty. 'In there!' The six of them stumbled forward, and water hissed out of the jets. It was cold, and stung their bodies, and they huddled together with little gasps and whimpers. Kalji found himself against the pretty girl, whose name was Rosa, and predictably had an erection.

'You!' Commandant Shackinarsky had come into the room. 'Out!' Kalji hesitated. 'You!' the Commandant snapped again. Kalji stepped from the water. The Commandant's hand moved, and was found to contain a rubber truncheon. This flicked the tip of Kalji's penis, and he gave a shriek of pain, and fell to his knees, clutching his genitals. 'There will no sexual contact in this orphanage,' Commandant Shackinarsky announced. 'Outside!'

They stumbled from the showers and into the open air, their skins rapidly drying in the hot sun. But here they found themselves facing some sixty boys and girls, like the guards, like Comrade Shackinarsky, wearing green uniforms, green sidecaps, and brown boots, standing stiffly to attention. In front of them was what looked like a very low iron vaulting horse: four uprights and two parallel crossbars, the crossbars set rather unusually wide apart. And standing beside the horse was a man with a cane. 'We will have discipline here,' Commandant Shackinarsky told them. 'You will all be caned.'

'But we have done nothing,' protested the girl Rosa, her body glowing with a combination of embarrassment and fear and indignation.

'Discipline means you will speak when you are spoken to,' Commandant Shackinarsky told her. 'This one first. Twelve strokes.'

Rosa gasped as two of the guards seized her arms and pulled her forward. They pushed her against the bar, which struck her neatly in the groin, so that her body fell forward. 'Hold the other bar,' the guard commanded, and Rosa wrapped her fingers around it, young breasts dangling, her hair clouding past her face.

'If you attempt to get up, your sentence will be doubled,' Commandant Shackinarsky ordered.

Rosa shivered, and the guard commenced to beat her upturned buttocks. Rosa screamed and writhed and stamped her feet, but she did not let go of the second bar. Now Batalji could not control an erection of his own, and hastily stepped round Kalji, who was still clutching his penis and weeping with pain, so as to be once removed from the Commandant. But after the twelfth stroke of the cane, when Rosa was allowed to release the bar – her fingers had to be prised loose – and told to stand up, he found the Commandant looking at him again. 'That one next,' she said. 'He is thinking of sex. Give him twelve, too.'

'I am Oleg. I am the boss here.' The four male orphans huddled together; the girls had been sent to a dormitory of their own. Oleg was at least sixteen, Batalji reckoned, and was some inches taller than any of them, as well as broader and thicker. But then, so were all the other five boys in the dormitory.

Oleg had heavy features, too, and twitching hands. He glared at them. 'So what're you crying about?' he demanded. 'A sore ass? Comrade Vera has six of us caned every day. It doesn't matter whether we have broken any rules or not. When new kids arrive, we old hands have a holiday. Now watch this.'

He showed them how to make their beds; an improperly made bed involved a caning. Then he led them downstairs to the communal dining hall, where all seventy orphans sat at long tables, with tin plates and mugs. They were all wearing green uniforms by now, and it was difficult to identify anyone, but at last Batalji spotted Rosa, and smiled at her. She was obviously still in considerable pain – perhaps she had never been caned before, and she was clearly not a horsewoman but a city dweller, so her ass would be soft, he supposed – but she managed a brief smile back before bending her head over her plate.

The food consisted of potatoes and onions. 'Do we ever get meat?' Kalji whispered. Apparently he came from a once-wealthy city family – his father had been a member of the Party before being expelled for his criticisms.

'Once a week,' Oleg told him. 'But it is too tough to eat, anyway. You just suck it.'

Kalji looked upset by this, but Batalji had only eaten meat on half a dozen occasions in his life, when for one reason or another there had been a huge feast on the steppes. There would have been meat at his marriage to Mortana. When he remembered that, he wanted to weep, and two tears trickled down his cheeks before he could stop himself.

'There is no room for crybabies here,' Oleg warned him.

After the meal Oleg showed them the laundry, where they would wash their clothes. They each had two shirts, two pairs of drawers, and two pairs of pants, one pair of boots, and one sidecap. They were not issued with socks. As far as Batalji could make out, the girls wore exactly the same.

They were also issued with a hairbrush and a toothbrush each. No other personal possessions were permitted. 'Kit inspection is once a week.' Oleg warned them. 'Your spare clothes must always be clean and folded, so.' He showed them.

Then it was time for their first class.

The instructor issued them with pencils and paper, rulers and erasers; Batalji had never seen any of these things before, had no idea what they were for. 'You will write your name, your age, your parents' names and ages when they died, at the head of the paper,' commanded the instructor.

Batalji stared at the white sheet with a slowly growing sense of panic. Then he looked at the instructor, who was a small man, and did not seem very aggressive. The instructor looked back at him. 'Why are you not writing, boy?'

Batalji licked his lips.

'Stand up!' the instructor commanded.

Batalji stood up, aware that everyone in the room – and there were girls as well as boys – was staring at him.

'Why are you not writing, boy?'

'Batalji licked his lips again. 'I cannot, Comrade Instructor.'

'Is there something the matter with your hand?'

'I cannot write, Comrade Instructor.'

'You are insubordinate.'

'I was never taught!' Batalji cried. 'I have never been to school.'

There was a ripple of laughter, immediately suppressed as the instructor glared around the room. Then he picked up a red card from his desk – there were several cards lying there, in different colours. 'Take this to the Commandant.'

Batalji left his desk and took the card. He looked at Oleg, in an endeavour to discover what the red card meant, but Oleg's face was stony. Batalji left the classroom, went along the corridor and down the stairs, encountered another of the instructors. 'Why are you not in class, boy?'

'I am to report to the Commandant, Comrade Instructor.'

'You are lying. You are a truant.'

'I have a card ...' Desperately, Batalji produced his red card.

The instructor grinned. 'That is twelve of the best. Let us make it twenty-four.' He felt in the breast pocket of his tunic and gave Batalji another red card. 'Off you go.'

Batalji wanted to scream a protest, but he took the card. His backside was still stinging from his earlier caning. The thought of receiving another twenty-four strokes ... He stumbled into the sunlight, looked from left to right, blinking, seeking some direction, and was accosted by another instructor, this one a woman. 'Boy, what are you doing out of the building?'

'I am to report to the Commandant. Can you direct me to her office, please, Comrade Instructor?'

'Boy, you are insubordinate. Do you think you can visit the Commandant whenever you choose?'

'I have these cards...' He held out the two red cards.

The instructress smiled. 'You are in deep shit. I will make it deeper, boy.' She gave him another red card. 'You will have no skin on your ass tomorrow.'

Batalji uttered a shriek of outrage, and hurled himself at her.

Commandant Shackinarsky surveyed Batalji, who stood before her desk, between two male instructors, his wrists manacled. On the desk was his file. 'I am empowered to have you shot,' she said. 'This is a military establishment, and you have committed mutiny. What have you to say?'

'I cannot read or write,' Batalji said. His sense of despair was so complete he even spoke quietly. 'I was never taught to read or write. I am to be punished for having never been taught to read or write. All I asked was the way to your office. I am to be punished for asking the way to your office.'

'You are insubordinate,' the Commandant said. 'Did I not tell you how to address me?'

Batalji sighed. 'Yes, Madame Comrade.'

'You are a shitbag Mongol from the steppes,' Commandant Shackinarsky told him. 'And I am supposed to make a human being out of such an animal. Your father was a deviant. Your entire family are deviants. It is the goodness of the State that grants you an education.'

'To be a soldier,' Batalji muttered.

'There is no finer purpose than to serve the State, with arms in your hands. But you must learn discipline. If I do not teach you discipline, the army will, and you will find them much more severe than us here.'

'But I have done nothing,' Batalji protested.

'You are breaking the rules now, by addressing me. You are a deviant, like your father. You will spend the next month in solitary confinement. During that time you will learn to read and write. I will instruct you myself. And every morning you will receive six strokes of the cane.'

Batalji wanted to protest again, as she could see. She smiled. 'I am at least saving you from being buggered. For a month.'

Batalji had no idea what she was talking about. He could imagine no worse fate than that with which he was now faced. Commandant Shackinarsky enjoyed her work. Batalji soon realised that she also enjoyed him. She enjoyed having him caned, but she also apparently enjoyed spending two hours with him every day teaching him to read and write, at least his name. She enjoyed taunting him, and once he could write made him write over and over again, 'My father was a deviant scoundrel'.

But some of her taunting was informative, for she told him about the Mongols, about how they had roamed the steppes for generations, in a way Baltomar and Selphine never had. Vera Shackinarsky dismissed his forebears as savages, and told him he was a savage too, but that rather appealed to him. And once upon a time they had been very successful savages indeed, who had overrun all the world, from China to the Danube.

Equally, soon he understood that she was interested in him sexually, from the way she usually visited the bathhouse when he was in there – as he was in solitary confinement he had to bathe when the others were in class – but he was too innocent to have any idea what she might want from him, especially as she had declared at their first meeting that there was to be no sex. He was therefore the more taken aback when, three days before he was due to be returned to his dormitory, and he was in her office laboriously picking his way through a text by Lenin, she suddenly took the book from his hands and snapped it shut, then sat on the desk beside him. 'I want you to suck me,' she commanded. Batalji goggled at her. 'Have you never had a woman?' she demanded. Batalji hesitated, then shook his head. 'You are lying,' Comrade Shackinarsky declared. 'Tell me about it, or I will have you caned.'

'It was my mother,' Batalji muttered.

'What did you say, boy?'

'It was my mother!' he said.

'You filthy little bastard!'

'They made me,' he shouted, now close to tears. 'The Commissars made me!'

Commandant Shackinarsky studied him for several seconds. 'You poor little boy,' she remarked at last. 'Presumably you did not enjoy that. Then I will teach you how to enjoy sex also, you little savage. And how to make a woman happy. Then the next time you fuck your mother she will enjoy it too, eh?' She stood up, pulled her skirt up round her waist, then slid her heavy green drawers past her hips and kicked them off. Then she sat on the desk again, her knees wide. 'Get in there and suck me,' she said. 'Use your tongue. Do not bite. If you bite me I will coat your prick in red pepper.'

Not really understanding what was happening to him, Batalji buried his head in the thick dark hair between her thighs, desperately thrusting his tongue in every direction. He felt her hands on his head, and she climaxed in great shuddering gasps. Then she pushed him away and slid off the desk. 'Now come in there,' she said, pointing to an inner room where there was a couch. 'And I will teach you how to fuck.'

Batalji didn't know whether he was standing on his head or his heels. What had happened to him, what he had been forced to do, had been utterly fascinating, had made him forget his misery, even if it brought back the memory of Selphine more clearly than ever ... and he could not help but wonder how much more enjoyable it might have been with Mortana, or even the girl Rosa, than with a woman old enough, by the standards of the steppes, to be his grandmother. But to have conquered the Commandant was a sufficient triumph, he reckoned.

Only he hadn't conquered her at all. The next morning he was marched into the courtyard as usual and caned, while she stood by and smiled. 'I thought you liked me,' he ventured, when he returned to her office; she could only cane him again for rudeness.

'Like you, you miserable savage shit?' she asked. 'I like your prick. Bring it here.'

*

Clearly her rules about sex did not apply to her personally. In fact Batalji quickly realised that they applied only to relations between the male and female inmates, presumably simply because dealing with pregnancies was a nuisance. Two days later he was returned to his dormitory. By then he had decided that he hated Madame Vera. But there did not seem anything he could do about her – until the day he could get hold of one of those automatic weapons. And he now discovered that solitary confinement, a daily caning, and a daily dose of Vera was heaven compared with the hell that was the dormitory. He understood this the moment he entered, and looked at Kalji, expecting a sympathetic greeting. But Kalji's vague air of intellectual superiority combined with defiance, had vanished, along, apparently, with his desire to be friends. Kalji now stood with stooped shoulders, glanced sideways, and gave anxious little smiles; he had been raped, by Oleg or one of the other seniors, every night since their arrival.

Now it was Batalji's turn. When he tried to fight them they beat him half unconscious, and then held him on his face and had him just the same; Kalji was one of those who held him down. When he told them that he had fucked the Commandant and was her favourite, Oleg merely laughed. 'Stupid shit,' he said. 'Comrade Vera has every boy in this place. And every girl, too.'

Oleg and his friends were interested only in sex. But then, so it seemed, was everyone else in the orphanage. A few days later Batalji happened to find himself standing next to Rosa as they waited in line for their food. 'Are you all right?' he whispered.

She glanced at him, then looked away again, giving an anxious glance at the senior female orphan, Tamara. Her ears glowed. And he realised that nothing was different in the girls' dormitories, either. He wondered if she had already been given private tuition by Madam Vera.

Life would have been unbearable – and several of the orphans did commit, or attempt, suicide every year – had not the sexual hell of the dormitories, the humiliations of the daily beatings, the misery of the heat in the summer and the cold in the winter, the poor food and the constant hunger, been alleviated by the lessons and instructions. For many of the orphans this was as great a hell as anything else, but for Batalji it was the fulfilment of a dream. Because they were being trained to fight. 'You're good for nothing else,' said their field instructor, an old soldier. 'You'll carry a gun for Mother Russia, and you'll die. You'll lie on the ground with your guts spilling out and ants crawling into your bellies.' He grinned at the terror in their faces. 'It's my business to make sure you take some of the buggers with you.'

'Who will they be, Comrade Instructor?' asked one of the boys.

'British, French, Americans, Germans. Oh yes, Germans,' the instructor said. 'NATO people. Capitalist swine. They hate us, because they're afraid of us. They'd like to bring us down. But they can't, because we're too strong for them. One day, we'll bring *them* down.'

And one day, I will bring you down, Batalji thought.

But for the time being he was happy to learn. All the orphans were destined for the army, girls as well as boys. Thus they trained together. They learned drill, from marching in step to standing absolutely still for upwards of an hour – the slightest movement was rewarded with a caning – to doing the goosestep, rifles held rigidly upright in one hand. 'Who knows?' the instructor grinned. 'One day you may be on guard duty outside Lenin's tomb.'

They went on route marches, winter and summer, armed with rifles and full bandoliers and heavy packs, staggering with exhaustion before their return, but knowing that to fall down was to be caned. They learned unarmed combat, fighting each other with a desperate intensity which sent several of them to the infirmary with broken bones, because not to fight one's hardest earned a caning. Batalji fought harder than anyone, and could beat anyone his own size and weight.

They underwent obstacle courses, again winter and summer, which involved fording rivers and swinging from trees. Some of the girls just could not do this, and were savagely beaten by their instructors, and then, being classified as useless, were put to work in the kitchens and cleaning the barracks. 'You are useless shitbags,' Commandant Vera told them. 'You will wind up sweeping the streets.' The girls wept.

They also learned to handle weapons, rifles and bayonets. Only in this regard was Batalji disappointed. The rifles were very old, breech-loading, bolt-action weapons such as had been used by the Mongols and Yakuts of the steppes. They were allowed nothing modern, and nothing automatic at all. 'Time for that,' their instructor told them, 'when you are proper soldiers. If shitbags like you can ever be proper soldiers.'

But he also taught them to shoot, and was pleased with Batalji, because Batalji, brought up on the steppes and with a gun always to hand, was already a crack shot. Comrade Vera summoned him to her office. 'Comrade Perone is pleased with you,' she said. 'You may be a success after all, Comrade Borjigin. Continue to please, and you will go far.'

As usual, she then sent him into the inner room. But by now Batalji understood the true facts of life, which were that one always surrendered, until one was strong enough to destroy one's enemy. He did not know when he would achieve that objective. But he did know that he was growing bigger and stronger every day, that he was already the best embryo soldier in the orphanage, and that there were times he was almost happy ... if he could forget about Oleg and Madame Vera.

The orphans were also required to receive political instruction, for two hours a day. This most of them found utterly boring, but again Batalji found it fascinating. He learned all the facets of the Marxist doctrine. He did not believe them himself – they had no application on the steppes – but he could see that his instructors believed them, and his instructors were representative of the regime.

He was most interested in the story of how the Bolsheviks gained power; not the political in-fighting which had preceded and followed their establishment, but the way they had survived the destructive wars which had followed, and which had been intended to crush them. 'Comrade Lenin's enemies were divided,' Comrade Perone explained. 'That is the secret of successful warfare, comrades. Divide your enemies, and take advantage of those divisions. Kornilov, Deniken, Yudenich, Kolchak ... they all wanted something different, and none of them would work with the other. While the so-called Allies were the most divided of all. We had British and Americans and French and Japanese and Czechs fighting against us. We were outnumbered and outgunned and outmanoeuvred. But we won. Because they too could not agree on what they were fighting for, what they were fighting against. There again is the secret, comrades. A man, an army, a country, is only strong when he is certain of both himself and his objectives. Once doubt enters the mind, defeat is certain. In the Western democracies, because of their system, there were always men who sympathised with our ideals, and other men who felt it was wrong to try to change our ideals, at least by force, and other men who just did not wish to go on fighting. While we had no doubts. We knew we had to fight, or die. And we knew that our system was the best, the only way. Comrade Lenin knew this. And so we triumphed.'

'Did Comrade Lenin command the Red Army himself, in the Great Civil War?' Batalji asked.

'Of course. Comrade Lenin commanded us in everything at that time.'

'My father says that the Red Army was commanded by Lev Trotsky,' Kalji objected.

Comrade Perone glared at him, then picked up a red card.

As Kalji, trembling, left the room, Batalji wondered if he would be invited into the inner room.

*

He doubted it. Kalji had become totally committed to the gay community within the dormitory. Batalji was committed to this community himself. He had no means of resisting it, and he held no positive views on sexual morality. The only woman he had ever properly serviced was Madame Vera, and it was impossible to become emotionally involved with her, except through hatred. He dreamed of Mortana, and of Rosa, often mixing up the two – and mixing them both up with Selphine – and of doing to them what Madame Vera had him do to her, but he did not know if he would ever achieve any of his dreams. And in the meantime there were his comrades in the dormitory, always randy, always eager to grab and to pull, sometimes even to caress and embrace.

But everything they did was at the behest of Oleg, who ruled them with a rod of iron, quite literally. He made them have sex with each other, to amuse him, and he made them have sex with him, whenever he needed servicing. It was this sexual slavery that Batalji hated, with a hatred which slowly mounted, as he himself grew and strengthened. He seemed to do this faster than the others, not in height, but in breadth and muscle power. After he had been in the orphanage a year, and was fifteen years old, he could run faster, and longer, and lift heavier weights, than any of the other inmates. He was still several inches shorter than Oleg, who was now seventeen and had an incipient beard, and was soon to leave to join the army, but he felt he was just as strong and tough. And he knew he hated, more than Oleg.

But the concept of doing something about his hatred was immense. It involved challenging authority, and Batalji had come to realise that authority was unchallengeable. It was simply too immense, too all-pervading, too powerful. He might never have taken the decision had not, only a month before Oleg was due to leave, some new orphans arrived. Amongst them was a Yakut boy named Almani Serhat; the Serhats were Selphine's clan.

Almani was a pretty boy, like all his family a throwback to some non-Mongol wanderer; like Selphine he had fair hair and aquiline features, blue eyes and a very white body. When he was shown into Oleg's dormitory, Oleg's eyes gleamed. Batalji was now one of the senior boys, and he showed Almani the ropes. Almani was overwhelmed to have found a friend he felt he could trust. 'Batalji Borjigin,' he said. 'Prince Batalji!'

'Prince?' Batalji was astonished.

'You are the only surviving male of the royal clan,' Almani explained. 'Did you not know this?'

Batalji had never thought about it. The royal Mongol clans did not officially exist, in the eyes of the Commissars. But he would be recognised as a prince by his own people, when he returned to them. If he ever returned to them. 'Do you know of my mother?' he asked, eagerly.

'Only that she is alive, and mourns her son.'

The sense of anger grew. He sat in a corner of the dormitory that night, and watched Almani dragged before Oleg. Oleg licked his lips. He had never had such a pretty boy before. 'Strip him,' he commanded. 'Let us see what he has.'

Almani looked at Batalji in terror as the other boys grasped him and pulled down his pants. Batalji's anger grew. He stood up, his shoulders hunched. 'No,' he said. Heads turned. Suddenly released, Almani fell to his knees. 'He is of my people,' Batalji said. 'He is my friend. If anyone is going to have him, it will be me.'

Oleg gazed at him, fingers twitching. But he had been aware over the past few months of Batalji's simmering anger. Just as he had watched the Mongol's growing strength. He feared a confrontation. 'Then take him,' he said. 'And give him to us after.'

'I will take him when I am ready,' Batalji said. 'Get into your bed, Almani.' Almani scrambled into his bed, pulled the blanket over him.

'He spites you, Oleg,' said one of the other boys.

Oleg glared at him.

'We have a new leader,' said another.

Oleg looked from face to face, and realised that he was

confronted with the most desperate of jungle situations – the law of succession. The confrontation he had hoped to avoid was upon him, and he had no alternative but to accept it: he had still a month to go before he left the orphanage. 'You'll take him now,' he said. 'And then give him to me.'

'When I am ready,' Batalji repeated.

The other boys hastily scrambled out of the way. Oleg hunched his shoulders just as Batalji had done, then lowered his head and charged. Batalji stood his ground, clasping his hands together to hit Oleg on the side of the head as he came close. Oleg grunted, but threw both arms round Batalji's waist, and with a gigantic effort swung Batalji from the floor. Batalji tightened his stomach muscles as the breath was forced from his body, and, still clasping his hands together, struck down twice more. Oleg continued to grunt, but was slowly tightening his grip, shaking Batalji from left to right as he did so. Batalji began to see red blotches before his eyes, and his breath was all gone. He needed to end it, quickly. Hitherto, when the boys had fought, it had always been with certain unwritten rules of conduct; they sought victory without destruction. But now it was time to destroy, or be forever beaten.

Batalji drove his hands downwards, found Oleg's face pressed against his own chest. His fingers slid over the nose and found the eyes, and he drove them in. Oleg screamed. His grip relaxed and he reared backwards. Batalji clasped his hands again and began hitting him, on the face and in the belly. Hands pressed to his eyes, Oleg fell to the floor. Batalji hit him again, on the nape of the neck, and Oleg slumped. Batalji kicked him in the ribs, and when Oleg rolled over, stamped on his groin. Oleg screamed again as his knees came up, then lay still as Batalji hit him again.

'What are you?' demanded Comrade Vera. 'A man or a beast? I will tell you, Comrade Borjigin: you are a beast. A monster from the steppes. You belong out there in the snow and the ice. You are a yeti!' She glared at him. 'Have you nothing to say?'

'It was a fight to the death, Madame Comrade.'

'You think you can fight, to the death, whenever you choose? Well, he is not dead, but he may as well be. He has lost the sight of one eye, and has three broken ribs. I should have you shot.' Batalji remained standing to attention. She had threatened to have him shot on his first day here. Besides, he could tell she admired him. 'There will have to be a report,' Vera said. 'The matter is out of my hands.'

Batalji realised for the first time that he might be in danger. On the other hand, he was suddenly master of the dormitory. And all the other dormitories as well. It was not that Oleg had been universally hated – there were too many potential Olegs in the orphanage – but that he had been universally feared, as the biggest and strongest and toughest of them all. Now he lay in the infirmary, moaning and weeping. Homage was due to the boy who had put him there. Almani looked at him with shining eyes, and Kalji followed him around like a faithful dog.

Even the girls acknowledged his supremacy. The next day he was approached by Tamara. Tamara was heavily built and had an incipient moustache. She was to the girls what Oleg had been to the boys, and they were all terrified of her. 'Well, Comrade Borjigin,' she said. 'I am told there has been a change. I would have you know that I have always admired you. Now I admire you more. Would you like one of my girls?'

'It is against the rules.'

Tamara grinned. 'Are you a man who is afraid of rules? I have seen you looking at Rosa. Would you like her? I will have her come to your dormitory tonight.'

'She never came to the dormitory when Oleg was there.'

'Oleg did not want her. He was not interested. But you . . . I can see that you are interested in all things.' She smiled at him. 'I would even come to you myself, if you wished.'

'I will have Rosa,' Batalji decided. If he was going to be shot, he might as well live life to the limit first. But he liked Rosa as much as he wanted her. 'What will happen to her if she becomes pregnant?'

'We will look after that,' Tamara assured him.

*

'You should escape,' Rosa whispered into his shoulder. 'Is it not possible to escape?'

Batalji had never considered it. And now that he did consider it, he reckoned it was not possible to escape. At least, not without everyone else knowing about it, as he would have to begin by sawing through the bars on the dormitory window. Besides, he could not believe he was actually going to be shot. Anyway, right this minute he did not wish to think about it. He had made all the other boys wait outside in the corridor so that he could enjoy Rosa all to himself.

His first woman! He could not count Vera Shackinarsky; she was an animal. A monster. Neither could he possibly count those dreadful, traumatic moments with his own mother. Rosa was not innocent. She was not even a virgin, although she claimed he was the first man she had known – no doubt Tamara's fingers had taken her hymen. But she submitted with a desperate earnestness, and her body was a wonderland of sexual fulfilment. At least, Batalji thought, I will be able to say that I am a man, when they put me against a wall.

The Commissar arrived the following week. By then Batalji had had Rosa on four more occasions, and felt he had nothing to lose. The Commissar sat at Comrade Shackinarsky's desk, while Vera stood beside him, sweating with anxiety. Batalji, standing before the desk between two of the guards, presumed she was afraid of what he might say. 'Borjigin,' the Commissar growled. 'Your father broke the law, and paid for it with his life.' He was a little man with horn-rimmed spectacles, and when he made notes he held his pen between the third and little fingers of his hand. Batalji was fascinated. 'Now *you* have broken the law. What have you to say, Comrade?'

'It was self-defence, Comrade Commissar.'

The Commissar glanced at Vera, who nodded enthusiastically. 'The boy Oleg has a bad reputation as a bully, Comrade Commissar. I have had to punish him on more than one occasion.'

The Commissar read the file. 'This is the file of a soldier,' he said.

'A born soldier, Comrade Commissar,' Vera said, even more enthusiastically. 'I have never seen such a shot.'

'We need good soldiers,' the Commissar said thoughtfully, and read some more. 'Sixteen years of age.'

'But big for his age,' Vera said proudly.

The Commissar raised his head to peer at Batalji, and Batalji inhaled to inflate his chest. The Commissar looked down at the file again. 'His academic record is poor.'

Vera bristled. 'He came here unable to read or write, Comrade Commissar. We have taught him these things, and a great many other things. He has much aptitude for learning.'

'Then he can learn in the army,' the Commissar said. 'He will be recruited immediately.'

'That is the perfect solution, Comrade Commissar,' Vera said.

But she was sad. The Commissar intended to take Batalji with him when he left next day, and he was sleeping in Vera's quarters. She caught the boys unawares by visiting their dormitory immediately after lights out, carrying a flashlight. They leapt to their feet, lining the walls of the corridor. 'What are you doing out here?' Vera demanded.

The boys looked at each other. 'Prince Batalji wished to be alone on his last night, Madame Comrade,' Almani ventured.

'Prince Batalji?'

'He is the last Borjigin, Madame Comrade.'

'Prince Batalji,' Vera snorted, and opened the door, sending the beam of her torch probing into the darkness. Rosa and Batalji sat up together; their arms were still round each other.

'Stand up!' Vera snapped.

Batalji hesitated. He knew he could strangle her before she could call for help. But he also knew he could not escape, and that Rosa would be executed beside him. So he stood up, the girl shivering against him; her hair tickled him as it shook.

'You savage,' Vera said. She did not specify which of them she was referring to. 'I will take your skin from your ass.'

'I made her come here, Madame Comrade,' Batalji said. 'I wished to have sex, before I joined the army.'

'Savage!' Vera said again, and hit him in the genitals with her stick. Batalji doubled up, and Rosa gave a little shriek of alarm. 'See what you can do with that,' Vera said, as Batalji sank to his knees, mumbling with pain.

She stamped from the room, past the gaping boys. As soon as she had gone down the stairs, they ran inside, lifted Batalji on to the bed. 'Is it very bad?' Almani asked.

Batalji shook his head, untruthfully, gritting his teeth against the pain so as not to cry out.

Rosa burst into tears.

'Just like Madame Comrade,' Kalji said, wonderingly. 'I saw her face when she left. She was crying, too.'

THE THIRD CHRONICLE

Moscow, October 2000

Sir Rodney Etherton stroked his moustache. 'It seems to me that we would be, shall we say, killing two birds with one stone, Ewfim. You wish to know what is happening inside Yakutiya, but you cannot find out, and none of your people are allowed in at the moment. Mr Stanton and his people also wish to find out what is happening. I can assure you that anything they discover will be made available to you before it is given to the world. Is that not so, Stanton?'

'Of course, Mr Ambassador,' Clive said, marvelling at the way the man could assume this demeanour of gracious patronage. Sir Rodney had been furious at being called upon to help, and had had to be persuaded by the big boys in France and England. Now he was all suave good intentions.

'And what makes you think a camera team will be allowed in?' inquired the Minister for Internal Affairs. 'They are very likely to be shot down and killed. This man Borjigin is an absolute savage, Mr Stanton. Perhaps you do not realise this.'

'Even savages can understand the value of publicity, Minister,' Clive said. 'Besides, I'm not so sure he is a savage. I've been reading about him. I'll admit he seems to hold human life cheap, but that has always been a Mongol trait. I believe I will be able to communicate with him.'

'Because you have always been successful, Mr Stanton, you believe that you always will be successful. You will not be able to land; Yakutsk Airport is closed, so far as we know.'

'By weather?'

'Only from time to time. It is closed because Borjigin will allow no one to land there.'

'They must be keeping radio communications open,' Clive said.

'That we do not know. They will not respond to our attempts to speak with them. The entire country, certainly Yakutsk itself, has disappeared off the map. And there is nothing we can do about it before next spring. We have asked the American Government to let us have satellite photographs of the area, but I doubt we will learn much from those.'

'How serious would it be if there was no communication with Borjigin until the spring?' asked the Ambassador.

'The spring in northern Siberia is May, Rodney. That is seven months away. By then, God knows what will have happened out there. There are foreign nationals in Yakutsk. Most especially, an American research team. The State Department has asked me to confirm that they are safe. I cannot do this.'

'Seems to me you have to let us go in, Minister,' Clive said. 'We'll talk him into opening his airport, or letting us land at one of the military fields.'

Ewfim Dolgorukov cracked his knuckles, uncertainly.

'When I asked how serious it might be if nothing is done about Borjigin until next spring,' Etherton said, 'I was not thinking of foreign nationals who may be in his power. That crops up with any dictatorial takeover. You may remember that we had the problem on a far more serious scale in Iraq, nine years ago. I was thinking more of the nuclear weapons you still have stored there.' Dolgorukov raised his eyebrows. Etherton smiled. 'Oh, we know they're there, Ewfim. With a delivery system.'

'Hm. Well ... the site is earmarked for the next series of de-arming and destruction, of course. And at present it is garrisoned. We have been able to make contact with the command centre, and the devices have been disarmed. I mean completely. They are not a threat.'

'At the moment. But if they have been disarmed on the spot, presumably the warheads are still there. Suppose Borjigin gets his hands on them? Even if they've been disarmed, he will surely be able to re-arm them?'

'That is not possible without expert help. This man and his followers are nomads from the steppes. What can they know of nuclear weapons? Anyway, it is not even possible for him to get hold of them. The site is well north of Yakutsk. As I say, it is strongly garrisoned. Borjigin would have to move a large number of men and fight a pitched battle to obtain those missiles, and that is simply not practical in Yakutiya in the winter. Even supposing such a savage is aware of their existence.'

'I hope you're right. Do you have any other important weapons out there?' Clive asked.

'All weapons are important, when they fall into the hands of an outlaw. But Yakutiya is not regarded, or I should say, *was* not regarded, as a critical area down to last week. There is a tank brigade based in Yakutsk itself.'

'T-84s?' The very latest Russian development.

'I'm afraid so.'

'Which is now presumably in the hands of the rebels?'

'The brigade is based on the Central Barracks in Yakutsk.'

'And Borjigin holds Yakutsk.'

'That does not mean he has taken the Central Barracks. That would have been a serious military operation. General Simonoslov, the Commanding Officer, was given orders not to become involved in local politics unless fired upon. We have lost contact with him for the moment.'

'Which doesn't sound too good.'

'We shall have to wait and see, Mr Stanton. In any event, one brigade ...'

'On the other hand, we *know* Borjigin controls the airport,' Etherton said. 'What about the Fulcrums? You have four squadrons based on Yakutsk, haven't you?'

Dolgorukov looked at Clive.

'I know what a Fulcrum is, Your Excellency,' Clive said. 'It is an MiG-29, your latest fighter-bomber. Are these Mark I, or Mark II?' Dolgorukov's expression gave him his answer. 'And you mean that Borjigin has control of four squadrons?' He gave a low whistle.

'There is also the oil,' Etherton remarked.

Clive, making notes, looked up. 'There is oil in Yakutiya?'

Dolgorukov sighed. 'That also is confidential, Mr Stanton. Yes, there was a strike last spring. Under the permafrost there is a veritable sea of oil. But it was only discovered a few months ago. We are negotiating now with various American companies to develop the fields, but nothing has been completed as yet, and nothing has been done.'

'But Borjigin knows about this oil?'

'I do not see how he can. As I said, it is confidential.'

'Minister, if Borjigin has seized power, he will have seized all the Government offices, and thus all the Government files. You are not going to tell me that President Taychin did not know of this oil strike?'

Dolgorukov hunched his shoulders.

'You *have* to let us go in, Minister,' Clive pressed.

'I can take no responsibility for your lives.'

'We do not expect you to. Let us charter an aircraft, and give us permission to fly into Yakutsk. That is all we ask.'

'And what happens if you arrive over Yakutsk Airport and are refused permission to land? You will not have enough fuel to make anywhere else, unless you intend to charter a jumbo.'

'Let us worry about that, Minister. As I have said, I do not believe Borjigin will turn us away.'

Etherton gave a brief smile. 'No matter what you charter, you will also need fuel just to leave here. And, barring that jumbo, somewhere to refuel. So that you *can*, if necessary, turn round and come back. Will you authorise that, Ewfim?'

Dolgorukov cracked some more knuckles. 'Sverdlovsk,' he muttered. 'You can fuel at Sverdlovsk. From Sverdlovsk you should be able to reach Yakutsk and get back, on one fuel load. I will give you the necessary authority.'

Clive leapt to his feat. 'Thank you, sir.' He frowned. 'Sverdlovsk. Wasn't that once known as Ekaterinburg?'

'Catherine's City, yes. It was named that in honour of the Empress Catherine II.'

'Then...'

'Yes, Mr Stanton. It is where the last Tsar and his family were executed. But you are just stopping there for fuel.' Dolgorukov pointed. 'Any information you obtain about the situation in Yakutsk will be brought to me before it is released.'

'You have my word.'

'I intend to make sure of it, Mr Stanton. You will be accompanied by one of my people. V. I. Kopylov. He knows Yakutiya.'

'So this is it,' Denise remarked.

'This cellar is exactly as it was, eighty-two years ago,' Kopylov told them; he was a little man who wore a heavy moustache and was very earnest. 'The Tsar and Tsarina sat in front, in straight chairs, with the Tsarevitch. The princesses stood behind, along with the doctor and a couple of other people. If you look closely at the walls, you can still see the bullet marks, and indeed the bloodstains.'

'After eighty-two years?' Being a director, Georges was a sceptic when it came to special effects. 'Are you saying the local tourist board doesn't freshen them up from time to time?'

'You mean they just sat there, and stood there, knowing they were about to be shot?' Denise asked.

'They did not know they were about to be shot, Mademoiselle l'Auberon,' Kopylov explained. 'They believed they were about to be moved to another prison, and were awaiting transport.'

'Those poor girls,' Denise commented. 'This place gives me

the creeps.' Outside it was snowing. It had been snowing while they landed, and was now snowing harder than ever. The pilot had flatly refused to take off until the blizzard was over, which was why Kopylov had taken them sightseeing. Denise stood on the pavement, her nose turning red, and gazed at the house. 'You know, I believed the story that at least one of the girls got away. When they proved that they had all died in that cellar, I was crushed.'

Henri kissed her on the cheek. 'You're a romantic.'

'She's going to need to be,' Georges remarked, 'if half of what that minister said is true.'

'Are we up?' Denise asked, opening her eyes as the plane levelled off.

'Just,' Clive grunted.

'I thought he wouldn't take off while it was snowing?' Georges asked, peering out of the window at the white mist which kept floating by.

'I crossed his palm with silver,' Clive confessed.

Denise was nestled against him; she had done that for most of the past week, and there were times when he had wondered why he had not accepted the inevitable, and wired Threlfall to tell him further progress was not possible until the spring. Then he could have carried Denise back to London, and married her ... But now they were on their way. Into the most remote region on earth, to interview a throwback from history.

'You know what puzzles me,' Denise remarked, over lunch, served by a heavy-set hostess who didn't seem to care much for her job. 'It's where did this Borjigin-bandit-character learn the military know-how to take over an entire country in one night.'

'I would say he learned it in Afghanistan,' Clive said. 'According to his file, he served there with the Soviet Army throughout the eighties.'

As he spoke, the starboard engines coughed.

CHAPTER 3

Afghanistan, 1979–86

The motorbike left a huge plume of yellow dust behind as it bounced over the beaten earth track west of the River Linde. Then it topped a rise, and Batalji put one foot down to survey the valley beneath him. He looked at an *ordu* of yurts, a corral of horses, and in the distance, a herd of reindeer.

He twisted the throttle, and guided the machine down the slope. The noise of the two-stroke engine alerted the camp, and men came out of the tents, many with weapons in their hands. They peered at the intruder, hostile, but not immediately ready to resist; he was in uniform and might be a Commissar. Batalji braked to a halt in a cloud of dust, and stepped off his machine. The men peered at him, half apprehensive, half in admiration. He wore the mottled yellow, brown and green fatigue dress of a private in the motor rifles, with a matching sidecap. His steel helmet hung from his shoulder. As a soldier on furlough, he was unarmed.

Batalji smiled at them. 'Is this not the camp of the Anhusats? I seek my mother, Selphine Borjigin. I am Batalji Borjigin.'

The men stared at him. Although he was no taller than they,

he seemed so much bigger. The uniform had much to do with this impression. Yet he *was* bigger, in the depth of his chest, the obvious power in his arms and shoulders and legs. 'Prince Batalji?' one of the men asked in awe.

Batalji grinned. 'Private Borjigin. Where is my mother? I was told that she was with you.'

'Batalji!' Selphine ran from her yurt, hair flying, feet bare. 'Batalji!'

'Mother!' He took her in his arms, held her close, lifting her from the ground while she kissed his mouth, his cheeks, his ear, his chin.

'Oh, Batalji! I had not thought ever to see you alive again.'

He smiled, and kissed her again. He would not tell her that there had been times, many more times since leaving the orphanage, when he had doubted his survival as well. Looking back, the orphanage, even Vera and Oleg, had been pleasant interludes on his path to hell. Which presumably was set to continue. But for these few days he had sidestepped into heaven. If he was accepted. 'Mother . . .'

Selphine kissed him some more. 'That is in the past. That is a score to settle with the Taychins, one day. And do you know, my son, my noble son, I am glad it happened. I would not have had it any other way. Having you inside me made those others seem as nothing.' She held him at arms' length, while a crowd formed around them. 'But . . . what are you doing here?'

'I have a furlough.' But now he could ask the question which dominated his mind. 'Is Mortana . . .?'

'Mortana and her father await you, Prince.'

A wedding was an occasion for an *ikhurdur*, or festival. A reindeer was slaughtered, there was singing and dancing, and even the children got drunk on vodka, while their elders poured libations on the ground in honour of the gods of the steppes.

Batalji drank little; he preferred to look at his wife. Mortana wore the traditional garb of a Mongol bride, a long dress of white silk, the braids of her hair laden with silver coins and tiny statuettes; her headdress was a cone of birch bark covered with silk, and supported over each ear by whorls of braided hair. Her face was exposed, calm and beautiful. Unlike his mother, she had never doubted her husband would come back to her. Yet thus far they had not spoken a word.

There were several clan chieftains present; it was almost a *kurultai*, an assembly of the Mongol khans. Khalim Anhusat made a speech, in which he acknowledged the supremacy of the Borjigins, hailed Batalji as Kha Khan, or ruler, and promised on behalf of his clan always to follow his command. Not everyone was pleased with his speech. Some of the other chieftains whispered to each other that they were being delivered into the leadership of a seventeen-year-old boy, who did not even live with them most of the time. 'But he is a soldier,' Khalim insisted, and presented his son-in-law with the symbol of his authority, the horsehair banner with the nine knots.

Batalji stood up. 'I wish to make a public acknowledgement of my gratitude to the Anhusats, and especially Khalim and his family, for their generosity in caring for my mother and stepmothers and sisters, following the murder of my father,' he said. 'Be sure that the Anhusats will always ride at my right hand, throughout my life. Yes, I am a soldier. I am a soldier in the Red Army, and I fight for the Commissars, now. But one day I will come to you, and I will say, let us now fight for the Yakka Mongols, and the Yakuts, and all the many people who will ride behind my horsehair banner. Then we will rid this land of the Commissars, and be our own people again, as we were in the past. Will you wait for me to come back to you?' The men gave a great shout of agreement, while the women clapped their hands, and the children gave high-pitched shrieks. Selphine's eyes shone with love and admiration.

Batalji looked from face to face. 'But now, my friends, my people . . . now I must claim my bride.'

Mortana stood up with a shriek of mock horror. Her brothers, Jalain and Jagnuth, clustered close to protect her, as Batalji leapt on to the table, scattering dishes, and jumped down on the far side. He swung his arms, and Mortana's brothers threw themselves to the earth as they acted out the age-old ritual. Batalji grasped Mortana's wrist, pulled her to him, ducked to drive his shoulder into her midriff and lift her from the ground. She gasped and screamed, as she was required to do, and he strode across to his yurt, and carried her inside. Traditionally he should have placed her on his horse and carried her off to his own *ordu*. But as he had no *ordu* of his own, tradition had to be abandoned. One of Mortana's sisters had followed them, and now she obligingly closed the flap; she would guard it until Batalji wished to come out.

Batalji took Mortana from his shoulders, and laid her on the blanket bed. Her headdress came off and her hair started to come down, and she nestled her head on it while she stared at him, lips slightly parted, breasts still heaving from the excitement. He wondered what she was thinking. Because she had waited for him, she was sixteen, old for a Mongol bride. And she seemed eager. But he knew nothing of her. Just as she knew nothing of him, less indeed. He at least knew what she had done with the three years since the day he had looked on her naked body by the stream. Her routine would have been unchanging, invariable. But she knew nothing of the ruthless sodomy in a darkened dormitory, or of Vera Shackinarsky's perverted lust, or of public canings in a school square. Nor did she know of the discipline practised in the Red Army.

And even less did she know of the savage anger which swept across him from time to time, made him seek only to hurt and to destroy – or that in such a mood he had once destroyed a man, with his bare hands.

Mortana licked her lips as she gazed at the intensity of his expression. 'I will honour you above all other men, my Prince,' she said.

It was the first time he had heard her speak; her voice was soft, and enticing. 'As I will honour you, my wife,' he told her, and pulled off her boots. Then, as she sat up, he gathered her gown and lifted it to her waist, to look at her, at the strong haunches of a horsewoman, the black forest which coated her groin, the slight pulse which animated her belly.

'Do I please you, my Prince?' she asked. Batalji knelt astride her legs, and slid his hands up her ribcage and under her bodice, to hold her breasts. These too were of a size to delight a man. 'I will bear you strong sons, my Prince,' she promised.

Batalji lifted the tunic over her head, and then she lay back, naked, to watch him undress in turn. Now she spread her legs, and waited for him to return.

'I will please you, my Prince,' she said again.

'Afghanistan,' Khalim said in mystification. 'Is it far to the south?'

'Very far,' Batalji assured him. 'It is a land of high mountains, yet great heat in the summer. It is not even within the Soviet Union.'

'Then why are you going there?' Selphine asked.

'They are our allies, Mother, and they are fighting a civil war. We are to help them.'

'Do you wish to go?'

'I am a soldier.'

Jalain Anhusat grinned, and slapped his new brother-in-law on the shoulder. 'You have all Yakutiya in which to hide. We will hide you, Batalji. You do not have to go to this faraway place.' Jalain was only a year older than Mortana, and thus the same age as Batalji himself.

'Would you hide me, and yourself, for the rest of your lives?' Batalji asked. 'The Commissars are too strong, we are too weak. We must wait for that to change.'

'That can never change,' Khalim said sadly. 'The Commissars are eternal.'

'Not so, Father. We were taught these things in school. There were no Commissars seventy years ago. Perhaps, some day, there will be no Commissars again. That is worth waiting for, eh?'

'It will never happen,' Khalim repeated, more dolefully than ever.

*

'You are going to fight, in a war.' Selphine sat between Batalji and Mortana for her son's last meal. 'Will you not be killed?'

'Not I, Mother.'

Selphine, if only thirty-three, no longer possessed the immortality-complex of youth. 'You will leave a young widow, and a grieving mother,' she grumbled. 'And an unavenged father, an unresolved insult to our honour. Perhaps Jalain is right, and it is better to live a fugitive, so long as one lives.'

Batalji reached across his mother to squeeze Mortana's hand. 'I will live,' he said. 'To avenge both you and Father. To conquer.'

The roof of the world, Batalji thought.

The motorised column had crossed the border immediately south of Termez, by the bridge over the River Amudar Ya, that which had been known to the ancients as the Oxus. They had been encouraged to exchange greetings with the turbaned warriors who had guarded the bridge, waving and cheering as the armoured personnel carriers laden with troops had rumbled across the steel spans. 'We are your friends,' Captain Gradchik had told the gaping crowds. 'We are your liberators.'

Batalji had stared at the veiled women. So had everyone else in his APC, except perhaps Private Koplin. Batalji's gaze had contained merely curiosity; he had never seen veiled women before. Most of his comrades were older. 'They'll give you the best fuck in the world,' Sergeant Ashansky had said.

Private Koplin had given a high-pitched giggle at the thought.

These men were his comrades, Batalji thought. He had trained beside them, slept with them, eaten with them, for over a year. He had run round and round a parade ground in full equipment with them, for some infringement dreamed up by Captain Gradchik, and he had suffered the lash with them for some supposed insubordination. He had shared their intimate thoughts and their sexual dreams. He knew their hatred, of all officers and Commissars; in that they were as one. But he also knew their fear, of their superiors far more than any enemy they might have to face.

Most of them were conscripts, and sought survival more than glory; in another year they would be back with their families. Only the NCOs were professionals, and the smattering of boys and young men who belonged to the army because they had nowhere else to go. Batalji was included in that group. The difference was that he *had* somewhere else to go. But the army wanted him here, where he could not cause trouble. Perhaps they had hoped he *would* desert when he had been given that furlough, then they could have hunted him down without hesitation. Now no doubt they hoped he would get his head blown off by some Afghan rebel. Yet he was content. He did not intend to get himself killed, and he knew that belonging had to come first; he could never hope to defeat this army – his dream – until he knew everything about it.

From the river and the border the road climbed, two, three, four thousand metres. Batalji had never known such mountains, which made even Yakutiya seem a plain.

It was high summer, and the heat during the day caused sweat to pour from the men as if they had been squeezed sponges, while at these altitudes the temperatures plummeted to below freezing at night. But what was most disturbing was the absence of vegetation. A few stunted trees, where there was a waterhole. Otherwise nothing but powdery white dust, the accumulation of centuries of erosion. The villages were occasional, the people fearful, staring at the huge tanks and the rumbling APCs. Herds of goats bayed at them, and vultures hovered overhead – waiting.

'This is a dead world,' growled Sergeant Ashansky.

'But filled with living things,' Captain Gradchik reminded him. '*Mujahedin.*'

On the third day one of the company's sentries was frozen to death come dawn. But that was better than two nights later, when they were in a relatively warm valley, and there was a summons to arms at first light. Then they found another of their sentries, wrists bound behind his back and still alive, just. His pants were round his ankles and he had been castrated, his genitals stuffed into his mouth, while he had slowly bled to death. He died soon after the alarm.

'*Mujahedin*,' said Captain Gradchik, hands on hips as he surveyed his horror-stricken men.

The captain called up a helicopter, which swooped overhead and to either side, and reported that there was a village over the next rise. 'Do you wish us to take it out?' asked the pilot of the gunship.

'We will look after our own business,' Captain Gradchik told him. 'Sergeant, take a platoon and avenge Private Scarpsi's death.'

Sergeant Ashansky pointed from man to man. The first man he pointed at was Private Borjigin. He did not like Borjigin; few real Russians did like the boy from the Asian steppes. But he knew there was no finer soldier in the regiment.

They tramped over the stony ground. Batalji had grown up in the great northern forests, and where there had not been forests, there had been grassy plains, at least in the summer. He found this high desert with its few stunted growths an alien place.

'You are going to kill,' Ashansky told them. 'You have never killed before, eh? Now you are going to learn how to do it. You will enjoy killing, once you get the knack of it.'

Ashansky had been around a long time. Twenty-four years earlier he had marched into Budapest. It was then he had learned to kill. Now he was eager to renew his acquaintance with death. The flankers, crouching on the next hilltop, were waving. Ashansky listened on his radio. 'In the dip,' he said. 'The village. That is our target.'

'How do we know they are *mujahedin*, Comrade Sergeant?' Koplin asked, face gleaming with sweat.

'Of course they are *mujahedin*,' Ashansky snapped. 'They

are all *mujahedin*.' They advanced to the escarpment, and looked down on the huts, the fires, the goats, listened to the animals bleating. Batalji knew instinctively that these were not *mujahedin*; the rebels would be on the move, not stationary – those huts were permanent. But he wanted to avenge poor Scarpsi as much as anyone. And he wanted to kill. He had never killed. But killing was to be his life, from now on.

Sergeant Ashansky extended his line along the ridge, then he blew his whistle, and the Russian soldiers ran down the hill, firing their Roschnoi Pulemet Detjarew light sub-machine-guns. There was a tremendous hubbub. Goats ran to and fro, dogs barked, people came out of their houses, eyes bleary from their midday siesta. Few fell in the wild shooting, as the Russians were running and firing from the hip. 'Halt!' shouted Sergeant Ashanksy. 'Cease firing.'

The men panted to a halt, stared at the villagers. There were old men, and old women, young women, and children. And dogs and chickens and goats. They stared at the Russians, and one of the old men came forward, speaking. '*Mujahedin*,' Ashansky accused. The old man protested, clearly denying the charge. 'Shoot them,' Ashansky commanded. 'Shoot them all. Leave the young women till last.'

The conscripts hesitated, looking from one to another. 'Shoot them, you shitbags!' bawled Ashansky. Batalji looked at the old man, standing in front of him, bewildered, as he knew no Russian. He thrust his RPD forward and squeezed the trigger.

Batalji had seen targets disintegrate when he had fired at them during training; he had never seen a man do so. And other men, and dogs and goats, as he sprayed bullets to and fro, pausing only to clip a fresh magazine to his gun. Now his comrades had started shooting as well, and men were falling all over the place, while slivers of stone and brick flew from the walls of the buildings, and the women and children screamed as they dived for shelter – several of them were hit as well. One of the Afghans managed to reach his rifle, and levelled it, but before he could squeeze the trigger he too had dissolved into a mass of flying red.

'Cease firing,' Ashansky bellowed, and the echoes died away into the surrounding hills. Even the dogs had stopped barking. The survivors had slunk off into the shadows. 'Fetch those women out,' Ashansky said. 'Cut off Scarpsi's prick, would they? We'll give them some pricks to remember.'

The women wailed and screamed as they were dragged out and stripped. Their clothes were surprisingly fine, thick cloth in a variety of colours, and heavily embroidered. There was also a good deal of gold jewellery, mainly bangles, to be torn off the thin brown arms. 'This one, Borjigin,' Ashansky said.

Batalji looked at the woman. She was not a day under sixty, he reckoned, and her long years in the sun and the wind and the heat and the cold had left her face and body a mass of wrinkled flesh; her breasts were mere bags. Only her thighs and legs were still firm and strong. Batalji grinned. 'You have her, Comrade Sergeant. She's not my type.' His gaze drifted to one of the girls, pretty, with a light brown body and flashing dark eyes.

'Listen, boy,' Ashansky said. 'I'm doing you a favour. I'm rewarding you for being the first man to open fire. You taught these conscripts a thing or two today, boy. Just as I expected you to. Now I offer you a long life. Do you not know the saying? Fuck a grandmother and you will live forever?' He grinned. 'How do you think I'm still alive? I fucked a grandmother in Budapest. Now get your prick into this one.'

'Mail!' Ashansky called the names. 'Borjigin!'

Batalji had never received a letter before in his life. Probably because he had never written one, and during his days in the orphanage his mother had not even known where he was. He took the envelope, thumbed it open. It was from Jagnuth, Mortana's younger brother; he was only thirteen. Batalji had no idea Jagnuth knew how to write. But the letters were carefully formed and perfectly legible, even if Batalji still read very slowly. Yet with an increasing mixture of delight and a sense of desolation that he was here, and Mortana was there.

'Who's dead?' Ashansky stood above him. 'Soldiers only get letters when one of their family has died.'

'My wife is pregnant,' Batalji said with a huge grin. 'I am to have a son!'

'Balls. It'll be a girl, and cost you money.'

'Is it possible to have leave, Sergeant?'

'Leave? You must be out of your tiny mind. You'll have leave when we've wiped out the *mujahedin*.'

So Batalji wrote to Mortana instead; Jagnuth would be able to read it to her. '*I do not know when I will be able to come to you,*' he wrote. '*My sergeant says it is when this war is over, which will be when the Afghan rebels have been defeated. As they will not surrender, to defeat them we must kill them all. We are doing this. I have never seen such killing. We kill them with bombs and napalm, and we kill them with bullets and grenades, and we kill them by poisoning their waterholes and wells and destroying their animals. I have never seen people treated so badly. I think they must hate us more than they hate the devil. But I do not think it can be too long before we kill them all.*'

'What are you?' demanded Captain Gradchik. 'Some kind of a lunatic?' He pounded the letter on the camp table before him. 'This letter is deviationist claptrap.'

Batalji, standing rigidly to attention before the Captain's tent, gulped. But he was also angry. It had never occurred to him that anyone save his family would read his letter, his very first letter, and to his wife. 'I wished my wife to know what is happening, sir.'

'Because she is a deviationist whore herself, eh? I know you Mongols.' Gradchik tore the sheet of paper into strips and threw them over his shoulder; they were immediately seized by the wind and scattered. 'I want to see no more letters from you, Borjigin.'

'I must write to my wife, Comrade Captain. She is pregnant.'

'So she is pregnant. She doesn't need to hear from you about it. Sergeant, give this man four hours extended heavy-duty drill.'

'You are a fool, boy,' Ashansky said, as he watched Batalji running round and round the encampment, pack bouncing on his back, RPD at the trail, sweat darkening his armpits and crotch and dripping from his hair. 'There are things one does not put in letters.'

You are right, Batalji thought. There are things that belong only in deeds, like one day ramming my knife up Gradchik's ass. 'Anyway,' Ashansky pointed out, 'there is no need for correspondence. If you are killed your wife will be informed. If she is not informed, you will still be alive, eh? And she will know that you will come back to her.' He shook his head. 'But getting into the Captain's bad books ... that is a serious matter.'

Batalji realised just how serious over the next few years. That winter they were encamped close to Kabul. The *mujahedin* did not cease their struggle because of the deep snow and the sub-zero temperatures, but like the Russians, they found it difficult to get about, and the Russians at least undertook no punitive expeditions. That meant there could be some local leave, and Batalji accompanied his comrades into the city, to wander through the immense central souk and stare at the veiled women, and the fierce-looking men, heavily armed, who walked beside them. 'They're all *mujahedin*, waiting to murder us,' Koplin muttered.

Koplin actually started the trouble, having read somewhere that all Afghans were ambidextrous. Unfortunately, the handsome young man he picked upon wasn't gay, and there was a fight, in which Batalji felt called upon to rescue Koplin, laying out a few Afghans in the process. That earned him more extra-duty drill, and this time Gradchik made out an 'incorrigible' report. Ashansky had recommended Batalji for a couple of corporal's stripes, but this was now forgotten, and when, next spring, certain selected privates were allowed to return to their homes for a furlough, Borjigin's name was conspicuously absent. Worse, there were no more letters from Jagnuth. Gradchik had made a report, and had received clearance to intercept any mail for Private Borjigin. As Mortana had to be just about due, Batalji was distraught with anxiety, and even contemplated desertion. But Ashansky, wise in the moods of the men he commanded, recognised the situation. 'You're not crazy, boy,' he said. 'Not like some. Desert, and you're done. For one thing, you'd never get out of Afghanistan. You'd have some pretty little bint making you eat your prick before you could say knife. And suppose you did get out? Then you'd be arrested and shot. What's a year or two? This war can't last forever. Then you'll be going home. Your daughter won't even recognise you now. She'll keep.'

'It is a son,' Batalji swore.

How long was forever? How many *mujahedin* were there? Winter became scorching summer, and summer became freezing winter again. The men muttered about how their action was being condemned at the United Nations; Ashansky dismissed that as capitalist-inspired rubbish. Batalji worried about this. He was impressed by what he had heard of the United Nations. Surely if all the other countries in the world condemned one national action, the condemned country had to yield. This was of course partly wishful thinking; he only wanted to get out of Afghanistan. But though the United Nations were condemning, they were not doing anything else. So the killing continued.

The Russian Army was officially doing nothing more than support the regime of Babrak Karmal, making sure his various garrisons were supplied with arms and ammunition, intending, by the very presence of eighty thousand well-armed and equipped men, to overawe the rebels. But as Karmal only controlled the cities, and then tenuously, moving supplies was a difficult matter. Even huge, heavily armed convoys were liable to be attacked, by people who possessed the knack of melting into the hills as soon as they had gained their victory. Counterattacks were launched, and those caught were savagely punished, without, as in Batalji's very first action, very much regard to whether or not they were actually *mujahedin*, but there always seemed more waiting to take their place – and more and more the rebels were being equipped with modern arms, from Pakistan. 'Napoleon fought a war like this once,' Ashansky said. 'In Spain.' The sergeant was steeped in military history.

'How did he win it?' Koplin asked.

'He lost it,' Ashansky told him.

Batalji reflected that if *he* had made a point like that, it would have cost him six hours of heavy-duty drill.

At times he felt quite desperate, in the absence of knowledge of what was happening in Yakutiya, in the absence of true information about what was happening in Afghanistan, in the growing feeling that even if he had raped the old woman he was still destined to leave his bones in this desolate and unfriendly country, fighting for a man he had never seen and, from what he heard, would not like. More and more his thoughts turned to desertion, even though he accepted Ashansky's estimation of his chances. But anything would have to be better than waiting to be killed by an unseen enemy. Perhaps this feeling was growing on the generals, as well. 'Full kit!' Ashansky announced. 'We are going to carry the fight to the bastards.'

It was the spring of 1986. Six years ago Batalji had been married. And it was six years since he had seen his bride. His child would be five years old. 'Quit moping,' Ashansky told him. 'This is going to be it. Seek and destroy, right up to the Pakistan border. Seek and destroy, boy.'

It was a massive operation, some twenty thousand men, a brigade of tanks, and a fleet of gunships, pressing south towards the frontiers of India and Pakistan. The motor infantry rumbled along in their APCs, RPDs at the ready.

Whenever a helicopter reported a village, the gunships went in first, followed by the tanks. The infantry came last to clean up any pockets of resistance. At least they had most of the available women – usually by the time they got there no men were left alive. 'We're showing the bastards,' Ashansky crowed as they moved out of Kandahar and into the Heda Mountains. 'But don't think it's going to be easy. A hundred and twenty-five years ago the British lost an entire army fighting in Afghanistan.'

'Did the British conquer Afghanistan, Comrade Sergeant?' Koplin asked.

'No. They found it too tough a nut to crack.' Ashansky observed the looks on the faces of his men, and added, 'But we're not the British. There aren't any nuts too tough for us, eh?'

Batalji accepted that he was probably right. If only because a hundred and twenty-five years ago the British would have lacked the equipment necessary for making a success of a campaign like this. He did not see how any army could hope to beat the Afghans in their own mountains without radios and gunships. Even the tanks were useless where the terrain was liable to go straight up or straight down, and the infantry had to work a lot harder, and take a lot more exercise, as the APCs were also useless. But the rebels could do nothing about the gunships, and village after village was obliterated, before the motor infantry moved in to clean up what was left. One day became much like another, a slow progress of death and destruction.

'You'd think the bastards would give up,' Koplin said, as they sat around their campfire, upwind of their latest triumph, which was now a shambles of burnt-out houses and bullet-riddled corpses. The soldiers were roasting goats; there was always plenty of meat available after a village had been wiped out.

'They haven't the sense to quit,' Ashansky said. 'But there can't be all that many of them left.' He was making out his sentry list, as the sun drooped into the mountains of the west.

The Russians had become so confident that the regiment had been split up into companies to carry out their search-and-destroy missions, but because they were operating in groups of seventy-odd men, it was necessary to be extra careful at night, when a fleet of gunships could not be promptly summoned by a word on the radio.

Batalji discovered he was one of the lucky ones this night; he was not on duty until four, which meant he would have most of the night snug in his sleeping bag. As was invariable with him, he fell asleep immediately. This was more than sheer exhaustion after a day's marching and killing. He had made a mental decision that he could do nothing about his own life until this war was finished. Therefore there was nothing to be thought about, save the war. That he was twenty-four years old, had not seen his wife or mother for six years, had never seen his child – did not even know if it was a boy or a girl – was irrelevant. He had accepted this as his destiny, and he knew that his family would be waiting for him, whenever he did manage to return.

The fact was, he was enjoying the life. Death and destruction appealed to the nomad in him. It was the ethic by which his forefathers had lived when they had been the most feared fighting force in the world. If that was to be his life, and he was determined that it should be, then he was getting a very good training for the future.

He awoke to find himself rolling, being impelled by some invisible force, while his ears were filled with screaming sound. He sat up, and there was another huge explosion, slightly further off; by its quick red glow he saw men falling about and sprawling on the ground. 'Mortars!' bawled Sergeant Ashansky. 'Where the fuck did the bastards get a mortar?'

'Fall back on the village,' Captain Gradchik shouted. 'They mean to assault. Fall back on the village.'

Batalji kicked off his sleeping bag, mentally cursing. He had taken off his boots, and they were nowhere to be seen in the darkness. More important, he had been blown away from his RPD. He crawled back towards where he had been sleeping, threw himself flat as there was another huge explosion. 'To the village,' Gradchik continued to shout. 'Form a perimeter, but hold your fire.'

Batalji found his weapon, and his haversack of ammunition and emergency rations and personal gear, including his helmet, but not his boots. He heard shots, and a scream from nearby. There were several small fires, started by mortar shells and by the scattering of the company's own fire, and in the flickering light men could be seen, easy targets for the snipers in the hills around them. The sentries were going to be strung up by the balls for letting the *mujahedin* get this close, Batalji thought. And then realised that if the poor bastards had been overrun, there would be nothing left to string them up by. The thought made his throat dry, as he crawled amidst the ruins and the dead bodies, and realised there were not more than thirty men around him. Half the company had been wiped out. Already.

'Form that perimeter,' Ashansky was saying, crawling himself as bullets whined and smashed into the houses. 'You, Borjigin, take the right flank. The very last of the houses. But do not fire until you see a target.'

'Has the Captain sent for help, Comrade Sergeant?' Koplin asked.

'We've lost the shitting radio,' Ashansky growled. 'We have to hold until dawn. There'll be a chopper over at dawn. There always is.'

Batalji crawled until he reached the last of the houses. Here he settled himself behind a broken wall, checked his weapon as best he could in the darkness. 'Who's next?' he asked. There was no reply. Maybe he'd crawled too far. But Ashansky had told him to hold the extreme right. It was up to the sergeant to space the perimeter properly.

The firing ceased, but the night was not quiet. There were wounded and dying men out there, screaming their agony and their fear – and there was nothing any of them could do about it. Presumably the *mujahedin* were now advancing, and advancing their mortar, too. And there was nothing they could do about that, either. Something landed on his head, and he turned, RPD thrust forward, his stomach churning as he thought an Afghan might have crept up behind him. Then something bounced off his hand, and something else splattered on his gun barrel. He looked up, into the darkness, and water struck him in the eye. That's all we need, he thought.

The rain became heavy. At least, by holding his head back and opening his mouth, he could alleviate his thirst. But at the same time a small worry began at the back of his brain. The *mujahedin* had not attacked before, in such force; their forte had always been attempting to cut off small parties, or capture a sleepy sentry. Perhaps they had only just got hold of a mortar. But equally perhaps they might have read the weather better than the Russians, who seldom bothered to read it at all, and knew that if there was low cloud on these mountains, the gunships would not be able to make their customary dawn sweeps. In that case ... There was an unearthly howl from in front of him, not far distant. 'Open fire,' Captain Gradchik shouted, from away to the left. 'Blast the buggers.'

Batalji did not join in the general burst of flame. Whoever was being tortured was also some distance to the left, and he did not like shooting blind. In any event, the hail of bullets had little effect; when it died, there was another horrible shriek of agony. Then silence. Except, in the distance, a scraping, rumbling sound. Motorised infantry? In the middle of the night? That was wishful thinking, born of fear. The sound was a mortar being dragged into position.

He realised that he could see his gun barrel. Then he could see the rocks in front of his position. He looked to his left, watched the village gradually emerge from the gloom. But he could see no movement there. There was no immediate movement in front of him either, save for the rain splashing into the dust, which was rapidly turning into mud. He was soaked through. He looked up at the sky. The clouds were very low; the peaks to either side were hidden. There was no possibility of a helicopter risking these hills in this weather, except in an emergency – and without a radio, the brigade would not know there was an emergency.

There was a whine and a huge crash from the village. Batalji watched stone and earth and bodies being thrown right and left. Almost before he had drawn his next breath there was another mortar hit. Now there was a good deal of noise from beside him, screams and curses and high-pitched voices. All hell was breaking loose over there. And now too the sniping began again, bullets thudding into the houses, seeking, and finding, human targets. But none were directed at the pile of stone amidst which he lay. When Gradchik had commanded his men to open fire during the night, the flashes of their guns must have been noted by the *mujahedin*. As Batalji had not fired, his position had not been identified.

Now his comrades were shooting back, at the gun-flashes of the enemy. Presumably they had been ordered to do so by the captain. But Batalji had not heard the order, and he decided not to act on his own. He knew the company was finished. They were outnumbered and in a hopeless position, without aerial support. It was now a matter of survival. Several more mortar shells crashed into the village, while the sniping was continuous. Batalji kept his head down, trying to melt into the rubbled stone of his position. He was abandoning his comrades. But they had never been *his* comrades. His comrades were out on the steppes. The men beside him he was sworn to destroy, one day. It seemed pointless to die with them, in utter futility.

A white flag emerged from the rubble of the village: someone's vest tied to a gun barrel. It was waved several times, and the Afghan firing ceased. For several minutes there was complete silence, save for the patter of the rain and the soughing of the wind. Then a voice called out, in broken Russian, 'You throw out your weapons, and come out with your hands up.' Batalji could not believe what was happening. It had been hammered into them throughout this campaign that one never surrendered to the *mujahedin*. Far better to blow out one's own brains than deliver one's living body into the hands of the Afghan women. But someone over there was actually preparing to do that.

He watched movement, and saw several men standing up. He peered into the drizzle, and made out Captain Gradchik, and Koplin, but not Ashansky. Ashansky must be dead; he would never have been a party to such madness. 'Throw out your guns,' the Afghan voice commanded.

There were now five men standing up. All that was left of the company, apart from Batalji himself. Now they threw their weapons on to the ground. Instantly the little plateau was crowded, as men emerged from the rocks, their rifles at the ready. They advanced on the Russians, surrounded them, poked at them with their gun muzzles, while others picked up the discarded equipment, went into the village and began searching for more. Soon there was a large pile of RPDs and ammunition, and the victorious Afghans fired several bursts into the air.

Not one of them had even looked at the stone pile where Batalji lay, motionless, peering through the stones. I am going to escape, he told himself. The *mujahedin* had won their victory, and got the Russian weapons, and they had got their prisoners ... There was surely nothing for them to stay here for – they would know that the moment the clouds lifted the gunships would be overhead: brigade would be wondering why Captain Gradchik's company had not reported in. But the Afghans were apparently sure the clouds were not going to lift, for a while, at any rate. Batalji heard high-pitched voices and matching laughter, and saw the women coming out of the rocks, their brightly coloured gowns heavy with the rain. They seemed to gleam, for most wore gold jewellery, some even had rings through their nostrils. But they also gleamed from the knives they carried.

Batalji watched Gradchik gesticulating, apparently arguing with his captors. He would now be realising what a terrible mistake he had made, as the women came up to them, and in turn began poking and prodding at them. Koplin's nerve was the first to break. He uttered a shriek, and burst through the people around him, running for the hills. The women whooped, and ran behind him, hardly restrained by their skirts. The men laughed, as they watched the sport. Koplin tripped and fell, and before he could recover the women were upon him. There were at least a dozen of them, and they rolled him on his back and began stripping away his clothes. Koplin screamed again and again, like a terrified horse. The women were all around him now, and Batalji could see nothing more than one kicking, naked leg. Then the screams reached a climax, and one of the women stood up, clutching the severed genitals in her bloodstained hand, yelling her triumph.

Koplin continued to moan and scream, but they were not done with him yet. Again they crowded round him, and the screams became even more animal, and then unintelligible. Batalji knew they had cut away his lips and eyelids, and then his tongue. He looked at the remaining Russians. They had fallen to their knees. Because the women had now left Koplin, a bleeding *thing*, still moving as the blood drained from his body. And now it was Gradchik's turn. The women dragged the captain from the group and stretched him on the earth. Now it was Gradchik who uttered unearthly screams. Batalji buried his head in his arms and closed his eyes. His throat was dry and his belly felt light. The thought of that happening to him . . .

The morning became a cacophony of horror as the other Russians were mutilated in turn. Batalji looked at his watch; it was half past nine, and the last screams had become moans, submerged in the high-pitched chatter and the loud laughter of the women as they wiped their bloody hands on their skirts, the shouts of the men as they shared out the weapons. They were leaving, abandoning their charnel house. It was a matter of only a few minutes more . . . Batalji heard a sound, close at hand, and behind him. He was certain his heart had missed a beat, and then resumed work with a rush which made him feel hot all over. Slowly he turned his head, and gazed at a young woman, hardly more than a girl. She stood beside the last of the houses, the only place from where his position was overlooked, and she was gazing at him.

He levelled his RPD, while the blood continued to pound in his temples. But shooting her would be a waste of time. He needed to put the gun muzzle in his own mouth, and squeeze the trigger. Quickly. But before he could make that irrevocable decision, the girl took him by surprise: she raised her right hand and put her finger against her lips. For the second time that morning Batalji could not believe his eyes: she did not mean to betray him?

He kept absolutely still, while she came towards him, embroidered gown swaying from side to side in time with her hips. He observed that she wore no jewellery – thus she was not married, or even betrothed. Yet she was handsome enough, in the aquiline fashion of her people. She came right up to him, while he scarcely dared to breathe, conscious always of the people behind him. She drew level with him, actually picking her way through the stones in which he was embedded; her skirt flicked his cheek, and he inhaled her scent, a curious mixture of freshness and stale sweat. Then she was past him, and approaching her people.

She was greeted with a chorus of laughter and shouted comment. Batalji gathered they were poking fun at her, why he did not know. He waited for her to turn round and point in his direction, but she did not. Slowly he began to breathe again. He had had never believed in miracles, but he had just witnessed one happening. Now the Afghans were definitely leaving. With continued shouts of triumph, and a few more shots fired into the air, they tramped back into their hills. The women followed behind, carrying various pieces of cloth and equipment they had taken from the dead Russians; several wore Russian helmets.

The girl who had seen him remained behind. No one seemed to care about that. Batalji watched her picking through the ruins and the dead bodies, apparently seeking something. Whatever it was, she did not seem to find it. She was wasting time.

Half an hour had passed since the last of her fellows had disappeared into the hills, before she came and squatted on the far side of his stone mound. In her hands she carried a discarded ammunition pouch, which she appeared to be examining with great care. 'Are you afraid, Russki?' she asked, her voice low, and to Batalji's ears intensely musical. And she spoke slowly enough for him to understand.

'I am very afraid,' he replied carefully.

'Will your people return here?'

'Yes. When the clouds lift.'

'Then you must stay here and wait for them.' Her nose wrinkled; the village exuded a slowly growing stench of death.

'And you?'

'I will wait with you.'

'I am grateful. Will you tell me why?'

'They think I am mad,' she said. 'Since I have been born, they think I am mad. I wish to leave this place. I wish to go to Kabul. Will you take me to Kabul?'

'Yes. Or I will see that you are sent there. What will you do in Kabul?'

She smiled again. 'Live.'

'How? Do you have relatives there?'

'I will live, in Kabul,' she said confidently, 'Have you food?'

'Yes.'

'Feed me,' she commanded.

He unslung his haversack and passed it to her. 'When can I move?'

'They are gone now.'

He wasn't sure whether or not to trust her judgement, but he was very cramped, and he needed to pee. Slowly he got up, stretched, watched her attempting to understand the intricacies of field rations. She raised her head, a packet of chocolate in her hand. 'This is good?'

'Yes.' He walked away from her, stood above the tattered bodies of Gradchik and Koplin. Gradchik still moved, but there was nothing Batalji could do for him or about him. His stomach rolled, and he went on to pee against a rock. He looked for his boots, but could not find them. When he turned round the girl was watching him, slowly masticating the chocolate. 'Why do your people do this?' he asked.

'Why do your people destroy our villages?' she riposted. She stood up, the haversack in her hands, and walked past the village, away from the dead bodies. He watched her hips swaying through the gown, and walked behind her. He was as any man fresh from the battleground, but he was more than that; he was whole and alive where by now he had expected to have suffered the most terrible of fates.

The girl sat down at the back of the village, where the air was relatively clear, and began taking more things out of his haversack. He squatted before her, watched her finger his razor, raising her head to look at him. 'For the chin,' he explained, drawing his finger down his own stubble.

She looked at his toothbrush equally curiously, and Batalji demonstrated. 'Wood is better,' she remarked.

He reached out and touched her cheek. She had saved his life. In the Mongol ethic that made him her slave. But he rather thought she would do better as *his* slave. He had a heady idea of taking her back to the steppes, and introducing her to Mortana. Mortana would not object. Her nostrils dilated; he could not tell whether she was pleased or angry, or perhaps afraid of his touch. 'My name is Batalji,' he said.

'I am Homaira.'

'Why have you no husband, Homaira?' Perhaps she suffered from Aids.

'Because I am mad, Batalji.'

'But you must have a father and mother.'

'They are dead.' Homaira found a packet of biscuits, and carefully opened them. Batalji had taken his hand away from her cheek, now he held her hand. Patiently she took the biscuit she had been holding with her other hand, and bit into it with sharp white teeth. He had a vision of her kneeling above him, knife in hand, smiling as she began to cut. Presumably she was still capable of that. 'Do you wish to lie with me?' she asked.

'Yes.'

She finished chewing her biscuit, carefully folded the paper around the rest of the packet, and then stood up, and with continued studied care, lifted her gown over her head and laid it on the ground to make a mattress.

Batalji opened his eyes, blinked, and looked at the sun, peeping through a break in the clouds. He looked at his watch; it was just past noon, and the sky was definitely clearing; it was quite warm. He sat up, suddenly alarmed, but Homaira was only a few feet away, using his toothbrush. He watched her naked perfection, squatting, half turned away from him, heavy breasts touching her knees; she was in fact no girl – he estimated her age as late twenties. But she was the first woman he had had without the use of brutal force in six years, and she had done much to restore his humanity.

She glanced at him, and put away the toothbrush; she was capable of embarrassment. She drew back her lips to expose her teeth. 'Good?'

'Yes,' he said. 'Very good.'

She stood up and came towards him, black hair swaying past her shoulders, then checked, looking up. Batalji looked up as well, and heard the distant chatter of a helicopter engine. 'Your people come,' Homaira observed. 'I saved your life, Batalji.'

'I shall not forget it,' he promised her.

He stood up, watched the machine swooping down between the hills. He wondered if the Afghans were still close enough to be watching it too, even as he thought there was no sight so sinister as a gunship, dropping lower and lower. But this one was his means of escape. He took off his blouse and waved it to and fro. The helicopter came closer, and passed overhead; he could see men peering down at him from the doorways. They were studying the situation, making sure there was no trap. He waved some more, and Homaira came to stand beside him. She did not wave, but obviously they could see her red and blue dress.

The helicopter came lower. Dust eddied upwards, and the machine came to rest. Instantly men leapt out, RPDs at the ready, while the two heavy machine-guns moved slowly to and fro, covering the adjacent hills. Batalji ran forward, stopped before the senior officer, a lieutenant, saluted. 'Private Borjigin, Comrade Lieutenant.'

The lieutenant looked past him, at the bodies of Gradchik and Koplin and the others, then at the village; he would have seen the bodies inside the ruins from the air. 'What happened here?'

'We were overrun, Comrade Lieutenant. The *mujahedin* had a mortar.'

'Why did you not radio for assistance?'

'The radio was lost in the first attack, Comrade Lieutenant.'

The lieutenant looked contemptuous of any command which could lose its radio. 'But you survived,' he remarked. 'And took a prisoner.'

Batalji turned his head to look at Homaira, who had advanced a few steps behind him, and now waited, her skirt fluttering in the breeze. 'She is not a prisoner, Comrade Lieutenant. She saved my life. I have promised her safe conduct to Kabul.'

'She is *mujahedin*?'

'Yes, Comrade Lieutenant. But she saved my life.'

'The men may have her, sergeant,' the lieutenant said.

Several of the soldiers whooped with joy, and ran at Homaira. She stood her ground, perhaps not realising what was about to happen to her. 'Comrade Lieutenant,' Batalji said, urgently, 'I have promised her . . .'

'Privates do not make promises,' the lieutenant pointed out.

'Batalji!' Homaira shouted. Batalji turned again, watched

her being seized and thrown to the ground, her dress pushed up to her chest while men pulled her legs apart. 'Batalji?'

'Bastards!' Batalji made to run forward, and was struck a blow on the side of the head by the sergeant. He fell to his knees, stunned, and heard the click of a pistol being cocked.

'He is obviously demented by the fate of his comrades,' the lieutenant said.

Batalji raised his head, watched the seething mass about Homaira. It reminded him of the seething mass around Gradchik and Koplin, that morning. But these were his comrades. No, he thought, never his comrades. They were finished. Homaira's brown body lay bruised and panting on the earth, while her tormentors pulled up their breeches. 'Let us get out of here, Sergeant,' the lieutenant said.

'Finish it,' the sergeant shouted.

Batalji's heart swelled until he thought it would burst. He rose to his knees, reaching for his RPD, and heard a burst of fire. Homaira's body kicked and rolled, and lay still. Batalji uttered a scream of maniacal outrage, and hurled himself at the lieutenant.

THE FOURTH CHRONICLE

Yakutiya, October 2000

'Oh, God! Oh, Jesus!' Denise l'Auberon bowed her head, her hands pressed to her face.

Clive made his way forward to the flight deck, where Kopylov and the hostess had already assembled, and the pilot was chattering into his radio. 'So where's the nearest airport?'

'Yakutsk. And that is six hundred miles away.'

'You mean we're flying over Yakutiya now?'

'We have just entered their airspace. We are trying to make contact with the ground, but they are not replying.'

'Have you made it clear that we are Western journalists, not Russian military.'

Kopylov nodded. 'But in any event, we are not going to reach the airport.' He pointed at the altimeter, which was steadily edging down as the remaining engine also lost power under the blanket of ice.

'Aren't there some military airstrips available?'

'None close enough. We are in contact with one north of Yakutsk, but that is even farther away.'

'But we're in contact. Doesn't that mean the base is still in the hands of the Russians, as opposed to the Yakuts?'

'Indeed. But they are powerless to help us at this moment.'

'Well, can't we turn back?'

'It is too far to the next airfield, with only one engine.'

Clive was not aware of being afraid. More he was irritated that his journey was going to be interrupted and delayed. 'So tell me what we're going to do?'

'Captain Orlov says he will have to put down. You must prepare for an emergency landing. Don't worry, he'll find a snowfield, and it will be a soft landing. He is jettisoning fuel now.'

Clive returned to the cabin, surveyed the frightened faces. 'Belly flop,' he said. 'I'm assured it's going to be soft. But we'd better take out our false teeth.' Georges put his plate in his pocket. Denise was hunched in her seat, praying. Clive sat beside her. 'It's going to be all right,' he told her. She didn't look at him, so he checked that her belt was secure, then adjusted his own.

The hostess came back to them. 'You know the drill.' She sat herself, strapped herself in, put her head down between her knees. Kopylov had also returned to the cabin.

The aircraft was now descending fast. Clive peered out of the window, but the snow was thicker than ever. Presumably the pilot could see ... His body shot forward and then back, and for a moment he thought he'd broken his neck. Denise uttered a long moan, and Henri was cursing.

The plane was slithering forward at, it seemed, tremendous speed; from the galley behind them came a series of crashes and thuds as equipment broke loose. Clive saw snow slewing past the window, then there was another sharp jerk and the movement stopped; Clive thought that Orlov was very good at his job.

The hostess and Kopylov were both on their feet. 'Out!'

The front doors were embedded in the snow, as the plane had tilted forward on to its nose. The hostess opened the rear door, and they pushed Denise through it. She gave a little shriek as she dropped several feet and then sank thigh-deep.

'God, it's *freezing*!' she shouted.

'Out, out,' the hostess was bellowing, so the men jumped beside Denise. The cold struck at them, and even breathing was difficult.

Orlov and the co-pilot appeared in the doorway above them.

'Is it going to blow?' Clive shouted, above the howling of the wind.

'No,' the pilot replied.

'Then let's get the hell back inside.' They lifted Denise up and then scrambled back into the plane; there was still some warmth in there. The door was shut, and they brushed snow from their clothes, shivering. 'Hot coffee, brandy, something,' Clive said.

Kopylov beckoned the hostess and they went back to the galley, where they could be heard picking their way through the debris. Orlov sat down and wiped his brow. He had a gash on his forehead, but did not appear even concussed. His co-pilot and the flight engineer both looked more concerned.

Henri was sorting through the camera and recording equipment, which was scattered about the cabin. 'It's mostly usable,' he said with great relief.

'Brandy!' Kopylov handed out plastic cups. Denise held hers in both hands, and gulped at it.

'Assets?' Clive suggested.

'We're alive.' Georges, having taken a swig of hot coffee, was hastily putting his plate back in.

'And the equipment is okay,' Henri pronounced.

'Do we know where we are?' Clive asked. The pilot nodded. 'Does anyone else?'

'I gave the map reference over the radio. I do not know who heard it.'

'But there's a chance someone will come along? When the snow stops?'

'Perhaps.'

'How long have we got?'

'There is no heating,' the pilot explained. 'We can make a

fire, with the gasolene and the fixtures, but that will not last long.'

'And that should be kept for when we hear an aircraft,' Kopylov pointed out.

'How long?' Clive asked again.

'The cabin will go below zero in perhaps twenty-four hours,' the captain said. 'Tatiana, issue everyone with blankets.'

The hostess obeyed.

'At least we have twenty-four hours of food,' Henri said.

They slept huddled together, after a cold meal. There was no longer any hot coffee. The pilot tried his radio, but could raise nothing but static; the main aerials had been damaged in the landing, and they were too low down, and surrounded by hills, for the VHF to be effective.

My last night on earth, maybe, Clive thought, his cheek resting on Denise's hair. Presumably within a day or two the snow would have completely covered the aircraft, and they would simply have disappeared. The snow was not going to go away for several months. He wondered how Holly would cope with Sintax, on a full-time basis? But he hadn't expected it to be this way.

Clive awoke to silence, raised his head, looked left and right. His companions, huddled beneath their blankets, were still fast asleep. But the wind had lost its whine, and although he could not see out of the windows, he was sure it had stopped snowing. Gently he disengaged himself from Denise's arms, laying her, still sleeping, on the seat, went to the exit in the rear. It opened easily enough, and he inhaled the freezing morning air while he looked out at the white world. It had indeed stopped snowing, but now the tail of the aircraft and one wing tip was all that was showing above the thick white carpet. And the snow stretched for as far as he could see, until the plain ended in trees perhaps a mile away. But even the trees seemed coated in white.

He closed the door, looked at Kopylov, who had also woken

up. It was very cold inside the plane, although still considerably warmer than the air temperature outside. 'We must hope, and pray,' Kopylov said.

'Do Russians pray?'

Kopylov's smile was grave. 'Russians have always prayed more than most people, even when there was officially no God. With a climate like this, and rulers such as we have had through most of our history, it has always been necessary to pray.'

The others awoke, the men with unshaven faces; Denise renewed her make-up. At least they could use the toilets. The captain and the hostess had been consulting. 'We have sufficient food for one good meal,' Orlov said. 'Or for three very small ones.'

'Well, if we are going to be frozen by tonight anyway, I vote for one good meal,' Henri said. The others opted for three small ones; they weren't very hungry anyway, and while there was life there was hope.

'Do you still wish to marry me?' Denise asked, sitting with Clive at the rear of the plane. She had, as usual, quite recovered her confidence now she was on the ground; it was not death she feared, only death by flying.

'Can't think of anything I'd rather do.'

'Can the captain marry us? Then we could honeymoon for a couple of hours.'

'I'll ask him.' He stood up, looked down at her. 'You're sure you want to do this?' They had already done a bit of honeymooning in the past two days, not to mention several times in the more distant past.

'Oh, yes. I'd hate to die unattached.'

Clive supposed that was as good a reason as any. He went up the corridor, and heard a rifle shot. Georges was on his feet. 'From out there.'

'People!' Denise shouted, marriage forgotten.

The captain and co-pilot were at the rear door, opening it again, very cautiously. Clive joined them, looked past them at the six men, mounted on shaggy ponies, wrapped up in heavy coats and boots and fur caps so that their faces were almost invisible, armed with assault rifles and a variety of other weapons as well, scattering snow as they approached, the ponies sinking to their haunches with every step, and yet, amazingly, always able to recover and flounder onwards.

'Yakuts!' the captain commented.

The doorway was crowded as the men came closer, halting when some fifty feet away from the crashed aircraft. 'Are they friends?' Denise asked.

'I will speak with them,' the captain decided. Clive felt like interfering, but decided against it; he was only a passenger.

The captain stepped into the doorway and waved. The horsemen gazed at him, and muttered to each other as they pointed at the markings on the one wing tip which showed out of the snow.

'We are from Moscow,' the captain called. 'We need your help. Will you help us?'

There was the crack of a rifle, and the captain gave a choking gasp and collapsed, out of the doorway into the snow.

'Down,' Kopylov shouted, but everyone had already fallen to the cabin floor.

'Shit!' Georges commented.

'Do we have any weapons?' Kopylov asked the co-pilot.

'None.'

'Then we are going to be murdered.'

'Back up,' Clive told them. 'Get behind the seats.'

They crawled past him, Denise panting beside him. 'You are not going to play the fucking hero,' she commented.

'We have to talk to them.'

She made a face and lay down, and he got to his hands and knees and crawled to the door. He could hear the Yakuts talking now; they had come closer, as there had been no return of fire.

'Listen to me,' he shouted in Russian. 'We are English journalists, and French. We are your friends. We need your help.' Several more shots slashed into the open doorway, and Clive pressed his cheek to the carpet.

'Clive, are you all right?' Denise shouted.

'So far. Friends,' he shouted. 'We are friends. We are unarmed. Help us.'

There was some more conversation, in a language he did not understand, then a voice said in Russian, 'You come out. Hands in the air. Come out.'

Clive looked over his shoulder. 'We have no option.' He stood up, took a deep breath, and stepped into the doorway, hands held high. The six men watched him, rifles thrust forward. Then he carefully lowered his hands to swing himself down, trying to avoid the captain's body, half buried in the snow.

'Catch me,' Denise said, and dropped into his arms. In her ski pants and heavy jacket and fur cap they would not immediately be able to tell she was a woman, Clive reflected thankfully. They could recognise the hostess as one, however, even if they did not immediately do anything about it.

'We need food, and water, and warm clothes,' Clive told them. 'And to send a message. You have a radio?'

The men gazed at them, broad faces expressionless, while the Russians attempted to look as much like English and French as possible.

'If we stand here we will freeze,' Denise complained, loudly, her breath misting, slapping her heavy gloves together.

The leader of the Yakut patrol made a decision. 'You come,' he said.

'Where?'

'To our camp.' He grinned. 'It is warm there.'

They gathered they were to ride one behind each of the Yakuts, but there were only six horses, and eight survivors. 'You stay,' said the Yakut spokesman to the co-pilot and flight engineer. The two men exchanged glances.

'If they stay they will freeze to death,' Clive protested.

'We will come back for them,' the Yakut said. 'Our camp is not far.'

Clive looked at the Russians, who shrugged. 'We will wait, Mr Stanton.'

They mounted up. Clive's pony was immediately behind

Denise, and he watched her being manhandled into position behind her rider with a great deal of tender loving care – the Yakuts had deduced her sex. He reflected that Denise was a worldly-wise woman, and would have to prove it now. His immediate priority was staying up behind his own rider as the ponies floundered through the snow towards the trees, and trying not to feel the cold. He had a heavy lined anorak over a sweater, as well as warm underwear and thick gloves, and still felt as if he were freezing, while the deerstalker he had brought along was totally ineffective – he had not expected to have to ride a horse in the snow.

He began to grow drowsy, while shivering and hugging the fur jacket in front of him, as much to keep warm as to stop himself from falling off. He lost track of time, was jerked awake when he heard noise, and the movement stopped. Then he did slide off, to land on his feet; his knees gave way and he knelt. The rest of the party were equally disorganised, as they either dismounted or were pushed from their seats. Denise was also on her knees, and Clive got up and went to her. 'You all right?' He helped her up.

'I don't know,' she said. 'He has very inquisitive fingers.'

Clive looked around them. They had reached the Yakut encampment, which he gathered was on the far side of the wood from where the plane had crashed. Here there were tents, and where the snow had been cleared, fires, and horses, and reindeer, and a large number of people; he felt some of them were women, but it was difficult to be certain, as they were all heavily wrapped up.

He faced a man who wore a star on his *schlem*; he might have been stepping back twenty-five years into the days of Soviet Russia. The man was only of medium height, but very powerfully built. What was disturbing was his youth. The face was strong, and yet curiously slack, as though the power of the mind behind it was dormant; the black eyes were sleepy. 'Are you the commandant?' Clive asked.

'I am Colonel Borjigin.'

'Borjigin? Are you related to Batalji Borjigin?'

'The Khan is my father. I am Barone Borjigin. You have violated our airspace.'

'We are television journalists, from Europe. From the EEC. We have come to interview your father, for western television,' Clive explained.

Barone Borjigin looked from face to face, then pointed at Kopylov and Tatiana. 'They are Russian.'

'Yes. They came to help us.'

'They have invaded our territory.'

'That is not so. We have no arms. We have come to speak with your father. He will wish to speak with us.'

'There are others in your party,' Barone commented.

'Yes. Your men murdered our pilot in cold blood. The co-pilot and flight engineer have remained with the plane. Your men said they would return for them. Or they will freeze.'

'Are they Russian?'

'Yes. They are Russian.'

Barone almost smiled. 'Then they will freeze. In there.'

He was pointing at the largest of the yurts, but Clive could not believe his ears. 'You cannot just abandon those men. Your people promised . . .'

'They had no authority,' Barone said. 'The Russians are our enemies. Any Russian entering our territory must be killed. My father has said this. In there.'

Clive looked at Georges and Henri. 'We had better do as he says,' Georges muttered. 'It may be possible to persuade him to change his mind.' Clive nodded, and held Denise's arm to guide her towards the tent.

'Not them,' Barone said. Kopylov had been walking with Tatiana. Now they were checked by some of the soldiers. 'You are Russian,' Barone said again.

'I am the guide for the party,' Kopylov said.

'Russian.' Barone spoke in Yakut, and men closed around the pair. Kopylov swore at them, and Tatiana screamed, but they were both dragged away to one of the tents.

'For God's sake!' Clive shouted, releasing Denise. 'What are you doing to them?'

'They will amuse my men,' Barone said. 'Then they will be executed.'

'You cannot *do* this,' Clive said. 'The laws of hospitality forbid you to do this.'

'They are Russians,' Barone said. 'There are no laws of hospitality for Russians. Inside.'

Clive was seized by four men and bundled into the tent. His every instinct was to fight them, but he knew they would be too strong for him, and there was Denise to be thought of. She was already in the tent, kneeling before one of several braziers which made the interior soporifically warm, hugging herself as circulation returned. He knelt beside her. 'I really didn't mean things to work out like this,' he muttered.

'Maybe there's a priest here can marry us, before they shoot us,' she suggested.

'There's more likely to be a shaman. But this character is not going to shoot us. Or he'd have already done so.'

He hoped he was right, squeezed her hand, as Barone Borjigin entered the tent followed by several of his officers. Slowly Barone took off his hat and cloak; underneath he wore Russian uniform, but with an insignia Clive had not seen before. He presumed the badge was meant to represent a lightning strike, but disturbingly, it was very similar to that worn by Hitler's SS during the Second World War. Now Barone seated himself on a reindeer-skin rug; incongruously, while a pistol holster hung on his right thigh, a sabre slapped his left. 'You have visas?' he asked.

'Well, no,' Clive said. 'You have no representatives in Moscow to grant us one. Anyway, we didn't know we needed them. We didn't need them to get to Moscow.'

'You were sent by Moscow?'

'We were sent by our principals in London and Paris. Your father, what he has done here in Yakutiya, is news. Our business is news. All we wish to do is report what has happened here, take some film, interview your father, and leave again.'

'How can you leave again? You have no plane.'

He appeared totally ingenuous. Yet he possessed the power of life and death; their lives and deaths! Clive knew he had to be patient and keep calm, even if he was bubbling with outrage at what had happened to the Russians. 'That is something I will have to negotiate with your father, when we meet. Your father will wish to meet with me.'

'Why?'

'Because I am a very famous man, known throughout the world. I can make the world understand what your father has done, perhaps support him.'

'Nothing like blowing your own trumpet,' Georges muttered in French.

But Barone Borjigin was stroking his chin. 'Very well,' he said at last. 'I will send you to my father. He will know what to do with you.'

Clive's heart gave a great bound of relief. 'We thank you, Colonel. When can we leave?'

'I will arrange it for tomorrow morning.'

'And the Russians?'

'They will be dead by then.' Barone smiled, a slow withdrawal of his upper lip from his teeth. 'I am being generous to you, Englishman. Now go with my people; they will feed you.' Denise got to her feet. 'Come here, woman,' Barone said.

Denise looked at Clive; she was not used to being ordered about, especially by someone very nearly young enough to be her son. 'Humour him,' Clive recommended, in French. He could not believe what was happening, but he knew their lives were still in danger.

Denise went forward. Barone waved his hand. 'Take off your hat.' Denise obeyed. 'Your jacket,' Barone commanded. Denise hesitated, then slowly unzipped her ski jacket and took it off. 'That.' Barone pointed at her multicoloured sweater.

Denise looked at Clive again. 'Our women do not undress before strangers, Colonel,' Clive said.

'But your woman is now my woman, eh?' Barone pointed out.

Clive took a step forward, and so did the waiting Yakut

officers. 'Wait!' Denise said. 'You told me to humour him.' She lifted the sweater over her head.

'You wear many clothes,' Barone remarked, gazing at her shirt. 'Now that, and that,' pointing at her pants.

'Now you look here,' Clive protested.

'Sssh,' Denise said, and stepped out of her ski pants. She was wearing long johns, and remained totally concealed. But Barone was gesturing again.

'Denise!' Clive said.

'I always wanted to be a stripper,' she told him. 'So where's the music?' She peeled off the woollen garment. She wore no bra, only a pair of knickers, and she did not wait for the command, but slid these down her thighs as well.

Barone gazed at her, nostrils dilating as he was clearly comparing her slender beauty with that of the more chunky Mongol women. 'The woman will stay with me,' he said. 'You others, go.'

'Not on your life!' Clive snapped, and looked down the barrel of a revolver, presented to him by one of Barone's aides.

'Don't be a fool, Clive,' Denise begged in French. 'He's only a boy.'

'He's an unmitigated thug,' Clive said.

'But still a boy.'

'What are you saying?' Barone demanded.

'That it will be a pleasure to stay with you, Colonel,' Denise said.

CHAPTER 4

The Steppes, Summer 1989

Jalain Anhusat raised his head, and held up his hand. The rest of the herdsmen also drew rein and listened. 'I heard a shout,' Jalain said.

They looked around them. It was summer on the steppes, and the grass was high, dotted with wild flowers. The herd was moving slowly to the east and the river, where the clans had already pitched their tents. The land undulated, some of the hills quite high, sheltering secluded valleys where the sun seldom reached. Then the cry came again, seeping across the landscape. 'It is a devil,' Pirale said.

'It is a man!' Jalain suddenly kicked his horse and sent it galloping towards the sound. 'It is the Prince!' he bellowed.

His cousins galloped behind him, the herd forgotten.

The man laid Batalji on the ground before his wife and mother, and Khalim Anhusat. 'Batalji!' Mortana screamed, throwing herself beside him, to hug and kiss him.

Batalji was bloodstained and sweat-stained, clearly exhausted and starving. Selphine, as alarmed as her daughter-in-law, fed him kumiss, and over the next few days watched the strength slowly flow back into those powerful limbs. It was ten years since she had seen him. 'Batalji,' she said. 'What have they done to you?'

Batalji gave a wolfish grin. 'Nothing I have not done to myself, Mother.'

'You have left the army?' They had stripped away his tattered, filthy clothing, but had been able to discern it had once been a uniform.

'Yes,' Batalji said. 'I have left the army. I have deserted.'

Selphine looked up, at Khalim and Jalain. 'Will they track you here?' Khalim asked.

'I do not know,' Batalji said. 'But ... yes. They can track a man anywhere.'

'We must do nothing suspicious,' Khalim said. 'We will conceal you, when it becomes necessary. But we must continue our movement, as normal.'

Mortana presented the boy. 'We have called him Barone, after your brother,' she explained. 'It was your mother's choice.'

The boy was nine years old, long-limbed and strong. 'I have dreamed of this moment, my Father Prince.'

Clearly he had been coached. Batalji looked at Mortana. 'We have done nothing but speak to him of you,' Mortana said, again carefully associating Selphine with herself.

'Then I am pleased.' Batalji stroked the boy's head. 'Tomorrow we will hunt together.'

'Next week, you mean,' Mortana objected. 'You are not strong enough, my lord.'

Batalji grinned. 'Stronger than you think. Leave us, boy. We will speak, tomorrow.'

Mortana gasped as she collapsed on her belly, her body seething, Batalji still inside her. 'You are stronger than you seem, my lord.' For the first time in their acquaintance – which in terms of actual time spent together was very brief – he had frightened her, in the urgency of his desire. Now, although spent, his hands continued to surge beneath her, massaging her breast and groin, moving back to seize her buttocks. 'Were there no women, in Afghanistan?' she asked.

Batalji rolled away from her, and glancing at him, she realised she had made a mistake. 'Will you tell me of them?' she asked.

'No,' Batalji said.

He would not speak of Homaira, but that evening he told Mortana and Selphine, Khalim and Jalain and Jagnuth, of how the army had treated him. 'I should have been shot,' he explained. 'For assaulting an officer. They preferred to send me to a punishment battalion.' He gazed into the distance, and shuddered. 'I was sentenced to four years, hard labour. We did every filthy job in the army, from burying the dead to digging latrines even where there already were latrines. To hesitate was to be flogged. But there were worse punishments. Because we could be punished at will. Many men went mad and attacked their officers, knowing they would be shot down. Others committed suicide.'

'But you survived, my son,' Selphine's eyes glowed.

'Yes, Mother. I made myself survive. Four years is not so long, I told myself. And when, after three of those years, the news came that the army was pulling out of Afghanistan, I felt sure of my survival.'

Khalim nodded. 'We have heard that this man Gorbachev will turn Russia upside down.'

'The army will not stand for that,' Batalji objected. 'It is the army which is the Soviet Union. It was not Gorbachev who pulled us out of Afghanistan. The army left because it was fighting a war which it could not win. It is a worse situation than the Americans were in, in Vietnam.' He stopped to remember what poor old Ashansky had said. The British had not been able to conquer Afghanistan. Nothing had changed. The odd thing was that *he* knew how to conquer Afghanistan. But he was unlikely ever to command a Russian army. Then he told them how, when they had returned to Russia, and he had applied for leave, he had been refused. 'Leave is not for rebels like you, Borjigin,' they had told him. 'So I left anyway,' he said.

'Where did you leave from?' Jagnuth asked.

'From our barracks in Orel.'

Jalain stared at him in disbelief. Having learned to read and write, he had also learned to read maps. 'That is more than three thousand miles,' he said.

'Yes,' Batalji said. They gazed at him as if he were a god.

'You walked three thousand miles to be with me,' Mortana said, snuggling against him that night.

'To be with my people,' Batalji corrected.

She was not offended. 'They worship you. A man who can walk three thousand miles is a god.'

He smiled into her hair. 'Sometimes I got a ride,' he confessed.

He had been away ten years. Now it seemed like a long nightmare. To sleep, without wondering if one would awake. To hold Mortana in his arms, knowing that she loved rather than hated him. To sit with his mother, with whom, however long their separation, he shared so much. To ride with his in-laws across the steppes, laughing and shooting and firing their guns at nothing particular. To fish in the river, and fear nothing from the cracking twig behind him. Above all, to have his son at his side; Barone had already been taught the essentials of Mongol manhood by his uncle, Jagnuth, but he wished to learn all over again, from his father. These were the good things in life. And after only a fortnight, Mortana told him, 'I am to bear you another son.'

'So soon?'

She laughed. 'It takes only a moment, my lord Prince. If that moment comes at the right time of the month.'

I have found paradise, he thought. After so long. It would take time, he knew, for the memories to become exorcised. He had but to close his eyes to feel the lash, the cold, to see Homaira's face before him, to hear the animal screams of Koplin as he had been castrated. But those horrors had eliminated the horrors of the orphanage. These present happinesses would, in time, eliminate the horrors of Afghanistan and the army. But it was time he lacked. A week later the gunships came.

Batalji was fishing with Barone when he heard the so-familiar chatter of the helicopter engines. 'Quickly!' He grasped the boy's hand, and pulled him into the bushes, then they stole back towards the encampment.

The rest of the clan had heard the sound too, and Khalim and Jalain and Jagnuth were galloping home as fast as they could, followed by the others. By the time Batalji reached the trees nearest to the camp, the gunships were on the ground, and the yurts were surrounded by soldiers. With them was Boris Taychin. Batalji pressed Barone to the earth, as he listened to what was being said.

'Batalji?' Khalim enquired. 'I know nothing of Batalji.'

'You are lying,' Boris Taychin told him. 'His movements have been tracked as far as the borders of Yakutiya. There can be only one place he is coming – here. And he has had time to reach here.'

'If he has not died on the way, Comrade Commissar,' Jalain suggested.

'That bastard? He has not died. He is here, somewhere. I know this. Now you listen to me: Batalji Borjigin is a deserter from the Red Army. He has killed six men to get to you. He is wanted for murder as well as desertion, and there is a list of other crimes longer than my arm. I intend to take him back to Yakutsk. Now, you either hand him over to me, or I will arrest you on charges of harbouring a deserter. The penalty for that is also death.' He glared at their faces, at the women, huddled together. 'I will give you ten seconds to tell me where I can find Batalji, then I will take you all back to Yakutsk for trial.'

Khalim looked at Selphine in consternation; it was an unthinkable choice. But Batalji knew there was no help for it. 'No matter what happens, you stay here,' he told Barone, and stood up. 'Wait. Is it me you are looking for?' He walked slowly across the open space towards the yurt, while the Russians gazed at him in consternation.

'They are all guilty of concealing a wanted criminal,' Taychin said.

'They did not know I am wanted,' Batalji said. 'I told them I had been discharged.' He held out his wrist for the handcuffs, looking at his mother. 'I am sorry, Mother,' he said. 'I am sorry, Mortana.' He used his eyes to will them not to speak of the boy.

'What will become of him?' Selphine asked.

'Why, he will be shot,' Boris Taychin told her. 'After due process of law, of course.' The coming of Gorbachev had made a difference; outlaws like the Borjigins could no longer be murdered in cold blood. But the end result would be the same, he had no doubt.

Jagnuth escorted Selphine and Mortana into Yakutsk. It was a long journey, made with desperate haste in the summer heat. Several of the other men came too, but they travelled separately. Jalain had gone on ahead. Jalain was the one who made plans, and determined how the plans were to be carried out.

The women insisted on going alone to the KGB building, where they waited for four hours before being admitted into Andrei Taychin's office. 'What are you doing here?' Andrei Taychin demanded. Andrei was in his sixties now, white-haired and white-moustached. But he had not changed with the times; Gorbachev might be doing his best to ruin the Soviet Union with his *perestroika* and his *glasnost*, but Andrei still preserved the attitude of a Commissar to non-Party members. 'Your husband was a deviationist, and your son is worse. His trial starts tomorrow. It will not take long. Then he will be executed.'

'What have you done to him?' Selphine asked.

Andrei Taychin snorted. 'It has not been necessary to do anything to him. His crimes are well known, and he has not denied them.'

'I wish to appeal for clemency,' Selphine said.

'Clemency!' Andrei Taychin laughed. 'For that thug?'

'We have heard that President Gorbachev is a good man,' Selphine persisted. 'All we ask is that he listens to our petition. My son is not a thug. He has been made so by mistreatment. You have taken away everything he has. You have no right to take away his life.'

'It is the law.'

'President Gorbachev...'

'President Gorbachev has no jurisdiction in Yakutiya,' Andrei Taychin said. 'Go away, woman, before I lose my temper.'

Selphine hesitated, and Mortana held her arm to stop her doing anything rash. Then the door opened, and Boris Taychin came in, accompanied by his wife, a tall, handsome woman in her early thirties. 'I apologise, Comrade Father,' Boris said. 'I did not mean to interrupt.' He looked at Selphine. 'You have allowed this ratbag in here?'

'She is just leaving,' Andrei said.

Selphine fell to her knees before Ludmilla Taychin. 'I have come to beg for my son's life. For the sake of his wife and his unborn child. For God's sake have mercy on me.'

'God,' Boris sneered. 'You don't believe in God.'

'I am begging you,' Selphine said to Ludmilla Taychin, hands clasped in front of her face. 'Please, madame ... have you no children of your own?'

Ludmilla's face was stony. 'No,' she said. 'I have no children of my own.' Selphine's shoulders slumped.

Andrei Taychin rang the bell on his desk. 'I will have you caned,' he decided. 'For embarrassing my daughter-in-law.'

Selphine uttered a great shriek, and leapt to her feet. She had no weapon, as both she and Mortana had been searched before being allowed into the palace, but she had her nails. She threw herself across the desk, reaching for Andrei Taychin's face. He leapt to his feet, knocking over his chair as he did so, while Boris ran forward and Mortana shrank against the wall.

Boris gripped Selphine's arms and pulled her back, but she tore herself free and turned on him, her face inhuman in its anger, her nails flailing at his cheeks. Ludmilla Taychin screamed, and the door burst open as the guards ran in. They seized both women, and dragged them to the door.

'Cane them!' Andrei Taychin shouted. 'Cane them till their asses bleed. But first, fuck them. Fuck them till they beg for mercy.'

Boris Taychin grinned. 'You'll excuse me, Comrade Father. Ludmilla. I will supervise this punishment myself.' He twined his fingers in Mortana's hair. 'Batalji's wife. You are a beauty.'

Mortana gasped. 'I am pregnant, Comrade.'

Boris Taychin's smile widened. 'Well, then, I will give your babe company.'

The men met in the house of Hilaim the wine merchant, coming secretly under the cover of darkness. By then the women were already there, Selphine and Mortana wrapped in their cloaks. The men only needed one glance at them to know what had happened to them. 'They have taken my baby,' Mortana sobbed.

'Being fucked a few times will not harm your baby,' Selphine told her. 'They are going to shoot my son.' She gazed at Jalain.

Jalain nodded. 'We will get him out.'

'How?' Pirale demanded. 'He is in the central gaol. The walls are several feet thick. There are a dozen men in the guardroom, machine-guns on the walls. There is no possibility of getting in, much less getting out, with Batalji.'

'I need two volunteers,' Jalain said. 'A pretty girl, and a determined man.'

'To get Batalji out?' Mortana raised her head. 'I will do anything.'

'You cannot volunteer,' Jalain told his sister. 'You are Batalji's wife, our Princess. These volunteers must sacrifice their lives.' The wine store was suddenly silent. 'Batalji is our Khan,' Jalain said. 'His life must be saved. Barone is too young to lead us. Batalji is the man who will lead us to freedom, one day. When that time comes, we must all be prepared to die for him, for the clan. Are we not prepared to die now? I would volunteer myself, but I must lead the rescue.'

'I will volunteer,' said one of the young men, Talane. 'Tell me what I must do.' Jalain told him. Talane swallowed. 'For Batalji,' he said.

Jalain looked over the other faces. 'I will volunteer,' said Rutka.

Jalain studied her. She was certainly attractive. 'You understand that you must die? There is no hope of survival.' The girl nodded. 'Then this is what you must do,' Jalain said.

It was dark again, the following day, when they left Hilaim's wine store. By then the first day of the trial had been completed. The prosecution had outlined the evidence against Batalji Borjigin, but there was more to come. The list of charges against him seemed endless. Pirale had left early, and was in court to see and hear what was happening, and more important, to make sure that Batalji was being kept in the cell beneath the courtroom for the night.

He was able to confirm this. They stole out of the shop. Mortana was sent with two of the men immediately to begin her journey back to the secret rendezvous in the forest. Talane went by himself to the International Hotel. He was wearing a suit, and no one questioned him as he entered the lobby and went straight to the lifts, without a moment's hesitation. 'Fifteen minutes,' Jalain said, and they took their positions on street corners close to the courthouse. The courthouse was situated three blocks up from the International Hotel. The streets were crowded with people in the early evening, and a dozen more made very little difference.

They waited. Jalain studied Rutka. She was only eighteen, which was a very young age to die, voluntarily, and he feared for her resolution. But she seemed absolutely determined, smiling and joking with the others in the party, and if she was definitely stouter than usual, she revealed no discomfort at the band of stolen Semtex secured around her waist.

There was a sudden whisper of alarm through the people, and they began to hurry towards the International Hotel, where a crowd was already gathered. 'There's a man on the top ledge,' they shouted. 'He's going to jump.'

Sirens wailed, as police and fire engines arrived, along with a TV camera crew. Jalain looked along the street, and saw searchlights playing on Talane as he stood on the ledge outside the staff quarters bedroom window he had used, back pressed against the sloping roof, gazing down at the gathering crowd some hundred feet below him. Policemen were shouting at him, and there were faces at the windows to either side of him. Talane moved further along the ledge so that they could not reach him. 'It is time,' Jalain said. He squeezed Rutka's hands and kissed her cheeks. She held his hands and pressed them against her breast for a moment – she had never known a man – then walked down the street.

They watched her from the corner, as she banged on the door. The eyehole was opened first, and then the door, as the men inside saw she was only a girl. Jalain had told her to say that she had come to see Batalji, but he knew they would not let her. On the other hand, they were certain to wish to play with her, on the pretence of searching her. So there were only a few seconds ... and there it was, a huge explosion, which blew out the entire front of the guardroom, scattering bodies into the air and along the street. Jalain ran forward, followed by Jagnuth and Selphine and the rest of the men. The noise had alarmed the crowd, but as they turned to find out what was happening, Talane, as instructed, jumped. There was a huge wail of consternation, and people surged forward to see the mangled remains of the demented young man.

Jagnuth and Selphine and their people were already in the shattered guardroom. There was no sign of Rutka, only blood and guts scattered far and wide. One of the guards was still alive, lying in a corner with both legs blown off. Selphine shot him in the head. Then they were inside, and at Batalji's cell.

THE FIFTH CHRONICLE

Yakutiya, October 2000

Clive awoke to a kick in the shoulder, looked up at one of Barone's lieutenants. 'It is time to leave,' the Mongol said.

Clive sat up, rubbed the back of his head. He was hungover. They had been wined and dined very well last night – but the wine had been entirely vodka. The Mongol officers had got drunk, and Clive and Georges and Henri had been able to think of nothing better than to join them; getting drunk blotted out the thoughts of what might be happening to Denise, of what might already have happened to Kopylov and Tatiana, of what the co-pilot and flight engineer might be thinking as they realised they had been abandoned to freeze to death. 'These people are savages,' Georges had muttered in French.

'They are Mongols, stripping off the veneer of civilisation imposed by the tsars and then the Communists,' Clive had pointed out.

'That doesn't make them any the more acceptable,' Georges grumbled. 'I hope you are going to report everything that has happened.'

'I intend to. Supposing we ever get back to do so.'

But the officer's words were at least promising. Clive kicked off his blanket and scrambled to his feet, joined by Georges and Henri. 'Where do we wash, and shave?' Henri asked.

'We leave now,' the officer said.

Orderlies were waiting to serve them steaming mugs of a yellowish liquid, which gave off a revolting smell. 'Breakfast?' Georges asked.

'Kumiss. It will give you strength.'

'It will give me something, I am certain,' Georges said. But he drank, and raised his eyebrows. 'Not too bad.'

As it was all they were apparently going to get, Clive drank as well, and found that the drink seemed to penetrate every part of his body. Even his brain, for it was distinctly alcoholic. The officer grinned. 'It keeps out the cold, eh? Come.'

They had been issued with fur coats and hats and boots at Barone's orders. These they put on, and left the tent they had been apportioned for the night. Waiting for them were a squad of mounted soldiers and several additional horses. At least they had a mount apiece, but . . . 'We are to ride, to Yakutsk?' Clive asked.

'That is six hundred miles,' Henri protested.

'In snow?' Georges added.

'It is the only way,' the officer pointed out.

'What about aircraft?'

'There is no landing place, in the snow.'

'Well, helicopters. Can't your colonel call up a chopper?'

'Our helicopters are at work, elsewhere. You go by horse, or you do not go.'

'Jesus! How long will it take?'

The officer shrugged. 'Two months. It is the only way.'

The three westerners exchanged glances. 'If it is the only way . . .' Georges said.

'I'm thinking of Denise. She won't be able to take such a journey. Where is she, anyway?'

They saw Barone leave his tent and come towards them. He looked extraordinarily pleased with himself. 'I have just heard on the radio,' he said. 'You are reported missing, and it is assumed you have crashed and are all dead. Is that not amusing?'

'I hope you've corrected the mistake,' Henri said.

'What mistake? Did you not crash?'

'But we are alive. Some of us.'

'You are dead,' Barone told him. 'Unless my father wills it that you should live. Now go.'

'We're waiting for Denise,' Clive said.

'The woman stays.'

'You have to be out of your tiny mind.'

'She interests me,' Barone explained, with utter simplicity, not taking offence.

'I can imagine. Do you suppose you can just appropriate a woman like that?'

'I am Barone Borjigin,' Barone said, even more simply.

'I think he means it,' Henri remarked in French.

'What are we to do?' Georges asked.

Clive knew there was nothing they *could* do. But he couldn't just abandon her. 'You said you have a radio. Can you not speak with your father on the radio? Or better yet, let me speak with him?'

'My father is too busy to speak with you, Englishman. You wish to speak with him, you must go to Yakutsk, and seek an audience.'

An audience! Clive thought. As if the damned man were a king or a pope. Yet he understood that further argument would lead nowhere – except that Barone might lose his temper and not let any of them go. Denise was going to have to prove just how big a girl she was. But two months... 'Where were you when the coup took place?' he asked.

'At my father's side.'

'Just over a week ago. And you are now on the border. How did you manage that?'

'I flew.'

'But you will not let us fly.'

'There is no place for an aircraft to land. I flew and jumped by parachute to join this *ordu* guarding the border. Now you must leave.'

Clive realised he was beaten. 'I wish to speak with the woman, before we go.'

'What for?' Barone asked.

'She is my woman.'

Barone frowned. 'Your wife?'

'My betrothed.'

Barone looked puzzled. 'She did not say this to me.'

'Did you ask her?'

Barone looked more puzzled yet. 'She is my woman now,' he declared.

'I am still entitled to say goodbye to her, surely,' Clive insisted.

Barone considered, then waved to one of his aides. A moment later Denise was let out. Like them, she had been wrapped in a heavy fur coat and fur boots, as well as a Mongol fur cap; it was difficult to be sure what else she had on, if anything. Her cheeks were flushed, and gave an impression of being mottled, and she glanced at each of their faces in turn, quickly, before looking away again. 'My God!' Henri said. 'What has he done to you?'

'Don't ask stupid questions,' Denise said.

Clive considered holding her hand, and decided against it, with Barone watching them. 'He wants to keep you here,' he said. Denise's tongue came out and circled her lips, then was hastily withdrawn before it froze. 'Listen,' Clive said. 'Can you stand it, for a while? We have been reported dead. There is no rescue mission on its way. Our only hope is to get to Batalji Borjigin, establish our credentials and our good intentions, and hope he'll treat us fairly. Getting you out of here will be our first priority.'

'How long?' she asked.

'Well . . . these people say it will take us two months to reach Yakutsk.'

'Two *months*?'

'We have to travel by horseback, apparently.'

'And two months back?'

'We'll try to see what we can arrange with Batalji. He *must* have helicopters. And he can send a message to his son by radio.'

'Four months,' she muttered, not convinced. 'And ...' She looked up. 'Suppose you don't *come* back.'

'I'll come back, Denise. Or I'll send for you. I'll get you out of this, I swear it. Can you stick it?'

'Four months,' she said again, and glanced at Barone. Then she drew a long breath and squared her shoulders. 'Come back, Clive. For God's sake, come back.' She forced a smile. 'We'll name the first one after you.'

'First, we wish to return to the aircraft,' Clive told Barone.

'Why?'

'Our equipment is there. Our cameras and our sound-recording gear.'

'You do not need cameras,' Barone told them, and grinned. 'If my father wishes you to have a picture of him, he will give you one.'

Clive grunted in frustrated anger; he had still hoped to be able to rescue the two Russians. 'I wish to protest, most strongly, against those two men being left to freeze to death,' he said.

Barone shrugged. 'They are Russians.'

'If we do not regain our equipment, it will be ruined,' Georges explained. 'It is very expensive equipment.'

'I did not ask you to bring it here,' Barone pointed out.

Georges gave up, but Clive was still prepared to try. 'Well, where are the other two Russians? Kopylov and the air hostess?'

'You ask too many questions, Englishman. But if you wish to know...' He led them into the wood, and the three Westerners gasped with horror. Kopylov's and Tatiana's naked bodies drooped from two stakes set in the snow. They had been impaled. 'They provided much sport for my men before they died,' Barone said.

CHAPTER FIVE

Yakutsk, Spring 1996

Andrei Taychin was seventy-one years old. But he could still bristle with anger, still send shivers up and down the spines of men standing before his desk; since he had become President of Yakutia his megalomania had grown. 'A convoy,' he said. 'An armed convoy on the Magadan Road, hijacked in broad daylight. Twenty-seven men killed. Ninety-six wounded. The rest demoralised. Weapons, ammunition, stolen. Now they have mortars and heavy machine-guns. How can this happen? You: General Arzhanov!'

'Borjigin knew the exact moment to strike, Your Excellency,' General Arzhanov attempted to explain. 'And he has so many men . . .'

'So many men,' Andrei Taychin sneered. 'If he has so many men, how is it that our helicopters never find these huge concentrations? You, General Simonoslov?'

'Well, Your Excellency, the forests . . .'

'Bah! It is an outrage. A continuous outrage. His escape was an outrage, seven years ago. You told me then that he would quickly be recaptured. Seven years ago.'

'It has taken longer than we had hoped, Your Excellency,' Arzhanov agreed. 'But when an outlaw commands men, and women, who are willing to die for him...'

'Then we should give them the opportunity of doing that on a more regular basis,' Andrei Taychin snapped. 'This is the last straw.'

'If we had more men...' Simonoslov suggested.

'There are no more men. I have applied to Moscow for additional forces, and they have refused to assist. They have troubles of their own. They are afraid of the Ukraine, and they have been having mutinies within their own army. They say they have no fuel to spare on chasing outlaws. They say we can use the garrison here in Yakutiya, however. What have you to say, Boris?'

Boris Taychin, now in his mid-fifties, had put on weight. But he was as quietly belligerent as ever. 'Tell me what you want done, Father.'

'Twenty years ago I sent you out to destroy Baltomar Borjigin.'

'I did this, Father.'

'But you let the cub Batalji live. That was a mistake. Now he is regarded as Khan by all the nomads. Well, I want him destroyed. I want all his people destroyed. Every man, every woman, every child who has ever supported him will be shot. Every animal belonging to their clans will be slaughtered.'

'You are speaking of destroying an entire people, Your Excellency,' Arzhanov protested. '*Our* people.'

'They are not our people if they support Borjigin.'

'The media will make a meal of it,' said Simonoslov. 'The United Nations...'

'I am not interested in the United Nations,' Andrei Taychin declared. 'Any more than they are interested in us. We are too far away from them. To get at us, they must first come through Russia, and Russia has told me I can handle this business any way I choose. Moscow will not allow the United Nations to interfere, even if they wish to do so. Boris, you have heard my orders. Choose a nomad *ordu* and destroy it. Utterly. That will bring this scoundrel out of hiding.'

*

Sartine panted as he fell from his horse, landed on his hands and knees before the Mongol *ordu*, deep in the forest. 'Planes,' he gasped. 'Gunships. Tanks. Our *ordu* is destroyed. Men, women and children shot. They are saying Stalin has come again.'

'Eat,' Batalji told him. 'And drink. And rest.'

The stricken man was helped away by the women and boys. 'What are we to do?' Jalain asked.

Jalain was in his middle thirties now, a grizzled, experienced guerrilla fighter. But then they all were, after seven years of outlawry. Batalji was in his mid-thirties now as well. In the context of the steppes, he feared he was growing old. And what did he have to show for it?

He could still remember, as if it were yesterday, the wild escape from the Yakutsk cell. They had got clear away from the city, because of the confusion and excitement over Talane's suicide. By the time Taychin's men had realised what had happened the Mongols were deep in the forests. Then the chase had been mounted in earnest. But those had been exhilarating days, as they had ridden, and hidden, and fought back whenever possible. He had had his mother and wife beside him, as well as his son. Men had died, on both sides, but he had lived as a true descendant of Genghis Khan was meant to live. As he had always intended to live.

The exhilaration had not lasted, of course. The life of an outlaw was in the main composed of boredom, and the constant strain of avoiding capture. At least there had been no question of betrayal. The entire nomad people had supported him, no matter what the cost. They had hidden him and his chosen band, and his women. And as time went by, his children. The girl, Shallane, had been born in 1990. They had feared for her, after her mother had been so brutally raped by Taychin's men, but she was a strong and healthy child. Then had come the other two boys, Tensan and Dorgat. These were both still hardly more than babes, but they would grow, as their brother Barone had grown. But Shallane, with her red-brown hair and wicked eyes, remained his favourite. Even at not quite six years old he could tell she would be a great beauty.

No one had ever asked his purpose. It was sufficient that a leader had arisen, who was prepared to defy the Commissars – the fact that they no longer called themselves Commissars meant nothing to the Yakuts: they remained the symbols of hated foreign rule. Not even his intimates, men like Jalain and Jagnuth, and Pirale, Haroun and Almani – who had himself deserted from the Red Army to follow the man he adored – not even old Khalim Anhusat himself, had ever asked where he was leading them. They too were merely happy to have been given the opportunity to live the life of their ancestors, whatever the dangers and hardships involved. Dangers and hardships were meat and drink to a Mongol.

Loyalty! He had possessed total loyalty. Mortana had never uttered a word of complaint, nor had her sisters. Only Selphine had ever doubted. She had not put her doubts into words, and she was the boldest spirit of them all. She rode beside her son to every raid, shot and killed like the best of his men. But her eyes always smouldered. Selphine sought more than a lifetime of outlawry. She sought revenge on the Taychins, father and son. That he knew. But he also knew she wanted more.

Then what did he want? Something more, as well. Without being sure what it could be. He wanted revenge, certainly. He wanted to destroy all the hated symbols of civilisation which defiled the land, not only because the factories and the roads and bridges, the airfields and the high-rise apartments in Yakutsk, were symbols of the Commissars, but because their destruction appealed to his deep-seated instincts: the land was for cattle and horses, and men, to roam across at will. Factories and apartment buildings imprisoned people, and blocked movement.

To accomplish that goal, he knew he must destroy the Taychins and all they stood for. Somehow. To that end, he was patiently accumulating both men and materiel. The raid on the military convoy had been his most successful coup to date. But it still left him far short of everything he needed. He was fighting a guerrilla war the only way he knew, the way the *mujahedin* had fought against the Russians, against himself. Raid and run, murder and melt into the forest. The *mujahedin* had done that for ten years, and they had won in the end; the Russians had pulled out of Afghanistan. But *had* the *mujahedin* won? Or had it been the change in the Russian leadership that had saved them? He didn't know. No one would ever know. So he continued the fight, endlessly, senselessly. And now the fight had brought this horrible retribution. An entire *ordu* destroyed. He knew his people were prepared to die for him. But now they had to ask, like Jalain, what are we to do? Simply die?

He turned round to look at them; men and women were watching him. He had no answer, only words. 'This is total war,' he said. 'It is them or us.'

'Then it must be them,' Selphine declared. 'Give us the word, and we will march on Yakutsk.'

'We will *ride* on Yakutsk!' Jagnuth cried.

Batalji smiled, sadly. They still dreamed of the past. And even if they understood the power of the gunships and the tanks, they had no concept of the real strength of the Red Army, even a demoralised and disorganised Red Army. But an army which could certainly fight on the defensive, as it would in Yakutsk, with far superior weapons to any he possessed. 'We still have a great deal to do before we can march, or ride, on Yakutsk,' he told them.

'Listen to me,' Selphine said. 'Is it not true that there is a missile site up in the north?'

'This is true.'

'Why do we not seize it, and the missiles. And force the Taychins to surrender by threatening to blow them out of existence.'

'That would bring the rest of the world down on our necks,' Batalji said. 'Equally it would require more strength than we possess. The site is garrisoned by a regiment of soldiers. And when we have seized the site, supposing we could, what do we know of missiles, and launchers? We would probably blow ourselves up. These things need to be planned, and our strength needs to be increased, while the Taychins are weakened. I have said, it is total war. We must carry the war to the enemy. To Yakutsk itself. But not by any frontal attack where we would merely be shot down. We must infiltrate into the city, and recruit there. Pirale, I make this your responsibility.' He looked around their faces, saw disappointment. 'We must also avenge the death of Sartine's people. I hereby condemn Andrei Taychin to death, and all his brood. Are you with me?' This time there was a huge shout of approval.

'How will we do this?' Selphine asked.

'That is what we must plan,' Batalji said. 'Jalain, you are my strong right arm. I put you in charge of the plan.'

They studied maps of the city. Batalji had only ever been to Yakutsk three times, and twice had been as a prisoner, first as a fourteen-year-old boy, and then as a deserter from the army. When he had returned in 1979 for his wedding, he had done nothing more than pass through, in his haste to reach the Anhusat's *ordu*. But Jalain had been to the city several times, and knew it fairly well. He was able to indicate the strong points; there did not seem many weak points.

'It is the Taychins we wish,' Selphine said. 'Once they are gone, their state will crumble. And I will kill them personally. Slowly.' Sometimes she could look quite demonic in her anger.

'Then the Taychins will be our target,' Batalji agreed.

It was necessary to wait, while Jalain reconnoitred. Jalain was his strong right arm, Batalji knew – his Subotai. Subotai had served Ghengis Khan in the same way and spirit, and been known as the Lion. 'I value your brother above all men,' he told Mortana, as they lay together in his yurt.

'As he loves you, above all other men,' she replied. And raised herself on her elbow to look at him. 'Now you will all be killed.' Batalji raised his eyebrows. 'You cannot fight the Taychins,' Mortana said. 'Surely these past six years have proved that. Batalji...' She held his hand. 'Can we not leave this place? There is all Asia in which we can hide. Jalain and Jagnuth, and Galina, and you and I, and the children...' She looked across the tent at where the four children lay sleeping in each other's arms. 'I could not bear to see them killed. Or Shallane...' She sighed.

'Boys can be raped as well,' Batalji told her. 'And there is nowhere we can go. Nowhere we *should* go. This is our land. The Taychins are interlopers. They are Russians. Do we not hate all Russians?'

'*All* Russians?' Mortana was doubtful.

'All Russians,' Batalji asserted. 'We will destroy them all. But we will begin with the Taychins.'

He left the planning to Jalain; he had a terrible fear of failure, of leading his people to disaster. His business was to win. Jalain's was to plan. 'Here is what we shall do,' Jalain said, spreading the map on the earth before the eager men. 'It will be May the first, and the Taychins still honour that date. It is the date of their great parade.'

'When all the troops will be accumulated on The Avenue,' Pirale objected.

'Yes, but I have discovered that their guns will not be loaded,' Jalain said.

'You mean they will have no ammunition at all?' Selphine enquired.

'Well, they will carry ammunition, of course, Princess. But in their belts, not in their magazines. In case of an accident, you understand. It will be up to us to make our move before they can load their weapons.'

'How long does it take a man to fit a clip into an AK-92?' Jagnuth demanded. 'Five seconds?'

'And what of the tanks?' Sartine asked.

'Because of the fuel rationing, there will be no tanks in this year's parade,' Jalain said, with great patience. 'They will remain at the Central Barracks. That is part of our plan. At the appointed hour, three things will happen: Force One will seize the television building, and make a broadcast that the Taychin regime has been removed; Force Two will attack the Central Barracks and seize the tanks.'

'We do not know how to drive tanks,' Almani protested.

'We will force their drivers to work for us, at gunpoint,' Jalain said.

'And Force Three?' Batalji asked, as quietly as ever.

'Force Three will be at the parade, and at the appointed moment it will open fire on the podium. Both Taychins will be there, with their wives. Once they are dead, we will overawe the parade. We will have loaded weapons, they will not. And their leaders will be dead. We will have the advantage.'

'There will be not less than two thousand soldiers in the parade,' Khalim commented. 'How many men have you allotted to the assassination?'

'Two hundred, my father. And they will be armed.'

'What with?' Pirale enquired. 'We cannot carry heavy machine-guns into the centre of Yakutsk without being found out.'

'We have RPGs and we have AK-92s. Those will be sufficient,' Jalain said patiently. 'The important thing is to get the Taychins. Once the Taychins are dead, and we turn our weapons on the soldiers, they will be forced to surrender.'

'And what of the spectators?' Jagnuth asked. 'They will be full of the secret police.'

'But not enough to resist us,' Jalain insisted. 'Obviously there is an element of risk. There has to be, in any attempted coup. But if all goes well, we will succeed.'

Everyone looked at Batalji. He had been content to let Jalain devise the plan, because Jalain knew so much more about Yakutsk, and the Taychins. It had been Jalain who had organised his escape, seven years before. Jalain was the thinker amongst them. And his plan *could* work. But Batalji did not like a plan which contained so many imponderables. Suppose both Taychins were not at the parade? Both Taychins always attended the May Day Parade, but suppose... Suppose the troops remaining in the barracks preferred to die than hand over the tanks? Surely men would wish to live, but suppose these preferred to die? Suppose the soldiers on parade were not overawed? Above all, there were not enough people on their side. 'Can we not recruit more people?' he asked. 'Have we no support in Yakutsk itself?'

'To attempt to recruit amongst the city-dwellers would be to risk betrayal,' Jalain explained.

Batalji stroked his chin. 'Then what of the *ordus*? Surely they are faithful to us.'

'I believe so,' Jalain said. 'But to recruit from amongst the *ordus* would be to alert the Taychins. Their agents keep a close watch on them, hoping to catch us. Any big movement of men away from the camps would make them suspicious.'

Again they waited. 'Give the word,' Selphine begged.

This is a poor plan, Batalji thought. It has been put together too quickly. One does not overthrow a regime after only a few weeks' planning. We have not enough people, and we are relying on everything happening as we hope, rather than *making* things happen as we intend. We should be aiming to eliminate all aspects of fortune, good or bad, and we should be certain of help from the inside. If we are going to rule this country, it has to be with the support of all the Yakuts, city-dwellers as well as nomads.

Jalain, for all his intellectual superiority, had not thought things through. He believed that their goal was the death of the Taychins. He believed that if they could do that, everything else would fall into place. But killing the Taychins was only opening the door to what came after. That was another weakness in the plan: they were timing their revolution for May, which left the whole summer ahead of them for the Russians to send men to Yakutiya to suppress them, and for the outlying garrisons to come to the support of their comrades.

There were so many other things Jalain had apparently not thought of. 'The airport,' Batalji said. 'You have said nothing about seizing the airport.'

'When Yakutsk is ours, so is the airport,' Jalain declared.

'And the war planes there? What if they take off?'

'Then they take off. They are not going to strafe Yakutsk, where their own people are.'

The faces around him were eager. Batalji understood that his people wanted action. That he might even begin to lose their support if he told them yet again to wait, and submit. And there was always the chance that Jalain's plan *might* succeed. 'May the first, then,' he said. 'The day of destiny.'

The Mongols gave another shout, and Selphine hugged her son.

Despite Batalji's apprehensions, 1 May was an invigorating date. It heralded the coming of spring. The ice on the Lena had melted, the country was turning green. Barone, who was now sixteen, assumed he would be accompanying his father and grandfather, his uncles and cousins. But Batalji told him he must stay with his mother and sister and younger brothers. 'Nothing is certain in war,' Batalji told him. 'You must be ready to take on the burden of leadership, should anything happen to me.'

Barone swelled with pride, which replaced his disappointment. Mortana wept.

They made their way into the city on 30 April. People were coming into Yakutsk from all over the country. The first of May was not only the parade; it was the date of the first fair of the year, when men and women emerged from their winter hibernation and exchanged views and news, and also offered their goods for sale. Batalji's people travelled in small groups and mingled with the nomads. Many of them were recognised, but these were their kinsmen, and there was no thought of betrayal.

Batalji travelled with Jalain and Jagnuth and his father-in-law and mother. All the men were heavily bearded, and Selphine kept a fold of her headdress across her face like any modest Yakut woman. They lodged for the night at the house of Hilaim the wine merchant, one of the few people Jalain felt he could trust. 'Should we not pray for success?' Batalji asked. 'Is there no shaman?'

'Shamans are forbidden to enter Yakutsk, Lord Prince,' Hilaim said.

'Are not shamans able to make themselves invisible?' Selphine enquired.

'They are all afraid,' Hilaim told her.

Selphine snorted her contempt for a wizard who could be afraid, but Batalji, looking from face to face, realised that they were all afraid, save perhaps for Selphine herself. Was he afraid? He thought he probably was; he was obsessed with the impending sense of failure.

Next morning they mingled with the crowds. They had synchronised their watches, and every man knew what he had to do, or said he did. Pirale and his group wandered towards the television station, Sartine and his people loitered around the army barracks. Batalji and the main body joined the throng on the newly created Avenue.

They sweated, for the sun was very hot. The crowd moved restlessly, waiting for something to happen. And at last there was a fanfare from the band, and several black automobiles drew up before the podium. Out stepped Andrei Taychin, followed by his wife, a small, grey-haired woman who looked around with utter contempt. Andrei Taychin led her up the steps, and at the top turned round to raise his hand to the watching crowd, who were dutifully clapping. Batalji watched, eyes narrowed, waiting for the emergence of Boris Taychin and his wife. But the car drove away, and from the next limousine there stepped General Simonoslov, the garrison commander, and his wife and children.

Batalji looked left and right, but he could not see Jalain, who had melted into the throng; he was alone with Selphine, Hilaim, and Almani and Jagnuth, his two personal aides who were also his bodyguards. The coup had been timed for fifteen minutes after the commencement of the parade – in itself an overcomplicated arrangement, in his opinion – and the parade was now beginning. No provision had been made for calling the action off, should there be any hitch. But Batalji regarded

Boris Taychin as far more dangerous than his elderly father. 'How can we stop it?' he muttered to his mother.

'Stop it?' Selphine was aghast.

'Boris is not there.'

She laughed. 'He will be there, soon enough. If not, we will get him afterwards, eh? And that whore of a wife.'

Batalji bit his lip; everyone was so confident, except him. And the parade had started. As Jalain had promised, it was not a big parade. Led by the band, it only consisted of two thousand soldiers, unsupported by either tanks or any other vehicles. Behind the soldiers were several thousand young people, representing the various youth groups which had developed out of the old, officially discarded, comsomol system. But they would surely be of no account.

Ten minutes had passed, and the troops were nearing The Avenue. Even above the blaring of the band the tramp of their boots echoes through the afternoon. Selphine had both hands beneath her cloak, wrapped round her rifle barrel. Batalji stood on tiptoe, searching for Jalain, but he was not to be seen in the crowd. He did see Jagnuth, now some distance away, but the younger brother was watching the podium intently, paying little attention to what was happening around him, and to attempt to attract him would be to give themselves away. Batalji could only look at his watch with a sinking feeling.

The second hand reached the fifteenth minute, and the morning burst into bloody confusion. Uttering a high-pitched scream, Jalain ran forward, followed by half a dozen men, firing from the hip. The officials on the podium were certainly taken by surprise; most of them fell to the floor of the stand while they scrabbled for their weapons. Selphine was running forward too, and Batalji could do nothing but follow her, while the lead in his belly seemed to double, while people scattered to and fro in front of them, and most followed the example of their president and threw themselves to the ground.

The band ceased playing in a chorus of discords, and the soldiers had stopped marching, while their officers bellowed orders. Most looked ready to turn and run, but a few reached for their cartridge belts. Batalji and Selphine burst out of the crowd, running towards the podium, where Jalain was standing, having seized the microphone of the loudspeaker. 'Batalji!' Jalain shouted, his voice reverberating across the square. 'Batalji! The day is ours. Speak to them!'

'Hurry!' Selphine snapped. Batalji wiped sweat from his forehead. The day is ours? he wanted to shout. How is that?

Even as he ran forward behind his mother, he heard deep reports from the direction of the Central Barracks; Pirale was running into serious opposition. But the soldiers were still hesitant, dissolving from their ranks, looking left and right. Batalji burst through the line of policemen restraining the crowd. One reached for his pistol, and Batalji shot him in the stomach. Then he and Selphine were running at the podium, to watch in horror as General Simonoslov suddenly reappeared, behind Jalain and his bodyguard, holding an assault rifle. The gun exploded, and the Yakuts fell left and right, blood flying through the still air. Jalain was on his hands and knees, blood flowing from his mouth; Simonoslov grabbed the loudspeaker. 'Soldiers of Yakutiya!' he shouted. 'Defend your city. Kill these scum who would overthrow your government.'

Batalji fired from the hip, and the General disappeared again, behind the podium. Batalji leapt on to the platform, Selphine at his shoulder. But the damage had been done. The troops had rallied, and were cramming magazines into their rifles; the police were drawing their weapons, and from the crowd there were emerging several members of the secret police, also armed. And when Batalji looked behind the podium, he saw that even the Taychins had not been hurt. Andrei and his wife were crawling out from beneath the stand, undignified to be sure, but very much alive. 'Bastards!' Selphine opened fire. Sara Taychin uttered a scream as the back of her gown dissolved into blood. Her husband scrambled to his feet and turned to face his enemies, drawing a pistol from inside his coat. Batalji cut him down with a single bullet in the breast, and was then struck himself, a hammer blow on the back, which pitched him on to his hands and knees.

Now it was Selphine's turn to scream, as she knelt beside her son. Those of Jalain's people who had survived were returning fire, but it was time to get away, if they could. Batalji, staggering more with shock than pain for the moment, pushed his mother off the back of the podium to join the fleeing spectators. He looked down at General Simonoslov, lying on the ground in a pool of blood, surrounded by his children and his wife, shouting and weeping. The General was not dead. Batalji hesitated. But to destroy the woman and her children would remind him too much of Afghanistan, and the revolt had failed, anyway. He hurried his mother into an alleyway, covered by the guns of Jalain's guards, and by Almani and Jagnuth, firing behind them, listened to the chatter of the automatic weapons, felt blood trickling down inside his coat. 'Jagnuth,' he gasped. 'Almani. Tell Pirale and the others to call it off. Tell them...' he fainted from loss of blood.

Khalim read off the list of the dead; it was headed by his own eldest son. Mortana and the other women beat their breasts and moaned their grief. Jagnuth and his cousins, Pirale and Sartine, even Almani the faithful, sat and glowered. Barone sat alone, his sister and brothers about his feet. He knew of the catastrophe only at second-hand. Selphine seethed, and stood before them. She was fifty years of age, yet she looked half that age; her body shimmered with emotion. 'What are you mourning?' she demanded. 'Our dead? I mourn them too. I mourn your son, Khalim; he was like a son to me. But he, and all the others, died the way Mongols are supposed to die, on their feet with weapons in their hands, facing their foes. That is death with honour. So we failed. Next time we will not fail. Tell us of the next time, Prince Batalji!'

Batalji lay on a bed of skins, and looked up at the giant trees, through which the sun was vainly attempting to force a way. He was not entirely sure where he was. Certainly he had little recollection of reaching here. His mind was a haze of exploding guns, shouting people, movement, and pain. But amazingly, the Mongols had fought their way out of the city, even if at a heavy cost in casualties. That was a measure of how near Jalain's plan had come to success, how disorganised the Taychin regime had been following the death of their leader and the wounding of General Simonoslov. Yet it had been a poor plan, ill-conceived and puny.

Even more amazingly, his people stood by him. Already, after three days of flight into the deepest recesses of the forest, harassed by gunships and mobile columns sent by Moscow, they were hearing news of whole *ordus* being destroyed by the command of Boris Taychin, out to take a terrible revenge for his father's and mother's murders. Yet this band of devoted warriors and their women would follow him anywhere, sacrifice themselves for him, if need be. They only required to be led. And now there was no one left to whom he could delegate that authority. He was the Khan.

He sat up, painfully; the bullet had broken his shoulder, and his entire left side was strapped up – three inches further to the right, and he would have been dead. 'I too grieve for our dead,' he said. 'For my brother-in-law. But he has shown us the way. Only he did not look far enough. The next time we will succeed.'

They raised their heads. 'Can there be a next time?' Khalim asked.

'There will be a next time, Father,' Batalji promised. 'But we must plan further than Jalain thought necessary. It will take time, but it will be time well spent.'

'Will they allow us time?' Jagnuth asked.

'I think so,' Batalji said.

'But while we wait, they will destroy our people,' Almani said.

'I do not think so. Many people saw me hit, did they not? And all they know since is that we have fled into the forest. The first thing you will do is let it be known that I have died of my wounds. If you do this convincingly, if the whole Yakut nation mourns my loss, Boris Taychin will believe it.'

'He will never believe it, without proof,' Selphine said.

'Then give him proof, Mother. Have a photograph taken, of me lying in state, and of my body being lowered into a grave, here in the forest. Boris Taychin will believe that.'

Khalim snapped his fingers. 'It might work.'

'But what will that accomplish, save to dispirit our people?' Jagnuth asked.

'It will buy us time, and more. When I am dead, we will all disappear. The revolt, and the Borjigins, will be finished. Forever, they will think. Then we will plan. And when our plans are complete, we will let a rumour seep through the forest and across the steppes, into Yakutsk and into Boris Taychin's very bedchamber, that Batalji Borjigin and his faithful *bahaturs*, Jagnuth Anhusat and Almani Serhat, have been seen, riding the steppes, with many men at their backs.'

'That will strike terror into the hearts of the Taychins,' Selphine said admiringly.

'But at the end of the day, they will still hold Yakutsk, they will still have the army and the tanks and the planes, they will still have the power,' Khalim said. 'We have lost nearly all our weapons. They will still have the power.'

'Not so, Father,' Batalji objected. 'The power lies with the people, and with the unexpected, and with careful planning. When we attack Boris Taychin, we will not do it at the beginning of summer; we will do it at the onset of winter, and we will have recruited many men, and we will attack from within. Listen to me, and I shall tell you how it will be done.'

THE SECOND PART

The Warlord

The blood-red blossom of war with a heart of fire.

Alfred, Lord Tennyson, *The May Queen*.

THE SIXTH CHRONICLE

Yakutsk, December 2000

'Do you know what day it is?' Georges mumbled.

'The day after yesterday,' Henri suggested, with determined humour.

'It is Christmas Eve,' Georges said gloomily.

'Well, I will bet this is the closest you have ever come to Santa Claus,' Henri told him. Clive had to admire the *élan* of the two Frenchmen. Of course they had both had considerable quantities of vodka to drink – whatever else might run short, their escort were never low on vodka – but Georges and Henri were like this even at the break of day, when they once again set off on their weary struggle through the snow.

The entire day was centred on reaching their next camp – obviously pre-selected by the Mongols, who seemed to know every inch of the route they were taking – when the tents were pitched and a fire was lit and it was possible to pretend, with the aid of the vodka, that one was warming up. Clive did not suppose he would ever be warm again.

He had endeavoured to keep his journal up to date, as no matter what had happened, and even if he was certainly presumed dead by now, he was still on assignment, and thus he knew that it was Christmas Eve; he had not told the others for fear of depressing them. He was certainly feeling depressed himself. He had lived all his adult life in an anxious rush from one country, one hotel, one aeroplane, to the next. Every moment counted. Even when he had been comfortably ensconced at home with Sintax he had watched the clock, knowing that a summons was coming closer with every tick of the second hand. But for the past nine weeks he had been forced to exist in a land where time apparently did not matter at all.

Nine weeks! With nothing to show for it save several close encounters with frostbite. They might have been travelling round and round in circles, for all he knew; the Mongols did not use maps – they seemed absolutely certain of their route and their whereabouts. All he knew was that they had climbed hills, and descended into valleys, that they had crossed frozen rivers and huddled before freezing blizzards, that they had ventured where he would have said no man could possibly hope to, in November and December in these latitudes, and survive. As the sun never rose above the horizon, and the stars were invisible behind the ever-present blanket of low cloud, it was not even possible to guess in which direction they were heading; he had to presume it was east.

Yet they had not only survived, but were in the best of health. As there did not appear to be any vitamins available, he would have anticipated scurvy at the very least, but the kumiss which was the main part of every meal was at once nourishing and apparently supplied them with everything essential. He would have supposed they had to suffer from frostbite, but in the Mongol furs, and looked after by their escorts, who smothered their faces with fat and oil, they travelled in comparative comfort, while at night the twelve men, all huddled together in one yurt, had been as snug as if in a centrally heated house. Throughout the nine weeks they had not once removed their clothing or bathed, but this was only obvious to the nostrils when in the warmth of the tent, and by then they were too exhausted to care, while with their shaggy beards it was now difficult to tell the Europeans from the Mongols. No doubt, Clive kept reminding himself, he should be looking on this journey as a scoop in itself, a marvellous story to be told when he regained civilisation. Save that he had no camera and no tape recorder ... and no camerawoman either. When he thought of what Denise was enduring his blood curdled ... and when he thought that, being Denise, she might even be enjoying it, the rest of him curdled as well.

While day drifted into day ... Captain Yetegei grinned at him. 'Tomorrow we come to Yakutsk,' he announced.

Clive had no idea they were anywhere close to civilisation. But the next morning they arrived on the banks of a wide river, completely frozen over. 'The Lena,' said the captain.

To their left was the airport, where a large number of aircraft were parked, snug under their covers. Clive did not need X-ray vision to be certain that amongst them were those four squadrons of MiG Fulcrums. Then they saw houses, and through the falling snow, realised they were approaching a city. A small city, to be sure, Clive reckoned, but he could make out the high-rise apartment blocks which were a feature of any Russian township, and then the factory chimneys which were a second feature; the Soviets had thought nothing of environmental problems when they had built their factories and apartments cheek by jowl. 'Those are ugly,' Yetegei said. 'The Khan will pull them down.'

'The factories, or the apartments?' Henri asked.

Yetegei shrugged. 'Maybe both.'

Now they were on a firm surface, invisible beneath the snow, but which Clive reckoned would be a road. They walked their horses through suburbs, composed mainly of high-rises; it was nearly noon, and there were people about, huddled up, hurrying; no one paid any attention to the group of horsemen. 'Do you know,' Henri remarked. 'I never expected to get here.'

Depression was forgotten, as they emerged on to The Avenue, and passed the International Hotel. The coup seemed to have been utterly successful. Of course it was ten weeks ago now, but there was little evidence of any damage, there were no tanks on the streets, and although every tenth person was a policeman, this was not altogether rare in a Russian republic. Only the flag was different to anything he had ever seen before; it was red, with a canton of yellow and black stripes. 'Is that the flag of Yakutiya?' Clive asked Yetegei.

'It is the flag of Yakutistan,' the captain replied. 'That is our name, now, Yakutistan.'

On their left was the broad drive up to the gates of the Presidential Palace, where again the red flag fluttered in the breeze and then dropped in the steady snowfall. Now there were several soldiers to be seen, on guard duty before the closed gates. They wore Russian army uniforms, but then, Clive supposed, they would. They were taken past the palace, and came to the university. Here they looked through the gates, and saw to their surprise a large number of young people, of both sexes, being drilled in the quadrangle, despite the weather; they carried wooden rifles and marched up and down, obeying the barked commands, and the occasional blows from the swagger sticks, of their instructors. 'It is better for young people to learn to defend the Motherland than to read books,' Yetegei remarked.

'Did the university students accept the change of government?' Clive asked.

Yetegei shrugged. 'It was necessary to shoot a few.'

Clive exchanged glances with Georges and Henri as they were guided down a side street. Now they saw the Central Barracks, but here again all was peaceful. To their surprise, however, they were taken up to the barracks and through the gates, which were again heavily guarded, while here at last they did see tanks, grouped in the courtyard, facing the building. 'Is there still resistance?' Georges asked.

'There is no resistance in Yakutsk,' Yetegei assured them. 'But the Russian garrison has been confined to these barracks, and it is best to make sure they stay there, eh?' Which indicated that the massacre had not been as wholesale as he had feared, Clive reflected, although he could not understand why some

Russians had been spared and others murdered out of hand.

'Then why have we been brought here?' Henri enquired. 'We are not Russians.'

'You are aliens,' Yetegei said. 'And aliens go to prison.'

'Now hold on a moment,' Clive said. 'Colonel Borjigin sent us to see the Khan. His father,' he added for good measure.

Yetegei grinned. 'The Khan is not here. You will stay in prison until he returns.'

CHAPTER 6

Yakutsk, December 2000

'Hi,' said the tall, gaunt man. 'Merry Christmas. I'm Jim Crawford. You guys don't look like Russians.'

'We're not,' Clive told him, and introduced Georges and Henri. 'You must be the research team.'

He was very relieved to see the Americans, not just because they were the Americans, but because they were looking perfectly fit and unharmed, and they were meeting in a large, clean, airy barracks hall, with no obvious evidence of restraint apart from the two guards on the door. 'Some of it,' Crawford agreed, a trifle grimly. 'What are you guys doing here?'

Clive explained. 'Hell,' said Al Mather. 'You mean you guys have lost a woman too?' Clive raised his eyebrows.

'There was a woman with our party,' Crawford explained. 'Rosemary Leigh. She was seized the night of the coup, and we haven't seen her since.'

'These people are womanisers,' Henri declared, indignantly.

'Let me get this straight,' Clive said. 'You have not seen this woman for ten weeks? And no one has told you what has happened to her? What about Borjigin himself? Haven't you spoken with him?'

'We haven't been allowed to see him. On the night of the coup we were confined in the hotel, like all the other guests. The following morning we were removed here, with all of our belongings, and here we've been ever since.'

'What about the other guests?'

'We haven't seen them either,' Mather said.

'Were they foreigners?'

'Nope. All the foreigners save for us idiots got out before the first snows. The hotel was pretty empty, but there were a few Russians.'

'Russians,' Georges said. 'Then they're all dead. These people do not like the Russians.'

'Christ, we know that,' Crawford said. 'But, Rosemary apart, we've been well enough treated since the coup was completed; they knocked us about a bit when we tried to help Rosemary, that was all. This place is warm, and clean, as you can see, and we're adequately fed and allowed the use of the gymnasium for an hour a day, so we've managed to keep ourselves fit.'

'You're not Russian,' Henri said gloomily.

'Have you been allowed to communicate with the States?' Clive asked.

'No. We've had absolutely no communication with the outside world. Ten weeks! I can't understand that. You people can't have been the only party of journalists trying to get in.'

'I rather suspect we were a trial case,' Clive said. 'And when we disappeared, nobody else was keen on trying.'

'But they can't do that!' Al protested. 'The world knows what happened here, right? They knew we were here. They knew you flew in. They can't just abandon us.'

'You must look out of the window more often, my friend,' Georges said. 'Even in normal times, there is little coming and going in and out of Yakutiya in the winter. There is nothing anyone can do in weather like this. With the airport closed, there is no way of getting in. The road to the south is blocked. If Borjigin has been making no response to radio signals, then the country is as effectively sealed off as if it were on another planet.'

'Until next April at the earliest,' Henri added, amused at the Americans' consternation.

'We have got to manage to obtain an interview with Borjigin,' Clive said. 'Forget about the news value; it seems to involve our lives. Or at least those of the two women. But the fellow who escorted us here, Yetegei, told us that the Khan isn't here.'

Crawford nodded. 'That bothers us, too. I met the guy, you know. We had an interview with him last summer, when he was still an outlaw. Quite a scoop, seeing as how no one was sure whether he was alive or dead. But he came across as quite a sensible fellow. No red-eyed bloodthirsty maniac.'

'You obviously didn't meet his son,' Georges commented.

'Anyway, even then he took a shine to Rosemary. That was plain as the nose on your face. So, we reckoned she was carried off to him as some kind of prize after the coup.'

'How primeval can you get?' Henri complained.

'And that didn't upset you?' Georges demanded.

'Sure it did, fella. But then we heard a rumour Borjigin had been shot. The soldiers here were full of it.'

'Shot?' Clive was aghast. 'You mean he's dead?'

'Well, he wasn't killed outright, so far as we could make out. But he was sure wounded. What bothers me is, suppose he has since died of his wounds? Maybe Rosemary was kind of immolated, or buried alive beside him.'

'You can't be serious.'

'Man, Borjigin may be all right, but the rest of these people are *primitive*,' Al told him. 'They may have a lot of sophisticated weapons but you should've seen them the day after the coup, dancing behind their shamans along The Avenue! We saw them when we were being brought down here. The Russian soldiers claim that some of the secret policemen taken prisoner were sacrificed to the gods of the steppes.'

'As for what they did to Taychin and his wife,' Joe Duncan said. 'Seems they strung Madame Taychin up, naked, from the balcony of the Presidential Palace, while Taychin . . . shit, man, they shot off his balls and then hung him beside her, still living, mind.'

'And you say Borjigin isn't a monster?'

'The soldiers think it was Borjigin's mother, the one they call Princess Selphine. Seems she was raped by Taychin personally many years ago, and she ain't the forgiving kind.'

'Quite a few people think that Princess Selphine is the one who's actually running the country,' Crawford remarked.

'Cheer us up,' Georges said. 'I'll bet she doesn't like gays either, Henri. What are you going to do?'

Henri grinned. 'Offer to fuck her if she looks at me twice.'

'But say,' Crawford said; the Americans had obviously been greatly cheered by the arrival of the Europeans. 'You fellows look as if you could do with a shave and a bath.'

'All mod cons in this gaol,' Al promised them.

They borrowed the Americans' razors, and while they bathed, Crawford told Clive as much as he knew of the actual revolt. 'It was timed to perfection,' he said. 'And worked out to perfection as well. Borjigin certainly learned from the last fiasco. The secret was the time of year, which effectively prevented the garrison, or the outlying garrisons, from reacting effectively in time, the immediate assassination of Boris Taychin, and perhaps most important of all, the seizing of General Simonoslov. The general is apparently very popular with his men. If he'd been killed, they might have fought to avenge him. But with him alive and yet a prisoner, his life on the line if they didn't obey him and lay down their arms, they obeyed him.'

'You think Borjigin masterminded it?'

'Absolutely.'

'And now he's dead,' Clive said sombrely.

'We don't know that,' Crawford pointed out. 'He could still be lying wounded, someplace.'

'But you liked him when you met him?'

Crawford considered. 'I wouldn't say I liked him. I saw immense power, immense anger, immense ambition. He frightened me.'

'Was this mother of his there too?'

'Oh, yes. She frightened me even more.'

'With reason, if what you've told me is true.'

'What are we going to do?' Georges asked at lunch, when they and the Americans sat down to a solid meal; although none of the food was fresh, there was as much vodka as they could drink.

'We have to find out what is going on, and we have to get to whoever is in authority,' Clive said.

'Don't you suppose the Americans have tried that?'

'I'm sure they have. But they were here when it happened. We've come in from outside. So we may have more clout. I have an idea.' He took a sheet from his notebook, and wrote a letter, in as good Russian as he could manage: *'To His Excellency Batalji Borjigin, President of Yakutistan.*

'Greetings, Your Excellency. My name is Clive Stanton. I am an internationally famous television correspondent. With me are two members of my team. The third member has been detained at the border by your son, Colonel Barone Borjigin.

'Your Excellency, our aircraft crashed on your border, nine weeks ago. Since then, the aircraft crew have been murdered, on the orders of your son, and we have been treated as prisoners. Your Excellency, the world is watching events here in Yakutistan. It may be that the weather has prevented any action from being taken against you, but this will change with the coming of spring, now only a few months away.

'Your Excellency, I was sent to Yakutistan to interview you, with a view to introducing you to the world. We are not hostile. Nor, at the moment, is our Government of the European Union. But it is a most powerful government, with many voices at the United Nations, and allied to the United States. Between them, the European Union and the United

States control two-thirds of the power of the world. They are not at this moment hostile to your government. They wish only to understand what has happened here.

'Would you oppose the entire world? China will not support you; the Chinese hate the people of the steppes. This is well known and attested by history.

'Your Excellency, I beg an interview with you. I and my people can help you to make your case before the world. Every day is vital, Your Excellency, for you, and for your people, and for your dream, whatever that may be.

'Your humble servant,

'Clive Stanton.'

'Now that should produce results,' Henri said, when the letter had been given to one of their guards.

It did. Only forty-eight hours later the section of the barracks occupied by the Westerners was invaded by a squad of heavily armed men. 'Oh-oh,' Crawford said. 'Seems you stirred the pot, Stanton.' Clive had shown him the letter before sending it.

'Which one of you is Stanton?' demanded the captain of the guard.

Clive stepped forward. 'I'm Stanton.'

'You come.' The captain stepped to one side and pointed at the door.

'Now hold on a moment,' Crawford said. 'Where are you taking him?'

The captain glanced at him, then turned back to Clive. 'You come, or we carry you.'

'Tie me a yellow ribbon,' Clive suggested, and went through the door.

Clive did not know what to expect, how confident to be. As Barone had not executed him, and as they had not been executed immediately on arriving in Yakutsk, and equally, as the Americans had not been executed, he felt there had been nothing in his letter to provoke the Mongols. Thus logic. But equally did he have to remember the utter contempt for human life and dignity which had been evident in the execution of the Russians, the appropriation of Denise, and the disappearance of the American woman. But, having provoked a response from their captors, there was no going back now, and for the moment at least he was not in any way ill-treated. He discovered this with relief, as he was escorted outside to a car, which slithered its way slowly along The Avenue to the Presidential Palace. It stopped at the gate to be inspected by the guards, who seemed in a hurry to regain the warmth, and then proceeded down the drive to come to a halt in front of the old-fashioned but imposing building.

Here there was another squad of guards, Clive looked at the still-bullet-scarred walls, the shattered windows, and the front door, boarded up against the cold, evidence that the Palace had fallen to an assault. In the downstairs hall there were yet more guards, and some of these were women. But they showed more curiosity towards the Englishman than hostility; clean-shaven and reasonably well groomed, Clive was very definitely of both a different race and a different culture.

He was led up the grand staircase, also bullet-chipped, and along a gallery. Doors and passages led away from the gallery in every direction, suggesting that the building was much larger than it appeared from the outside. Clive was marched into a spacious office, and made to stand before a desk. The man seated behind the desk was a surprise. He wore green Russian army uniform, with the same lightning-flash insignia as Barone, but was yellow-haired and aquilinely handsome of feature, not in the least like the Mongols standing to either side. 'You are Mr Clive Stanton?' he asked, his voice quiet. 'You wrote a letter to the Khan?'

'That is correct.'

The man considered him for several seconds, then he nodded, and stood up. 'The Princess wishes to see you.'

He walked to the door, and waited. Clive glanced at his guards, then followed. They went back on to the gallery. 'Am I allowed to ask your name?'

'I am Colonel Almani Serhat.'

They arrived before another flight of stairs. 'Doesn't this place have an elevator?' Clive asked.

'There is an elevator, but it is not functioning. Many things in Yakutsk are not functioning, because of the revolution.'

'I've gathered that. Why cannot I see the Khan?'

'The Khan is not here,' Almani said.

'I have heard he was wounded in the revolution.'

'He is recovered now. He is campaigning.'

'In this weather?'

Almani, climbing the stairs with vigorous steps, glanced over his shoulder. 'It is the best weather, for us. Our horses can move, where tanks cannot.'

'I've observed that,' Clive agreed. 'But who is the Khan campaigning against?'

They had reached an upper floor, the stairs ending in a spacious corridor, patrolled by several guards – and these were all women. They looked at Clive as if they would enjoy having him for breakfast. 'You ask too many questions,' Almani told him, and spoke to the women in Yakut. One of them replied, and then opened a door. 'You go in there, and wait,' Almani told him.

'You mean you're leaving me here?' Clive enquired, suddenly apprehensive.

'I will see you later. Perhaps,' he added with sinister enigmatism. He returned to the stairs, and Clive looked at the women. One gestured at the door with her machine-pistol, and he went through. This was another large room, comfortably furnished, but here too there were bullet marks on the walls, and the lock of the door had been shot away. Surely Batalji Borjigin, with the whole resources of the city at his disposal, could have found a locksmith, even if he perhaps had not had the time to institute a general redecoration? Campaigning, Clive thought, in December! Borjigin was after those atomic warheads! Thus the situation might be far more serious than anyone supposed.

One of the women had come in with him, and now she pointed to one of several settees. Clive sat down. The woman closed the door and leaned against it, her hands crossed in front of the crotch of her pants, the machine pistol thrusting upwards from between her clasped fingers like a phallic symbol. Like everyone else in this new state, she seemed very young; Clive did not suppose she was much over twenty. She was not pretty, although her broad Mongol features were quite attractive. The face was not especially hostile, but she never took her eyes from his, and he did not doubt that she would shoot him without hesitation if he did anything she did not like.

The inner door opened. Clive started to rise, and then sat again; he had been joined by three children. Two of them were small boys, five or six, he supposed. Their sister – for they were clearly related – was perhaps ten. She was small and slender, but *her* face was extremely pretty, surprisingly small-featured – she made him think of Colonel Serhat – framed in a mass of curling tawny-brown hair. Clive glanced at his guard, but her expression never changed.

The little girl led her brothers across the room to stand in front of him. She said something in Yakut, and was answered by the guard. The girl stared at him. 'Who are you?' she asked in Russian.

'My name is Clive Stanton. Who are you?'

'I am Shallane Borjigin.' Her voice, if high, was filled with confidence, which gave it a startling resonance. 'I am the daughter of the Khan. I am a princess.'

'Then I am honoured, Your Highness.' Clive hastily dismissed the possibility that this was the princess who had sent for him; that would be simply too bizarre for even this bizarre country.

Princess Shallane gazed at him for several more seconds. Then she asked, 'Will you scream when you die, Stanton?'

Clive managed a smile. 'Very probably, Princess. Will you?'

Shallane Borjigin tossed her head. 'I am not going to die, Stanton.'

'That is a very sound philosophy. I shall endeavour to adopt it myself.'

'You will die,' she told him, 'when . . .'

The inner door opened again, and this time Clive did stand up as two women came in. They both wore pants and smocks, and there was no suggestion of rank, yet he immediately knew who they were – even if the girl at the door had not come to attention. The younger of the two women was clearly the mother of the three children, and thus was Mortana Borjigin. She was in her late thirties, a trifle heavy of body although her face was as attractive as her daughter's and she had the same magnificent hair, escaping from a bandanna. The other woman was much older, but equally much more striking. She had the tawny-gold hair of Almani Serhat, and the same surprisingly aquiline features as her granddaughter, and if the hair was streaked with grey and the face with wind wrinkles, she was still a beautiful woman, taller than her daughter-in-law, and moved vigorously.

He bowed to them both, and a piece of paper floated to the floor in front of him. His piece of paper. 'Pick it up,' Selphine commanded, in Russian. Clive obeyed, feeling the tension tightening his muscles; this was the crunch. 'You wrote that,' Selphine said.

'Yes, I did, Your Highness.'

'That is a threat to the Khan. To his people. How dare you utter threats to the Khan?'

Clive refused to lower his gaze. 'It is a statement of the truth, Your Highness. I think the Khan will understand this, when he returns, and listens to what I have to say.'

Selphine glared at him, then spoke to the girl on the door. The girl promptly opened the door and called her companions. They filed into the room, six young women, not one a day over twenty-five, Clive estimated, and all now regarding him with hostility. Mortana spoke to her mother-in-law in Yakut, her voice soft. Selphine replied brusquely, with a dismissive wave of her hand. Shallane clapped her hands. My God, Clive thought; I have just been condemned to death!

He looked left and right as Selphine gave another command. The girls came forward. Selphine stretched out her hand, and one of them gave her a machine-pistol. This she pointed at Clive's head. 'I am a very good shot,' she said. 'There is none better in Yakutistan.' She glanced around the room. 'Watch.'

Clive looked at the ornate fireplace, decorated with tiny cherubs. Selphine raised the gun and squeezed the trigger, once, and one of the cherub's heads disintegrated; the wall behind splintered. 'Do you think that was a good shot, Stanton?'

Clive had to lick his lips to obtain some saliva, even as he wondered just how much of the damage to this building had occurred during the revolt, and how much since, if all of these people were so trigger-happy. 'Yes, Your Highness.'

The pistol was again pointing at his head. 'If you attempt to resist, I will shoot you.' The pistol barrel slowly drooped, until it was aimed at his pelvis. 'After I have shot you,' Selphine said, 'you will take several hours to die. They will be very painful hours.'

'And then you will scream,' the child Shallane told him. Mortana made a brusque remark to her daughter, and Shallane pouted.

'Now tell me the truth,' Selphine said. 'You came here from Moscow.'

'Yes,' Clive said, endeavouring not to look at the seven young women who stood around him, two to either side of the settee and three behind it. Never had he felt so vulnerable, not even when he had been captured by Bedouin tribesmen in the southern Sahara and kept prisoner for several days.

'Moscow sent you,' Selphine said.

'No. I was sent by my employers, the Anglo-French Television Network.'

'Do not lie to me, Stanton.'

'That is not a lie, Your Highness.'

'Why should some television company send you to Yakutistan, in October?'

'What has happened here, but especially your son, Your Highness, is news. I, my company, deal in news. It is my business to interview the people who make news. That is why I was sent here.'

'You are lying.'

'It is the truth. Why do you not send a radio message to Moscow, asking for my credentials?'

'Moscow will say what it has been agreed they will say,' Selphine pointed out, contemptuously. 'You have come here to give my son an ultimatum. Admit it.'

'That is not true,' Clive protested, as earnestly as he could, every second growing more certain of the hostility around him. Only Mortana seemed to have the least sympathy for him, and she was clearly entirely subordinate to her mother-in-law.

'We do not like liars in Yakutistan,' Selphine said. 'In there with him.'

The young woman seized his arms to drag him to his feet. Clive toyed with the idea of resisting them; he was as big, and as strong, as any three of them – but there were seven of them. There was also Selphine and her machine-pistol, and he suspected that even if there was a general scrummage, she would not hesitate to shoot her own guards to get at him, if she felt it necessary. Besides, he could only survive these people, and save Denise, not to mention Georges and Henri, by conviction rather than force. So he allowed himself to be pulled and pushed towards a doorway on the far side of the room, and through it, into what appeared to be a spare bedroom; it was well enough furnished with table and chairs and a bureau against the wall, but there was only a mattress on the bed. What was sinister was that there were cords tied to each of the four iron uprights.

The women chattered amongst themselves as they threw him on to the bed and began to strip him. Now he did resist them, involuntarily, for they were not the least gentle, but there were too many of them, and all the while he was aware of Selphine, standing beside the bed, pointing her pistol at him. She had no doubt about the outcome, and soon enough he was exhausted and naked, sprawled on the bed, unable to fight any longer as he was rolled on his back and his wrists and ankles secured to the four bedposts and drawn tight.

The girls stood around the bed to admire their handiwork;

they were panting and dishevelled, and one or two were rubbing breast or belly or buttock where he had got in a punch or a squeeze – but they seemed pleased with themselves, and grinned as they exchanged reminiscences. But they were also curious, as was Selphine herself. 'I have seen men like you,' she remarked, standing beside the bed. 'Are you a Jew, or a Moslem? There is no place for Jews or Moslems in Yakutistan.'

'I am neither,' Clive said, trying to speak normally. 'I was born in the tropics, and my parents chose circumcision for reasons of health.'

'You are a born liar,' Selphine remarked, and flicked him with her finger. To his disgust, he began to have an erection. He had been around a long time, and in and out of more beds than he cared to remember, but this was the first time he had ever been gang-raped. Although he suspected that the rape had not yet started to happen, and the sight of him was likely to encourage them. But only Selphine mattered.

She gave an order in Yakut, and the girls laughed. One of them went to a corner of the room and came back with an armful of pillows. Four of them knelt on the bed and seized his thighs to lift him from the mattress as far as they could; the others began stuffing the pillows under his buttocks. He had been tightly tied before; now he was jacked up until he was held absolutely rigid, arched away from the mattress, the cords biting into his wrists and ankles. The only free part of him was his penis, now standing proud. Six of the girls moved away; the seventh knelt on the bed, and held him, making sure he remained erect. He turned his head, uncertain what was going to happen next, wondering if he was in some kind of utterly camp massage parlour, and saw that Mortana and the children had also come into the room, Shallane again clapping her hands at the sight of his naked body.

Selphine stood beside the bed, looking down at him. 'I can shoot the top off your prick at twenty feet,' she said.

'I believe you,' Clive assured her, desperately trying to stop himself screaming.

'I did that to Boris Taychin,' Selphine said proudly. 'I will do it to any man who seeks to harm my son.'

'I wish to help your son. You must believe me.'

'You are lying again.' She spoke to the girl, and walked away from the bed. Despite the warm female fingers Clive had started to retract as he sweated with apprehension. Now the girl shifted her hand down the stem, to grasp him two inches from the glans, so that the now soft flesh remained visible. She made Clive think of a child preparing to eat an ice-cream cone. But she was nervous herself; there were beads of sweat at her temples, and she was no longer smiling.

'This is a very difficult shot,' Selphine explained, levelling the pistol. 'The slightest mistake, and I will shoot away Yorcka's fingers as well. I would not like to do that.'

My God, Clive thought; I have only seconds to live, as a man. Or perhaps to live at all. 'I am here to help your son,' he said, amazed at the calmness of his voice. 'Shoot me, and your cause is lost.'

There was a moment of silence, and Clive shut his eyes. Then he realised that the girl's hand had gone, and he heard movement. He opened his eyes, and saw the other women leaving the room. 'Isn't he going to scream?' Shallane asked, wistfully.

'Later,' Selphine promised. The door closed behind them, and he was alone, except for Selphine. He did not know if he was any closer to saving his life, but at least some of the humiliation was diminished.

Selphine stood by the bed. 'You are a brave man,' she remarked. 'And a cunning one. You seek to preserve your miserable life by frightening me. You say your death will harm my son? Are you that powerful? You do not look powerful.'

'Yes, I am powerful,' Clive told her. 'I work for the most powerful organisation in the world, the international media. Without them, you are nothing. With them on your side, you can scale mountains.'

'We have already scaled mountains,' Selphine said. She

rested her left hand on his stomach, and suddenly closed the fingers. Even stretched tight, there was too much loose flesh there. 'You are not fit,' she commented.

Confidence was slowly flowing back into Clive's system; she was no longer sounding like a woman in the mood to shoot away a man's balls. 'I admit it,' he said. 'Not as fit as I should be, anyway.'

'Strong men need to be strong all over.'

Clive realised that he had to regain the initiative. Or indeed, obtain it for the first time. He remembered Henri's words. 'Try me,' he suggested.

They gazed at each other, Clive acutely aware that he was again erecting; partly this was his position, spreadeagled and jacked into the air, which was in itself stimulating. But the nearness of the woman, the thought of her, was not less so. He wondered how old she was, tried to calculate. At least fifty-four. But it was difficult to envisage.

'Do you suppose,' she said, 'that if I release you, you will be able to overpower me, and somehow make your escape?'

'I know that is not possible,' he said.

'My women would cut you into little pieces. Slowly,' Selphine said.

'I am entirely in your power,' Clive acknowledged.

She stared at him for several seconds. Then she looked at his penis. 'You have a big prick,' she remarked. 'It is bigger than Boris Taychin's. But not so big as my son's.' She walked across the room and placed the machine-pistol on the table. Then she undressed. To his surprise she wore nothing under her pants and blouse, and no stockings inside the soft boots she kicked off. Her body was firm and strong, heavy-breasted and wide-hipped; muscles rippled in her arms and in her thighs as she moved.

She came back to the bed, and pulled the pillows out from beneath him. His body sank to the mattress, and he sighed as some of the pressure was taken from his wrists and ankles, although immediately he suffered an agony of pins and needles in his feet and hands. 'Thank you,' he said.

'I can always put them back,' she reminded him, and crawled on to the bed to sit astride him. He had hoped she would release him, but she was not ready for that yet, apparently. 'Do I not attract you?'

'You attract me very much, Princess. But it's been a fairly traumatic half an hour for me. If you'd release me...' Because he was not hard enough to enter her.

'Then you would attack me.'

'You have just pointed out that that would be suicidal, Princess.'

'Then what would you do to me, if I released you?'

'I would make love to you.'

'You mean you would fuck me?'

'Yes. But I would also make love to you.'

Her gaze shrouded him for several seconds, then she got off him again, went to the bureau, opened a drawer, and took out a long, sharp-bladed knife. Clive could not resist a sucking-in of his breath as he wondered just what other purposes that knife had been used for in the past. Selphine returned to the bed and cut the cords securing his wrists. Immediately he sat up, to rub the tortured flesh. She released his feet as well, and he brought them up too, hugging himself. Selphine sat beside him, her shoulder against his, her golden-brown hair flopping over them both. Her skin was very white – obviously there was no temptation to sunbathe in Yakutistan – but it was also firm; she smelt of health and cleanliness, although she was not wearing perfume.

Clive Stanton had never made love to a woman seventeen years older than himself, but she was as attractive as any women he had ever known, although she was remarkably hairy. More attractive than even Denise. But now was not the time to think of Denise. He put his arm round her, and held her against him, kissed her mouth. It remained closed, but when he licked her lips she opened them. Then he had to lick her teeth as well to find her tongue. She pulled her head back.

'Why do you wish to do this?'

'Do Mongol women not kiss?'

She made a *moue*. 'Perhaps. You are forward.'

Like a whore, he thought, she would let him fuck her, but not kiss her. But he had to conquer her, utterly. He kissed her again, and touched her breasts. She rippled, like a snake, and his hand slid down her side to her buttocks. He lay back, pulled her with him, sought the warmth between her legs. Once again her head reared up, and she frowned at him. 'What are you doing?'

'Making love to you.'

'With your hand?'

'Listen, Selphine,' he said. 'You may be the boss in this land, but in my land a woman takes what is coming in bed.'

A total lie. But she accepted it, lay down again, her eyes widening as he stroked her, her breath beginning to pant, her breasts to heave. 'This is unnatural,' she gasped, as she climaxed.

'This is just the beginning,' he said, and got between her legs.

Her heavy breaths slowly subsided. 'You are a man amongst men,' she muttered.

Clive made a mental note not to let her ever get too close to Georges, who Denise had told him was a master masturbator of women. 'You are a beautiful woman,' he countered.

She gazed at him. 'Are you telling the truth?'

'Yes,' he said, and realised that he was. Because beauty did not truly lie in hair and legs, in breasts and buttocks, or in youth. It lay in the person, and this woman, by repute the most bloodthirsty woman on earth, was beautiful.

'Then you shall be mine,' she said. 'I need a man. It is too long since I have had one, lovingly. Do you know how many times I have been raped?'

'No.'

She laughed, a low, throaty gurgle, which made him think of a lioness. Which, he supposed, was appropriate enough. 'Neither do I. I have lost count. Do you know that I was once raped by my own son?' Another laugh. 'He was forced to do it, by Boris Taychin. Well, that is avenged. And do you know, it made us very close. But he will not be back for another month. How old are you, Stanton?'

'Thirty-seven.'

She had been lying on him. Now she rolled off and sat up, her legs over the side of the mattress. 'You are younger than my son! But I would have had you younger yet. You are a virile man.' She smiled. 'Even if your body is soft. You say you can help my son?'

'If he wishes it. And if he will help me.'

'You would attempt to make terms?'

'But I must look after my people. My camerawoman was take prisoner by your grandson, when we crashed.'

Selphine laughed. 'Barone is insatiable.'

'That is not civilised conduct,' Clive argued.

'Am I interested in civilised conduct?'

'Your son has to be, if he would set himself up as a ruler of a country.'

'Ha! Do you not know that he is a descendant of the Genghis Kha Khan, greatest of men?'

'I know this.'

'Then you will know that the Genghis Khan made his own laws. He had no need to obey the laws of other countries.'

'This is a different world to that of the thirteenth century,' Clive pointed out.

'You speak of things I do not understand,' Selphine grumbled. 'So Barone took a woman from your party. That is the right of the conqueror.' She frowned at him. 'Was she your woman?'

'We were to be married.'

'And you expect me to get her back for you? You are mine, now.'

If the international media ever get to know of this, Clive thought, my reputation is ruined. 'I accept that,' he said. 'But I would still like her to be brought back to Yakutsk.'

'Why? Do you think I will let you fuck her?'

'Your grandson is ill-treating her.'

'Ha! We shall see.' She crawled back beside him. 'You are slow.'

'I am thirty-seven years old. There is also the matter of the American woman, Rosemary Leigh.'

'Leigh? *You* are insatiable. But you cannot have Leigh. She belongs to the Khan.'

'Because he took her, on the night of the coup. You will say that was the right of the conqueror. Again, Your Highness, it is not civilised merely to appropriate women at will.'

Selphine snorted, and got off the bed, began to dress. 'You speak of things you do not know, Stanton. Dress yourself.'

Clive obeyed.

'Now come.' She led him out of the room and into the corridor. The guards were still there, watching him with dormant hostility. At least Princess Shallane and her brothers had disappeared.

Selphine led Clive along the corridor, down a flight of steps, and along another corridor. He gathered that they were now deep in the recesses of the palace, and down here there was no evidence of any damage sustained in the coup. They arrived before double doors, guarded by two women. At the sight of Selphine they opened the doors, and she went in, beckoning Clive to follow her. 'There,' she said, pointing. 'Your American friend, Rosemary Leigh.'

THE SEVENTH CHRONICLE

Yakutsk, December 2000

The woman, who had been reclining on a settee reading a book, got up. Clive had not known what to expect, was surprised by Rosemary Leigh's height and obvious health and fitness. By the complete absence of any indication that she might have been ill-treated over the past nine weeks, or indeed that she was unhappy with her situation. And by her attractiveness; the golden hair was brushed into straight perfection past her shoulders, the broad features were oddly beautiful. Equally was he surprised by her clothes: in a land where all the women appeared to wear pants, she wore a dress, and high-heeled shoes. At least it enabled him to establish that her legs were as good as the rest of her.

'This man is an English journalist named Clive Stanton,' Selphine said. 'He wishes to speak with you. He wishes to *rescue* you, from the clutches of my son.'

Rosemary Leigh raised her eyebrows. 'A knight in shining armour,' she suggested, in English.

Selphine snorted. 'Speak with him. But remember, he is mine. And you, Stanton, remember that she is the Khan's. To take the Khan's woman is to suffer castration, and then the slow death.' She smiled. 'I would not like that. Speak with her, and then come to me.' She closed the door behind her.

'Clive Stanton. I've heard of you,' Rosemary Leigh said. 'You're the TV personality.'

'I've heard of you, too,' he agreed. 'From Jim Crawford, and Al Mather, and Joe Duncan.'

She sat down and waved her hand at him to do the same. 'Are they all right?'

Clive wandered round the room, examining the light fixtures, checking behind the pictures on the walls, pausing for several seconds before a full-length mirror. 'What's behind this wall?'

'I have no idea.'

'It's not a part of this apartment?'

'This apartment goes thataway. What are you looking for?'

'Bugs. I imagine the place is full of them. As for this mirror ... I'm probably looking at Selphine right this minute.' He blew his reflection a kiss.

'It must be very exhausting, having to be suspicious all the time,' Rosemary remarked.

'You don't think it's necessary?'

'I don't see what you propose to do about it if we are being recorded, or overlooked, or whatever. Unless you intend to sit there like a dummy and not say anything. I asked you about Jim and Al and Joe.'

Clive sat down. 'They're fine. But pretty worried about you. They reckon you have been at best raped, at worst murdered.'

'They're very protective.'

'Couldn't you let them know you're ... well, at least you haven't been murdered.'

She gave a quick, almost secretive smile. 'I haven't even been raped, Mr Stanton. Would you like some tea?'

'Thank you.'

She rang a silver bell on the coffee table. Instantly a

maidservant appeared; she was very like the guards, save that she was not armed. 'Tea, Yana,' Rosemary said, in Russian. The girl bowed, and withdrew. 'What brings a famous TV journalist to Yakutistan?' Rosemary asked.

'Batalji Borjigin.'

'I'm surprised you got in.'

'We nearly didn't.'

'So what are you going to tell the outside world about Batalji?' The maidservant placed a tray of tea before her, and she poured.

'I didn't know Americans took tea,' Clive ventured.

'We can adapt. In the more remote parts of Russia the choice seems to lie between tea and vodka.'

There was so much he wanted to ask her, but while she was being entirely polite and even friendly, there was something wrong with her demeanour; she was just too relaxed, too unaware of her position. And she hadn't actually answered his first question. He would have to press her, as he didn't know how long Selphine was going to allow them together.

'You were saying?' she remarked.

'I don't know if I'm going to tell the outside world anything,' Clive confessed. 'I and my camera team are prisoners. So are your colleagues. So are you. You *are* a prisoner, you know.'

'I guess I am.'

'But it doesn't bother you. You say you weren't raped by Borjigin? Are you trying to say he's keeping you locked away in this palace as some kind of decoration?'

'You don't think that's a kind of personal question?'

'It's my business, to ask personal questions. And I think it's very relevant to our situation. According to Crawford, you were presented to Borjigin on the night of the coup, as a kind of victor's prize. Is that true?'

Rosemary considered. 'I'd say that's true. He had a bullet wound. He wanted a bit of comfort. I was elected.'

'Crawford said you were dragged from the International Hotel, screaming and shouting – and naked save for a coat.'

Rosemary poured more tea. 'Well, wouldn't you scream and

shout in those circumstances? I had no idea where they were taking me, or what they were going to do to me when we got there.'

'But it all turned out all right.'

She raised her head. 'Yes, Mr Stanton, it did.'

'And now you're quite happy, is that it? Are you going to tell me that Borjigin has never fucked you?'

Her face was cold. 'That is entirely my business.'

He leaned forward. 'Listen: this man is an unmitigated thug.'

'There are women who would say all men are unmitigated thugs, or would be, given the circumstances and the opportunity. Batalji had both.'

'There are degrees of thuggery. He just appropriated you. I don't see how an educated, intelligent, presumably liberated American woman can accept that.'

'What would you recommend I do about it, Mr Stanton?'

A breakthrough at last? 'Then you'd like to get out of his clutches?'

'I didn't say that.'

'For Jesus' sake! You mean to stay here for the rest of your life? At his beck and call? The man is a mass murderer. He's even worse than that. As for the rest of them . . . Do you know what his mother did to Boris Taychin and his wife on the night of the coup?'

'She told me. She's a very good shot.'

'And that doesn't bother you at all? She had the idea of doing the same thing to me.'

Rosemary gave a faint smile. 'Don't tell me she missed? Your voice isn't high enough for a hit.'

Suddenly he was angry. 'You think this is one hell of a joke, right? You sit here, in complete comfort, in the midst of the most bloodthirsty regime in the world . . .'

She got up, abruptly, and he wondered if she was going to ring for help. Instead she walked to the table and took a cigarette from the box there, flicked a lighter. 'Do you want one?'

'I don't.'

She shrugged. 'I shouldn't. But there are times ... it's better than shooting dope, right? Listen, Mr Bigshot Stanton, you seem to have come here with some preconceived ideas. You can't apply London or New York standards of behaviour to the steppes, especially steppes which have seen as much blood as these have. The Taychins ruled this republic like the old-time Commissars. They *were* old-time Commissars. The Gestapo or the KGB had nothing to teach them. Step out of line, and you were shot, what was left of you after they'd had you in their dungeons for a bit. Batalji's father stepped out of line.'

'He wasn't unique.'

'I'd say this event was, I hope. They made Batalji bugger his own mother. Try imagining that, Stanton. Then they packed him off to a state orphanage, to enjoy a bit of rape himself. Then he went to Afghanistan. The regime really worked at making him into a thug.'

'And succeeded.'

'You're wrong. They made him realise who and what he was: a Mongol prince. A direct descendant of Genghis Khan! They inspired him to recreate the greatness of his people.'

'What you are saying is that he is mad.'

'Look around you. This is his land, now.'

'An empty wasteland perched on the edge of nowhere, knee-deep in snow?'

She smiled, and stubbed out her cigarette. 'That was Siberia when Genghis rode out of it, too.'

'You don't mean he seriously thinks he can take over Russia?'

'I don't know what he thinks. He's certainly taken over Yakutistan.'

'Until next spring, and Russia marches against him.'

'That kind of next spring isn't going to come, Stanton. Batalji's people are now armed and ready. They are happy to die for him. Do you know that two young people committed suicide to get him out of prison, eleven years ago?'

'I heard about it.'

'Well, that's the kind of support he can call on, throughout this country. Now they want to fight for him. It would take a bigger army, and far bigger resources, than Moscow presently possesses to take Yakutistan back. I don't think they'll ever try. I think they'll negotiate. Batalji has a lot going for him. He has oil and natural gas, which Moscow desperately needs.'

'So you are entirely on Batalji's side. What has he done to you?'

She laughed. 'Witchcraft?' She sat down with a rustle of silk. 'Sure, he scared the pants off me at first. Sure, I knew I was for his bed, and sure, I was revolted at the idea. But when you can't do much about something I reckon your best bet is to put up with it until you can, if you follow me. And then ... it wasn't like what I'd expected. He was pretty sick for a while. He'd been shot leading the assault on Taychin in this very palace. The wound was clean enough, but he'd lost a lot of blood, and he wouldn't take it easy until he was sure he'd won. So fever set in and everyone was pretty upset. All this while my business was just to be there, so he could look at me, and give that funny smile of his. I felt like a nurse.'

'What did his wife have to say about this?'

'I haven't asked her. But this guy is a Mongol prince. Monogamy cuts no ice with him, or with his people. They'd be pretty upset if they discovered he only had one woman in his life. Anyway, time was when he was feeling better, so ... I don't know why I'm telling you all this.'

'I asked,' Clive reminded her. 'And I think you wanted to get it off your chest.'

She considered. 'Maybe I do have a guilt complex. But ... he's one hell of a man, Stanton. More of a man than anyone I've ever met.'

'You're in love with him?' Clive couldn't believe his ears.

She sat down again. 'Have you ever been in love, Stanton? I mean, in love? I'm not talking about the hots.'

Clive's turn to consider. Presumably if he'd been in that kind of romantic love with Denise he'd have insisted on dying beside her rather than give her to Barone. 'I suppose I'd have to say no.'

'Then you have no right to ask any questions. Batalji . . .' She shrugged. 'As you're alive, I imagine you'll get to meet him. You'll have to form your own judgement.'

'You mean you're expecting me to fall in love with him as well.'

She grinned. 'Could be.'

'I'll have to play that as it comes. Meanwhile, do you give any thought to your friends?'

'Selphine told me they're alive and well. You've just confirmed that. Batalji will let them go come the spring.'

'You have his word on that.'

'Yes, Stanton. I have his word.'

'But you'll be staying.'

'I think maybe I will.'

'Okay. You're one hundred per cent Batalji's girl. I'd like to ask for your help.'

'As long as you don't rub him up the wrong way, I'd say he'll give you your interview. He's quite amenable to publicity. But I shouldn't think you'll be able to leave either, until the spring. He's not meaning to reopen the airport before then. Anyway, what's your hurry. I kind of got the idea Selphine has something going for you.'

'That,' Clive said, 'is the least of my worries. But I have a camerawoman, who, like you, has been appropriated by a Borjigin. Barone, to be exact.'

'A camerawoman. Is she important to you?'

'She happens to be my camerawoman, yes. That is important. But more than that, we're going to be married.'

'That's important,' Rosemary said.

'I want to get her out of Barone's clutches.'

'I can imagine you would. Mind you, when you do, you may find she's changed a bit.'

'Will you help me?'

'I'm a prisoner, like you, like her, Stanton. You keep reminding me of that.'

'But you're Batalji's current favourite. I'm asking for your help, Miss Leigh. You could talk to Selphine, or Mortana. They must have some influence over Barone.'

'No one has any influence over Barone, Stanton. Except his father. You'll have to ask him.' She rang her bell for the maid. 'Mr Stanton is leaving. Give my love to the boys,' she said.

CHAPTER 7

Yakutsk, Spring 2001

An army made its way through the snow. Mainly it followed the River Lena, for the ice was thick enough to support the heaviest kibitka, and the surface was relatively smooth. But this was a Mongol army; snow and ice were irritations, not hazards.

The army stretched for several miles. Half a mile in front of the main body was the advance guard, commanded by General Pirale, some five hundred men, mounted on their shaggy ponies. Their presence, in a land so completely appropriated by Batalji Borjigin, was a testimony to his caution; he kept in touch with both Yakutsk and his border by radio, but he knew that it was possible to fake radio conversations, and he had no intention of ever falling into the Taychin's mistake of complacency. The main body was also mounted. In this weather and in this terrain, mechanised vehicles were a liability rather than an asset, as the Russian garrisons had found out. They had been unable to start their tanks; their mechanically controlled heavy guns had seized, their gunships and fighter-bombers had been unable to take off. No one had ever contemplated having to fight a war virtually in the Arctic Circle, in midwinter. Nobody had ever supposed the Mongols would again unite.

Batalji rode with the main body. Jagnuth Anhusat, his chief of staff, was at his shoulder, together with Generals Haroun and Carowan. The seven thousand men following them were, like the advance guard, armed only with light automatic weapons; that had been all they had needed to gain the victory. That, and their ability to survive, and fight, in the snow. Behind the main body came the kibitkas, mounted on sleds, and also drawn by the Mongol ponies, twelve to a team. These not only contained the army's logistical necessities, but the wounded, both Mongol and Russian. Batalji had promised the Russians their lives, and repatriation to Russia, if they surrendered; he had taken General Simonoslov with him on the campaign to encourage their resistance to be brief. Now they walked behind the wagons, stumbling in the snow, but thankful to be alive.

And that they were soldiers. For behind them, driven by the whips of the rearguard, came those members of Boris Taychin's secret police captured in the garrison posts. There were only a dozen of them; their comrades had fought with fanatical fury, and when surrender had become inevitable, most had blown out their own brains rather than face Mongol captivity. Now the survivors also stumbled along, each man and woman – there were two women – wearing a *kang*, the wide wooden collar locked to the neck; the prisoners' wrists were secured to iron loops on the underside of the *kang*, so that they were helpless to resist any mistreatment, or even to attend to their clothing. Their guards, who constantly poked them with sticks and beat them when they fell down, who would open their jackets to allow the freezing air to turn their flesh blue, did not attend to them either; within their uniforms they had turned into moving cesspools.

But they were well fed on kumiss, and if they were all suffering in some degree from frostbite, they were capable of feeling, and understanding; Batalji wanted them alive when they came to Yakutsk. And there it was.

*

People left their houses and high-rise flats to crowd the pavements and cheer the army as it marched through the snowbound streets. The troops marched to the beat of a drum, but no music, which made the entry more dramatic.

Batalji had radioed ahead to let Almani know that the campaign had been concluded, and the crowds screamed and clapped their approbation of the victors, booed and hissed and bellowed threats and imprecations at the Russians and even more at the secret police. Yakutsk, normally such a quiet, hidden place after the first snows fell, had never known a day like it. The procession marched up to the gates of the Presidential Palace, where Batalji and Jagnuth pulled their horses out of the line. Waiting for them, also mounted, was Almani, and the three Mongol leaders saluted while their forces and prisoners wheeled and marched past them, heading now for the Central Barracks.

Only when the last man had passed, his hand still raised in salute, did Batalji allow himself to look up at the balcony, where his mother and his wife, his children, and the American woman stood. They were almost unrecognisable beneath their heavy fur coats and hats, but he waved to them all, before walking his horse towards them. They left the balcony and ran down the interior staircase to greet him in the entry hall, winter clothing thrown carelessly aside. He scooped his children from the floor first, to hug them and kiss them, then took Mortana into his arms, held her there for several seconds. His mother came next. 'Did you get them?' Selphine asked.

Batalji kissed her. 'They are guarded by Sartine, and a hand-picked detachment.'

'The warheads?'

'Had been disarmed.'

'Then they are useless.'

Batalji grinned. 'I do not think so.'

'I have videos for you.'

He nodded. 'Soon.' He released her and looked at Rosemary, who waited some distance behind the family. He walked towards her.

'My congratulations,' she said.

'It was not difficult.' He held her hand, led her towards the stairs.

She did not dare look at Mortana. 'Batalji,' she protested. 'Your family. Your wife.'

'It is you I wish, now,' he said.

'But . . . you've been away from them for five months.'

'If I do not fuck you, now, I will explode,' he told her.

Rosemary realised she was shaking as Batalji led her up the stairs. But it was caused more by excitement than fear, although fear was involved.

She had not lied to Clive Stanton in attempting to explain her reaction to her situation. But neither had she told him the whole truth. She supposed she had been psychologically shocked by what had happened last October. To be dragged from her bed, to all intents and purposes naked, and delivered to a warlord whose eyes had in any event frightened her, had been the most traumatic experience of her life.

It had been a singularly trouble-free life, down to that moment. She was an only child of two successful lawyers; there had been no crises in her girlhood, and, blessed with strength and health, she had cruised through high school and college. Born into the AIDS situation, losing one's virginity had been a much more considered matter than, apparently, it had been in her mother's generation; both partners needed to know and respect each other, even if neither had marriage in mind. Yet it was a necessary step in the business of being adult. And when it was done, she had not really wanted to take it much further. Her first affair had lasted several months, and done little more than convince her that she didn't really like the guy. There had been a couple more, but with them, too, she had been more concerned with her career as a social and cultural historian, and coming home to someone wasn't necessarily the pleasure lyricists pretended. Above all, she had fiercely defended her privacy, her freedom of action, her individuality.

Thus the maturity of thirty had brought with it the realisation that perhaps she did not have sufficient capacity to share to be the marrying kind. This had not bothered her. She would have liked a child, because she felt she did possess a deep mothering instinct – but even there she wondered if she could give enough to be a good mother. Above all, she had prided herself on her level-headedness. As she had told Stanton, one rolled with the punches until one perceived the opportunity to get up off the floor and do some punching of one's own. She had fought Batalji's goons instinctively, because she had been shocked out of her normal complacency. But the fighting had been brief; she could see no point in perhaps incurring a broken arm or worse where she had no hope of success. She had anticipated rape, brutal and ugly. Thus she had overreacted to the wounded warlord, who had come across as an almost noble figure, certainly in his treatment of her.

By the time she had learned of the ghastly deaths of Boris Taychin, and his wife and mistress, the horrible executions of his secret policemen, she had already been sucked into the orbit of Batalji's personality, and her own immortality-complex had reasserted itself. Such things were not likely to happen to her, and she had been promised they would not happen to her associates, either. Thus she had not wanted to have her private adventure interrupted. She assumed she was now stuck in Yakutsk until the spring, and in October that had seemed a long way away. That suited her. When news had come from Barone that a planeload of Western journalists had crash-landed just inside Yakutistan's western borders, she had been vaguely annoyed; her past – which was also no doubt her future – was attempting to catch up with her present, far sooner than she had anticipated or wished. Batalji had merely grinned and told her they would not be a nuisance. She had not heard of them again for more than two months.

She had always known that she would go to Batalji's bed eventually, had perhaps anticipated it. And been shocked again by the animal sexuality of the man. And yet, because she had not resisted, she had received no bruises that had not faded within a few hours, and she had been left feeling that for the first time in her life she had been possessed, utterly and without end. It had been a disturbing, frightening, and yet oddly exhilarating feeling. She had wanted it again, even if she would never have admitted it to herself. Instead he had rolled her on her back, and smiled at her, and said, 'I must leave you now.'

She remembered sitting up and pushing hair from her eyes in consternation. At that moment she did not wish to be returned to face Jim Crawford and Al Mather and Joe Duncan; they were men who belonged to a different civilisation; they would be afraid for her; therefore they would have to ask questions. Batalji had kissed her mouth, for the first time. 'I have to campaign,' he said. 'It is not enough to claim this country. It must be taken, and held. But I will return to you. Until then, you will be in the care of my mother, and my wife.'

Then she had been afraid, and it must have shown in her eyes. He had held her chin to raise her head. 'They will deal well with you, Rosemary,' he had said. 'As long as you deal well with them. You are mine. Remember that. This palace is your home, your only home, until I will otherwise.' The fear had remained, as the Khan had ridden out of the city, accompanied by his brother-in-law and his faithful *bahaturs*, his *kiyat*, or Raging Torrents, the men who had helped him bring off the coup in the first place. Only Almani Serhat, Selphine's cousin, and Batalji's boon companion, had remained, as governor of the city.

Rosemary had been unable to believe that a woman like Mortana, a child of the steppes, who had fought beside her husband and no doubt killed beside him as well, could accept the presence of an alien woman in her very own home. She had read about harems, but they had been in different ages, certainly different cultures. It was difficult to accept that she was now part of an alien culture herself. Yet there she had been, Rosemary Leigh, as much incarcerated in a harem as any odalisque of the past. Only this was a strange harem. There were no eunuchs, and no other inmates. She was entirely surrounded by women, but these were guards and servants. Mortana ignored her completely, for which she was grateful.

Selphine visited her occasionally, but Rosemary knew this was to make sure she remained in good health and her beauty was not in any way impaired – Selphine wished her to bear a child for Batalji, something she simply could not contemplate, even if, as she was allowed no protection, it was extremely likely to happen once the Khan returned from his campaign.

She had no contact with the outside world, was made to exercise every day, was locked into her rooms twenty hours in every day as well, and was never allowed outside the Palace grounds. Granted that she lived in a five-room apartment, with bathroom taps made of gold, slept on satin sheets and had the use of three television sets and endless videos, that dressmakers had created a whole new wardrobe for her, that her food was of the best and she could have got drunk on vodka every night had she chosen to do so, that she was allowed to use the Presidential Library, and take whichever books she wished back to her apartment... she was still as utterly a prisoner as if she had been in an American gaol. Yet even that had not bothered her, because Batalji was coming back. The only time she had really been upset was when Selphine had so oddly brought the English journalist to visit her. It was useless trying to fathom Selphine's reasons for doing so. Often enough, Rosemary reckoned the boss lady – because Selphine was certainly that – had *no* reason for her actions, but just wished to be amused. On that occasion she had certainly stirred Rosemary up, by putting her into a position where she was forced to defend herself and her actions, while all the while knowing that in some people's eyes, they were indefensible.

The odd thing was that Clive Stanton had not come across as one of those people. But he was a journalist attempting to do a job of work, and it was his business to probe. She had resented that. Not that it mattered. She had not heard from him or of him again. And now he was less than ever relevant: Batalji was back, and she was following him to her apartment, like the slave she was. Whatever had happened to her much-vaunted independence?

*

Batalji closed the door. There was a woman guard in the corridor, standing rigidly to attention; she would see they were not interrupted. Nor would anyone dare listen in to what Batalji might be saying, or attempt to oversee him – not even Selphine would risk that. 'Bathe me,' Batalji said. 'Hot water. I have not had a bath in weeks.'

Rosemary turned on the golden taps in the bathroom, undressed him, nose wrinkling; here in the heated apartment his words were self-evident. Yet he wanted to be clean before coming to her bed. That relieved her, even as it intrigued her. This man was a savage, but inside this savage there was a gentleman trying to escape. She tested the water.

'Hot!' he commanded.

'It's too hot for me.'

He got in; water bubbled over the lip and splashed on to the tiled floor. 'Bathe me.'

Rosemary stripped, took the soap, and knelt beside him. Instantly his arm went round her, caressing her shoulders and breasts, slipping down her spine to find her buttocks and slide between. He loved every aspect of her, sexually. When she soaped his chest he pulled her head forward to nuzzle her golden hair. Her hair had fascinated him from their very first meeting; he had been quite upset that her pubes were somewhat darker. He lay back with a sigh as she washed his thighs and genitals; he was already fully erect. 'I dreamed of you, on the steppes,' he said.

She raised her head in surprise, and he grinned. 'Can warriors not dream?' He held her face and kissed her mouth. All his movements were sudden, abrupt, unheralded. 'Why are you not pregnant?'

'It was hardly likely to happen after one fuck.'

'I want you to give me a son. You have a big, strong body.' He pulled one of her nipples. 'Big breasts. These are made to suckle warriors.'

She found she was breathing heavily; he had this effect on her, the constant uncertainty whether he was going to be gentle or brutal. But it was also because she realised he was serious.

'I don't know if it will be possible.'

He frowned, and stood up, scattering water. 'You think I am impotent? I am Batalji Borjigin.'

'I mean, it may take time, and I have things to do.'

He stepped from the bath, and the floor was flooded. 'What things?'

'Well, I have my home to go to, my parents, my career...'

'Your home is here. Your career is to be my woman. If you miss your parents, I will send for them to come here.'

Rosemary decided not even to try to imagine her mother's reaction to life in Yakutistan. Besides, he was being ridiculous if he supposed she was going to spend the rest of her life here. 'Now you listen...'

He put one arm round her shoulders, and with the other swept her legs from the floor before she realised what was happening. He was far stronger than he looked, carried her nine and a half stones with no effort at all. He left the bathroom and entered the bedroom. 'You're all wet,' she protested.

He grinned, and threw her on to the bed. She rolled, checked herself just before she fell off the other side, sat up, pulling hair from her face. 'Just who do you think you are?'

He grinned as he crawled on to the bed beside her, soaking the sheets and mattress. 'I know who I am. Batalji Borjigin.'

'Winston Churchill once said that an iron curtain had descended across Eastern Europe. I have to tell you, ladies and gentlemen, that a curtain of snow and ice has descended across Yakutiya. Behind that curtain, a million and a half people have just disappeared. Obviously they are going to reappear when the thaw comes, but what will we find? We know there has been a *coup d'état*. We know that the leader of the coup is a wild and dangerous man, a murderer and a robber. We know that there was massive bloodshed at the time of the coup. These are serious matters, ladies and gentlemen.' The speaker paused, and took a drink of water. The members of the Russian Parliament stirred, as the television camera played across their faces.

Batalji, sprawled on a settee watching the screen, asked, 'Do you know any of those people?'

'No,' Rosemary said. She sat on his right, Selphine, who had the video remote-control panel, on his left.

'But there are more serious matters yet,' the speaker continued. 'Only last week a radio message was received from our base at Ugumun that they were under attack. Under attack, ladies and gentlemen, in January, in northern Siberia. We are told that the Red Army is impotent to do anything about this revolt until next May, because of the weather. But the rebels are not impotent, it seems. Then we heard the base had surrendered. That base, ladies and gentlemen, is a missile launch site. This site is now in the hands of Batalji Borjigin. No matter that the garrison assured us that the warheads were disarmed before they surrendered. They are now in the hands if Borjigin, and we may be sure that he will have them re-armed, in the very near future. But our Government says it can do nothing about the situation, until next summer, at the earliest.'

Selphine pressed the mute button. 'There were many more speeches like that.'

'When was the debate recorded?' Batalji asked.

'January the twenty-third.'

'Let me hear the Government reply.' Selphine pressed Fast Forward, then Play.

'The Government is doing all it can to open negotiations with the Borjigin regime,' the spokeswoman was saying. 'We are prepared to talk, we are prepared to listen. We have announced this, time and again, over the radio, and on television. But there has been absolutely no response from whoever is in power in Yakutsk. The airport is closed, and anyone attempting to land has been fired upon. It is even possible that the missing European television crew was shot down last October, and did not truly come down in a blizzard. If the Borjigin Government has taken over all Russian military installations in the country, then it has obtained several surface-to-air missile launchers which could have been used to bring down the chartered aircraft. It also has obtained control of four squadrons of Fulcrum Mark II fighter-bombers, equipped with air-to-air missiles. Again, we have asked for information, and have received in return nothing but silence. You ask us why we have taken no action. A look at the map, and the weather map, should make the answer obvious. Deputy Kalminin chooses to poke fun at us, pointing out that the Mongols have been able to campaign during the winter, and we have not. But these people are riding horses. They are setting warfare back a thousand years.'

There was a ripple of not entirely good-humoured laughter.

'We can assure you,' the speaker went on, 'that as soon as the weather improves we will press Mr Borjigin very closely, but you must understand that to take military action, as has been suggested here today, against a republic which has always enjoyed virtual autonomy, is a very serious matter . . .' This time there were boos, which took some time to settle. 'Needless to say,' the spokeswoman protested, 'we are in consultation with our fellow members of the CIS, and with representatives of the European Union, and we have also consulted with the United Nations. There is no doubt that Borjigin will wish to negotiate his independence. He needs our help to develop his oil. He needs a market for his coal. He will come to us, and very shortly.'

Batalji waved his hand, and his mother switched the video off. 'When was that recorded?'

'Also January the twenty-third.'

'Three months,' Batalji mused. 'Have you nothing more recent?'

'There have been various debates. But none much different to that.'

'What about Europe, the United Nations?'

'There have been several references . . .' Selphine tapped the row of videos on the table in front of her, selected one, and fed it into the machine.

The speaker was a dapper-looking middle-aged man, speaking English to a group of journalists; his words were subtitled into Russian at the foot of the screen. 'We regard the situation in Yakutiya as an internal matter for the Russian Government,' he said. 'Of course we deplore bloodshed and any form of violent change of government, but it remains to be seen whether this coup has the support of a majority of the people of that country. If it does, then you may presume that the State Department will incline towards recognition of the Borjigin Government.'

'Who is that?' Batalji asked.

'Just a spokesman for the American Government,' Rosemary told him. 'But if what he says is true, you've got it made.'

Batalji scratched his nose. Rosemary understood that he did not properly evaluate the strength of the United States, never having come into contact with it at first-hand; when American troops had been restoring peace in the Persian Gulf and Yugoslavia in the nineties he had been an outlaw on the run, far from television sets or even proper radio reception, and he had little knowledge of history. Selphine waved her hand for silence, as the State Department spokesman was replying to another question.

'Well, of course we are interested in discovering what happened to the research team, and we would take a very grave view of the situation if any harm has befallen them. But in the absence of any information we are presuming that they are alive and well and will be allowed to leave Yakutiya whenever the airport or the main highway out of the country is reopened.' Batalji winked at Rosemary. 'But I'm afraid,' the spokesman went on, 'that we cannot be so sanguine about the European television camera crew which went missing right after the coup last October. There was a severe blizzard over central Asia at the moment it disappeared, and this is almost certainly the cause of its crash.'

'There have been rumours that the aircraft was shot down by a SAM,' said one of the journalists. 'Which would account for the fact that nothing has been heard of them since.'

'The State Department regards such rumours as specious,' the spokesman said. 'The pilot of the aircraft reported clearly, immediately before the crash, that he had lost an engine because of the weather. However, I need hardly tell you that if the aircraft crashed into a remote area of Siberia in the middle of a blizzard there would be no hope of survival for the passengers and crew. Nor would there be any chance of a rescue team finding the wreckage, even supposing one was looking. That is a tragedy. But our policy must be to wait and see, before taking any action.'

Selphine switched off the set.

'That is all they ever do,' Batalji said. 'Wait and see. They did nothing about Afghanistan. They did nothing about Georgia. They did nothing about Yugoslavia until tens of thousands of people had been killed.'

'They did something about Iraq,' Rosemary pointed out.

'Again, after a long time. And they acted against Iraq not because of Kuwait, but because they feared Saddam Hussein might have nuclear weapons.'

'You have just obtained nuclear weapons.'

Batalji grinned. 'No one is sure about that. And I must keep them guessing until I am ready. Now tell me, Mother, about these journalists. When last I heard, Barone was sending them to Yakutsk. Did they ever get here?'

'They arrived in December,' Selphine said.

'And where are they now?'

'I have confined them with the Americans.' Rosemary gazed at the older woman, but Selphine was totally relaxed. 'I thought of executing them, but I changed my mind. Their leader is an interesting man. He is apparently a famous journalist, named Stanton. He has come to interview you.'

'And he is unharmed?'

Again Rosemary looked at Selphine. 'Yes,' Selphine said. 'I have said, I find him interesting. I have had several meetings with him.'

Batalji threw back his head and uttered a roar of laugher. 'Does he still have his balls?'

'I think you would do well to see him,' Selphine recommended, not taking offence. 'You do not have to let him publish his interview.'

Batalji looked at Rosemary.

'I agree with the Princess,' Rosemary said.

'Do you know this man?'

For a third time Rosemary looked at Selphine. 'The Princess brought him to see me.'

'Why?' Batalji looked at his mother.

Selphine shrugged. 'I wished to see his reaction. Her reaction. He was worried about her.'

'And about another Western woman, who is being held prisoner by Barone,' Rosemary put in.

Batalji gave another roar of laughter. 'He is insatiable.'

'It is not how Westerners expect their women to be treated,' Rosemary said quietly.

Batalji gazed at her for several seconds. Then he said, 'This man, is he intelligent?'

'I would say, very.'

Batalji looked at his mother.

'Yes,' Selphine said. 'He is very learned. He has travelled everywhere, and seen everything.'

'That is what he says,' Batalji pointed out.

'It is true,' Rosemary said.

'I will speak with this man,' Batalji agreed. 'Tomorrow. After the executions.'

Rosemary caught her breath. 'You are not going to execute all of these people?'

'The soldiers, no. I think some of them are going to join my army, and work for me. They are technicians. They will teach my people how to use their tanks. I have captured all their pilots, as well. They will teach my people how to fly. I have promised them their lives if they will do these things, and they have agreed. But I have captured twelve of Taychin's secret police.'

'They will be executed in public,' Selphine said, eyes gleaming.

'That is barbarous,' Rosemary protested. 'It will tell the world that you are a savage.' She bit her lip, wondering if she had said too much.

But Batalji merely grinned. 'You saw the videos, Romy. The world already thinks I am a savage.'

'But to shoot men, in public . . .'

'I am not going to shoot them,' Batalji said.

'Shooting is too good for such as them,' Selphine said.

Rosemary looked from face to face. 'Then how . . .'

'They will be impaled,' Batalji told her.

'Im . . . you can't be serious!'

'This is the best punishment for creatures such as they.'

'You must be out of your mind,' she shouted. 'Batalji, this is two thousand and one, not twelve hundred and one.'

'You mean you in the West have lost the true meaning of life, and death,' Batalji said. 'You have abolished capital punishment, yet you treat death as if it were nothing. You watch television programmes, cops and robbers, in which men are shot down by the score, and you say to yourself, they will get up as soon as the camera moves on. You watch someone truly die, peacefully, and you say, he is not dead. He will rise again. Or if he was a bad man, he will suffer in the hereafter; it is not our place to punish him now. I heard of these things when I was in the army. You in the West have trivialised death, because you are so afraid of it. What nonsense. Death is nothing to be afraid of. But neither is it a trivial matter. It is the supreme moment of anyone's life. And then, when a man is dead, he is dead. There is no hereafter. It is the manner of his dying that matters. How he behaves, how he suffers. How he is made to suffer. To shoot those people would be nothing, nothing, compared with the hours, days, weeks of suffering they have inflicted upon my people over the years, the men and women, and children, they have tortured to death in their secret chambers. If I was truly barbarious, do you know what I would do? I would treat them as my forefathers treated their enemies, and condemn them to the death of a thousand cuts. Do you know what that is, Romy?'

Rosemary sighed. She did not wish to know what that was.

'The culprit is stripped and enclosed in a coat of chain mail,' Selphine said gleefully. 'It is a specially made coat, and the links are an inch apart, thus when it is drawn tight, parts of his flesh bulge through. One of these parts is then cut away by the executioner. The bleeding is stopped, and the culprit is secured, fed and given wine to drink, until the following day, when he is again placed in the coat, and another piece is cut away. I have heard it said that there have actually been men who have lived out the whole thousand cuts – nearly three years of having bits chopped off them every morning. Oh, it must have been a splendid thing.'

'You are nauseating,' Rosemary snapped.

Selphine raised her eyebrows.

'But you will see that impalement is a much less unpleasant fate,' Batalji said. 'The important thing about it is that it is at once painful and humiliating. People who have seen an impalement do not forget it, and this is important, because they will know that to cross me will mean such a fate for them.'

'Do you think that will deter them?' Rosemary cried. 'In the West it has been proved that the threat of execution is not a deterrent to murder.'

'That is nonsense,' Batalji argued. 'Of course it would be a deterrent, if everyone who considered committing murder knew for certain that he or she would be executed. It is not a deterrent because no one who commits murder believes he is going to be caught. That is all. And when he is caught, he believes his lawyers may well enable him to escape condemnation.'

'That is it,' Rosemary said urgently. 'Due process of law. These men have not been tried.'

'There is no necessity for a trial,' Batalji said. 'They were wearing the uniforms of the secret police when they were captured. There is no doubt of their guilt. Nor have they denied it.'

'The world will still condemn *you*,' Rosemary said, 'if you have these men executed without at trial. For God's sake, Batalji, even Stalin had trials.'

'And the world laughed at him,' Batalji said. 'The world! What do I care about the world, Romy? My world is here, in Yakutistan.'

'You must deal with the world, some time.'

'I will deal with the world when I am ready, and in my own way. Right now, I am to deal with my people, and their enemies. Those men are the enemies of my people. My people will watch them die, and know that their Khan can and will defend them against their enemies.'

'Batalji...' Rosemary slipped from the settee to kneel on the carpet. 'I am begging you. If you have any regard for me at all... spare those men. Or at least put them on trial.'

Batalji drove his fingers into her hair, and raised her head. 'I adore you, Romy. But you are interfering in matters of which you know nothing. Those men will die, tomorrow morning.'

THE EIGHTH CHRONICLE

Yakutsk, Spring 2001

'Up, gentlemen, up!' The guard, nicknamed Joe by the Americans because of his walrus moustache, was actually a very friendly fellow – since he had realised that Clive Stanton had been raised to the rank of Selphine Borjigin's lover. Now he stood in the doorway of the barracks and grinned at them. 'Today is a special day.'

'To do with that rumpus yesterday?' Jim Crawford asked, as he rolled out of his bunk.

'Yesterday, the Khan returned,' Joe announced. 'He has won a great victory.'

'Over what?' Al Mather demanded. 'The snow?'

'A great victory,' Joe repeated. 'You come. You shave and dress, and then you come.' He turned smartly, and marched back through the door.

'What do you reckon?' Jim asked Clive, who had also been aroused.

Clive scratched his head. 'I suppose you could say it's crunch time.'

'If she's told him,' Jim said, optimistically.

They had become good friends over the four months of their captivity, and there had in any event been no point in keeping the reason for his repeated mysterious summonses to the Presidential Palace secret. Clive himself remained in a state of total unreality. That he, Clive Stanton, should have dropped entirely out of circulation for six months, that he should be a prisoner and yet kept in relatively comfortable surroundings ... and that he should have become some kind of stud for a bloodstained warlady ... He would have a personal scoop to relate, when he got out of here. If he dared. And if he was ever going to get out of here. With the return of his mistress's son, that was suddenly a real question.

But it was the damage to his self-esteem – some would have said his arrogance – which he feared was irredeemable. There had been moments when he had wanted to insult Selphine, even hit her, or, probably most conclusive of all, laugh at her. He had done none of these things. So perhaps, having always considered himself as brave as any other man, he was a coward after all. On the other hand, he had never denied he enjoyed sex, when given the opportunity, and if Selphine Borjigin was in her mid-fifties, she was also as compelling as any woman he had ever met. She had only ever had the one child, which had left her fully developed but not weakened her in any way. Her body was hard-muscled from her years in the saddle. She had young breasts and a hard ass, powerful legs, and a luxuriance of hair, although since taking up her habit of watching endless videos of Western women, she had begun to shave her legs and armpits. She smelt naturally sweet, and having the run of Ludmilla Taychin's apartment and belongings, was constantly experimenting with the expensive perfumes the late president's wife had had flown in from Paris, just as she enjoyed wearing Ludmilla Taychin's gowns, after her dressmakers had altered them, usually inadequately.

Sexually she was a dream, he supposed, in her total lack of inhibition, her humour, her willingness to submit ... in bed. But he could never make the mistake of assuming, or even hoping, that she was fond of him as a man rather than a body of a sort she had not previously encountered, and with which she enjoyed playing. Just as he could never forget what she had done to Boris Taychin, and almost done to him. He was having a forced affair with a savage monster. And yet, a savage who was of enormous interest, just for her savagery, and the fact that she had been turned loose in a modern world of which she had no inkling. She would spend hours washing her own clothes just for the thrill of seeing the machine fill with water. Equally would she prowl the kitchens, inspecting the microwave ovens and the electric cookers, opening the dishwashers halfway through their cycle to see how they worked.

Most of all, however, she would take him to the control room, situated in the Palace basement, where there were banks of computers and television sets and radio monitors and radar receivers, all switched on and working, operated by a handful of men and women previously employed by the Taychins, who had made their peace with the new regime. Having seen so little television in her life, Selphine was fascinated by it, would watch it by the hour. She had the sense to understand that what was happening in the outer world might well be of use to her son, and having discovered the enormous video library possessed by the Taychins, she was accumulating a stock of recordings of Russian parliamentary debates and various items of world news which interested her. But she was also fascinated by the soaps pumped out by Moscow Television – often bought from one of the American networks and often more than ten years old – and would stay up all night to watch an especially interesting episode of *Dallas* or *Dynasty*.

And to study the people. 'Do women in the West really dress like that?' she asked him. And when he said yes, she commented, 'They eat too much.'

She had the fascinated curiosity of a child. But then he felt that went for all of the Mongols. When he thought of Barone . . . But he didn't want to think of Barone, because that meant thinking of Denise. Denise had now been six months in the clutches of that youthful monster. Even for Denise that was a long time. And he had no idea whether she was alive or dead.

But perhaps Denise had become as reconciled to her position

as that strange American woman. Clive had not seen Rosemary Leigh either, since their one meeting, and then he had been too conscious of Selphine's unseen presence properly to take in more than an impression of an unusually strong personality added to an unusually attractive physical presence ... But she had apparently surrendered to Batalji, hook, line and sinker. More likely she was just suffering a long nervous breakdown from having endured such a horrendous fate, and was refusing to admit it to herself.

He had only seen Mortana and her children once or twice, in passing, as he was taken in and out of the Palace. The girl Shallane had waved to him, contemptuously, and he had waved back.

His situation was incredible. But this entire situation was incredible. And yet, he was no less fascinated by the new rulers of Yakutistan than Selphine was by the outside world. They had pulled off a remarkable coup, conceived in the brain of one man. Save for that one man – and possibly Almani Serhat, who, he gathered, had also served in the Red Army – they knew nothing of the outside world. They were making no attempt to create a viable state, that he could see – simply because that one man was absent. No doubt life in Yakutsk came to a complete standstill every winter in any event. But the business of living, and creating exports, had to go on. Coal was being mined, he knew; but the paper and other wood-product factories had shut down. Yet it did not appear that any of the Taychin laws had been changed or rescinded, or even that there was no longer a secret police; only the policemen had changed, and even there it was the faces which had changed, not the uniforms. Nothing else. Because Batalji was not here. Everything emanated from Batalji Borjigin. Everything waited on Batalji Borjigin. And everyone seemed content to do so. And now he was back. The man whose mother had chosen a Western journalist as her lover. At least for the time being.

Joe waited for them outside the barracks. 'Wrap up,' he told them. 'We are going outside.' The six men pulled on their heavy coats and went into the courtyard, to find that the entire captive garrison had been turned out as well, watched by the tanks and the rifles of the Mongol soldiery, who were massed facing them, and also spread out around the huge courtyard. Just inside the gates was another large gathering, civilians who had been allowed in, or marshalled and forced in, Clive supposed. Their breath steamed, and they stamped their feet against the cold, chattering to each other, controlled by mounted Mongol soldiers armed with swords as well as rifles.

There was also a band – playing discordant music and surmounted by a huge cloud of steam from the heavy breaths – which now gave a roll of drums. All heads turned, to look at the procession of horsemen which had proceeded down The Avenue from the Presidential Palace, and was now entering the barracks courtyard. Horsemen, and horsewomen, Clive observed, recognising Selphine and Mortana, as well as Mortana's children, even the two small boys controlling their mounts with the expertise of veterans. And at the back, seated somewhat uneasily, was Rosemary Leigh.

'Well, there's a sight for sore eyes,' Jim muttered. 'But say, she's looking all right.'

'I told you that,' Clive reminded him. But he was more interested in the men. He recognised only one of them, Almani Serhat, but there could be no doubt about the one who rode in front: Batalji Borjigin! Clive narrowed his eyes as he stared. Like all the others, Batalji was well wrapped up in furs, but having made allowance for that Clive could tell he was a big man, if clearly not very tall. His face was exposed, and even at a distance Clive could get some idea of the strength in it. But not of the personality. Batalji looked sleepy, his eyes half closed against the wind.

The official party took their places, in front of the band, which now stopped playing. The man on Batalji's right held the standard, a staff with nine horse-tails floating from it. The troops stood to attention, and so did the Russian prisoners. The civilians shuffled their feet and rubbed their gloved hands together, but they too were quiet. Jim nudged Clive, and they watched another procession emerge from the barracks behind them. This marched quickly, because although the guards were as warmly clad as everyone else, the twelve prisoners in the centre were naked from the waist down, and stumbled in the snow, their legs and thighs and genitals rapidly turning blue – and two of them were women.

'Jesus Christ!' Al Mather muttered. Henri rubbed the back of his hand across his face.

The prisoners were marched forward until they stood immediately before Batalji. He looked at them, and one of the women fell to her knees, shouting something unintelligible. Batalji raised his hand, and the kneeling woman was dragged out in front of her fellows. A saddle had been placed on the snow, and the woman was forced to lie across this, face down. Her legs were pulled apart and held there, and other guards stepped forward, two carrying an eight-foot-long wooden pole with sharpened ends, and the third a mallet. 'Jesus!' Al muttered again. 'This can't be real.'

But it was. Clive swallowed to empty his mouth of a sudden flow of saliva. This was what had happened to Kopylov and Tatiana the hostess. After they had 'amused' their captors for a night. He wondered if those secret policemen and policewomen had also amused their guards for the night.

The sharpened tip of the pole was thrust into the woman's anus. Immediately she screamed, and frantically writhed against the six pairs of hands holding her down. When the pole was well embedded, the executioner stood up, and glanced at Batalji. Batalji nodded, and the man swung his mallet against the base of the pole. The scream that followed was the most unearthly sound Clive had ever heard. 'I am going to be sick,' Georges said.

At least it was fairly quick. There were two more animal-like screams, and then the woman's head dropped. Clive saw that the sharp end of the pole had been driven right through her body, so that it protruded through her chest, exactly as with Kopylov and Tatiana. Now several men lifted the pole, with the woman's body hanging from it, and thrust it into the ground; the hole, dug earlier that morning, had been hidden in the snow. Now the ground around the pole was stamped down to hold it firmly upright, so that the woman drooped there, hideously and piteously obscene.

And the next woman was being dragged forward, while the men waited their turn.

CHAPTER 8

Yakutsk, Spring 2001

The six men sat at their communal table and stared at their food. Only the jugs of vodka had been touched; these had been emptied. Before their eyes floated the constant vision of the twelve bodies, now hoisted in a row on their stakes in the courtyard, not a hundred yards away from where they sat.

'What do you think it *feels* like,' Henri said, 'to have a piece of wood stuffed up your ass?'

'Shut up,' Georges recommended.

Al held up his empty vodka jug. 'Christ, I can't even get pissed.'

'You've seen it all, Clive,' Jim said. 'What do you reckon?'

'That we have stumbled back five hundred years into history,' Clive said. 'At least.'

'Rosemary sleeps with that guy,' Al remarked.

'Not willingly,' Jim snapped. 'You'll never convince me of that.' He looked at Clive for support.

'Not willingly,' Clive said, hopefully.

'Man, Romy doesn't sleep with *anyone* willingly,' Al pointed out, with a feeble attempt at humour.

Joe appeared in the doorway. 'You, Stanton! The Khan wishes you.'

'Oh, Christ,' Georges muttered.

Clive swallowed the last of his vodka, stood up. Joe came into the room, looked at the table, picked up a sausage and bit into it. 'You don't like this food?' he demanded. He had stood beside them at the executions.

'Not today,' Al said.

Clive went to the door, turned back. 'See you in the funnies, eh?'

Joe led him along the corridor. 'The Khan is a great man,' he said. 'You remember this, eh, Mr Stanton?'

'I don't think I am going to be allowed to forget it,' Clive muttered. But at least there was a limousine waiting for him. That didn't suggest he was about to be executed, immediately. He tried to avoid looking at the twelve bodies, as the chains clicked through the snow, and up the presidential drive. Just as on one of his visits to Selphine, he thought. Maybe they'd got it wrong.

His guards handed him over to the presidential women. He was quite familiar with most of these now, and gave them as confident a smile as he could manage. 'His Excellency lunches,' Yorcka told him, and led him up the great staircase to the first floor, and then into the state dining room, which Batalji apparently used for domestic meals as well.

Yorcka paused in the doorway; Clive, at her shoulder, immediately felt very small as he looked into the room, which was crowded. He estimated the table had been designed to seat about forty people, and there were some twenty present, scattered round it in a careless fashion; presumably there had been place settings once, but these had been disarranged in the gusto with which the meal had been consumed; food was also scattered the length of the polished surface, along with cutlery, crockery and vodka – several of the jugs had been overturned.

There was also debris on the floor. Clive reckoned that only dogs were lacking to make it a perfect replica of a medieval baronial hall on a feast day. Dogs and servants, for there were none to be seen. Yet someone must have served the meal.

Of the people seated around the table, half a dozen were Mongol officers, wearing uniform, but with their tunics and the shirts beneath opened, to expose their chests. Again the only one of them he recognised was Almani Serhat, but by relating them to Almani's insignia he gathered the others were at least colonels. Then there were half a dozen children. He recognised Shallane and the two boys, Tensan and Dorgat, but not the other three.

There were five women. Selphine, of course, and Mortana, and two other clearly Mongol women he had not seen before – and Rosemary Leigh. All were very fashionably if inappropriately dressed, in that although it was lunchtime they wore evening gowns, but the Mongol women were as drunk as their menfolk. Rosemary's cheeks were pink enough to suggest she had also drunk a lot, but Clive did not feel she was drunk. She was trying to forget the morning. But they were all irrelevant, for at the head of the table there sat Batalji Borjigin.

There had been a great deal of noise and chatter, but this ceased at Clive's entrance, and all heads turned to look at him. 'The man, Stanton,' Yorcka announced.

'He didn't scream,' Shallane shouted. 'You never screamed.'

Clive had already decided that it would not do to be overawed by these people – or at least to let them guess he was overawed. 'That's because I have had nothing to scream about, Princess.'

Selphine was on her feet, and coming towards him. She wore a red gown, something else obviously appropriated from Tamara Taychin's wardrobe, for it hung loosely by two straps from her shoulders, somewhat like a sack, and when she moved it exposed her breasts. But she was compelling as ever, shrouded in the mass of tawny hair which fell around her like a shawl. 'Stanton,' she said. 'I saw you, this morning, at the execution. Was that not a pretty sight?'

'I found it a sickening sight, Princess.'

'Ha ha,' she shouted. 'You people from the West are soft.

Except where it matters, eh? Come!' She grasped his arm and led him the length of the table, to stand beside her son. 'This is the man Stanton, Batalji. Stanton, this is the Khan!'

Clive stood to attention, while he gazed at Batalji, and Batalji gazed at him. The Khan was every bit as big as he had supposed, with enormously powerful shoulders and fingers which looked capable of bending the silver cutlery scattered before him. There was nothing classically strong about his face; his forehead was low, crowded with somewhat shaggy hair, but this was a national characteristic; his nose and chin were rounded rather than thrusting; his mouth was curiously soft, when he was smiling, as he was smiling now. But his eyes were flat; they were not smiling. And his whole demeanour, so relaxed – his fingers, resting on the table, never moved as he surveyed Clive in turn – indicated tremendous power of mind as well as muscle. 'Your Excellency,' Clive said.

Batalji continued to study him for some seconds. Then he said, 'I have heard you are a famous man.'

'In the West, yes,' Clive agreed.

'Do you know many famous men?'

'Yes.'

'Now you know another. I have heard you have come here to interview me.' Batalji gestured at a vacant chair, close to him, next to Mortana. 'Interview me.'

'I have no equipment.'

'You need equipment, to interview me?'

'What I ask you, and what you say to me in reply, must be recorded, Your Excellency. Or there would be no point to it. People pay to see my interviews, and hear them.'

'You came here, from the West, without your equipment?'

'My equipment was in my plane, which crash-landed in a blizzard on your borders. Your son would not let me bring it with me, so I assume it is still in the plane. It will be ruined by now.'

Batalji gazed at him for several seconds, then he pointed to the chair again and said, 'We shall record your interview. Later. Tell me what you wish to know?'

Obviously an unrecorded interview was both a waste of time and would ruin any proper interview that might follow; second time around Batalji would have had time to think about his answers – he would not be caught by surprise by any question. On the other hand, clearly now was a time to concentrate on survival rather than professional precision. The question was, how to conduct such an interview, where all of the safeguards normally afforded to a journalist were lacking. Clive glanced at the waiting people; they were quiet, and all seemed interested in what he had to say ... even the children. Again he understood that these people would respect a man who behaved like a man, and have nothing but contempt for any dissembling. He sat down. 'Very well, Your Excellency. You have overthrown the Taychin Government, and I understand that you are now the master of Yakutiya.'

'It is now called Yakutistan,' Selphine interrupted.

'As you say, Princess. Now, Your Excellency, I have read a great deal about you ...'

'How?' Batalji demanded.

'You are a famous man, as you just reminded me. My company, every newspaper or television company in the world, has a file on you. And I should think most national governments, as well.'

Batalji frowned, and looked at his officers.

'What does your file say?' Almani asked, speaking as quietly as ever.

'It contains everything that is known about President Borjigin. The murder of his father, his confinement in a state orphanage, his service in Afghanistan, his desertion, his outlawry, his attempted coup in 1996, his assassination of Andrei Taychin.'

'What does it say about me?' Selphine demanded. She had not thought to ask that before.

'Only that you are the President's mother,' Clive told her.

'Ha! They do not know, in the West, how I have suffered.'

'So you have read about me,' Batalji said. 'Why?'

'To attempt to understand you. I was going to say, you may have had strong personal reasons for wishing to overthrow the

Taychins. But now that you have done so, you are the head of a state. My viewers would be interested to know what are your plans for this state.'

'That is my son's business,' Selphine snapped.

Clive continued to look at Batalji. 'Have you told your people what you intend for them, Your Excellency? For example, the form of government you intend to institute? I can understand that the country remains for the moment under martial law and military rule. But this cannot endure. People in the West will wish to know if you intend to institute a democratic form of government, or if you intend to continue a military dictatorship.'

Batalji stroked his chin. 'My people know nothing of democracy. Nor do they wish it.'

'Have you asked them, Your Excellency?'

There was a rustle around the table. 'My people wish only to be led, by me,' Batalji said. 'I was chosen Kha Khan by the *kurultai* . . . do you know what a *kurultai* is?'

'Yes, Your Excellency. It is an assembly of all the khans of all the clans.'

'That is correct,' Batalji acknowledged, with some surprise. 'Well, I was chosen Kha Khan by the *kurultai*, twenty years ago. I was eighteen years old, and I was chosen Kha Khan. This is because I am Batalji Borjigin. In my veins runs the royal blood of the Mongols. In my veins runs the blood of Temujin, the Man of Steel, the Genghis Khan!'

'With respect, Your Excellency, were *all* the clan chieftains present at this *kurultai*?'

There was another rustle of annoyance round the table, but Batalji's face remained relaxed. 'Enough were present, Englishman. I am the Kha Khan. My people know this. They expect to be led, by their Khan.'

'Such a government will not be approved by the West, Your Excellency. By the United Nations.'

'Why not? My people have always chosen as their khans have told them to.'

'But not all the khans were present, Your Excellency. And

then, the election took place twenty years ago. No government can endure for twenty years without seeking a fresh mandate from its people. The United Nations will insist on this.'

'The United Nations,' remarked one of the generals, contemptuously. From his close resemblance to Mortana, Clive estimated the speaker had to be her brother.

'Your Excellency, gentlemen, no country can exist in a vacuum. You will need to trade. As soon as the ice melts, a matter of weeks, now, you will wish to sell your coal, sitting there on your docks. You will also wish to develop your oil. Yakutistan could be a very rich nation. It has many things that the rest of the world would like to buy. But if the United Nations were to put an economic boycott upon you, then you would be unable to sell your goods. How would you survive?'

'Our people survived for centuries without foreign trade,' Jagnuth argued.

'Centuries ago,' Clive riposted. 'Times have changed, General. You need an army. A modern army has to have transport, as well as tanks and aircraft. These things need support, in parts and mechanical understanding and constant updating to keep abreast of other weapons. They also need oil. You have the oil, but how are you going to develop it and refine it without foreign aid, foreign money, foreign enterprise?'

'And these things are controlled by the United Nations?' Almani asked.

'In the long run, yes.'

'Will the United Nations be so interested in us, here on the steppes?' Batalji asked.

'They are interested now, Your Excellency.'

'You saw this, on the video,' Selphine reminded her son.

'They merely wish to know if I am governing with the will of my people,' Batalji said. 'I am.'

'How can you prove that?' Clive asked. 'The only accepted way, in the modern world, for a leader to prove that he is the choice of at least a majority of his people, is to hold a general election or a referendum. That is to say, to go through the democratic process.'

'Ha, ha,' Jagnuth laughed. 'Then we will have an election. The people will vote how we tell them to vote. They have always voted how the Commissars told them to vote. Now they will do as we tell them.'

'Are you saying that there are no undemocratic governments in the world?' Batalji asked.

'No, Your Excellency. There are several. But they do not belong to the concert of nations.'

'China is not a democracy,' Almani said.

'It pretends to be.'

'It is as much a democracy as was Soviet Russia. People vote the way they are told. The world trades with China, as they did with Soviet Russia. It accepts it into ... what was your term? The concert of nations. As it accepted Soviet Russia. Why should the world not trade with us, and accept us, if we tell our people how to vote?'

'I agree the situation is not satisfactory,' Clive said. 'But Soviet Russia was a superpower, and China is the most populous nation on earth.'

'What you are saying is, that the United Nations, like all human organisations everywhere, yields to power. Then we will just have to become powerful.' Batalji studied Clive. 'You do not believe we can do this?'

Clive took a deep breath. 'No, Your Excellency. I do not believe you can do this, at least not in time. I believe you need to work out very carefully, but very quickly, where you are going. Russia is opposed to you. This I am sure you know.'

Batalji nodded. 'But Russia is helpless. Russia is bankrupt. It has to accept us, as we will not yield to anything but military force, and Russia has no money to afford a war.'

'Russia is still a great military power, Your Excellency. It needs financing, I agree. But it may well obtain such finance from the West, if it is felt that here in Yakutistan there is a military dictatorship which is violating human rights, and which may cause trouble to its neighbours.'

'Human rights?' Jagnuth demanded.

Clive took another deep breath. 'It is a violation of human

rights to kidnap women and use them as slaves.' He stared at Batalji. 'It is a violation of human rights to imprison foreign nationals where they have broken no laws. Above all it is a violation of human rights to condemn people without trial, and then to execute them in so barbarous a fashion as impalement. Many people in the West would say it is a violation of human rights to execute people at all.'

There was an uproar, as all the generals started shouting at once. Batalji waved his hand, and the noise slowly subsided. Clive looked at Rosemary. Compared with the Mongol women, her high-necked blue gown was demure. And she seemed as relaxed and confident as ever. But she had watched those executions as well. There had to be considerable turmoil behind that handsome façade. 'Is what he says true?' Batalji asked her.

'Yes,' Rosemary said. 'That is how it will be regarded in the West.'

'So, they will condemn us, and they will talk,' Almani said. 'They may even impose sanctions. We can live without foreign trade. They will not do more. We have seen this, in Afghanistan, in Yugoslavia. They will never interfere militarily.'

Batalji turned his sleepy eyes upon Almani for a moment, then he abruptly pushed back his chair and stood up. 'You come,' he told Clive. 'And you.' He beckoned Rosemary.

Selphine also got up, but Batalji waved her back to her seat. 'I will talk with these alone,' he said.

Selphine looked very annoyed, but she sat down.

Batalji left the dining room, the women guards standing to attention as he passed. He went up the stairs and along several corridors, before opening a door into what Clive, following with Rosemary, immediately guessed had to be the warlord's private apartment. He paused in the doorway in surprise. The room was empty of conventional furniture, but there was a huge pile of rugs and blankets in the centre of the floor; this was apparently Batalji's bed. There was a table, two straight chairs, and a chest. On the table there were several books.

Weapons hung on the walls, from modern machine-pistols to well-worn rifles and old yataghans. There was no television set or video or music centre; nothing to indicate that this man ever relaxed. Except for the presence of Rosemary.

Batalji went to the wall, and took down one of the yataghans. With great expertise he swung it once or twice. 'I used this sword as a boy. I used it on the night I took this city, six months ago. Have you ever used a yataghan, Stanton?'

'I'm afraid not.'

'Try this one.'

Without warning Batalji threw the weapon. Clive's every instinct was to hurl himself to one side, but instead he stood his ground, and managed to catch the haft, in both hands, gasping as he saw that the blade was honed to a razor sharpness. Behind him he heard Rosemary's sharp intake of breath. Batalji grinned, came across the room, and took the weapon back. 'A coward would have jumped aside. A fool would have lost an arm.' He replaced the yataghan on its hooks. 'I have been told you have a woman with your party.'

'Yes. My cameraperson.'

'What is this, cameraperson?'

Having got his breath back, Clive grinned. 'In the West, Your Excellency, it is not proper to designate the sexes, certainly where someone of either sex is capable of doing the same job.'

Batalji looked genuinely puzzled. 'You cannot tell the difference between men and women, in the West?'

'Well . . .' Clive scratched his head, and looked at Rosemary.

'It's to do with women's lib,' Rosemary attempted to explain. 'In the West, women are as good as men.'

Batalji looked from one to the other. 'You agree with this, Stanton?'

'I don't have much choice. The bottom line is a legal matter.'

Batalji laughed. 'You could not defeat Rosemary in unarmed combat?'

'You'd have to work at it,' Rosemary retorted in English.

Now Batalji's laugh was louder. 'Do you think you could defeat *me* in unarmed combat, Rosemary?'

'No,' Rosemary said. 'I do not think I could defeat you in unarmed combat, Batalji.'

'Then you are not my equal.'

'In primitive circumstances, perhaps not. But with the use of modern technology, which does not depend upon unarmed combat, I can be your equal.'

'That is rubbish,' Batalji declared. 'At the end of the day, it will always depend upon a man's strength. You may as well say that night is as bright as day because you have an electric light on. Switch off the electricity or have a power failure, revert to nature, and it is dark again. Tell me of this woman, this cameraperson. Is she beautiful?'

'I think so.'

'Then where is she? She is not in the prison with you.'

'She was appropriated by your son, Barone, Your Excellency. I was speaking of her just now when I referred to your violation of human rights, or accepted international behaviour.'

'Ha, ha,' Batalji said. 'I thought you were speaking of Rosemary.'

'So did I,' Rosemary remarked, coldly.

'I would like to get Mademoiselle l'Auberon back,' Clive said. 'Just as quickly as possible.'

Batalji gave a roar of laughter. 'To stop her human rights being violated, eh? Very well, I will send to my son and command him to deliver the woman to Yakutsk.'

Clive could not believe his ears. Just like that? 'Thank you, Your Excellency.'

'Come.' Batalji left the room. Clive and Rosemary looked at each other. He wanted to establish a relationship here, some kind of empathy, because there could be no doubt that Batalji valued her opinions. But her gaze remained cold. She turned and followed her master.

Batalji led them downstairs into the communications room.

The television screens glowed, and the radios crackled, but if it was the middle of the afternoon in Yakutsk, it was still early morning in Moscow, and hardly dawn in Europe; America still slept. One of the women telegraphers presented Batalji with a pile of notes, which he glanced at before throwing them on the floor; the telegrapher obediently knelt and began scooping them up. 'Moscow keeps calling us, calling me,' Batalji said, and grinned. 'But I do not reply.'

'Is that because you cannot think of anything to say?'

Rosemary again caught her breath, but Batalji was grinning. 'I will have something to say, in due course. They wish me to go to them, for a conference. They must think I am a fool.'

'Will they not give you safe conduct?'

'You also think I am a fool, Stanton. Safe conduct. I have seen Moscow at work, remember? I fought for them once.' A look of utter ferocity crossed his face, then cleared as quickly as it had come. 'Videos. Play those videos.' He threw himself on the settee before the screen, and Rosemary sat beside him. Instantly his arm went round her, his fingers seeping under her arm to close on her breast. She gave an embarrassed cough, but then the lights went down and pictures began to flicker on the screen. 'Who are these people?' Batalji asked. 'Rosemary does not know their names. Do you know their names, Stanton?'

It was a news programme, several days old, Clive estimated, but it was still good to see news. 'Yes,' he said. 'It is a conference of European heads of state. The man on the right is the Prime Minister of Great Britain, the one on the left is the Chancellor of Germany. In the middle are the President of France, and the Prime Minister of Spain.'

'These men all rule their countries?'

'Yes, Your Excellency.'

'Then why are two of them called prime minister, one a president, and one a chancellor? Is not a president senior to a prime minister? That is so in Russia.'

'They are all words which mean roughly the same thing in the West, Your Excellency. They are each an elected head of state.'

'Have you no kings in the West?'

'Indeed, Your Excellency. There is a monarch in Spain and in England. But they are titular heads. They do not actually rule.'

Batalji brooded at the screen for several minutes. Then he asked, 'What should I call myself as ruler of Yakutistan, in your opinion, Stanton?'

'That depends on how you intend to rule, Your Excellency.'

'It is your opinion that I should speak with those men?'

'I believe you will have to, eventually.'

Batalji stared at the screen. 'I do not wish to speak with anyone from Moscow,' he said at last. 'Is it possible to speak with those men, and not Moscow?'

Clive seized his opportunity. 'I might be able to arrange it for you.'

'You? How can you do this?'

'I know those men.'

Batalji looked back at the screen, and pointed. 'You know those prime ministers and chancellors and presidents? You have met them?'

'I have interviewed them all, Your Excellency.'

'Ha, ha! Next you will be telling me that you have met the President of the United States!'

'As a matter of fact, I have.'

'How can that be? He has just been elected.'

'I interviewed him last year, when he first announced his candidacy. But I had met him before that; he has been in politics a long time.'

Batalji studied him. Then he said, 'What do you like to do best, Stanton? When you are not working?'

'I play a bit of golf.'

'What is this, golf?' Batalji looked at Rosemary.

'It is a game,' Rosemary explained.

'Game?'

'Something people do to relax,' Clive suggested.

'Ha, ha! When I wish to relax, I get drunk, and I have a woman. Stanton, you and I will get drunk, and have a woman. I like you, Stanton. Does that not please you?'

'It pleases me very much,' Clive said. 'Which woman do you have in mind?' He could not stop himself glancing at Rosemary.

'You must be out of your tiny mind,' Rosemary snapped, in English.

'You would like her?' Batalji asked. 'Well, perhaps later. Right now she is what I wish. Do you like fucking my mother?'

'I ... ah ... your mother has been very kind to me,' Clive said cautiously.

'My mother? My mother has never been kind to anyone in her life,' Batalji said. 'She was never even kind to me, when I was a child. She is not a kind woman. I have no objection to you fucking her, Stanton, when she wishes it. A woman must be fucked, eh? But I do not wish her to be with us, today. She will be telling us what to do all the time. There is a woman.' He pointed at the telegrapher. 'Do you like that woman?'

She was a plump, pretty young woman, dark-haired and buxom, wearing green uniform skirt and blouse, stockings and high-heeled shoes, who giggled nervously as she saw her master looking at her. 'She is very attractive,' Clive said.

'Then you shall have her. What is your name, woman?'

'Nita, Your Excellency.'

'You are relieved of duty,' Batalji told her. 'Come.'

'Batalji!' Rosemary protested.

'Do you not like this woman?'

'I have nothing against her. But you cannot mean to ... well, for us to be together. The four of us.'

'Yes, I mean this. We will inspire one another, eh?'

'It won't inspire me,' Rosemary snapped. 'We don't do that kind of thing in the West. Well, maybe some people do. But I don't.' She looked at Clive. 'Tell him, Stanton,' she said in English.

'Tell him what?'

'Shit! I thought it was asking too much for you to be a gentleman.'

'You know something?' Batalji remarked. 'I think she likes you, Stanton.'

'Like *him*?' Rosemary snorted.

Batalji grinned. 'You are too vehement in your dislike of him. We will go to your apartment.' He went to the door, where one of the women was on guard. 'Bring vodka,' he said.

He led the way to Rosemary's apartment, Rosemary following. She did not look at Clive, and her ears were pink; he estimated it was a combination of anger and embarrassment. The telegrapher walked beside him. She did not look the least embarrassed, only a little apprehensive. 'Are you a Yakut, Nita?' he asked her.

'No, Your Excellency. I am Russian. His Excellency employs me because I am good at telegraphy.'

She spoke simply. Clive wondered if she knew what had happened to her compatriots that morning; if perhaps she had been there, but like everyone else was just content to obey the Khan. Who was he to carp? he wondered. Was he not doing exactly the same thing? Batalji threw open the door and went into Rosemary's apartment. Rosemary followed him, stood just within the doorway, looking uncertain. Clive and Nita were almost pushed aside by several women hurrying in the trays on which there were six bottles of vodka and four glasses.

My God, Clive thought, if he means us to drink all of that ... The trays were placed on the table, the women bowed, and hurried out again. The door was closed. Batalji had already removed his tunic and shirt, to reveal a barrel-chest, thickly coated in hair. 'Pour,' he commaneded.

Rosemary and Nita went to the table together, and filled the glasses. 'Do you do this often?' Clive asked in English.

Rosemary made a face at him, gave Batalji a glass. Nita brought one to Clive. 'To a happy evening,' Batalji announced. 'It is good to be home.' He drank half of his glass. Nita followed his example. Rosemary and Clive sipped theirs.

Batalji sat down and stretched out his legs. 'One each.' The two women each straddled a leg to grasp a boot, and were kicked away as Batalji's feet came free. Clive noted with surprise that the warlord did not wear socks, and then remembered that the Red Army did not wear socks either, and Batalji had begun life as a soldier. 'Out there, in the snow, is where a man belongs,' Batalji said. 'But it is still good to get back to one's yurt, and one's woman. Is this not a splendid yurt, Stanton?'

'The best, Your Excellency.' Clive drank some more vodka.

Batalji had finished his glass, and Nita hurried back to the table to fill it. Rosemary was unbuckling the warlord's belt, and pulling off his pants. Clive thought he would give several thousand pounds to be able to get into her brain, at this moment.

'Why do you not undress?' Batalji demanded. 'Are you afraid of these women?' Clive undressed. Nita hurried to help him, smiling at him. 'What is that?' Batalji demanded. 'Are you a Moslem?'

'It's because he is Jewish,' Rosemary suggested.

'I am neither Moslem nor Jewish,' Clive said with a sigh. 'I was born in the tropics. In the tropics it is customary to circumcise boys when they are babies, as a guard against disease.'

'Is that why they do it?' Batalji was interested. 'You are not as big as me.'

'Well, Your Excellency, as we say in the West, it's not what you have, but how you use it.'

'Ha, ha,' Batalji shouted. 'We shall see.' He pointed. 'Strip.' The women obeyed, Rosemary turning her back on Clive. But even from behind he could tell she was a most desirable sexual animal, and in any event, Batalji held her arm to turn her round. She made Nita look like a young girl. 'Now,' Batalji said. 'you know what I like you to do, first.'

'No,' Rosemary muttered. 'Please, Batalji.'

'Do it.'

'I hate you!' she shouted. 'You are a despicable pervert!'

Batalji merely grinned. 'Is she not beautiful when she is angry, Stanton? But she is more beautiful yet when she is coming. You!' He pointed at Nita. 'Lie down and play with yourself. Lie beside her. You!' He pointed at Rosemary. 'Do it, or I will give you to Stanton.' Another grin. 'If you do not please me, I will give you to Stanton anyway.'

Clive reflected that he might as well have done so, as Rosemary's thigh rubbed against his as she sat astride Batalji, working her body while the warlord played with her breasts. More orthodoxly, Clive was lying on Nita, who was giving delighted little squeals, even if she had been a little alarmed when she had realised how he intended to enter her. But now he was spent; whether she had had another orgasm he didn't know. But he rather thought Rosemary had, as her body flopped forward, lying on Batalji's chest, shoulders rising and falling as she gasped.

Batalji heaved her off. It was a big bed, but his movement was so violent she rolled across it and fell out, landing on the carpet with a thump. Batalji got up, went to the table, and refilled his empty glass. He filled Clive's as well. Clive also got up. He was exhausted, but more emotionally than physically. He didn't want to look at the two women. 'That was good, eh?' Batalji asked. 'Now we get drunk, and then we fuck them again.'

'You mean we're not drunk yet?' Clive asked. The room was swaying around him. As for fucking them again . . .

'On one bottle of vodka, split between four?' Batalji seemed genuinely surprised, as he opened the second bottle. 'You like Rosemary, eh?'

'She is a very attractive woman,' Clive said cautiously.

'Ha, ha. Next time I will give her to you.'

'You mean you'll give him my dead body,' Rosemary muttered, in English; she was still lying on the floor.

'A woman is more amusing when she hates you,' Batalji commented, sitting at the table and drinking vodka. He gestured Clive to a seat as well.

'I have an idea you hate women, Your Excellency,' Clive said.

'Hate them? I love them. All women. I love them all.'

'Then why do you enjoy ill-treating them?'

'I do not ill-treat Rosemary. There is not a mark on her body that is not caused by love.'

'You treat her as a slave.'

Batalji raised his eyebrows. 'She *is* a slave. My slave.'

'Your Excellency...'

'I know.' Batalji refilled his glass. 'Human rights. I am violating her human rights. And I must care about human rights.' He pointed. 'Genghis Khan never cared for human rights. He killed people. Thousands and thousands of people. He destroyed whole countries. Whole empires.'

'With respect, Your Excellency, that was eight hundred years ago.'

'What is eight hundred years? Are we not the same people now, as then?'

'No, Your Excellency. We are more civilised.'

'Ha, ha, you think so? I have read of what happened in the Second World War. I was taught that at the orphanage. And then I saw for myself what the Red Army was doing in Afghanistan. That is more civilised?'

'I think the difference is that nowadays we know that kind of behaviour is wrong, where in Genghis Khan's day it was accepted as an aspect of warfare. That has got to be a step in the right direction.'

Batalji brooded, and drank. 'If I let you leave Yakutistan, what will you do?'

'I will return to Europe. But I will not leave without my people. All of my people. And the Americans.' He looked at Rosemary, who had got off the floor and was sitting on the bed, where Nita lay, uncertain if she was allowed to move, or if the men would be coming back. Rosemary's strong body sagged, and her yellow hair drifted past her face and on to her knees. But she was watching them as well; when she caught Clive's gaze, she flushed.

'I meant, what would you tell them?'

Clive took a deep breath. 'What I have seen here.'

Batalji glanced at him. 'Then they will call me a savage.'

'Yes, Your Excellency, they will.' Because that is what you are, Clive thought.

'I would prefer it if you worked for me,' Batalji said.

THE NINTH CHRONICLE

Yakutsk, Spring 2001

When Clive awoke, he had no idea where he was. As opposed to the barracks in which he had spent the last four months, where the beds, if not uncomfortable, had been far from luxurious, he found himself nestling in a very soft mattress in the middle of a huge four-poster. That the bed was going up and down and swinging round and round for a moment seemed irrelevant. Then it became very relevant indeed. He sat up, saw an open door into a bathroom, staggered at it, and just reached the toilet before being violently sick.

His head was now moving faster than the bed, and the top of his skull was opening and closing with fearsome crashes. It was some minutes before he could move, then he managed to drape himself across the basin, and run cold water over his head and face.

How much vodka had he drunk last night? At least a bottle. The miracle was that he was alive. And could remember anything of it. But he could remember the women, Rosemary Leigh, certainly, all of that proud beauty so absolutely at the mercy of their lust ... and then ... He staggered back to the bed, lay down, and sat up again as the room began to rock.

And as memory became more vivid. Batalji himself? It had happened, the warlord laughing as he recalled what he had been made to suffer in the state orphanage. While Rosemary Leigh . . . The door opened, and Batalji came in. The Khan was fully dressed, in his green Russian uniform, carried a holster on one hip, while his yataghan hung over the other. He might have been about to go to war. And he looked absolutely fit and in command of himself. 'Still in bed?' he demanded. 'You Westerners cannot drink.'

Clive gazed at him. If they had shared anything, it had not altered Batalji's demeanour in the least. Therefore he must maintain his own. 'That is absolutely right,' he acknowledged.

'Thank God! Has it ever occurred to you that you are drinking yourself to death?'

'Bah! A man must die of something. And he dies when his time comes, not before.'

'It's a philosophy.'

'So, have you considered my proposal? I wish your answer.'

Clive scratched his head. 'You mean you really did make that proposal?' Because if he had, then everything else had to have really happened, as well.

'You cannot remember?'

'Not very clearly. It was around then that I got really drunk.'

'Ha, ha. It was then that you became truly entertaining. Are you sure that you cannot remember?'

'I am not at all sure that I *want* to remember,' Clive confessed.

'Ha, ha. I did not bugger you. We were both too drunk. But we loved. Or I did. You were reluctant. I can respect that. That does not mean I cannot love you, Stanton. I want you at my side. Now give me your answer.'

'You wish me to work for you,' Clive said slowly, wanting to get it absolutely straight. 'What as?'

'There is much I need to do.' Batalji sat on the bed beside him. 'More than I thought. My associates do not understand this, except perhaps Almani. He is the only one of them, apart from myself, who has ever been to Moscow, seen what lies in the West. None of us has ever been to Europe.' He brooded. 'My mother understands nothing of the West. She has done nothing but watch television for the past six months, but she cannot tell the difference between what is play-acting and what is real.'

'I've observed that,' Clive agreed.

'But I know that a great deal needs to be done. I wish you to tell me everything.'

'Will you do what I tell you?'

Batalji grinned. 'That depends what you tell me.'

'And if I tell you everything I think should be done, will you allow me and my team, and the Americans, to leave Yakutsk?'

'We will discuss this,' Batalji said.

'The surest way to attract international condemnation is to play the hostage game. Saddam Hussein tried it, and look where it got him.'

'I have said we will discuss this. I will send women to you, and they will bathe you and feed you, and then you and I will sit down together and discuss this.'

'What about Denise?'

'Your woman? I have dispatched an aircraft this morning. She will be here for dinner. You see, I am prepared to discuss everything with you. Now . . .' His head jerked as the door was thrown open.

Three men stood there. They wore uniform, and carried automatic pistols. Clive had never been personally confronted by assassins before, but he knew immediately that he was now. He began to roll across the bed, violently, even as he knew there could be no escape. 'Savage!' said one of the men, in Russian, and fired at Batalji. But his eye had been distracted by Clive's movement, and the bullet thumped into the bedclothes. Before he could recover, Batalji had drawn his own weapon and shot him in the chest. Then he fired again, and the second man dropped, blood spewing from his mouth.

The third man was firing in turn. He did not hit Batalji, but the Khan turned so violently that he fell over the side of the bed, hitting the floor with a thump that winded him and caused him to lose his grip on his gun, which flew across the floor. Clive had fallen off the other side of the bed, and the two of them gazed at the assassin, who stood above the Khan, baring his teeth. 'You impaled my brother,' he gritted, levelling his pistol.

Clive held his breath. Was this fantastic dream about to end? He looked at Batalji, but the Khan seemed totally unafraid. 'Then your brother was one of Taychin's secret police,' he said, quietly. 'Are you admitting that you, too, were a secret policeman?'

'Does it matter?' The man's finger was white on the trigger.

'Indeed it does,' Batalji told him. 'It will make a difference to how you die.' He slowly pushed himself up from the floor. 'Do you wish to be impaled as well? If you shoot me, they will cut off your balls first, slowly, and then shove the stake up your ass.' The man licked his lips. The gun was still levelled, but it was wavering. Batalji reached his feet. 'Whereas if you are sensible,' he said, his voice still low and caressing, 'you could join your compatriots in being repatriated to Russia. Would you not like that?'

The man slowly lowered the gun, his face a picture of indecision. 'I think you should give me that,' Batalji said. 'Before you do something stupid.'

'You will send me home?' the man asked. 'This is your word?'

'This is my word,' Batalji said. The man reversed the gun, and held it out. Batalji took it, looked at it, then raised it and shot him twice in the head. 'I will send you home,' he said. 'In a box.' He glanced at Clive. 'Go and have a bath. You look terrible.'

The women came in to attend to Clive, and to provide him with a breakfast which consisted mainly of kumiss. Their ministrations plus the fermented brew made him feel a great deal better, but his head was still spinning with what had happened, his own brush with death, and more than anything the way Batalji had handled the situation. Now he could understand something of what Rosemary had been trying to convey, last December. But he still had a big decision to make. Batalji wanted his expertise as an observer of government and statesmanship, hopefully more than his body. Well, Clive was not above giving him that, especially if it meant the rescue of Denise.

But could he contemplate working for a monster? Even if the monster was at once the most charming, talented, bold and ambitious man he had ever met?

Batalji sat behind the walnut desk in the huge presidential office. He appeared to have suffered no reaction at all to his experience of that morning, although the several other man present were all in a state of considerable agitation. 'Sit down,' the Khan said. 'And you, leave us.'

The men filed from the room. Jagnuth and Almani hesitated, but a wave of Batalji's hand had them following the others. Batalji grinned. 'They think you will attempt to assassinate me.'

'Have you found out how those men got into the Palace?' Clive asked.

'Poor security. Oh, those responsible will be punished, and I have instructed Almani to overhaul the entire system. When I think what I had to go through to reach Boris Taychin, and those three just walked in, simply because they were wearing uniform! Shit!'

'But it does raise an interesting point,' Clive said. 'suppose you had been killed? Who would be your successor?'

'My eldest son, Barone.'

'Then believe me, Your Excellency, I intend to do everything that is humanly possible to keep you alive.'

Batalji nodded. 'Barone is a savage. It was his upbringing. It was a difficult time.' Clive decided against making the obvious remark. 'Now, you have thought over my proposal?'

'Yes, Your Excellency. But I must establish certain things

first. You must understand that if I give you everything you wish, and *then* ask for a quid pro quo, I will be in an inferior position.'

'Quid pro quo?'

'Something of equal value in exchange.'

'Ah! I understand that. But do you understand that to the West you are dead, killed in a plane crash? Were I to execute you, and your companions, including this woman you are so interested in, no one would be any the wiser.'

Clive hoped his expression didn't change. 'And you would be no further ahead.'

'I am sure I would be able to find another adviser, Stanton.' Batalji grinned. 'Do not misunderstand me. I like you. I like the way you speak. I even like the way you drink. I feel I can trust you. I merely wish to point out that it would be to your advantage to work with me, rather than against me. However, tell me what you wish.'

'The release of my companions, and the Americans.'

'They will be released when you have agreed to work for me. Listen to what I am offering you, Stanton. I need more than your advice. I need someone to persuade the West to give me the breathing space to create a viable nation here in Yakutistan. I think you could be that person. You tell me you know the Western leaders. You will know the ones to speak with, the ones to persuade. Most important, I want Russia off my back. I do not think they are in a position to attempt to reconquer Yakutistan. But I must be sure.'

'You are asking me to be your ambassador to the West? To the United Nations?'

'Call it whatever you wish. Now listen, agree to this and I will give you whatever you wish. A house, a car, money, women . . . listen, I will give you Rosemary Leigh. I saw the way you looked at her. Agree, and she is yours.' Clive could not stop himself laughing. Batalji frowned. 'I have made a joke?'

'I am sure you have not, Your Excellency. But that is not the way we do things in the West. I already have a home, and a car, and a large income. As for Rosemary Leigh, we just do not give each other women. Women go where they wish, with whom they wish. You are welcome to give me Miss Leigh, as that is the custom here in Yakutistan. But I shall merely take her back to the States and let her get on with her life.'

Batalji frowned at him for several seconds. Then he said, 'Then what is it you wish, to work for me?'

Clive drew a long breath: he had never expected to find himself in such a position, and had to think very fast. 'I would first of all have to inform my present employers that I and my team are alive and unharmed, and will be returning. Once that is done, I will be free to assist you. I cannot expect you to follow all the advice I give you, but I cannot help you if you will accept none of it. If you wish understanding from the West, you must undertake certain actions that can be approved by the West.'

'You mean I must hold elections,' Batalji said.

'Certainly. With Western observers present. Then you must draw up, or have drawn up, a code of laws.'

'There is already a law in Yakutistan.'

'Taychin law, which is an extension of Soviet law.'

'Ha, ha, you are right. I will draw up my own laws. Genghis Khan drew up his own code of law. It was called the *yassa*. I will draw upon my own *yassa*.'

Clive had never read the original *yassa*, but he could imagine both what it contained and what Batalji's would be likely to contain. And omit! 'If you wish to be friends with the West, you must have a code of law which respects civil rights, that is, prohibits arbitrary arrest, prohibits conviction without a fair and open trial, allows every citizen in a country to know his rights.'

'Can you draw up such a law?'

Clive shook his head. 'I am not a lawyer. However, I know several lawyers of international repute who might be prepared to undertake such a task, if they could be certain that you would accept at least most of their proposals. Then you would have to consider trade with the West, and your part in the international scene.'

'You mean we would join the United Nations.'

'You would *apply* to join the United Nations. I am not sure you would be accepted until you have held your elections and instituted an acceptable code of law. And I am sure that Russia will oppose your admittance. But that can be overcome if you can prove you are ruling with the consent of the majority of your people, and if you comply with the requirements of a civilised state.'

'You mean we would not be able to trade until then?'

'No, I think you would be able to trade right away. The world needs Yakutistan's oil. But you will need Western expertise and Western finance to get the oil out of the ground. Moscow wishes to help you do this.'

'No!' For the first time Batalji was vehement. 'Not Moscow. You will arrange help from the West. You spoke of finance. This is a poor country. It will need financial help.'

'With respect, Your Excellency, if your oil reserves are as great as I have heard reported, you could become as rich as Saudi Arabia.'

'That is in the future. I am speaking of now. What of the International Monetary Fund? Do they not give money to developing nations?'

'Like the United Nations, the IMF would need to be sure that you are a practising democracy with a developed civil rights programme, and also that you are capable of handling vast sums of money without spending it either on your personal pleasure or on far-out social schemes which you simply cannot afford. This has happened too often with Third World countries. Which brings us to the question of armaments. You have too many of them.'

Batalji appeared genuinely surprised. 'A nation must be able, and prepared, to defend itself.'

'Absolutely. But I have gained the impression that your entire nation is under arms.'

'We have just fought a revolution.'

'Nonetheless, an army which comprises at least fifty per cent of the population is not going to make anyone in the West feel very happy. Then there is the question that most of your hardware belongs to Russia.'

'You will have to arrange that with them. I must have planes, and I must have tanks. As soon as I have money, I will pay for these things. But the planes and tanks in Yakutistan stay in Yakutistan.' Batalji gave one of his grins. 'They are welcome to come to Yakutistan and reclaim their weapons, if they wish. If they can.'

'Just now you said you wanted peace with Russia.'

'Certainly I wish peace with Russia. But not at any price.'

'What you mean is, the peace will have to be at your price, Your Excellency. Am I to take it that you also intend to hold on to your nuclear weapons?'

'I have no nuclear weapons. It is the Russians who have nuclear weapons.'

'Nonetheless, Your Excellency, the missile bases in Yakutistan are now in your possession, are they not?'

'The missiles have been disarmed. By the Russians.'

'The West would wish them handed over, or destroyed under supervision.' Batalji shrugged. 'You mean you would have no objection?' Clive was surprised, and relieved.

'What have I to do with nuclear weapons? I am not going to war with anyone.'

'Those are the words that will most please the West, Your Excellency.'

'Then I also am pleased. But I must put all of these proposals before my officers.' Batalji grinned. 'And my mother. Can you write out what you have said, in Russian?'

'No. But I can write it out in English, and have it written out in French by my associates. I am sure that amongst the survivors of Taychin's Government, or the university students, you will find some people who can speak either English or French.'

Batalji nodded. 'Then go and write out what you have said; I will have the necessary translators found. A car will take you back to your barracks. It will bring you back here to me this evening, when you have completed the transcript. Your woman will be here by then, and you will be rewarded.'

CHAPTER 9

Yakutsk, Spring 2001

Batalji summoned Jagnuth, and told him the gist of what he had discussed with Clive. 'Thus I have a mission for you. How many missiles are there at Ugumun?'

'Twenty-four.'

'Then what I wish you to do, Jagnuth, is take a company of picked men, and some of the prisoners to do the hard work, and move six of the missiles to a new location. You select it. When you get there, bury them and their warheads, making sure that they are properly insulated. Then put a guard on the site, under an officer you can trust, kill the prisoners who did the job, and return here.'

Jagnuth plucked at his lip. 'I will need perhaps a hundred prisoners, if I am to dig into the permafrost. That will mean fifty guards. My men can kill the prisoners, but I cannot ask them to kill themselves.'

'We will dispose of them when they return here. The important thing is to swear them to secrecy until then.'

Jagnuth nodded. 'But also, I do not think it will be practical to move the missiles until the thaw.'

'I understand this. They will be moved the moment there is a thaw. That should be in a few weeks' time.'

'What do you intend to do with these missiles?'

Batalji grinned. 'It appears that we are about to embark on a period of negotiating with the West. It will do no harm for us to have an ace up our sleeve, eh? Six aces. But no one must know they are there, except you and me, Jagnuth.'

'What are you going to do?' Jim Crawford asked. 'I know Batalji seems to have guts to spare, but I don't think you can really trust this fellow, you know. A Mongol regards deceit as a way of life, save where he has given his word, and Batalji doesn't seem to have made any promises.'

Clive nodded. 'I know that. But how the hell else am I going to get us all out of this mess?'

'You don't think it might be an idea to stall another couple of weeks?' Al suggested. 'Once the weather breaks, and the road from the south becomes open, it'll be possible for the West to put a lot of pressure on our friend.'

'Why should they do that?' Clive asked him. 'As far as the West is concerned, this is none of their business right now. Last October there was a coup. Since then, nothing. The Russians may be agitated, but no one else is. So a European camera crew got itself killed trying to get in. They were fools to try, and were warned of the risks. So four Americans are stuck. There's been no suggestion that they are hostages, but even if they are so considered, America didn't exactly invade Lebanon when her nationals were being held there, back in the eighties and early nineties, and in that situation she *knew* they were being held as hostages. No, as I see it, no one is going to be interested in doing anything about this situation until and unless Batalji does something first, so if we are going to get out of there, we have to do it ourselves . . . even if it involves *making* Batalji do something.'

Crawford studied him. 'I've a notion you like the guy. Impalements and all.'

'I'd have to say yes, I do like him. Some things about him. He's an unmitigated thug with the upbringing and behavioural habits of a savage, but he has the instincts of a leader, and he's damned intelligent. But I'll tell you something, Jim: I'm more afraid of him. I don't think we ever want to forget that he claims descent from Genghis Khan, and is proud of it.'

'So what?' Al asked. 'You're not gonna say that he's about to lead a horde of sword-waving horsemen riding out of the steppes, shooting bows and arrows? Or that if he does it's gonna cause any problems, nowadays?'

'I don't think all that many of his people have swords, nowadays,' Clive retorted. 'Or bows and arrows. But there are enough assault rifles to go round.'

'And a brigade of tanks, and a few squadrons of fighter-bombers,' Al scoffed. 'Big deal.'

'And a missile delivery system?' Henri asked.

'He doesn't know how that works, and anyway, he's agreed to surrender it, according to Stanton.'

'Yes,' Clive said thoughtfully. 'I still think we always want to remember that Genghis Khan was around fifty when he first stepped into history. Batalji is only thirty-eight.'

'I was terrified when I heard.' Selphine sat, cross-legged on a pile of cushions, in the huge drawing room which had once been the Taychins' reception room. Here too there continued to be evidence of the coup, but it remained a most elegant room, with its gilt mirrors, only one of which was shattered, and gilt chandeliers, its thick-pile Persian carpets. It was well furnished, with settees and chairs as well as ornamental tables, but Selphine preferred to sit on the floor.

Batalji lounged on a settee. 'For me, or for Stanton?'

'For you both. You could both have been killed. What are you going to do?'

Batalji chose deliberately to misunderstand her. 'Stanton has told me of many things I must do.'

Selphine snorted. 'Is Stanton then your father? Your lord? Your master?'

Another lazy grin. 'Rather had I supposed he was *your* lord and master, Mother.'

'Ha! He is different. I find him amusing. I do not take his advice.'

'I think he will be a useful aide. Did not Genghis Khan learn much about the world, and statecraft, from the Chinese philosopher, Ye-lu Ch'u-ts'ai? This man Stanton has much to offer. He tells me I must make my own *yassa*. But he has told me many other things as well. I can use this man. I *will* use him.'

'To use him you will have to trust him.'

'That will not be necessary, Mother. He will do what I wish because I will make him.' The telephone jangled, and Batalji picked it up. 'Yes,' he said. 'Send her here immediately.' He replaced the phone and smiled at his mother. 'One of the reasons he will do as I ask has just arrived.'

Guards stood to attention as the double doors were thrown open, and Denise was escorted into the room. Selphine had remained with her son, and she continued to sit on her pile of skins and rugs. Batalji however stood up, and waved the escort away. The double doors closed again.

Batalji stared at Denise, and Denise returned his stare; she allowed Selphine hardly a glance. The Khan thought he had seldom seen a more attractive sight, because even wrapped up as she still was in her furs, he could tell she was a small woman, and that she was possessed of totally unusual features, from a Mongol point of view; she had the aquiline beauty of a Serhat. She might have been a reincarnation of his own mother as a girl, save that Selphine's nose was bigger – Denise's nose was small and chiselled, a thing of utter beauty. Clive Stanton's woman, he thought. 'Do you speak Russian?' he asked.

'I have learned,' Denise replied.

Her voice was low and musical. The foreign accent was a delight. And it was totally lacking in either fear or servility. Batalji felt like a small boy who has just been given a marvellous present. 'Are you not warm?' he asked.

Denise took off her fur hat, and auburn hair tumbled past her shoulders: it had not been cut for six months. Batalji caught his breath. He had never seen hair that colour. Then she took off her coat, looked left and right, and threw it across the back of a chair. She wore a loose woolly sweater over a white shirt, and white ski pants. The pants clung to every contour of her hips, buttocks, thighs, knees and calves. She might have been naked. He had only seen such physical perfection in very young Afghan girls, but Denise was no young girl – the swell of the bodice of her sweater told him that.

She understood his interest, but did not flush. Rather she half smiled, and for the first time looked at Selphine, who was speechless; Selphine could tell that her son had fallen in love, at first sight.

'What would you like?' Batalji asked.

'I should like to sit down,' Denise replied.

'Then please do so. I meant, would you like some tea? I will send for tea.'

Selphine snorted. The Khan of Yakutistan was behaving like a lovesick boy. Denise sat down. 'I would prefer brandy.'

'Brandy! Yes.' Batalji went to the sideboard, hunted through the bottles and decanters; he himself only ever drank vodka.

'Where are my friends?' Denise asked. 'Are they dead?'

'Your friends are alive,' Batalji assured her. 'And looking forward to meeting you again.' He handed her a tumbler of brandy, filled to the brim; he had taken one for himself. 'Welcome to Yakutsk.'

'Thank you.' Denise looked at the tumbler, sipped, and made a face. 'I would like a cigarette.'

'A cigarette! Yes . . .' He looked at his mother.

Selphine pointed at the sideboard. 'There are cigarettes in that box.'

Batalji opened the box, held it out. Denise took a cigarette, held it to her nose, and sniffed. 'My God!'

'There is something wrong with the cigarette?'

'How long have you had them?'

Batalji again looked at his mother. 'They were there when we came here, six months ago,' Selphine said.

Denise replaced the cigarette in the box. Batalji downed half his glass, and gave a little gasp; it was stronger than vodka. 'You like this brandy?'

'Not this brandy,' Denise said. 'It is shit. I can see why you drink it in tumblers. Do you make it yourself?'

Batalji looked totally disconcerted, while Selphine uttered another snort. 'This woman is not afraid of you,' she remarked in Yakut.

Batalji gave her an impatient glance. 'The man Stanton is especially anxious to see you,' he told Denise.

Denise held her shapely nose between thumb and forefinger, and drank some more brandy. 'And I am anxious to see him,' she agreed. 'I intend to scratch out both his eyes.'

'Eh?'

'Stanton told me he would send for me as soon as he reached civilisation,' Denise said. 'When did he get here?'

'Four months ago,' Selphine said.

'Four months! And for all of that time I have been left with that ...'

'The Khan's son,' Selphine said. 'What were you saying about him?'

'I was going to say that he is a lecherous asshole, who has as much idea how to treat a lady as a dog.'

Selphine began to laugh. 'Did my son ill-treat you?' Batalji asked.

Denise shrugged. 'He fucked me morning, noon and night.'

'Do you not like being fucked?' Selphine asked, apparently ingenuously.

'Not three times a day, at least not by the same man. There is a limit.' She looked at Batalji, holding up her empty glass. 'Do *you* know how to treat a lady?'

'He has never known any ladies,' Selphine pointed out. 'I thought you did not like the brandy?'

'It is growing on me.'

Batalji poured; his brain was seething. He was certain of only one thing: he had to possess this woman. He gave her the glass, allowed his fingers to touch hers for a moment. 'Stanton says you are a cameraperson. He says you came here to photograph me. I gave orders for your equipment to be brought with you to Yakutsk. Is it in working order?'

'I doubt it. It has been frozen solid for six months. With the two aircrew. Your son murdered them, you know. As well as two others. He is a murdering shit.'

'Do you realise you are speaking of the next Khan of Yakutistan?' Selphine demanded.

'If that is the case,' Denise replied, coolly, 'then the devil help you all. Because God won't.'

Selphine was as speechless as Batalji had been earlier. 'We have cameras here in Yakutsk for you to see,' Batalji said.

'I use my own camcorder,' Denise told me. 'Or nothing.'

Batalji scratched his head. 'You must be hungry,' he said.

'Yes. When do I see Stanton? And Georges and Henri?'

'After we have eaten.'

'I will call the others,' Selphine said.

'No,' Batalji said. 'Mademoiselle l'Auberon and I will dine alone.'

Selphine left with a good deal of snorting, and Batalji escorted Denise to the great dinning room. 'I don't like that woman,' Denise remarked.

'She is my mother.'

'That explains a great deal. Well, I don't think she likes me, either.'

'I am certain of it.' Batalji wondered if she could be shocked out of her amazing arrogance. 'If I gave you to her, do you know what she would do to you? She would cut off your breasts, for a start. Then she would cut off your fingers and toes, and your nose, and tear out your tongue, and then she would gouge out your eyes. Finally she would thrust a sharp stake up your ass.'

'If you are trying to save food by putting me off my dinner,' Denise told him. 'Forget it. I could eat a horse.' She entered the dining room. 'You really are the Khan of this dump?'

'Dump?'

'Well, you wouldn't call Yakutiya a country, now would you?'

'It is now called Yakutistan, and it is a country. It will be a famous country, soon.' He gestured her to the sideboards, which were laden with dishes. 'Help yourself.'

Denise sat down, exactly in the centre of the huge table. 'I prefer to be helped. Show me that you are a gentleman.'

Batalji hesitated. 'You know I can have you whipped?' he asked.

'And then start cutting bits off me? Why should you want to do that, Mr Khan? Once I'm gone, I'm gone. You won't find another one like me, you know.'

Batalji was very afraid she might be right. 'My name is Batalji,' he said. 'Call me Batalji.' He went to the sideboard. 'I don't know what you wish to eat.'

'I will eat whatever you are eating,' Denise said. 'See? I am prepared to trust you.' Batalji filled two plates, came back to sit beside her. 'Is there no wine?' Denise asked.

'There is vodka.' He fetched the jug.

'You drink vodka with your meal?' she asked. 'You are no better than your son.'

Batalji filled her glass, sat beside her again, leaned across, and touched the front of her sweater. Denise ate some sausage, her expression somewhat distasteful. Batalji's hand slid down to her waist, and moved beneath the sweater. Denise finished chewing, swallowed, and drank some vodka. She gave a little shudder. Batalji released the waistband of her ski pants and slipped his hand over her nylon-clad stomach. Denise started on another mouthful.

Batalji's hand slipped up again, under shirt and sweater, and found her breasts, to hold them, lightly but possessively. In their size and weight they were everything he had ever wanted in a woman's breasts. Denise turned her head to look at him. 'I wish to fuck you,' he said.

'Well,' she said, and took another mouthful. 'You will have to wait until after dinner.'

The Europeans ate their dinner in gloomy silence, and after the meal, sat in more gloomy silence, watching the minutes tick away. 'Something has gone wrong,' Henri complained.

'The flight has been delayed, that is all,' Georges argued.

'Or Barone has refused to let her go.'

'Barone would not dare defy his father,' Georges argued.

'This woman must be something very special,' Jim Crawford remarked.

'She is,' Clive acknowledged.

'To all three of you?'

'Yes,' Henri said.

Joe stood in the doorway. 'You are summoned to the Palace, Mr Stanton.'

Clive swallowed the last of his vodka. 'Wish me luck.' It was now quite late in the evening, but the Palace was a blaze of light. By now he was a familiar figure, and there were no formalities before he was hurried up the stairs and along corridors, in a direction he had not been before. He had not arrived at his destination when he and his guards encountered Selphine.

'Ha!' she commented. 'You have lost her, Stanton. And I have lost my son. That woman is a witch. Did you know that, Stanton?'

'Which woman, Princess?'

'One day,' Selphine said, 'I will have her. One day. She has bewitched my son. One day...'

A door opened further down the corridor. 'Mother,' Batalji said. 'Why do you not go to bed? Come here, Stanton.'

Clive glanced at Selphine, at her expression of mingled anger and dejection, and then followed Batalji into one of the many reception rooms with which this palace abounded. Here there was no evidence at all of violence or disruption, just masses of gilt and mirrors – the Taychins' idea of beauty. And the inevitable ornate desk, behind which Batalji sat, waving Clive to a chair in front of him. 'I have decided what we will do,' Batalji announced.

Clive wanted to ask whether Denise had arrived, but decided to be patient. 'I have considered what you said to me, last night and this morning,' Batalji went on. 'Much of it makes good sense. I am going to try to co-operate with you, but you must be prepared to co-operate with me.'

'I have here the draft of the proposals I made.'

Batalji nodded. 'I will have them studied. Now, to begin with, I know you wish to inform your people in the West that you are still alive, and that you and all of your people are well. Tomorrow evening you will make a telecast to the West. I have here a draft of what you will say, but you may put it into your own words.'

Clive took the paper, scanned it. He spoke Russian much better than he read it, but the gist was simple enough. He was required to inform the world firstly that he and his team were alive and being well treated by the people of Yakutistan; that they were not in any sense prisoners, but were merely waiting for an improvement in the weather before leaving. Batalji's ingenuousness almost made him smile: they had waited six months for an improvement in the weather? Secondly he was to tell the world that the coup had been made necessary by the tyrannical and undemocratic methods, the systematic abuse of civil rights, employed by the Taychin regime. He had to smile at that.

Thirdly he was to say that the coup had been entirely successful, supported as it had been by the vast majority of the people of Yakutistan; the Russian garrison had surrendered after very little resistance, and would be repatriated to Russia as soon as weather conditions permitted. Fourthly, he was to say that regrettably, members of the Taychin secret police had attempted to resist the will of the people and had been killed. This resistance had been led by Boris Taychin himself, and he had died in the storming of the Presidential Palace. His wife had died at her husband's side. That at least was true, Clive reflected.

Finally, he was to inform the world that while the new government in Yakutistan desired to be friends with all men, to trade with them and to take its place upon the international stage, it was determined to defend its hard-won independence, which it appealed to the rest of the world to recognise. There was no mention of impalements or condemning innocent people to freeze to death. 'Well?' Batalji demanded when Clive raised his head.

'It is brilliant. Unfortunately, it is not entirely true.'

'Truth is a point of view. Will you broadcast that?'

Clive considered, and temporised. 'I do not yet know, for instance, that all of my party is safe and well. Has Mademoiselle l'Auberon been delivered here?'

'Yes. I said that she would be, and she has.'

'I would need to see her before I make this broadcast.'

'You will. Are there any other points?'

'You have actually mentioned nothing of the release of my team and the Americans. If you consider truth to be a point of view, then presumably an improvement in the weather is also a point of view.'

'The Americans, and your French associates, will be allowed to leave as soon as you have made the broadcast and arrangements have been made with Moscow for the safe landing of one of my aircraft.'

Clive gave a brief smile. 'Moscow will say it is one of *their* aircraft.'

'I understand this. Which is why I say that arrangements will have to be made.'

'You say the Frenchmen and the Americans. That leaves the two women and myself.'

'I am still hoping you will act as my ambassador to the West, to the United Nations. The women will remain here until you have carried out your assignment.'

'You mean to keep two Western women as hostages? That is no way to win acceptance from the West.'

Batalji smiled. 'The two women will stay in Yakutistan of their own free will, Stanton. You will tell the world this. When you have completed your assignment, I will endeavour to *persuade* Mademoiselle l'Auberon and Miss Leigh to leave Yakutistan, if you still wish them to do so. I am not promising that I will be successful.'

'I'm afraid I will have to hear that from their own mouths, Your Excellency.'

'If you are satisfied that they are staying of their own free will, will you act as my envoy?'

'If you will promise me that there will be no more impalements. No more executions at all, and that all these repatriations of which you speak will be carried out.' He was yielding principal here, but he did not see that he had too much alternative. The important thing was to keep Batalji playing until he had got the women out.

'For a man who is entirely at my mercy, you make a great many conditions, Stanton.'

'Am I at your mercy, Your Excellency? Or are you understanding that you are at the mercy of world opinion, which I am going to have to persuade to accept you? I cannot persuade the world to accept a monster.'

Batalji stroked his chin. 'I am still creating a government, a nation here, Stanton. Most of my people are behind me. But there are always dissident elements, in any society. If any attempt is made, by an individual or by a group of individuals, acting on their own or in the name of Moscow or the CIA or anyone else, to overthrow my government, I will kill them. If you expect me to do otherwise, you are a fool.'

'I understand that you must preserve your government, Your Excellency. But unnecessary killing is still anathema to the West. We would expect you to arrest the conspirators where possible, and produce them for trial. As for whether they should then be executed, is a matter of debate. But in any event, they should be executed as humanely as possible. Impalement is barbaric and unacceptable.'

'I will note what you say. But there is also the point that I am hoping not all the Russian prisoners will choose to go home. They have many skills that I need. In particular I need the tank crews and the aircraft pilots and mechanics. These, and other technicians, I am endeavouring to persuade to remain here in Yakutistan, and work for me.'

'Endeavouring to persuade?'

Batalji grinned. 'I am offering them very good salaries, Stanton. You cannot object to that. Just as I am offering you a great deal to work for me.'

'Most of the things you are offering I cannot accept,' Clive pointed out. 'And now you tell me you are keeping the two women...'

Batalji raised his finger. 'They are remaining of their own free will.'

'Well, that I am waiting to be told.'

'Of course,' Batalji said. 'Shall we go?'

Female guards stood to attention, and Batalji opened a door; Clive discovered that they were entering yet another apartment he had not visited before. Here as usual were opulent if essentially tawdry furnishings, and pleasant odours. 'This is where Boris Taychin kept his chief mistress,' Batalji explained.

'Are you trying to tell me you have attempted to appropriate Mademoiselle l'Auberon as well?' Clive demanded.

Batalji grinned. 'You will have to ask her.' He opened an inner door, showed Clive into a bedroom. Against the far wall there was a king-size divan bed, with pink sheets, scattered and rumpled. In the centre of the bed lay Denise. 'Ah!' Batalji said. 'She is asleep. But she has had an exhausting time of it.'

Clive glanced at him, then looked at the bed again. Denise was naked, and in the overheated room had kicked off her covers; lying on her side, facing them, she made an utterly entrancing sight. 'She has been your mistress, has she not?' Batalji asked. 'You may go closer.'

Clive approached the bed, footfalls deadened by the soft carpet. Strands of Denise's hair had flopped across her face, and these fluttered as she breathed. There were one or two slight discolourations on her flesh, but nothing that might not have been caused by shared lovemaking. Certainly she had not recently been beaten in any way, nor were there any marks of arms and legs having been tied, or even gripped very hard. Behind him the door closed. Batalji had left him alone with her. Clive had no doubt that the room was bugged, as it had belonged to the Taychins. On the other hand, he had no objection to Batalji listening to what he had to say, because he would not be able to understand any of it.

He sat on the bed, touched her shoulder. Denise stirred and

stretched. 'Denise,' Clive said in French. 'Wake up.'

Denise rolled on to her back, and stretched again. Clive thought that she and Sintax would make a good pair. Oh, if only they *were* going to make a good pair. 'Denise,' he said again.

Denise half smiled, although her eyes remained closed. 'Shit,' she commented. 'Not again, so soon. You are worse than that son of yours.'

He shook her shoulder. 'It's me, Clive.'

Denise opened her eyes, identified him, and closed her eyes again. 'Don't tell me I am to be shared between you.'

'You mean Batalji has fucked you?'

Denise opened her eyes again. 'Why do men always ask stupid questions? Listen, Clive, darling, I am very tired. I was fast asleep, you know. There was no wine for dinner. Only vodka. Let me sleep, and I will talk with you tomorrow.'

'It has to be now, Denise.' She rolled across the bed, got up, went to the bathroom, and washed her face. 'That was exactly how I felt this morning,' Clive told her. 'Denise. If you wish, you can leave this place, with me.'

Denise appeared in the bathroom doorway, patting her face with a towel. 'I am ruining my complexion,' she remarked. 'Leave this place? To go where?'

'Back to Paris.'

'Paris,' she said dreamily. 'It seems so long ago that I was in Paris.'

'Well, I shall be leaving in a few days. Georges and Henri are going even sooner.'

She knelt beside him on the bed. 'Are they all right? Georges and Henri?'

'They're fine. Are *you* all right?'

'Do I not look all right?'

'You mean you survived Barone?'

'He was a boy,' Denise said scornfully.

'And now his father?'

'Ah,' Denise said, and lay down again to do some more stretching.

Clive had an enormous urge to join her. But not with Batalji watching. 'So,' he said. 'We will leave together, eh? And then we will get married.'

Denise sat up. 'I don't think marriage is something one wants to rush into,' she said.

'For God's sake! How long have we known each other?'

'Seven years.'

'And in that time . . .'

'You have fucked me seventeen times. I keep a diary.'

'Oh? I had no idea it was that often.'

'You see? You are bored with me already.'

'Absolutely not. I adore you. And you could say we've made a start. Always begin as you mean to go on, I say.'

Denise got out of bed and went to the dressing table. Clive followed her. He had not really taken in the dressing table before. Now he saw it was covered in jewellery. From amongst the several pieces Denise picked up a bracelet and handed it to him. 'Do you like that?'

It was a thick, heavy gold band, encrusted with . . . He bent lower. 'Are those garnets and citrines?'

'You are an asshole,' Denise told him. 'Those are rubies and topaz.' She slipped it on to her arm, extending the arm so that the jewels caught the light. 'The Khan says it belonged to Madame Taychin. She had some very nice pieces.'

'Aren't you a little old to be accepting bribes?'

'Now I know you are bored with me. Calling me old!' She tried on a diamond solitaire ring, made a *moue*. 'She must have had big fingers. But the size can be reduced.'

'Denise . . .' Clive caught her hands. 'Listen to me. I am leaving here, and I am taking you with me. Right?'

Denise raised her head. Her eyes, like her face, were expressionless. 'I wish to stay here, for a while,' she said.

'For God's sake . . .' He was getting angry. 'Just to sleep with Batalji and wear his stolen jewellery? What are you, some kind of whore?'

'Would you mind letting go of me?'

'Not until I've talked some sense into you.'

'I wish you to let go of me,' Denise said. 'So that I may slap your face.' Clive let go of her, and she slapped his face. Then she took off the jewellery and went back to bed. 'Get out,' she said.

Clive stood above her. 'Okay, I apologise. I spoke right out of turn. Denise, you must see that you cannot stay here. You're ... you're just too valuable a human being to become the mistress of a Mongol bandit.'

'I am going to be his Queen,' Denise said, lying on her back and closing her eyes. 'He wants me to bear him a son. I have never had a child. I think it is time. He says if I bear him a son, he will raise me above all other women in Yakutistan. I think that sounds rather attractive. I am prepared to give it a whirl.'

'And get your throat cut?' Denise opened her eyes. Clive knelt on the bed beside her. 'Listen. Batalji's mother hates you.'

'Oh, I know that. My throat is the last part of me she wants to cut. But she can never harm me. Batalji will see to that.'

'Then what about Mortana? She may come across as a softie, at least when compared with her mother-in-law, but she's a Yakut, a woman of the steppes. How do you think she's going to react if you start producing children for her husband? And if Batalji starts making you number one?'

'I haven't met this woman.'

'I have.'

'Well, Batalji tells me she understand that he needs more sons. I can believe that. Barone is an asshole.'

Clive sighed. 'Batalji already has a Western mistress. Did you know that?'

'Some American woman. He is disappointed in her. She has not given him any children. American women do not know about sex, really. They are too hung up on it.'

'She happens to be the incumbent. How do you think *she* is going to react?'

Denise smiled. 'You will have to tell me. Batalji says he has given her to you.'

'He keeps saying things like that. Do you really suppose I can accept such a situation?'

'I think you should. She may not know much about it, but Batalji says she's a big girl. You could have a lot of fun with her. So what are you afraid of? What people will say when you go home? Why go home? Stay here and enjoy yourself. We're in Shangri-la. Why knock it?'

Clive actually felt like hitting her. Denise! 'Shangri-la! Are you aware that this new lover of yours has a nasty little habit of impaling people?'

'He's primitive,' Denise agreed. 'But, he's primitive in bed. That's not so bad.'

Clive stood up. 'Denise, what the hell has got into you? When last I saw you, you were a responsible member of the human race. Believe me, I'm sorry I didn't manage to get you out of there before six months. But . . .'

'I have just remembered,' Denise said. 'I am going to scratch out both of your eyes.'

'Just tell me what has happened to you,' he begged. 'Explain it so I'll understand.'

Denise sat up and brought in her legs to assume the lotus position. 'I am not sure I can explain it to myself. I know that you and Georges and Henri think I am a totally liberated woman. I think, by the standards of the West, I am. But are there any Western liberated women? We speak of liberation, but what do we mean? To be able to stick up a middle figuer at men? What is liberated about that, if you are a true woman? When in exchange you are forced to take on all the duties and responsibilities of a man? I don't call that liberation. Do you know of what I have always dreamed? It is of not having to work, not having to watch my figure, not having to open letters or go to places I don't feel like going or wear clothes I don't feel like wearing. All I have ever wanted to do was eat, drink, sleep, fuck . . . and wear nice things when I felt like wearing them. Batalji is allowing me to do what I want to do. As I said, I think I will give it a whirl.'

'I'd give you that freedom, Denise. I just never understood it was what you really wanted.'

'Dear Clive.' She blew him a kiss. 'You might wish to give

me those things, but you couldn't. Because you are just as much a prisoner of your environment as anyone in the West. Batalji has broken out of his environment.'

'And when you do get fat, and he grows tired of you? As he seems to have grown tired of Miss Leigh?'

Denise lay down again. 'He will not grow tired of me, once I bear a child for him. That is where the American has failed.'

Clive gave up. As Selphine had said, he had lost her. At least for the time being. Perhaps by the time he came back from his mission ... because with Denise remaining, he would have to come back. 'Anyway,' she said, with charming inconsistency, 'I have my career to think of.'

'You have just told me you don't want a career.'

'I don't want to have to work. That doesn't mean I can't have a career. Batalji has promised me the scoop of a lifetime. All my life I have been the one who cranked the camera, eh? While you have got the name and the fame. Well, this is going to be my show. Batalji says I can photograph him all I like. Him, and Yakutistan, and everything in it. It will make me famous.'

'You don't have a camera any more.'

'Batalji has promised me the most expensive camcorder in the world.'

He went to the door, and there paused. He had one last arrow in his quiver. 'You seem damned confident you can become pregnant by Batalji. How come you didn't by Barone?'

Denise did not open her eyes. 'Barone was a boy,' she said.

Clive closed the door behind himself and stood in the corridor, watched by three of the women guards. After a few minutes Batalji came hurrying along. 'I assume you were watching?' Clive asked.

'The wonders of modern science, Stanton. I was even able to get the gist of your conversation.'

Clive nodded. 'That figures. Okay, Your Excellency, you have won this round.'

'Now, come and visit Rosemary,' Batalji said. 'Or are you too tired?'

'You can't pretend that *she*'s going to want to stay here, after being thrown over for Denise.'

'I have told you, she is yours.'

'And I have told you that I don't want her.'

'No, no, my friend,' Batalji said. 'What you have told me is that you do not feel able to take her, because of your mores. But I insist. It is best for me to provide you with two important reasons for returning to Yakutistan in triumph, your mission completed.'

'Your Excellency,' Clive said. 'We have a saying in the West, that you can lead a horse to water, but you cannot make him drink.'

Batalji grinned. 'Not even if he knows that if he does not, the water will become very muddied?' Clive frowned at him. 'Barone is very upset at losing Mademoiselle l'Auberon,' Batalji said. 'He has asked for Miss Leigh. It seems he has developed a liking for Western women. It seems to me that you and Miss Leigh need to discuss this situation. Very urgently.'

THE TENTH CHRONICLE

Yakutsk, Spring 2001

It was now three o'clock in the morning, but time did not seem to matter to Batalji. 'I assume you will again be watching and listening?' Clive asked.

'A ruler must know what is going on,' Batalji said, apparently seriously. 'I think how you get on will prove how useful as ambassador you are going to be. I would say you have some very persuasive arguments to put to her.'

Clive sighed, opened the door and went into the darkened apartment, began switching on lights. He was riding a roller coaster which had no end. Yet he could step off it any time he wished. Denise had made her bed and was prepared to lie on it, quite literally. He had nothing going for Rosemary Leigh. If she was destined for Barone's bed, then that was fate and it was probably what she deserved. He could pay lip service to Batalji, make his broadcast, flee this country, and then tell the truth.

But there was more involved than his dislike for dishonesty, or his undoubtedly outdated feelings of chivalry towards the two women. As he had tried to tell Crawford and Mather, there was something stirring out here on the steppes. Something immense, and rather frightening. It was absurd to suppose that not much more than a million primitives could possibly frighten the world. But then, no doubt the great empires of Persia and India, reeking of wealth and corruption, confident in their apparent power, had felt the same way in the twelfth and thirteenth centuries. It had taken only a few clean cuts on the sword, wielded by a man who cared nothing for their value and did not care whether he himself lived or died, to sweep those empires away. Had anything changed?

He stood in the bedroom doorway, looked at Rosemary Leigh. Like Denise she was just waking up as the light shone in her face. Like Denise, she stretched, and like Denise she had kicked the covers away from her naked body. But there the resemblance ended. Denise was like an awakening cat. Rosemary Leigh made him think of an awakening lioness.

'What the hell are you doing here?' she demanded, reaching for the sheet and drawing it to her throat. 'Do you know what time it is?'

He went up to the bed, sat on the end. 'Would you like to hear a bedtime story? It'll wake you up.'

Rosemary reached for the phone. 'I need help,' she said. 'This guy Stanton has somehow got loose and is in my room. Come and get him.' She listened, her expression one of incredulity, staring at Clive. Then she replaced the phone. 'Batalji sent you?'

'Would you like to hear my story?' Rosemary sank back down into the bed, the sheet held to her throat. Clive told her what he knew of the events of the past twenty-four hours. 'You are quite entitled to say it is my fault,' he agreed in advance. 'After all, I introduced Denise to Batalji. But ... there it is. Willy-nilly, we have swopped partners.'

'You try to get into this bed, and I'll kick you in the balls.'

'You don't seem to understand,' Clive explained. 'It's me, or Barone.'

'What?' She sat up, the sheet forgotten.

'Barone is upset at having to give up Denise, so he wants a

swap. Batalji has no objection to that, but he figures you might do more for me than Barone. He's going to hold you here as hostage for my being a good boy when I leave, on the basis that I shall be coming back to claim you.'

'That shit,' she commented. 'That absolute shit!'

'I think you should know that this apartment is bugged, both visually and audibly, and that Batalji is watching us and listening to us right this minute. He may just have someone with him who speaks English.' Rosemary looked at the light fittings and the mirrors. 'I have no idea where the camera is,' Clive told her. 'I looked the last time I was here, remember? But I know it's there. He wants to make sure that I learn to appreciate your charms before I leave ... just to make sure I come back.'

'And you think the whole thing is one big joke, is that it?'

'I don't like you any more than you like me, Miss Leigh. It would actually relieve me a great deal if you opted for Barone. Then I wouldn't have to be responsible for you.'

Rosemary Leigh glared at him, and lay down again. 'How do I know you are going to come back, anyway?' she asked.

'Denise, darling.'

'Fuck Denise.'

'That is what I would dearly like to do. Unfortunately, Batalji has done it first, and intends to keep on doing it first.'

'And you're still going to work for him? Impalements and all? You're a fucking coward as well as a lecherous asshole.'

'I don't have much choice. But I may as well tell you that with every word you utter, the concept of saving *your* asshole grows less attractive.'

Suddenly she smiled. 'If you hate me that much, you won't even be able to get it up.'

Clive smiled back. 'Try me.'

She shrugged, a magnificent sight. 'Seems like I don't have a hell of a lot of choice, either.'

'Well, I have to hand it to you, Clive,' Jim Crawford said.

The Americans, as well as Georges and Henri, had been

given their European clothes as well as all their luggage, and a car was waiting to take them to the airport. 'I'd like to know how the hell you did it,' Al said. 'I'm grateful, mind.'

Clive shrugged. 'I agreed to work for him.'

'I can imagine what that cost,' Crawford said. 'But . . . we're still grateful. What about the girls?'

'I'm afraid the deal is that they stay here until I return. With whatever goodies I can raise for Batalji.'

'Suppose you don't get any?'

'I have to get something. And you fellows are going to have to help me. So, keep quiet about things like the executions, at least until the girls are out.'

'You're sure they're coming out?'

'If it is humanly possible, I will get them out, Jim. I can't say more than that. But until I do, or until I have definitely failed, we have to play ball with Batalji. Now here is a list of people in the States I need to see. Can I leave that with you? Remember, Rosemary's life is on the line.' Crawford nodded, thoughtfully. 'She'd also be grateful if you'd call her folks and reassure them,' Clive added. 'I'll be seeing them myself when I follow, of course.'

'And just what will be happening to Rosemary and your French friend while they're left here alone?' Al asked. 'You say the Frenchwoman has already been raped by this guy Barone. And Rosemary . . .'

'Has been Batalji's mistress for the past six months. I can only tell you that they are both unharmed, and don't seem too unhappy with their situations.'

He thought that might even be true. It was certainly true about Denise. As for Rosemary Leigh . . . He kept telling himself that it had really happened, because it was difficult to be certain. He had been very tired, and terribly aware that he was putting on a display. Clive Stanton, the principal in a sex show for a savage from the steppes. But he hadn't been the principal. Having made her decision, Rosemary Leigh had held nothing back. No doubt she did loathe him, as she had told him several times. Thus she had intended to milk him dry, leave him in no doubt that when it came to sex he was in the little league, and at the same time show the watching Batalji what he was throwing over. But he had also felt she was expiating her own guilt. She knew she had surrendered to the sheer masculinity of Batalji, and she hated herself for it. Because of that hatred, she now loathed the entire masculine sex. Either way, he was now utterly bound up with this regime. But he couldn't explain that to these decent men, whose only mistake was that they had been in Yakutsk at the wrong time. He knew they felt he was cavalierly risking his life for the two women – one day they might learn the truth.

'Your telephone call to London is through, Mr Stanton,' said Nita. In addition to all his other problems, she had been appointed his personal assistant, as she spoke English.

'Clive? My God, Clive!' Threlfall sounded like a man who had just learned he had won the national lottery. 'I caught your broadcast! Terrific! Do you know you're officially dead, old man? There's even been a memorial service for you at the Abbey.'

'I hope you recorded what was said,' Clive remarked.

'All good, dear boy. All good. I never knew you were such a perfect specimen. Now, when are you coming out?'

'In a couple of days. Have you contacted my parents?'

'They're overwhelmed. They can hardly wait to see you.'

'What about Holly Barnett?'

'She contacted me, to find out if it's true. Two days! Right. I've arranged everything. There are full-scale interviews on all channels, with transatlantic hook-ups. The publishers want your book in three months, so . . .'

'What book?'

'The one you're about to start writing.'

'That will have to wait.'

'Wait? They're paying a quarter of a million. And the *Sunday Times* has bought first rights for another quarter. And . . .'

'Philip, old boy,' Clive said. 'I am not writing any books right now. Nor am I wasting a lot of time appearing on TV chat shows. When I come back I have work to do.'

'Of course you have, my dear fellow. That's what I'm trying to tell you.'

'And I am trying to tell you that I no longer work for Anglo-French Television.'

There was a moment's silence. 'Say again?' Threlfall said.

'I am now working for President Borjigin. He has appointed me his ambassador to the West.'

'Good God!'

'Now, I need to have a meeting with the Foreign Secretary. Will you arrange it, please?'

'Well, I say, old man, if you are no longer . . .'

'Listen,' Clive said. 'If you play ball with me, I will play ball with you. I'll give you an exclusive interview on my impressions here.' Well, some of them, anyway, he thought. 'How about it, old man?'

'The Ambassador to Russia is on the other line, Mr Stanton,' Nita told him.

'Have to go,' Clive told Threlfall. 'Don't let me down on this.'

'You will be accompanied by Colonel Serhat, and the woman Nita,' Batalji told Clive.

'Don't you ever get tired of picking women for me?' Clive asked.

'A man should always have a woman close by,' Batalji said seriously. 'Knowing that she is there allows him to concentrate on what he has to do. Wishing a woman was there distracts him from his tasks.' Clive really couldn't argue with that very simple masculine philosophy. 'And you have much to do that is of great importance to Yakutistan, and to me,' Batalji added, staring at him. Clive nodded. He had not before seen Batalji so serious. 'And to you, and the women,' Batalji added.

'If I am going to make promises on your behalf,' Clive reminded him. 'I want to be certain those promises will be kept.'

Batalji grinned. 'Am I not a man of my word? Now go and spend a last night with Rosemary. You leave tomorrow morning.'

*

'You *are* coming back?' Rosemary asked.

'Don't tell me you're going to miss me?'

'I am not going to miss you,' she said. 'I just want to feel that one day I am going to get out of this hole.'

'Don't despair. I'm hoping Batalji will get tired of Denise and want to switch back again.'

She stuck out her tongue at him.

CHAPTER 10

The West, Summer 2001

'So you will appreciate, Mr President, that President Borjigin is prepared to co-operate in every possible way,' Clive said, as persuasively as he could. 'Of course he regrets the bloodshed involved in his takeover of the Taychin Government, but it was inevitable.'

President Anatole Boroslov looked at Sir Rodney Etherton. 'Her Majesty's Government feels that these are positive developments, sir,' Etherton said. 'If your troops are really being repatriated . . .'

'Borjigin is keeping their weapons,' Boroslov remarked, his voice deep. He was a man beset with all the problems bequeathed by the Yeltsin Government, to which was added the constantly increasing friction with the Ukraine. The Yakutiya crisis was just about the last straw.

'For which he will pay a negotiated price, sir,' Clive put in.

'What with? And who negotiates? You tell me he wishes to co-operate? I have invited him to come to Moscow. He refuses. Instead he has sent you. An Englishman. That is co-operation?'

'I am accredited, sir.'

'Borjigin has no right to accredit anyone. He is an outlaw and a rebel.'

'Well, sir, obviously the first thing President Borjigin requires is recognition. Whatever he may have been in the past, I cannot see any great difficulty in this. Yakutistan has always been virtually independent. The Taychin regime was a hangover from the bad days of Soviet rule, as I am sure you know, Mr President. President Borjigin has the backing of the vast majority of his people, which he is prepared to prove by holding elections the moment the independence of Yakutistan is recognized. Now, I have explained, sir, that he is willing to permit trade between your two countries. He has coal to sell, and soon he will have oil . . .'

'It is the oil of which I wish to speak,' Boroslov said.

'I am sorry, sir, but President Borjigin wishes to negotiate with Western companies to develop his resources. He is prepared to negotiate a price for his coal, however . . .'

'That coal was paid for, last September. And was never delivered.'

'It was paid for to the Taychin Government, Mr President. Thus its delivery was overtaken by events. President Borjigin is prepared to renegotiate that sale . . . Perhaps it can be used as a part of the purchase price of the planes and tanks he wishes to buy . . .' President Boroslov waved his hand, dismissively.

'Poor chap,' Etherton commented as he entertained Clive to a whisky in his office. 'There is damn all he can do. But he wants to do *something*. Borjigin has been an absolute pain in the neck to the Russians for the past ten years and more. I hope your man understands this.'

'He does,' Clive said. 'Which is why he intends to hang on to those weapons.'

'Hm,' Etherton commented. 'If he has already been paid for that coal, he is acting the outlaw all over again, you know.'

'Financially, he is in a precarious position, at least for the moment. As to what happened to the money paid to the

Taychins, I do not know. All Batalji knows is that he has a large amount of coal he wishes to sell . . .'

'You mean to exchange for weapons he has obtained illegally.'

'Well, sir, he is hardly interested in being paid for it in Russian roubles. He wants hard currency, or its equivalent.'

'Tell me straight, Stanton: is he sound?'

'I believe he is, Your Excellency.' He had better be, he thought.

'Yes. Well, I have arranged for you to be debriefed by the FO as soon as you reach London, so . . .'

'You'll pardon me, Your Excellency, but I am not going to be debriefed by anyone.' Etherton raised his eyebrows. 'You have seen my papers, Sir Rodney,' Clive said. 'I am the accredited envoy-at-large for the Government of Yakutistan. I have no intention of having any private meetings with FO personnel. However, if you would arrange a meeting for me with the Foreign Secretary or the Prime Minister, then I should be grateful.'

Etherton stared at him. 'I was *going* to invite you to dinner,' he remarked.

'What do you think of the situation?' asked President Boroslov of his Minister of the Interior.

Ewfim Dolgorukov stroked his chin. 'Stanton is either a scoundrel or a fool.'

'He is neither of those, Ewfim,' Boroslov said. 'He is an idealist, which means he is a dangerous man. Not in himself, but in what he believes he can accomplish. What he *wishes* to accomplish.'

Dolgorukov cracked a knuckle. 'Do you wish him . . . ah . . .'

'I have said, he is not dangerous in himself. He merely has to be monitored very carefully. No, the danger lies in his source of ideas, his source of power. Tell me, Ewfim, was not Batalji Borjigin condemned to death in 1989?'

'In absentia, certainly. After his escape from prison in

Yakutsk. He was condemned again, in absentia, following his assassination of Andrei Taychin.'

'But the sentence has never been carried out.'

Dolgorukov cracked some more knuckles, uneasily. 'It is generally supposed that those days are history, Anatole.'

'Nothing is ever history, in political matters,' Boroslov told him. 'There are merely changing circumstances. I am sure there are one or two retired KGB people who are capable of taking out Batalji Borjigin.'

'It will not be easy,' Dolgorukov muttered. 'At the moment, Yakutiya is impregnable. And Borjigin will be well guarded.'

'I did not say it had to be done tomorrow, Ewfim. Again, times will soon change. The snows are melting, and Borjigin wishes to encourage trade and have experts assist him to develop his oil. Yakutiya is going to become accessible all over again, and as time goes by, as he is recognised by the West, and by us, as we do not seem to have any choice in the matter, Borjigin is going to become more confident and less paranoid. Then he becomes more vulnerable.'

'Yes, but he is still only one man.'

'He is *the* man, Ewfim. That has always been obvious, and the man Stanton has just confirmed it. Borjigin was the heart and soul of the revolt. He is now the heart and soul of the state he has set up. Without him, it will be nothing. Without him, the nomads will simply fade away and go back to their herds and their wandering. Find me the man to rid the world of this convicted murderer and robber and deserter. In the utmost secrecy, of course. And when the time is right, or necessary. It may be possible to deal with Borjigin. Who knows? But if it is not, then we must be prepared. We must have our man chosen, primed, and targeted.'

'Or woman,' Dolgorukov said thoughtfully.

'Eh?'

'There are only four known facts about Batalji Borjigin, Anatole. One is that he is a monster when aroused. The second is that he is a born soldier. The third is that he drinks like a fish. And the fourth is that he is a womaniser in the class of Casanova. I will find you an assassin. Give me a month.'

'Home,' Clive said, ushering Nita and Almani into the flat.

'But this is very nice,' Almani said. 'Very large. How many people live here?'

'One man and one cat. Actually, it has two bedrooms. I'm afraid you and Nita will have to share.'

'My instructions are not to let you out of my sight,' Nita reminded him. 'And besides, do you not like me any more?'

'Oh, I do. But this is Holly.'

He had telephoned from Moscow, and Holly now emerged from the kitchen, Sintax in her arms. 'We thought you were dead,' she remarked, placing the cat on the floor.

Holly had dark hair and very white skin. She suggested domesticity rather than dynamism, which was probably why she had lasted longer than any of Clive's female acquaintances. She also liked cats, and was prepared to be taken advantage of. Sintax walked across the room, sniffed Clive's trouser leg, and rubbed herself against it. 'She loves you,' Holly commented.

Clive scooped the cat up to give it a hug. 'This is Colonel Serhat, and Captain Strilenka,' he explained. 'They love me, too.'

'Am I allowed to take my cat back to Yakutistan?' Clive asked at dinner.

'But of course,' Almani said. 'There are not enough cats in Yakutistan.'

'I'm afraid Sintax is not going to be able to help you there. Would you be prepared to hold on to the girl for another few weeks?' he asked Holly. 'I'll pick her up on my way back.'

Holly had spent the evening warming to Almani, although she still regarded Nita with suspicion. 'I might. If I can come to Yakutistan with you too.'

'You'd probably find it a bit hot ... at this time of year,' he told her.

*

John Stanton was a heavier, greyer version of his son, in contrast to his wife Elizabeth, who was small and compact – once, Clive suspected, his mother had been an English version of Denise, which might explain a lot of things. 'Oh, Clive,' she said, sitting with her arm around him. 'When are you going to give it up?'

'Not for a while, I'm afraid, Ma. I have too much to do.'

'The chap on TV was saying that you're working for this fellow Bor-whatever,' John Stanton said. 'You're not a politician.'

'I am one now, Pa. At least, a diplomat, I hope.'

'But you're not a Russian, either.' John Stanton peered at his son. 'You haven't given up British nationality, I hope.'

'No, Pa. Things like that don't matter to Batalji Borjigin.'

'But you're not going to live there?' Elizabeth Stanton pressed.

'Only for a little while,' Clive promised her. 'Until the job is done.'

The Foreign Secretary studied Clive, stroking his chin. 'If I may say so, Stanton,' he remarked. 'That was a remarkable adventure. But you make this man Borjigin sound like a paragon. That doesn't tie in with what we know of his past.'

'He is not a paragon, sir. He is a very hard man, and he can be ruthless. The way he eliminated the Taychin regime proves that. He is also as bold as a lion; I've seen him fighting for his life. But he genuinely wants to be a legitimate member of the international community.'

'You mean, he desperately needs money,' the Foreign Secretary commented. 'I am sure you know that this Government has already invested some considerable sum in the Russian economy. I doubt my colleagues will be interested in extending any aid to a regime which is, to say the least, unstable.'

'Foreign Secretary, I would describe the Borjigin Government as the most stable in the world, at this moment.'

'What you mean is, it is a dictatorship.'

'It is President Borjigin's most earnest wish to hold elections not later than next summer. Sir, I quite accept that the United Kingdom may not be interested in financing the regime, but I would assume you have no objections to trading links?'

'And trading credits, Stanton?'

'They would be useful. But I assume you are aware that Yakutistan has immense oil reserves?'

'I have heard rumours. They are not yet proven.'

'Oh, they are proven, Foreign Secretary. You check with our man in Moscow.'

'Even if proven,' the Foreign Secretary said, 'they still have to be developed.'

'That is one of the reasons for my embassy,' Clive said. 'There is a possibility that President Borjigin may be interested in having the development undertaken by a British Consortium.'

The two men looked at each other for several seconds. 'In return for trade credits,' the Foreign Secretary said.

'Amongst other things.'

'Perhaps you should tell me what these other things are, Mr Stanton.'

'These people never say yes, or no, you understand,' Clive explained to Almani. 'Like a good woman, it is always maybe. I think recognition of Batalji's Government is certain. Trade credits, for a limited amount, are probable, following recognition. Sponsorship for membership of the United Nations is also likely, but after a reasonable period of time.'

'What is a reasonable period of time?' Almani asked.

'A couple of years. The Foreign Secretary suggests that Yakustistan, like the other members of the CIS in the beginning, permit Russia to represent it for the time being.'

'Yakutistan is not a member of the CIS,' Almani pointed out. 'And we could never permit Russia to represent our interests.'

'It really would be to your advantage to get over that psychological hump and join the union.'

'What about weapons?'

'Now that is going to be difficult in England. The Government is dead against selling weapons to Third World countries.'

'We are not a Third World country.'
'I'm afraid you are to the British Government.'
'Are there no private arms manufacturers?'
'Oh, indeed. But after what happened in Iraq, licences to export arms, or anything which could be converted into arms, are very hard to come by. Don't take this too seriously: Britain isn't the only country in the world.'
'I am glad of that. Where do we go from here?'
'Paris.'

'Do you know,' Henri said, sipping his aperitif. 'I sometimes find it hard to believe it all actually happened. But for Denise . . .'
'Denise is having the time of her life,' Clive told him. 'Now, Georges, what have you fixed up for me?'

'Incredible,' remarked the Foreign Minister. 'Georges Delaart told me something of it, of course, Monsieur Stanton, but he did not know it all. But . . .' He raised his finger. 'Monsieur Delaart also told me that this outlaw chieftain is holding a Frenchwoman against her will. That is not tolerable.'
'Georges is incorrect, Your Excellency,' Clive said. 'Mademoiselle l'Auberon has remained in Yakutistan entirely of her own free will. She is compiling a film documentary of the accomplishments of the new government.' He always endeavoured to stay as close to the truth as possible.
The Minister frowned. 'You are certain of this?'
'She is living in the Presidential Palace in Yakutsk. You may telephone her there for confirmation.'
'In the Presidential Palace? *Mon Dieu*!'
'President Borjigin is a very approachable man, Your Excellency. He does not stand on ceremony.'
'Hm. Yes, I shall telephone. Now, you wish credits, and support for a seat at the United Nations. Yes. Hm.'
'And arms, Your Excellency.'
The Minister gave him a hard look. 'Why do you need arms?'

'Your Excellency, President Borjigin is still regarded as an outlaw by Moscow. He is afraid that Russia may attempt to overthrow him by force.'

'I am sure they would not consider that,' the Minister protested. 'It would become a matter for the United Nations.'

'Which is why President Borjigin is anxious to join that body, Your Excellency. But the United Nations, with respect, is not an absolute safeguard, as I am sure you understand.'

'They talk too much, and do too little,' the Minister agreed. 'When it comes to using force, certainly. Hm. What does your President wish?'

'Your Excellency, Yakutistan is defended by four fighter squadrons and a brigade of tanks. President Borjigin seeks only defensive weapons. He does not wish to fight anyone. But ... your Rafale fighter-aircraft would answer many of his problems.'

'Hm,' the Minister said. 'Hm.'

'What is this Rafale?' Almani asked.

'We are having a demonstration tomorrow. Basically, it is the French answer to the Fulcrum, or the Lockheed F-22. But, unlike both of those, it is a strictly defensive weapon. Where the Fulcrum is armed, in addition to its thirty-millimetre cannon, with air-to-air missiles, and also carries cluster bombs, the Rafale is armed only with an equivalent cannon system, and two Magic missiles. It is not as fast, either; thirteen hundred miles per hour as against the Fulcrum's fifteen. But it is a good plane. A plane. And a lot cheaper than the Fulcrum or the Lockheed.'

'Is the Lockheed as good as the Fulcrum?' Nita asked.

'It is as well armed. But it isn't as fast.' Clive glanced at her. 'You won't get any of those, I shouldn't think.'

'I was but comparing them,' she said quietly. 'Is there nothing better than these?'

'Now you're getting into what is called the European aircraft,' Clive said. 'That carries a thousand-pound bomb, as well as additional fuel tanks, to make it an offensive as well as a defensive weapon. But the British Government aren't interested in selling any to Yakutistan.'

'Is not Spain a partner in developing this project?' Almani asked.

'I'd say things have changed, Clive, in your direction, since the last time we met,' remarked the Secretary of State, Walter Ingraham.

'I'm still not sure whether I'm coming or going,' Clive admitted.

'Yes, well, I guess you know we have certain procedures for granting recognition. Now from what you say, Borjigin seems to have fulfilled at least some of those. But we'd be interested in free elections.'

'These are promised. But recognition has to come first.'

'Weapons, no way. Sponsorship of the UN, well, I agree with your British friends: we need a cooling-down period. Finance, well, I understand Jim Crawford has some people lined up who want to meet you. I don't think I can offer you any government aid, but if you can do a deal with private enterprise, good luck. What I really want from you, Clive, is some idea of where this Borjigin fellow thinks he's going. Okay, he feels he and his people had a rough deal from the Taychins. I'm not going to argue with that. The Taychins have been a blot on the Russian landscape for a hell of a long time. No one's going to weep over them. Now you say Borjigin wants to wear a white hat, and be seen to do so. That's great. But does he have any idea how to run a country?'

Clive grinned. 'He's learning.'

'How fast? He's refusing to have anything to do with Moscow. Can he really feed his people, develop any kind of social programme, without dealing through Moscow? Especially if he's dreaming about guns before butter.'

'I don't think the Yakuts have ever had a great deal of help from Moscow, Mr Secretary. The fact is that they still have a pretty primitive standard of living, by our values. But I can tell you they're not dying of malnutrition. Would you believe I lived virtually off kumiss alone for several weeks, and I'm as fit as a horse? The steppe people have lived like that for centuries. As for guns, well, you can't blame him for being a little edgy. He is completely hedged in by hostility. Russia to the west, several mainly Moslem CIS states to the south, China to the east. And the Arctic Ocean to the north. That's not a particularly friendly environment.'

'Talking about China, have you had any reaction from Peking?'

'I was hoping you'd tell me,' Clive said.

'Not a murmur. I guess they're watching the situation, though. They know they're not going to get any sympathy from us if there's a border clash, after this latest round of arrests in Hong Kong. What about Borjigin's financial situation? He hasn't any hard currency, for a start.'

'That's why he needs credits. He will have hard currency, when he starts exporting his oil.'

'When. If it's there.'

'Moscow thinks it's there. That's one of the things that makes Batalji want to be able to defend himself.'

The Secretary stroked his chin. 'Clive, you know as well as I, that at the end of the day politics comes down to personalities. Sure, it's sometimes necessary to do business with someone you don't like. But that never lasts too long. Life is one hell of a lot simpler when you and the person you're negotiating with are on the same wavelength. Right?'

Clive nodded. 'I can't argue with that.'

'Then give me the short answer to this question: Is Borjigin on our wavelength?'

'The short answer would be no.' Clive held up his finger as the Secretary would have interrupted. 'You have to understand his background, Walter. Father murdered before his eyes; mother raped, by him amongst others – he was forced to it; state orphanage during the Soviet days; Afghanistan; desertion; outlawry ... Now, Walter, have you, or any member of the Administration, got anything like that in your background?'

'No, thank God. But I take your point. You mean his is a whole different ball game.'

'Exactly. To him there are his family and followers, and there are enemies. There are no other shades in his spectrum. Fortunately, one hundred per cent of the inhabitants of Yakutistan are his followers.'

'I can't buy that, unless you mean he's killed off all the opposition.'

'Warm. But they weren't too numerous.'

'Jesus! And you expect us to do business with someone like that?'

'As you said, it's not always possible to like the chap you're facing across a table. But Batalji has this going for him: he wants to get that tiger off his back. He wants to be accepted.'

'And you like him. That's pretty damned obvious.'

'He grows on one. Right now, he's a dictator. But he's not like any dictator I've ever come across, or read about. He's not a fist-waving, vegetarian fanatic, like Hitler. He's not a pompous ass, like Mussolini, although he's probably just as compulsive a womaniser. He doesn't regard his thoughts as important, like Mao. Perhaps most important of all, he's not constantly surrounded by bodyguards; his palace is filled with guards, but they're all nubile young women. He can take care of himself. I've seen him do it.'

'So why do his people follow him?'

'He freed them from the Taychins. From the rule of Moscow. Moscow may be full of good intentions right now, but to people like the Yakuts it's still the place the Commissars came from, arresting, shooting, and worst of all, regimenting.'

'They're gonna want more, pretty soon.'

'That's why it's up to us to see that they get more.'

'Just to keep your friend up there?'

'To stop Yakutistan degenerating into a frozen desert. If they're determined never to return to rule from Moscow, even to the extent of fighting if need be, and we don't give them the tools to preserve that independence . . . That leaves China.'

The Secretary of State considered. 'Tell me this ... Do you trust him?'

Clive grinned. 'I have to. It's my life on the line.'

'That's something else you have to explain to me. Clive, you are just about the top of your profession, worldwide. I'm not going to ask what you earn, but it has to be well up into six figures, maybe seven. But the word is that you've given all this up to be Borjigin's ambassador to the West. You said your life is on the line. But it can't be if you just shove two fingers into the air and get back to work. Or are you afraid of assassination?'

Clive chose his words with care; this man was too dedicated to his work to be interested in talk of helpless women. 'Shall I say that after a lifetime of presenting and interpreting history, I'm just a little interested in making some?' And that wasn't a lie, either.

'It's a point. But I don't reckon it's all of it.'

'I could add, I'm just a little bit afraid, as well,' Clive said. And that was the least lie of all.

Batalji sat at breakfast with his wife and mother, while Shallane and her two brothers played around the table. Outside the sun shone and the snow was melting; everywhere was the sound of rushing water. It was the best time of year.

Jagnuth came in. 'I have had a report from Pirale. The road south is open. I await your instructions.'

'About what?'

'Well ... exactly where you wish roadblocks erected. And how many *tumans* you will be sending down there. Who will command.' A *tuman* was the old Mongol division of ten thousand men, into which the Yakut army had been organised.

'We shall send no *tumans* to the south,' Batalji said, lazily.

Jagmuth looked at Selphine. 'That is the road any invading army must follow; they cannot come across the steppes.'

'There will be no invading army.' Batalji tapped the letter on the table in front of him. 'From Almani. It came yesterday.'

'Stanton has worked wonders,' Selphine said. 'I always knew

he was a man to be trusted. I knew it the moment I laid eyes on him.' Mortana smiled. 'It is true,' Selphine snapped. 'It was necessary to make sure. But I never doubted.'

'What is so good that he has accomplished?' Jagnuth asked.

Batalji picked up the letter. 'Item: The Republic of Yakutistan is recognised as independent by the Republic of Russia. It is assumed that the Republic of Yakutistan will become a member of the Commonwealth of Independent States.'

'Never!' Jagnuth declared.

'It is sometimes necessary to bend a little, Jagnuth, before straightening again more firmly than before. As, for example, it is very necessary for us to be represented at the United Nations. Our own membership may be a little delayed, according to Almani, but in the meantime, Russia is prepared to represent our interests. The important thing is our recognition and acceptance by Moscow, which effectively rules out any question of military intervention.'

'Ha!' Jagnuth commented. 'Next you will be telling me that we are going to hand back their tanks and planes.'

Batalji read. 'Item: A conference will be held in Moscow, attended by the Presidents of both Russia and Yakutistan, to settle all trade differences between the two republics, and to negotiate the sale of certain military items to the Republic of Yakutistan.'

'You will go to Moscow? They will arrest you and shoot you.'

'I am going as an international leader, with all the safeguards necessary. The eyes of the whole world will be upon this meeting. There is nothing to fear.'

'And they will let us keep the weapons?'

'That has been tacitly agreed, yes. On condition I agree to the destruction of all atomic warheads on Yakut territory. I am of course going to agree to this.' Batalji gazed at Jagnuth, and Jagnuth gazed back. This time the younger man made no comment. Batalji read. 'Item: The American–Canadian Oil Company, known as AmCak, is sending representatives to Yakutsk to negotiate a concession for the development of the

Yakut oil reserves. AmCak is prepared to work in partnership with the Government of Yakutistan, in return for a fifty-one per cent share of the company to be set up, and which will be known as AmCakYu, or ACY for short. These people love initials.'

'Fifty-one per cent?' Jagnuth shouted. 'That means we have no control over our own oil.'

Batalji smiled. 'Item: The French Government is sending a military mission to discuss the possible sale of several squadrons of Rafale fighter-interceptors to the Government of Yakutistan. Such a sale to be backed up by a full logistical and support system, including trainers, mechanics, and spare parts.'

'What is this plane?'

'It is one of the very latest aircraft. It is regarded as a defensive weapon. Almani says it is not as effective as the Fulcrum, but beggars cannot be choosers, eh? And he is working on obtaining at least the plans for something better. Item: The German Government is sending an industrial mission to investigate, with the Government of Yakutistan, the building of factories . . .'

'Factories,' Jagnuth sneered. 'We already have factories. I thought we were going to pull all the factories down. And the high-rises.'

'We shall,' Batalji agreed. 'When we are ready. These factories are for the making of consumer items, such as washing machines and dishwashers and television sets.'

'Dishwashers?' Jagnuth was even more contemptuous.

Batalji smiled. 'They will also build a factory to manufacture the machine tools necessary for making these consumer goods. And they will teach our people how to make these things, and use them, too. Did you know, Jagnuth, that the same machine tool which is needed to make a dishwasher can also be used to make a tank, or an aeroplane? Or a helicopter? Item: A British engineering firm is coming to discuss the building of four new hydro-electric stations. We have sufficient water power to drive the world. Quite apart from our oil and our natural gas and our coal. They are speaking of us as potentially the richest nation in the world. There are several more items, all to our advantage.'

'Stanton has even set up a deal with an American tour company,' Selphine said. 'It will bring tourists to Yakutistan. We have not had tourists before. They have much money.'

'Why should anyone wish to come to Yakutistan?' Jagnuth demanded. 'We have no beaches. And not that much sun.'

'What is the phrase Stanton uses? We are off the beaten track. The people of the West are jaded with their beaches and their sun. They want to adventure. I am going to organise adventures for them,' Selphine said. 'Treks through the forests. Bear hunts. Reindeer round-ups. I have learned all about it, from television.'

'Television! Tourists! Dishwashers!' Jagnuth looked at his sister. 'I suppose you wish a dishwasher.'

'I have three,' Mortana told him.

Jagnuth waved his arms. 'Where is our dream? Where is the dream of which we spoke, in the forests, over the years, Batalji? Your dream, of re-creating the empire of Genghis Khan, of leading the Mongol people back to the glory of eight hundred years ago? Is that dream all sunk into a mess of tourists and dishwashers?'

Batalji glanced at the women and the children, then he got up, threw his arm round Jagnuth's shoulders, and walked with him on to the balcony overlooking The Avenue. 'I am not a man who forgets my dreams, Jagnuth,' he said. 'But to recreate our past, we must become strong. And to become strong, we need the West. For the moment.' He grinned. 'It is a moment that will soon pass. Then we shall resume our Course, the Course of history.'

'And Stanton? Does he understand about the Course?'

'Of course not. When the people learn what he has accomplished, they will think of him as some kind of hero. All the best heroes are also martyrs,' Batalji said. 'His name will live forever in our annals, beside Ye-lu Ch'u-ts'ai.'

THE THIRD PART

Genghis Khan

And Caesar's spirit, ranging for revenge,
With Até by his side, come hot from hell,
Shall in these confines, with a monarch's voice,
Cry 'Havoc!' and let slip the dogs of war

William Shakespeare, *Julius Caesar*

THE ELEVENTH CHRONICLE

Yakutistan, Summer 2004

The helicopter blades rotated, and the gunship lifted from the ground; the other five machines of the squadron were already airborne. The men who remained standing beneath it came to attention, even if their coats and hair were rippled by the downdraft. 'Thirty million barrels a day,' Batalji shouted above the roar, looking down to give a last wave, and then across the landscape at the drilling rigs which dotted the tundra. 'And they say that can be doubled if we need to. That is good, eh?'

'It's bloody marvellous,' Clive agreed. The helicopter flew along the pipeline to the refinery, which had been laid almost before the first wellhead had been drilled. Both the pipeline and the wells had cost lives, as Batalji had driven the projects forward regardless of the weather. But that was Batalji's way, and now Yakutistan had become a major oil producer. More than three billion barrels a year, at half-production! 'What are you going to do with all that money?' Clive asked.

Batalji grinned. 'Pay my debts to begin with. But there is so much to be done. You will guide me, eh?'

'You reckon you still need my guidance, Batalji?' But he knew what the answer would be; their intimacy was illustrated by his ability to call the President by his Christian name, a privilege allowed to only two other men, Jagnuth and Almani, in all Yakutistan.

'I will always need your guidance, Clive,' Batalji said. 'Without you, none of this would have been possible.'

They left the pipeline and swung over the hills. It was high summer, and even on the hills all was green. Beneath them, the nomads tended their herds, pausing to look up and wave as the helicopter squadron – Batalji never travelled with fewer than six machines – swooped low over them to wave back. 'They are a happy people,' Clive remarked.

'And you sound surprised that they should be. Is this because the people in the West are not happy?'

'Not this happy. And frankly, while I know that your people worship you, I don't see what they have to be happy about. In that degree.'

Batalji gave one of his huge grins. 'I have made them happy. I know no one from the West can understand this. Their journalists, their tourists, their experts, come to Yakutistan, and poke around, and ask questions, and scratch their heads and go away again. They say, but you have no true social security system, your hospitals are primitive, your education standards are low, your university is not up to scratch and is anyway only half full. Your women have no rights, your economy remains at a barter level, you are spending too much of your GNP on armaments. And to top it all, you have an appalling climate. Yet your people are happy. This is a mystery to them.'

'I believe someone is writing a book about it,' Clive said.

'Ha, ha. But does he understand it? Do *you* understand it, Clive? My people are happy because I have given them their freedom. It is something your people will never understand. They talk about freedom, but they do not understand it, because they are not free. They are the meanest slaves, crushed by the weight of their taxes, their mortgages, their petty rules.

Almani tells me that when he was in Moscow he got a parking ticket. All your people live in fear of getting parking tickets. There are no parking tickets in Yakutsk. People park where they choose.'

'Yes, but you only have a few hundred cars,' Clive protested. 'When you have as many cars per capita as in the West...'

'Why should we have too many cars? People living in cities do not need cars. What is wrong with walking, or riding a horse? Do you know why your people are all dying of heart disease? It is because they do not take any exercise. Every man should walk at least a mile every day. I am not talking about senseless jogging. I am talking about purposeful walking, to get from one important point to another. All women too,' he added in a lower tone.

Clive knew he was thinking about Denise, who was no believer in exercise. The amazing thing about Denise was that she did not appear to put on weight, and remained as healthily beautiful as he had ever known her, even with forty in sight. Every time he saw her, which was quite often as Batalji had become a great thrower of dinner parties, he was more amazed, and more envious of his employer. Denise undoubtedly took all the exercise she needed on her back or her knees, and thrived on it.

Did he still want her, after she had become the plaything of an Asiatic warlord? He wanted her more than ever. It was not merely that she was the first woman he had made up his mind that he *did* want, above all others; it was also the desire of a man for something he had lost. Forever. Even if she were to be returned to him, which was always possible where Batalji was concerned, he doubted he would be able to accept her – he could never be sure whether she *was* Batalji's plaything ... or whether the situation was grotesquely reversed.

'Tell me about the Chinese Foreign Minister,' Batalji said. 'He arrives tomorrow morning, does he not?'

'I will have Nita send you over a complete itinerary. But I don't think you should receive him personally.'

'Why not? China is the only country in the world which has

not yet recognised my government. Now they wish to do so. Why shouldn't we seize the opportunity? I cannot understand why they have waited this long.'

'Well ... they're a cautious people. Or at least a cautious government. They have a long history of hostility to the Soviet Union, to Russia in general.' He smiled. 'They also have an even longer memory of your ancestors conquering them. More seriously, Batalji, their Foreign Minister is coming to Yakutsk with some specific ideas in mind.'

'Tell me. I am not yielding one inch of my territory.'

'He won't be looking for territory. He will be looking for support.'

'A billion people wish support from two million?'

'Right now, China is totally isolated,' Clive told him. 'She is the most populous country on earth, but not the most powerful, and she is by far the most unpopular. I don't think, when they took over Hong Kong so gleefully seven years ago, that they had any idea just what a thorny bush they were wrapping their hands around. Well, neither did the West, of course. But then, the West never does recognise thorns until they are actually jabbed in the finger. The Chinese saw only a vast opening in the world money markets; the West saw only, via those money markets, a vast opening of trade with a billion consumer-goods-starved people. Neither understood the nature of the opposing beast. I think it is safe to say that the Chinese leadership understands Western morality rather less than Western leadership understands Yakut contentment with your rule. Obviously all those Hong Kong activists who objected to Chinese repression back in the Tienanmen Square days were recorded on film; obviously the Chinese Government was going to make sure they didn't cause any more trouble; and obviously the time-honoured way to clean up the mess is to have a few *agents provocateurs* stir up trouble, and then crush that trouble with massive force, arresting or shooting all the known dissidents. Yet somehow the West believed, or pretended to believe, that it wasn't going to happen.'

'And now it has happened. But the United Nations does nothing about it.'

'The United Nations has no mandate for interfering in the internal affairs of member nations. It can criticise, of course, but China has her permanent seat on the Security Council and can simply veto any discussion of the matter. On the other hand, other member nations can take their own measures, and the United States in particular, but backed by Britain, which of course has quite a guilt complex about Hong Kong as they were the ones who gave it back to the Chinese, are talking about various trade sanctions until the human rights position improves. So China would like all the friends it can find, and Yakutistan is an obvious choice, not only because you share a border but especially since you have withdrawn from the CIS.'

'Hm,' Batalji commented.

'There is also the point that quite a few Chinese dissidents have fled across our border. Yuan may want them back. I hope you will not agree to that.' Batalji stroked his chin. 'As to whether you wish to be seen to support a regime which the rest of the world is coming to abhor ... I don't think that would be good for our international relations, right now.'

'We are producing thirty million barrels of oil a day. Can international criticism harm us?'

'It might lead to a withdrawal of some foreign capital. Some foreign technicians, too.'

'But I no longer need foreign capital, or technicians. I have my own capital, and my own technicians, now.' Batalji grinned. 'I will receive the Chinese Foreign Minister. We will have a state banquet. It must be a month since we have had a state banquet. You will bring Rosemary, eh?'

'Ah,' Clive said, 'I would like to discuss Rosemary with you.'

'You wish to let her go.'

'Have I not served you faithfully and well?'

'No one has served me better.'

'And I will continue to do so, Batalji. Not only because I have great respect for you and what you are doing, but because . . .' He grinned. 'I like to think I can keep you out of trouble, and thus save the world a great deal of trouble as well.'

'My Ye-lu Ch'u-ts'ai.' Batalji grinned in turn.

'Thus there is no longer any need to hold someone hostage for my good behaviour. Surely. And she has now been here for nearly four years.'

'She does not enjoy being fucked by you?'

'I don't know. Sometimes I think she does. What she does not enjoy is being held a prisoner here in Yakutistan. If you were to let her go home . . . I am sure it could be arranged that there would be no leaking of bedroom secrets. I don't think she would wish to, anyway.'

'And you would spend more time with my mother, eh? Do you tell her my secrets?'

'Do you tell *me* your secrets?' Clive countered.

Batalji laughed. 'I trust you, Clive. But I do not trust my mother. Remember this. It is not that I think she would ever betray me. But she is too inquisitive. It is not good for a woman to be inquisitive, and nearly all of them are. I give you permission to send Rosemary home, if that is what you wish to do. But remember what I told you: if he is to do great things, a man must have a woman, always waiting for him, for when he needs her. Of course, there is always Nita . . .'

Clive had been given a building of his own for use as the Foreign Ministry. Here Nita controlled his staff and ran his communications centre. When he reached his office she placed before him all the telegrams and the latest news from around the world: he had been away for a fortnight on his tour of inspection with Batalji. 'We concentrate on the Chinese visit,' he told her. 'Let me see the itinerary. It will have to be expanded.'

'Yes, sir. The Princess wishes to see you, sir. The moment you returned, she said.' Nita's features seemed to screw themselves up; she understood that it was a measure of the topsy-turvy state of affairs in Yakutistan that while he was widely accepted to be perhaps the second most powerful man in the country, he remained at the beck and call of the most powerful woman.

But then, so did *the* most powerful man. Batalji's so far tentative attempts to keep his decision and plans secret from his mother were doomed to failure as long as she remained in the very centre of Yakut affairs, and as long as she was determined always to stand at her son's shoulder ... and as long as Batalji was afraid of her. Because he was. She was the only person on earth he feared, Clive estimated. He got up. 'I will be back this afternoon.'

'There is also a message from Miss Leigh,' Nita said. 'She too wishes to see you immediately on your return.'

They exchanged glances. Clive had also been given a house of his own, in which Rosemary had been installed. He had no reason to think that she loathed him any the less for having been his mistress for three years, but she had accepted the situation – as he had been away a large part of that time anyway he had not been a nuisance, and she had taken to Sintax. On the other hand, she was inclined to treat him as a husband. 'Well,' he said. 'I have some good news for her. But she'll have to keep until after the Princess.'

His car was waiting to drive him to the Palace; Batalji might consider it unnecessary for the majority of the inhabitants of Yakutsk to own cars, but he believed his ministers should travel in style. But as usual, a drive through the streets of Yakutsk was a revelation, especially in August. The heat was intense in the city, and the place was a huge bustle. Not only were there ships alongside the quays loading coal, and tourists wandering along The Avenue with their cameras, the inhabitants were also out in force, seeing what they could obtain today.

The Yakut economy was something else that was not understood in the West, because it was based on the simplest of all trading methods: barter. Over the past three years, Batalji had used a part of his trading credits to import consumer goods, and he had not hesitated to borrow to bring in more –

everyone in the world had quickly learned that Yakutistan possessed the world's largest proven oil reserves, and the banks had queued up to lend the regime money.

It followed, therefore, to Western eyes, that the country had to be in the grip of a runaway inflationary spiral. In fact, very few people in Yakutsk had ever heard of the word inflation. Batalji had simply bypassed the slow progress of centuries, and eliminated cash. If one wanted a washing machine or a dishwasher, one went along to the store which imported them – and which in the best old Soviet tradition was state-owned – and one bartered. Time was the currency in Yakutistan. A dishwasher cost sixty hours. In theory one had a choice as to how those hours could be spent; in practice, the choice came down to one of two or three options. Every able-bodied man, and every able-bodied woman, between the ages of sixteen and sixty, was required to do fourteen hours a week military training; it followed that a month's military training by itself would very nearly earn a dishwasher. But there were other jobs available, from road-sweeping through working in the factories or the mines, to road-mending. Every hour spent working from the country, as Batalji put it, was recorded in a little booklet. When major purchases were made, a fresh booklet was issued and marked off as each work session was completed. But if one preferred one could work 'loose', as it was termed, and receive a booklet for that too. This would be marked off, like an old wartime ration book, for the purchase of small items. Cash was quite unnecessary, as all medical treatment, all ordinary food, and all alcohol was free and supplied by the Government – again marked off on one's personal booklet as it was purchased, to insure no one received too much.

It was an amazingly simple, and, in the short-term, effective system, ruling out as it did any temptation to commit ordinary theft, as there was nothing to steal – quite apart from the horrendous punishments, such as the loss of a hand or an eye, meted out for such crimes – and no opportunity to get drunk and become disorderly, as one's book was marked off on entry into a public bar, and each person limited to four drinks per evening. This did not of course apply to the Mongol aristocracy, who got drunk every night in the privacy of their palaces. Equally it was not possible to run into debt, for copies of each man's or woman's chosen work contract were sent to their selected employer, be he army quartermaster or building foreman, and anyone who did not turn up at the appointed time was promptly arrested, unless he or she possessed a valid medical certificate. Only the nomads on the steppes were exempt from the system; they put in yearly claims for everything they needed, and after careful examination, they received most of what they required, free of charge.

Of course the system was only practical where the government had more money than it knew what to do with and thus could afford to own everything. Equally it was only practical where people were being raised from such a primitive level that any rise in their standard of living was greeted with acclaim; obviously the moment the Yakuts began to wonder why the goods they could obtain were strictly controlled, why, for instance, they could all have dishwashers and washing machines and television sets, but not cars, and why every one of them was being trained as a soldier, there were going to be problems. Advertising was strictly controlled, and both TV channels were government-owned, but that also could not obtain forever.

But for the moment the people of Yakutistan appeared totally devoted to the man who had given them this freedom. Not even the university students were dissenting from the way the country was governed – they were in any event not allowed to debate, only to attend their lectures and pass their examinations and drill – and of course the total absence of income or any other form of taxation apart from the corvée was a great attraction for people who had always accepted that life was a hard physical grind. But yet there was that cloud on the horizon . . . even if it did not appear to bother Batalji.

Clive was by now such a regular and privileged visitor at the Palace that he could come and go as he pleased. Guards stood to attention, but no one asked his business or his destination as he went up the stairs and along the corridors to Selphine's apartment. Save that before he got there he encountered Mortana and her daughter, apparently on their way to the stables, for they both wore boots and carried riding crops – the Mongol women invariably wore pants suitable for riding, on all occasions. 'Highness!' Clive saluted.

'Stanton!' Mortana smiled at him. Clive felt she liked him, and he was pleased about that, because he genuinely liked her. She was the ideal wife for a khan, big and strong, healthy and good-humoured. It was a tragedy that her husband preferred the petite sophistication of a Western woman – and there was no longer any pretence about it: after three years Denise had been no more able to give him children than Rosemary had been after six months. But Batalji still preferred the Frenchwoman's company. Clive had no idea whether or not he still slept with Mortana at all. Yet she continued to smile.

As did Shallane. Shallane was fourteen, as tall as her mother but with the continued slenderness of her grandmother; she entirely lacked puppy fat. And unlike her mother, her smile glittered; she, more than any of them, made him think of a predatory cat. 'Will you scream when you die?' she had asked him on the occasion of their first meeting.

'I did not know you had returned,' Mortana said. 'Is . . .' She hesitated.

'The Khan returned also, Highness. But I think he went to the barracks, to see General Anhusat.'

'Ah!' Mortana could at least take comfort from the fact that her brother remained the army chief of staff.

'Then where are you going, Stanton?' Shallane demanded.

It was a pleasant thought, Clive reflected, that within a couple of years this hoyden would be married to some rough Mongol warrior, and would have to learn a thing or two about the facts of life – and he was not thinking merely in sexual terms. The surprise was that Batalji had not yet selected a husband for her – fourteen was certainly a marriageable age for a Mongol woman. But he would, soon enough. Then she would become pregnant ... and maybe she'd start to become a human being, although he doubted it. But she remained Batalji's daughter, and his favourite child. Her elder brother Barone was a general, although aged only twenty-five, and both Tensan and Dorgat were being schooled, mainly as soldiers, but it was Shallane who brought a smile to her father's face. 'I am going to visit your grandmother,' he explained.

'She snaps her fingers,' Shallane said contemptuously, 'and you go running, prick waggling.'

'Shallane!' Mortana remonstrated. But that was as far as she would go; she also knew how much Batalji adored his daughter.

'Am I allowed to reply, Highness?' Clive asked.

'Well, of course you are, Stanton. What will you say to her?'

'I was simply going to ask Princess Shallane, Highness, if she did not also go running whenever the Princess Selphine snapped her fingers ... and she does not even have a prick *to* waggle.'

'One day, Stanton,' Shallane said. 'When my father is tired of you, I am going to hear you *scream*!'

'I should advise against holding your breath, Princess. Highness!' He continued on his way, trying to convince himself that he was not both angry ... and afraid.

'Stanton!' Selphine reclined in the middle of a huge heart-shaped bed with pink sheets – she had recently been watching several old Jayne Mansfield movies. She wore gold lamé pyjamas – which he had bought her in Paris on his last visit – with the jacket open. There was a bank of six television sets along the wall opposite the bed, each one with a different video playing, although all the sounds were muted; Clive knew that Selphine liked watching her favourites over and over again, only turning up the volume when it was a conversation she wanted to recall. 'When did you get back?'

'Not an hour ago, Princess.'

'Come here and kiss me.' Clive sat on the bed and was hugged into her embrace, slid his hands over her satin-like skin. 'Have you seen the bitch yet?'

She used the word indiscriminately when referring to either Denise or Rosemary, but the answer was the same in either case. 'I came directly here, Princess.'

'And where is my son?'

'He went straight to the barracks for a meeting with General Anhusat. It is to do with the arrival of the Chinese Foreign Minister, tomorrow.'

'Ha! The Chinese Foreign Minister. Lock the door.'

Clive raised his eyebrows, as Selphine did not as a rule care about privacy, but he obeyed. 'What I have to say must be a secret, between you and me,' Selphine said. Clive glanced at the wall mirror, and Selphine smiled. 'Not even Batalji would dare bug my apartment, Stanton. Come here.'

He sat beside her on the bed. 'You have been to the oilfield. Is it true that we are now in full production?'

'We could produce more, but we are pumping out thirty million barrels a day.'

'What does that mean?'

'It means that Yakutistan is now one of the richest states in the world.'

'The richest state in the world,' Selphine mused. 'You also went to the Complex?' The Complex was the name for a highly secret group of factories situated to the west of Yakutsk, on the River Linde, where Clive knew the Borjigins and Anhusats had grazed their flocks during earlier summers. Here there was all the water-power to generate electricity any plant manager could wish, and the Complex was in production twenty-four hours a day. 'What is the turn-out there?'

'A tank every day, a plane every week. A missile every month. It is as if the country were at war.'

'What do you tell the Western diplomats who ask about it?'

'Very few of them even know of it. For the rest, it is an arms factory. Most countries have arms factories. No one knows how hard they are working, how much they are producing. No one is allowed to know.'

'And this does not concern them? Concern you?'

'It does not concern the West, at the moment. They are

delighted that Batalji has handed over his atomic weapons to be destroyed. They are content that his government received such a massive majority in the elections. They are pleased with the stability of the country, and its prosperity. And of course they wish our oil.'

'*Our* oil!' Selphine sneered. 'You are a Mongol, now?'

'By adoption, yes, Princess.'

'And you have no idea what Batalji is doing?'

'I would say he is making a very good job of running his country. Which is one reason I am working for him. I think he is a phenomenon.'

'You are a fool, Stanton.' Selphine got out of bed and strode to and fro, hair flying. 'Tell me, is it not true that General Simonoslov has reported that not all of the atomic warheads or their launchers have been handed over?'

'There was some such report.'

'What has been done about it?'

'The report was given to the United Nations and I was questioned about it. I referred the question to Batalji himself, and he replied that he knew nothing about it. He captured the missile site, put it under guard, and it stayed under guard until the United Nations team visited it and took the missiles away last year. If there is a discrepancy between the number of warheads originally on the site and the number found by the United Nations team, then it is a Russian affair.'

Selphine paused in front of him, hands on her hips; wisps of hair drifted across her face and these she blew away with pursed lips. 'You honestly believe that? You honestly trust my son?'

Clive knew he had to choose his words carefully. One could never tell when Selphine was laying traps. But why should she? Only because Batalji had told her to. And why should Batalji wish to entrap him? Clive had no false modesty regarding the success he had been as Batalji's representative in the West, and, thus, how valuable he was to the warlord. 'It is my business to trust my employer, Princess.'

'Ha! Batalji trusts nobody. He does not even trust me any more.' Which was the root of her anger, Clive knew. 'Let me tell you something, Stanton,' Selphine said. 'Batalji intends to conquer Russia.' She waved her arm. 'All of Russia.'

'That is simply not possible, Princess. Two million people cannot conquer two hundred million.'

'Then tell me why he is building weapons as if, as you have just said, the country were at war?'

'Batalji remains fearful that Russia intends to attack Yakutistan, Princess. He is a little paranoid about this, I'm afraid, but...'

'Tell me why he has been so anxious to become self-sufficient in oil just as rapidly as possible?'

'It is the dream of every nation to become self-sufficient in oil, Princess. Besides, he needs the money, desperately; his foreign debts are enormous.'

'Ha! Tell me why he is concealing a number of atomic warheads.'

'I have just explained...'

'You have explained nothing, Stanton. You have mouthed what Batalji has told you to say.'

'Princess, it is just not possible to make off with half a dozen atom bombs, complete with their launchers and ancillary equipment, without somebody knowing about it. It would in any event take a large number of men and vehicles just to move them. May I point out that the first UN observers, invited by Batalji, arrived in the summer of 2001? They were taken straightaway to the launching site. To have removed part of the site before their arrival would have involved an immense exercise, in winter. The very winter he took over the state.'

'My son captured the site in winter, did he not? Explain to me about the hundred and twenty Russian soldiers who were never repatriated?'

'Batalji himself has explained that, Princess. They staged a revolt...'

'And were all killed. That at least is correct. Explain to me about the fifty Mongol soldiers who accompanied Jagnuth to the north four winters ago, and have never been heard of since.'

'I hope you are not saying what I think you are saying, Princess.'

'I am saying that I do not think you know my son very well, Stanton, however intimate you may be with him. No one knows Batalji the way I do. But he is afraid I will disapprove of his plans.'

'As you do,' Clive said, hopefully.

'I wish to know what they are.'

'In order to dissuade him,' Clive said, more hopefully yet. 'You must understand, Princess, that for Yakutistan to go to war with anyone would be a total disaster. Everything your son has achieved, everything he has created, would be wiped out. *You* would be wiped out, and all of your grandchildren.'

Selphine threw herself across the bed. 'Do you not think Batalji has considered this?'

'I am sure he has, that is why I cannot believe he means to to to war with anyone. But if he has any ideas in that direction, he must be dissuaded.'

'By me? Ha! We are Mongols. Fighting is in our blood. It is all our ancestors did, make war. But I want to know, Stanton. You must find out, and tell me. I make that your most important charge. Now come to me. You have been away too long.' She rolled on to her back, arms outstretched.

It was dusk before Clive left the Palace. He went straight to his house, where his servants bowed and his guards stood to attention. 'Madam awaits Your Excellency,' said Kasmir, his butler.

'Are there any messages?'

'This came from the Ministry, Your Excellency.'

Clive took the bulky envelope – it was from Nita with the revisions he had asked for – and went up the stairs. His brain was spinning. It normally was, after several hours with Selphine, but today it was rotating somewhat faster than usual. It was very tempting to dismiss her suspicions as the ramblings of a jealous woman determined to regain her old intimacy with her son, to reflect on the very solid achievements Batalji had accomplished over the past four years, the way he had gone out of his way to be accepted by the world community, and most important of all, the way he had always accepted his Foreign Minister's advice, at least on external matters. Since leaving the CIS the previous autumn, Yakutistan now had its seat in the United Nations, had representatives on most world bodies, was recognised, gladly, as an oasis of stability in the constantly fluctuating politics of Asia. Batalji's desire to be well armed had not been overly criticised, in view of his proximity to China, at a period when China was again becoming the outlaw nation. Of course there was going to be some criticism of the Khan's decision to seek closer relations with the giant Communist state ... but the West still regarded the presence of a determinedly independent and militarily strong Yakutistan as very useful.

He frowned as he reflected that in seeking a *rapprochement* with China, the Khan was going *against* his Foreign Minister's advice, for the first time. Yet there was no one in the whole world prepared to question Batalji's motives for doing anything, right this minute ... save his own mother. But what *had* happened to those so conveniently forgotten Russian prisoners, and their guards?

He knocked on the door of Rosemary's suite, entered. She had been sitting by the window, looking out at the river, which flowed past the street on which the house was situated, but she rose at his entry. She wore a dress, as usual, in her determination to be different from the people around her, and with her hair tied in a chiffon scarf on the nape of her neck looked most attractively feminine. Whatever their very odd relationship, she was always worth coming home to. But today her expression was even more defiant than usual. 'I came as soon as I could,' he said.

'Beggars can't be choosers.'

He went to the sideboard. 'Drink?'

'Thank you, no.' He raised his eyebrows, but poured himself a vodka. Rosemary sat down again, crossed her legs. 'How was your trip?'

'Exhausting, as ever.' He sat opposite her. 'But it gave me

a rare opportunity to have a private chat with Batalji, away from affairs of state.' She waited, hands folded in her lap, and he realised that here too there was something going on of which he was not fully aware. 'You're to go home' he said.

Her head came up, sharply.

'I've been working on this, for some time,' Clive explained. 'I think, when he gave you to me, just as when he took Denise, Batalji was simply enjoying his power, the idea that he could command people to do anything he chose, and they would have to obey. Now he's simmered down. He has realised that the possession of power entails as much responsibility in its exercise as enjoyment. I suppose you might say he's growing up.'

Rosemary did not speak, remained gazing at him.

'So,' Clive said, 'he's agreed that if you wish to return to the States, you may do so. Whenever you choose.'

'The prisoner has been reprieved,' she remarked.

'If you wish to put it that way.'

'After three and a half years,' she said, thoughtfully. 'Six months as his plaything, and three years as yours. Now I imagine you are also tired of me, so out I go. Back to where I belong. Where do I belong, Stanton?'

'Okay, there's been a four-year break in your career ... You'll have no trouble at all in resuming it. Jim Crawford has given me his word on that.'

'I suppose you meet Jim every time you visit the States.'

'I try to, certainly.'

'And you discuss me.'

'Well, of course. He worries about you.'

'Does he worry more, or less, when you tell him how you fuck me?'

'I am sorry about that. I have told you so. But I do not discuss our private life with anyone.'

'Which fuck are you sorry about?'

'All of them.' She turned to gaze at him. 'Don't get me wrong,' he said. 'You're a lovely woman. Fucking you is a joy. It's more of a joy when I feel you are enjoying it too. But those occasions have been few and far between, so ...'

'It's a kick in the butt and next stop New York.'

'For God's sake! Don't you want to go? You've always given a pretty good impression of being unable to wait until you could get out of here.'

Rosemary left the room, banging the door behind her. Clive finished his drink, and followed her into the bedroom, reflecting that he never would understand women. Rosemary had thrown herself across the bed, face down, disturbing Sintax, who had been asleep on the pillows. The cat had stalked down to the bottom of the mattress, and was staring at him. 'Don't you start,' Clive warned, and then realised that Rosemary was crying. Rosemary Leigh? He knelt on the bed. 'For God's sake,' he remarked again. 'Romy? Oh, shit!'

She rolled over and sat up, reached for a tissue from the box on the bedside table and blew her nose.

'I know it sounds a little abrupt,' Clive said. 'But I've been working on it for so long it just sort of came out.'

She sniffed. 'But you never thought of telling me first.'

'I didn't want to get your hopes up.'

'But now you want me to go.'

'*You* want to go. Remember?'

'I never said that.'

They gazed at each other, and he reached out to dab a last tear from her cheek. 'I'm not sure if you did or not. But you certainly gave that impression.'

'Do you think I enjoy being treated as a slave?'

'I have never treated you as a slave ...'

'Or as a punching bag, or a sack of sexual coal.'

He sighed, and lay down, his arm outstretched to tickle Sintax. 'I apologise. There were times I thought you enjoyed it.' She didn't immediately reply, so he glanced at her.

'Someone once said that if two people lived together for a year they'd have to either love each other or hate each other at the end of that time.'

Clive sat up again. 'And you mean you don't hate me? Romy ...' He took her in his arms, but her hands came up against his chest.

'I want you to marry me.'

'Sure I'll marry you, sweetheart.'

'Because you love me,' Rosemary added.

'I do love you. As you said . . .'

'More than anyone else.'

'I love you. I wish I could find out what brought this on, though.'

'You great gink,' she muttered. 'I'm pregnant.'

For a moment he was speechless; fatherhood had never been one of his great aims in life. 'You have to be joking.'

'I wish I were, in view of your reaction.'

He ignored her hands, pulled her against him, kissed her. 'I am absolutely delighted.'

'So you'll see I have a point of view.'

'Absolutely. But . . . after four years?'

'I guess I just got careless. You were here so seldom . . .'

'I think that's tremendous. Of course we'll get married. But . . . you're sure you want to have the baby here?'

'I want to have the baby where the father is, Clive. I have some very old-fashioned ideas.'

'I love them all. You mean, seriously, you don't want to go home?'

'Only if you'll come with me. I mean, for good.'

'I can't do that right now. I'm committed. To Yakutistan, to finishing what I've begun . . . to Batalji. It could be a long time. You're sure you want to wait that long? It would mean the baby growing up here, perhaps.'

'He'll be growing up with his father. I can't go home right now. Not on my lonesome, anyhow. Clive, the whole world knows that I've been locked up in Yakutistan for four years.'

'We've deliberately played it down. Made it seem you're carrying on your work here. Your friends won't let you down.'

'But you told my parents the truth, right?'

'In confidence. I told them you would get out, some time.'

'Confidence, shit! They'll have told their friends, and their friends will have told the media . . . If I haven't been front-page news it's simply because I'm not important enough. But when I go home, bingo, they'll be offering me millions for my story, just as if I was some hostage coming back from the Middle East. Right? Life as a warlord's mistress! I don't want that. Even less do I want it for my baby. When I leave Yakutistan, it's going to be at your side, and you are going to answer all of the questions, and keep those hounds off my back. Right? So, as long as you intend to keep on working for Batalji...' She smiled, and kissed him. 'I like it here. Cross my heart. But it'd be fun to be married.'

'Leave that one with me. Just let me get this Chinese FM out of the way, then I'll have a word with the boss.'

He got up, and she held his hand. 'You happy with this?'

'I'm happier than I have ever been before in my life,' Clive told her.

Ewfim Dolgorukov sat before the desk of the Russian President. 'What do you think of the news from Yakutsk?'

'That Borjigin is now in full oil production?' Boroslov asked, wearily.

'That amongst others. His receiving the Chinese Foreign Minister, for instance.' Dolgorukov frowned at his employer; the President did not appear to be concentrating. 'I think you should know that I have the person you requested me to find, three years ago. She is, as you wished, primed and ready. I had supposed we would have used her before now. But in these circumstances...'

Boroslov sighed, and thrust a piece of paper across the desk. Dolgorukov picked it up, studied it, then raised his head. 'But this...'

'Is virtually an ultimatum from Kiev. Yes. It arrived last night. And you expect me to be interested in disposing of Borjigin at this moment?' He gave a brief, humourless laugh. 'If Obolonsky really mean to go to war, we may need Borjigin and his Mongol hordes. Keep your assassin on ice for a while longer, Ewfim.'

CHAPTER 11

Yakutsk, Summer 2004

Batalji sat at the table and surveyed the map. Barone stood at his shoulder, Almani sat on his right, Jagnuth on his left. No one else was present at this most private meeting of the Mongol chieftains. 'The news arrived this morning,' Almani said.

'If Russia and the Ukraine go to war . . .' Barone muttered.

'It is too soon,' Batalji snapped. He tapped the map. 'It is not yet decisive, and we are not ready. We need another year. We must join the other members of the CIS in demanding mediation. More, we must lead in this. Peace is what we must preach.'

'For how long?' Barone demanded.

'Until next year, certainly,' his father insisted. 'We need to keep the oil flowing for the next three months. Then we shall be into winter. During the winter our preparations will be completed. During the winter we will start our moves. But we do not wish war between Russia and the Ukraine to commence before next spring.'

'Next spring is still too soon,' Jagnuth muttered.

Batalji looked at his brother-in-law; no one else, not even Almani, knew of the existence, much less the whereabouts, of the atomic warheads, which had been re-armed and targeted – Almani was as brave as a lion and as loyal as a *bahatur* should be, but he was not actually a relative. 'Next spring we will be ready,' Batalji said. 'We cannot wait forever.'

'Will the Russians accept our mediation?' Barone asked.

'I will send Stanton. The whole world respects Stanton.'

'Stanton!' Barone's tone was distasteful. 'I do not understand how you so trust that man.'

'Has he not served me, us, honestly and well?' Batalji asked, patiently.

'Ha! Simply because you have held his woman hostage. When he tires of her . . .'

Batalji smiled. 'He is already tired of her. He has asked permission to send her back to America.'

'Permission you have refused, Father.'

'No, no, I have told him she may go. As you have said, she is of no value once he has tired of her.'

Barone's eyes gleamed. 'Then give her to me, Father. Give me the American woman.'

Batalji smiled. 'Do you not have twelve women already?'

'None like the American. You took my Frenchwoman. I asked for the American in exchange. You said you needed her to coerce Stanton. If you no longer need her for that purpose, then she should be mine.'

'I have told Stanton he may send her home,' Batalji said, quietly. 'Stanton trusts me as much as I trust him. That is how it should be. He is our greatest asset, until we begin our Course. After that . . . well, we shall see.'

'Does he know of the Course?' Almani asked.

'No. He would oppose it.'

'And when he finds out, you think he will still work for you?'

'For as long as I desire it, yes. I intend to bind him more closely to me than ever. I have long had this in mind. He is a man, like any other man. He can be bound to me like any other man.' He grinned at them. 'Like you.'

'We love you, and we are of your flesh,' Jagnuth protested.

'Stanton loves me. More, in many ways he regards me as his own creation, because I have always done what he has recommended. I don't think he realises that I understand this. Like all Westerners he is very arrogant. Now I shall make him of my flesh as well, and he will be faithful forever.' He grinned. 'Besides, I intend to set a collar upon him, so that he will never be free of me again.'

There was a considerable diplomatic corps already in residence in Yakutsk, as most of the Western countries, as well as those in southern Asia and in Africa, had sought representation at the court of the Mongol phenomenon. That he actually ruled as a king rather than an elected president did not make him any the less attractive to the West. Besides, while the world at large was busily condemning Chinese excesses in Hong Kong, it remained aware that the colossus had to be dealt with at every level, and unofficial contacts with Mr Yuan Shu-pi were useful. Thus the ambassadors and chargés d'affaires and their wives had all accepted their invitations to the state dinner being held at the Presidential Palace in honour of Mr Yuan.

Batalji, and Selphine, had spent a great deal of time studying videos of Western state occasions, and no expense was spared when the Khan entertained, even if he sometimes got his ethnic ideas confused. Thus the guests entered the floodlit Palace gardens down the long, curving drive, past the huge plaque which commemorated the start of the revolution, where Batalji had himself killed the four guards and blown open the gates; each side of the driveway was lined with members of Batalji's élite guard, wearing green uniforms with the forked lightning insignia and standing rigidly to attention, rifles at the present. At the steps, the guests were greeted by white-coated major-domos, and escorted up to the huge front doors by the women guards of the Palace interior, who wore the same uniforms as their male counterparts, save for knee-length skirts instead of pants. All trace of the damage caused by the revolution had long disappeared; Clive had insisted upon that: all the lifts were now working again.

Inside the huge reception hall an orchestra was playing, and more women were waiting to escort the guests to the foot of the grand staircase, at the top of which Batalji stood, wearing, like his men, a plain green uniform, although with red tabs at his collar, and gold epaulettes. A single gold medal, hanging from a black and crimson ribbon, lay on his breast, and it was a medal worn by most of his associates; everyone who had taken part in the Day of the Revolution was entitled to wear it.

Thus Selphine, standing on her son's left, in a crimson evening gown with a breathtaking *décolletage,* also wore it; its weight sagged the gown and brought her left nipple perilously close to exposure, but those of the guests who had attended previous functions at the palace knew this was only a temporary display of modesty – when Selphine got drunk she was liable to strip at least to the waist, and require her guests to follow her example: the more modest had to make a point of leaving early. On Batalji's right there waited Mortana, wearing a high-necked blue gown, a regal if overweight figure, her hair gathered on the top of her head and secured there by a diamond tiara, in strong contrast to her mother-in-law, whose tawny mane was as ever loose on her shoulders.

To everyone's surprise, beside Mortana was the Princess Shallane. This was the first time the Princess had attended an official function, and most people knew she was only just fourteen years old. But even if it was several years since she had lived on the steppes, she was none the less a child of the wilderness, who had ridden her pony bareback through the snow before she was six years old, and her body was already sturdily developed, very like Mortana's at that age. Her gold-coloured gown was as modest as her mother's, but like her grandmother, whom she so closely resembled both in features and colouring, she wore her hair loose.

The line was completed by Denise l'Auberon. Denise's position, and her appearance at official functions, had caused quite a stir three years ago; the position of official *mâtresse en titre* had supposedly disappeared with the French Revolution. But no visitor to Yakutistan could fail to realise, very rapidly, that he had stepped into a world in which past and present, and perhaps even future, were fascinatingly, and disturbingly, mingled. Denise greeted each guest with the aplomb of a hostess, unaffected by the nearness of Mortana, who was apparently equally unaffected by her. Denise remained exquisitely lovely. If she had turned her back on the Paris she adored for the sake of being a warlord's mistress, she had imported as much of Paris as was practical to Yakutsk; her gown was *haute couture*, her perfume was De Berens Number 1. Her now very long auburn hair – Batalji would not let her cut it – was, like Mortana's, upswept to expose the classic beauty of her face, and if her gown had a cleavage, it was totally modest when compared with Selphine's – Denise had never found it necessary to advertise her wares. Watching Batalji, surrounded by his four favourite women, it was easy to see why he wore such a contented look all of the time.

Beyond the reception line there was a huge room filled with waitresses, who wore white silk blouses and black silk pants, with red sashes, and offered either drinks or canapés. Here one mingled with the other guests, had one's wife ogled by Barone Borjigin, or greeted courteously by Almani Serhat and his wife, or boisterously by Jagnuth Anhusat and his wife. It was understood that, after the Khan himself, these were the three most powerful men in the land, and their various personalities had to be accepted. But there was a fourth man to be sought out and cultivated. Clive Stanton, unlike the Mongol chieftains, preferred black tie to uniform, and thus made the more contrasting figure. He stood to the rear of the throng, Rosemary Leigh at his side. Again, Rosemary's position had necessarily been accepted by the foreign diplomats, in this country where conventional morality had no meaning, but with her height and striking looks, as well as her ability to speak Russian fluently – added to the reputation of having once been Batalji's mistress – she was well worth a conversation.

But tonight Clive was the more important. 'What do you think of the news from the Ukraine?' asked the British Ambassador, Basil Easterbrook.

'I think it means they have finally got fed up with being bullied by Moscow,' Clive told him.

'Yes, but mobilisation . . . HM Government is very upset, I can tell you. We intend to raise the matter in the United Nations. We would like to know where Yakutistan stands.'

'Yakutistan stands for peace.'

'Will you be able to maintain that point of view, should the whole of the CIS become involved?'

'Yakutistan is no longer a member of the CIS, Basil,' Clive reminded him. 'We have no intention of being drawn into any conflict to decide who is top dog amongst the republics. But I can tell you that as soon as Yuan goes home I am leaving for Moscow to attempt to restore some sanity there.'

'I am sure HM Government will be very relieved,' Easterbrook said. The notes of a gong drifted through the room, and the ambassador gave Rosemary a little bow. 'I believe I am taking you in, Miss Leigh.'

'Why, thank you, Your Excellency. Who have you got, Clive?'

'Ah . . .' Clive glanced at the note which had been given him as he entered the Palace, but which he had not yet bothered to read. 'Oh, God Almighty! Shallane.'

Clive made his way across the room to where Shallane waited with her mother and father. He had greeted her on arriving, of course, and been rewarded with one of her secret smiles. Now he received another as he bowed over her head. 'Ha, ha,' Batalji remarked. 'You make a pretty pair, Clive. Be sure she does not eat too much.'

Shallane put out her tongue at her father, and he put his out in return. Their intimacy was a delight to watch; it was a human side to Batalji's character that both pleased and astonished. 'What he really means is, you mustn't let me drink too much,' Shallane confided as they went in.

'If I was your father, I wouldn't let you drink at all,' Clive told her.

'If you were my father, I would have cut your throat long

ago,' she riposted. 'And then drunk your blood. That is what Grandmama says they used to do in the old days.'

'Very old days,' Clive reminded her, and showed her to her chair, on her father's right hand, which meant that Clive himself was only one seat removed from the head of the table. Selphine sat on Batalji's left, as she always did, Mortana was on Clive's right. Denise and Rosemary were lost further down the table.

As with all of Batalji's dinner parties, food, vodka, and conversation flowed. However unsophisticated, Shallane was surprisingly knowledgeable of the outside world, but then, she watched almost as much television as her grandmother. 'I look forward to visiting Paris,' she told the French Ambassador, seated across the table from her. 'I want to climb to the top of the Eiffel Tower.'

'I am sure Paris looks forward to receiving Your Highness,' the ambassador replied, gallantly. 'But I assure you, there is an elevator.'

'I intend to climb the stairs,' Shallane informed him. 'Do I look like an old woman?'

'Heaven forbid, Princess. When do you expect to travel abroad?'

Shallane smiled. 'Soon,' she promised.

'My little girl is ready to fly the coop,' Mortana said to Clive. Her face was wistful. 'Circumstances conspired against us, and I was sixteen before Batalji took me to his yurt. Too old.'

Clive tried to think of a suitable reply, was arrested by Batalji getting to his feet. Immediately the table was quiet; the waitresses stopped moving.

'My friends!' Batalji said. 'We are gathered here tonight to welcome Mr Yuan, who comes to us as representative of the People's Republic of China. Mr Yuan and I intend to hold fruitful talks over the next few days, talks which will influence the future of Asia, and Asia, my friends, is the world. But before we get down to serious business, it is my pleasure tonight to make an announcement of the greatest importance to my family and to my country, and, thus, to Asia and the world. I wish to announce that my daughter, the Princess Shallane, is to be married.' There was a gasp, and then a storm of applause, while Shallane stood up and made a little bow.

'That was a well-kept secret,' Clive whispered to Mortana, and then frowned, because for all their conversation he suddenly had a suspicion the secret had been kept from her as well.

'Now,' Batalji said. 'I know you are all eager to learn the name of the fortunate man on whom I am about to bestow my most treasured possession. Who else, I ask you, but my most treasured companion, and mentor and, I may add, my conscience. Ladies and gentlemen, I give you ... the Foreign Secretary, Clive Stanton.'

THE TWELFTH CHRONICLE

Yakutsk, Summer 2004

The noise was tremendous as the Mongol chieftains, obviously primed by the Khan, shouted and cheered and banged their glasses and knives on the table, so that the foreign diplomats could hardly do less. Mortana put her arms round Clive and kissed him. He stared across the table at Selphine, who looked like a snake about to strike; she equally could have had no idea what Batalji had been planning. Beside her, Mr Yuan was smiling benignly, obviously totally confused as to what was going on. Then Clive looked at Batalji, who was grinning at him. 'You will be my son,' Batalji said.

Clive felt fingers biting into his arm, and looked down, at Shallane. Her mouth was open, her tongue showing as she smiled. 'Will you make me scream, Stanton?' she asked.

The rest of the evening was a confused kaleidoscope. Batalji saw that everyone got drunk, with the exception of Rosemary, who had disappeared during the congratulations. 'I must go after her,' Clive muttered; he had just drunk several toasts in rapid succession, and the room was spinning about him.

'Don't be a fool,' Denise said, grasping his arm as he would have lurched to the doorway.

He looked down at her, blinked. 'You don't understand...'

'I do understand. And so must she. Batalji says she is going home anyway. Let her be insulted.'

'You don't understand,' he said again, and was then seized by several arms and pushed on to the table, where his feet broke and scattered the priceless crockery, and the people around him cheered.

'The bride!' they shouted. 'Let us have the bride!' Laughing, Shallane was pushed up beside him, a full glass of vodka overflowing down her gown. 'A kiss!' they shouted. 'A betrothal kiss!'

Shallane turned her face up, and he lowered his head to hers. I must stop this, he thought. I must tell them all now that it is impossible. This girl is young enough to be my daughter. I also hate her, and she hates me. And I am in love, and about to become a father. I must... Shallane's tongue pushed its way into his mouth. 'Make me scream, Stanton,' she whispered. 'Make me scream.'

'Hoist the bride,' they shouted. 'Hoist the bride.'

Shallane came against him, one leg wrapped itself around him to give him a purchase. He grasped her buttocks and lifted her up, and she turned herself to sit on his shoulder, holding on to his head with her other arm raised on high, while he staggered to and fro, destroying more crockery, scattering knives and forks and fruit, and finally stepped right off the table.

Shallane gave a dainty shriek and jumped from his shoulders. Jagnuth and Almani caught Clive before he hit the floor, and the assembly cheered, while Barone grinned as he held another jug of vodka to Clive's lips.

It was the middle of the following afternoon before Clive could get Batalji alone. Batalji was in a high good humour, and, as usual, revealed not a trace of a hangover. 'Now, Clive,' he said, waving his Foreign Minister to a chair before his desk. 'I think this Chinese thing is going off very well. So you can leave Yuan with me. I want you on the plane to Moscow this evening. This is most important. There must be no war between Russia and the Ukraine at this time.'

'I will do everything I can,' Clive promised. 'Batalji, we have to talk.'

Batalji grinned. 'About your wedding. Don't worry, it will not take place until next spring: Shallane will be nearly fifteen then.'

'Batalji, I cannot marry Shallane.'

'I know she is very young. But fully mature.'

'She hates me.'

Batalji grinned. 'Then you must teach her to love you. Whether she hates you or not, as you will be her husband, she will please you. I don't expect you to love her at this moment. Perhaps I don't expect you to love her at all. But she will please you. And this will please me.'

'I understand this, and I am flattered. Believe me. Were all things equal, I would be happy to do as you wish. But there is Rosemary to be considered.'

Batalji raised his eyebrows. 'Are you not sending her home?'

'She does not wish to go. She wishes me to marry her. She is bearing my child.'

Batalji gazed at him for several seconds. Then he said, 'Congratulations. She never managed to bear a child for me. Neither has Denise,' he said thoughtfully. 'I wonder if that wound I received, eight years ago ... but no matter. I congratulate you. Shallane will also bear you strong sons.'

'Yes, but Rosemary...'

'You are welcome to become a Moslem and marry her as well, Clive. But not until after you have married Shallane. My daughter must be your principal wife.'

'I have no desire to become a Moslem.'

'Then just take her as a wife. After Shallane. I give you my permission.'

'Batalji ... people just don't do that sort of thing. Not in a civilised community. The world will call you a savage.'

Batalji grinned. 'They will call you a savage as well, Clive. And they already consider me a savage. But a useful savage. I will tell you what the world will do: it will smile, benignly, as it has smiled, benignly, at everything I have accomplished. Everything you have accomplished, as well. I do not mind about this, and neither should you. Here in Yakutistan we make up our own rules as we go along. I don't intend that should change. And listen to me, Clive. Do you suppose I am just making you a present of a pretty little girl to warm your bed and as a reward for your services? I am making you a present of the most valuable jewel I possess. Don't misunderstand me. Once you are wed, she is yours. I will not have her come running back to me screaming of your ill-treatment. That is not the Mongol way, and Shallane understands this. Which is why I have said she will please you, or you have my permission to beat her as any Mongol husband would do. But she will also bear you those sons of whom I spoke. My grandsons, fathered by you, Clive. They will take their places behind my own sons. Who knows, if they please me, I will set them *alongside* my own sons. Life is a strange business, Clive: you could finish your life as the father of the ruler of Yakutistan.'

'You look at the future in too grand a manner, Batalji.'

'That is the only way to rule, Clive. You will not fail me in this. Rosemary will understand. She will make a fine mother. And I will make you a promise: I will make your son by Rosemary a prince, inferior only to my own sons and your sons by Shallane. If it is a girl, she will be a princess. Now, go and prepare to leave this afternoon.'

Clive stood up. 'Am I allowed to take Rosemary with me?'

Batalji gave one of his quiet smiles. 'I think, in all the circumstances, Clive, it would be best if she remained here.'

Rosemary sat in the garden, Sintax on her lap, enjoying the suddenly strong sun, while a team of men attempted to repair the damage done by the winter frosts; gardening in Yakutsk was an act of faith, but the plants always seemed to come back to life with the arrival of the sun, and flowers were blooming everywhere.

Clive sat beside her, and she glanced at him, and then away again. 'How was she?'

'It's not something one finds out in advance, with a khan's daughter.'

'The very idea is obscene.'

'I agree with you. But it is going to happen.'

'Because Batalji says so? Aren't you ever going to stand up to him? Oh, I know: you can't walk away from your responsibilities.'

'I can't walk away from you, either.'

'I thought you had already done that.'

'Try listening.' He repeated his conversation with Batalji. 'I'm afraid I came over a bit strong,' he explained. 'So now he reckons you should stay here for a while, just to make sure I don't do a runner.'

'Your friend,' she said bitterly.

'And yours, my darling. So ... would you like to be wife number two? Or, in fact, number one. Batalji and Shallane are certainly not interested in a Christian ceremony. So ... after my marriage to Shallane, you and I could be married, by a Christian priest.'

'There isn't one in Yakutsk.'

'There's a Russian Orthodox priest. Or Easterbrook could probably do it, for God's sake. Or we'll bloody well fly one in. Batalji isn't going to object. And then you'll be my legal wife.'

'While you're married illegally to someone else. That has got to be the most bizarre arrangement I have ever heard.'

'Wouldn't you say we are living in a bizarre society? Don't you want your son to be a prince?'

'A prince of outlaws? A prince of thieves?'

'What do you wish to do?'

'My wishes seem to be limited, darling. I'll take what I can get.' She held his hands. 'You're not going to go falling in love with that little spitfire, are you?'

Clive grinned. 'Batalji has promised me that once we're married, she's mine. I intend to knock some sense into her.'

'While loving every knock. Okay. It's a man's world, here in Yakutistan. You just remember that.'

'Well?' Selphine demanded. 'You have betrayed me.'

'I was as surprised as you, Princess. I should think that was obvious, to everyone.'

'Yes, it was obvious to everyone,' Selphine growled. 'Batalji has put a chain around your neck, secured to a tiger cub.'

'I promise you, she will be kept on a leash.'

'You don't know her as I do,' Selphine grumbled. 'She is an utter savage, and devoted to her father.'

'I am not in a position to defy the Khan, as you well know, Princess.'

'Ha,' Selphine growled. 'My only son. Do you know how often I wish that Baltomar's loins had been fruitful just one more time?'

'Now you are speaking treason.'

'Will you betray me, Stanton?'

'No, Princess. I would but ask you to be cautious. And reassure you. Your son has the makings of greatness in him. Perhaps it is in the nature of greatness to be extravagant, both of deed and word and gift. I know he seeks to bind me closer to him. But I am content that this should be so. He will never let you down. As I will never let him down.'

Selphine gazed at him for several seconds. 'It is you who have the seeds of greatness, Stanton,' she said at last. 'Those who serve can also be great, you know. By the quality of their servitude. I say only this to you: however many women Batalji presents to you, and there may be many more, for Batalji is a child of the steppes, to whom possession of women is in itself regarded as a sign of greatness, remain faithful to me, and I will remain faithful to you, and ensure your greatness. Betray me, and I will destroy you, in the name of my son.'

CHAPTER 12

Yakutsk, 2004-5

Batalji looked up as Shallane entered. It became chilly outside as soon as the evening drew in, and the girl still wore her fur coat and hat; concealed beneath the voluminous garments she looked older than her fourteen years. 'He has gone,' she announced.

'Did you bid him a fond farewell?'

'Of course, Papa. He is my betrothed.'

She went round the desk, and Batalji pushed his chair back so that she could sit on his knee. 'Did Denise film it?'

'Oh yes. She was filming constantly.'

'Excellent. We will send that video to all the television stations in the world, that everyone may know of your betrothal.'

She squirmed on his knee. 'Papa! Why do I have to marry Stanton?'

'Because I want you to.'

'But *why* do you want me to. I do not like him. He doesn't like me. I don't want to be fucked by Stanton.'

'Who do you want to be fucked by?'

'You.' He laughed, and kissed her nose. 'You are the Khan,' she told him. 'You can do anything. You can fuck anyone you choose.'

'And I will fuck you, one of these fine days. But you will be a virgin when you go to Stanton's bed.'

'Then I will be with child, and swell and be ugly.'

'And then you will be a mother, and fulfilled, and happy.'

'Never with Stanton.'

'Listen to me,' Batalji said. 'You will marry Stanton, and you will please him, and more important yet, when you are married to him, you will never let him out of your sight.' Shallane pulled her head back to frown at her father. 'Where he goes, you will go. Whatever he says, you will remember, so that you can tell me. Will you do this for me?'

'I will do anything for you, Papa. For how long must I do this thing?'

Batalji took off her hat and stroked the curling tawny hair. 'It will not be for very long. Can you keep a secret?'

'I can keep *your* secret, Papa.'

'No one knows of this. And no one must know of it. If anyone ever does, I will be very angry with you. You will never sit upon my knee again.'

'No one will ever know of it, Papa, not even if they tear me apart with wild horses.'

Batalji kissed her again. 'Then you and I will share this secret. Stanton is of great importance to me. But I do not trust him. I trust him even less in relation to my plans for the future. You will be my right arm, beside Stanton at all times. And one day, when I no longer need him, you will kill him for me. Would you like to do that?'

Shallane's eyes shone. 'When, Papa? When?'

'I will tell you when. But it will not be long now. Only a few years. Perhaps a few months. You will still be a young girl. And then, when you have carried out this task for me, I will let you choose any man in Yakutistan, any man in Russia, any man in Asia, any man in the world, to be your husband.'

Shallane hugged him. 'I will choose you, Papa.'

'I have said any man, Shallane, when the time comes.'

She bounced off his knee, went to the door, looked over her shoulder. 'Can I kill Stanton any way I choose?'

Batalji laughed. 'Of course. Providing you don't let him know what you are doing. Or he might kill you first.'

Shallane blew her father a kiss.

Batalji sat behind his desk in the huge control room of the military barracks, and surveyed the twelve men who stood before him. None of them were Mongols: they were from the south, dark-complexioned and big-nosed, tall and heavy-shouldered. They were members of that Moslem population which, over the centuries, had overflowed into southern Yakutistan and made its home there. Thus their wives and families still lived there.

Almani stood beside them; he had personally chosen every one. 'You know what you have to do?' Batalji asked.

'We know, Great Khan.'

'Have you been told the rewards you will receive when you have succeeded?'

'All the gold we may lift in our arms, using whatever utensil we choose,' they replied.

'Have you been told the punishment your families will suffer if you betray me?'

'They will suffer the death of a thousand cuts, Great Khan.'

'Now tell me what you have to do. Where are you going? You.'

'My companion and I are to go into Kazakhstan, Great Khan,' replied the man at whom Batalji was pointing.

'You.'

'My companion and I are to go to Kirghizia, Great Khan.'

'You.'

'My companion and I are to go to Azerbaijan, Great Khan.'

'You.'

'My companion and I are to go to Turkmenistan, Great Khan.'

'You.'

'My companion and I are to go to Uzbekistan, Great Khan.'

'And you.'

'My companion and I are to go to Krasnoyarskiy, Great Khan.'

'Your duties?'

'We are to contact our friends. We are to promise them great rewards, if they follow the course, and we are to give them sufficient money to whet their appetites. We are to tell them to await the word of the Khan, and then to act. We will not tell them how to act until we receive the word of the Khan.'

'You understand that there is not much time. Especially in Krasnoyarskiy, there is not much time.'

'We understand, Great Khan.'

'Then go about your duties.' The men bowed, and filed from the room. Batalji looked at Almani. 'What of the others?'

'My agents have worked well,' Almani told him. 'We have sufficient members of the Parliaments of both Krasnoyarskiy and Kazakhstan in our pay. In particular, General Morodosky, who commands the Kazakh army, is in our pay.'

'Tell me of the emigration. Are there problems?'

'As yet, no. Those of our people I have sent south and southwest are good Moslems. Or at least, they pretend to be. And there are not very many of them, as yet. No one is objecting.'

'They will eventually, when the numbers grow,' Jagnuth remarked. He was standing on the far side of the room.

'Then part of our Course may be conducted for us,' Batalji pointed out. 'Are your people ready for the manoeuvres?'

'Yes,' Jagnuth said. 'You have not told me if you wish foreign observers to be there.'

'Are your people good enough?'

'They are good enough.'

'Then invite the foreign attachés. And Mr Yuan. Let them see what our Yakut army is capable of.' Batalji leaned back in his chair. 'It is all going very well.'

'You understand,' Jagnuth said, 'that once you give the word, Batalji, there can be no going back.'

'Are you afraid, Jagnuth? You were never afraid before,' Betalji pointed out.

'I am not afraid now,' Jagnuth protested. 'I am concerned. You have done great things, Batalji. It seems senseless to risk it all now.'

'Risk what?' Batalji asked.

'Well, the prosperity of Yakutistan. The love of your people. Your standing in the international community.'

'Like my mother, Jagnuth, you have been watching too much Western television,' Batalji said. 'You are allowing yourself to grow soft, to think of your wife and family, instead of the will of destiny. Do you oppose the Course?'

'Of course I don't, Batalji. But...'

'You speak of the prosperity of Yakutistan. Can a nation ever be prosperous while it is covered in snow for eight months of the year? You talk of the love of my people. My people love me because I overthrew the Taychins, because I have given them material things they never before possessed, and because I am the descendant of Genghis Khan. The first two are transient. Now every household has its dishwasher and its washing machine and its television set. Now they all want cars. Soon they will all want to travel. Then they will no longer wish to be soldiers. Then all they will remember is that I am a descendant of Genghis Khan, and they will ask, what is this descendant of Genghis Khan, who sits on his ass in the Presidential Palace and grows fat and rich? How can he be a descendant of Genghis Khan?'

'Your people will always love you. Did not Talane and Rutka die for you?'

'Yes. They died because we were at war with the Taychins. Well, soon we will be at war again, and my people will have the opportunity to die for me all over again.'

'What you are planning is too big, too immense,' Jagnuth protested. 'Suppose we are defeated at any stage? It will mean the end of us all, of everything we have created.'

'Was Genghis Khan ever defeated?'

'That was a different time, different people, different weapons, different political systems, a different...' He checked what he was going to say.

'A different man?' Batalji asked softly. 'I am a better man, because I know more than did Temujin. I have learned more. But one particular thing I have learned is that the world has not really changed, except to our advantage. You forget that I have seen this world in action, and Stanton has told me more. Stanton has told me of the ease with which Hitler conquered Europe, with which Stalin took over most of Hitler's empire. I have seen for myself how reluctant the West, the United Nations, are to interfere in the affairs of other states. Equally do I know there are many people who consider that the break-up of the old Soviet Union was a bad thing, that it jeopardises world trade as well as world peace. Many of those people are in the various armies of the CIS, especially Russia. There are many people in the world who will welcome the Course, if we hoodwink them into believing we are the injured party, and if we are quick and clean and decisive about what we do. And if we are ruthless enough. We will not fail.'

'It is a demographic impossibility, for two million people to conquer two hundred and fifty million,' Jagnuth insisted.

'Two hundred and fifty million?'

'That is approximately the population of the CIS.'

Batalji grinned. 'And then there are a hundred million in China, and seven hundred and fifty million in the subcontinent. Do you know, those odds are more in our favour than when Genghis Khan set forth?'

Batalji himself was at the airport to greet his returning Foreign Secretary. As was Denise, to film their meeting, at which Batalji embraced Clive, hugging him close before escorting him to the waiting limousine. It was high summer, and Yakutsk basked in the sun. Crowds lined the street to greet their Khan, whose car was escorted by a squadron of Mongol horsemen, carrying lances from which horse-tails floated in the breeze. 'I wasn't that successful,' Clive confessed.

Batalji grinned. 'You have arranged both a cease-fire and a conference.'

'I don't have all that much confidence in the cease-fire, and the conference can't be convened for another three months. Then it will drag on throughout the winter, and we shall probably be back where we started next year. The plain fact is that the Russians and the Ukrainians hate each other. It goes back a long time. The Ukrainians tried to grab independence back in 1918, after the Russian defeat in World War One. And there is a considerable body of thought which holds that if Hitler had offered them some kind of autonomy in 1941, instead of treating them as a conquered people, he would have won the war – at least against the Soviet Union.'

'The important thing is that we, you, Clive, have kept them from each other's throats. That is all we can do, endeavour to keep the peace. The world is most appreciative. There have been telegrams of congratulations from all over the place. Even from our friend Yuan. Peace is the thing.' Clive gave him a sidelong glance; Batalji was uttering sentiments he would have said were the last any Mongol truly believed. Batalji grinned. 'Would you not agree that we have too much to do here to get involved in a war?'

'There would be no necessity for us to become involved,' Clive said.

'I do not agree. I believe that if the CIS ever falls apart, and it has showing increasing signs of doing this over the past few years, then we will be involved. There are too many corrupt governments in the CIS. In all the world, perhaps.'

'Yes,' Clive said drily. There was, of course, no reason for Batalji's Government to be corrupt; it owned everything anyway. 'I saw the videos of your manoeuvres. They were very impressive.'

'You must tell Jagnuth. He will be very pleased.'

'Who exactly were they intended to impress? Yuan?'

'He was impressed, certainly,' Batalji agreed. 'I think, in times like these, it is necessary to let the whole world know that Yakutistan will defend itself to the last drop of its blood, if it ever has to.'

Clive nodded. 'There was a good deal of comment amongst the ministers in Moscow. One of the Russian generals worked out that you had three quarters of a million people under arms.'

'Give or take a thousand,' Batalji agreed.

'Out of a population of two point one million.'

'We are a nation of fighters. I wish people to remember that.'

'The experts are wondering just how you did it.'

'I gave a week's holiday,' Batalji said ingenuously.

Clive decided to leave that subject; he had a more important one on his mind. 'I'd like to talk to you about this emigration problem.'

'What emigration problem?' Batalji asked, carelessly.

'You are not aware that something like six thousand Yakuts have fled Yakutistan since the spring? This is according to a report given me by Nita.'

'And she should know,' Batalji agreed, more carelessly yet.

'This doesn't bother you?'

'Six thousand people? I have a few left.'

'It is surely a sign of discontent. You are giving your people everything you think they should have. But from the start I have wondered whether that is the best way to go about it. Paternalistic states have been tried before, in Europe. All that has resulted has been a collapse of the human will to work hard enough to achieve anything.'

'You are thinking of socialistic experiments, such as Sweden or Britain thirty years ago,' Batalji said. He was always surprising Clive by the scope of the reading he had done since seizing power and having access to the Taychins' library. 'That was caused by the high taxes necessary to *pay* for paternalism,' Batalji argued. 'My people have no taxes.'

'Yet six thousand of your people, with their families, have upped and moved, mainly into Krasnoyarskiy. A Russian republic, Batalji. Surely that indicates something is wrong here.'

'Or six thousand people find it so,' Batalji agreed.

Clive sighed. 'What is even more disturbing is that according to Nita's report these people are drawn from amongst the best educated and most intelligent of your people. That is very bad.'

'What would you have me do, Clive? Patrol my borders with armed guards and give them orders to shoot anyone trying to leave? Like East Germany in the seventies and eighties? Would that please your friends in the West?'

'Of course not. What I am suggesting is that we endeavour to find out the cause of this emigration.'

Batalji squeezed his hand. 'I make that your charge.'

'But you refuse to worry about it.'

'What have I to worry about? The oil is flowing, the sun is shining, and I am content. I expect my people to be content also. If they are not, let them leave. There will be more for those who remain.'

'Even oil-rich states can go bankrupt, Batalji. Especially if they suffer a brain-drain.'

Batalji gave his sleepy smile. 'Yakutistan will never go bankrupt, Clive. Because you will always be standing at my shoulder, admonishing me, checking me, keeping my feet upon the straight and narrow, eh? Now, I tell you what we are going to do. We are going to go home, and we are going to get in some of the girls, and we are going to get drunk. You have had a great triumph, in organising this conference, in being appointed its convenor and chairman. It is a great triumph for Yakutistan. I wish you to know how pleased I am. How grateful. Now you must rest and relax for a while. This time next year you will be married, eh? You will be my son-in-law. I am looking forward to that.'

In the spring of 2005, even before the snows melted, Yakutsk was *en fête*. Red banners, crossed with black and yellow stripes, flew from every house, fluttered from every tree, lined every fence and hoarding. Foreign dignitaries arrived by the planeload. No heads of state were present, but almost every country in the world wished to be represented at the wedding of the Khan's daughter.

Three months before the wedding, Rosemary gave birth to

a baby boy. What with chairing the conference trying to arrange peace between Russia and the Ukraine, which kept breaking up as the cease-fire was broken and having to be rearranged, Clive had been unable to spend as much time with her over the winter as he would have liked, but he was delighted with the relationship which had sprung up between them, perhaps enhanced by the bizarre situation hanging over their heads. But that in itself deepened their mental intimacy; while Rosemary accepted that he had to go through a form of marriage with Shallane, she took refuge in the fact that it would not really be any marriage recognised by their society, and that their own marriage would take place later on in the year; with his usual sleepy good humour Batalji had supported that plan enthusiastically, and told them by all means import a priest to solemnise the event later on in the year. 'How may a man live with only one woman?' he had asked, giving one of his huge laughs.

For Clive himself, his situation was heady. In the short space of five years he had jumped from being one of the best-known and respected journalists in the world to being one of the best-known and respected diplomats in the world. He felt he had brought a fresh outlook to the international political scene by his straight talking, and he knew that most of his fellow diplomats had no doubt at all that he was the guiding force behind Batalji's search for respectability and prosperity; if they could still find a great deal to criticise in Yakut policy and social conditions, they were prepared to accept Clive's insistence that, dealing with a people and a government which had emerged from such total primitiveness, they simply had to be patient, and that the vital factor was to overcome Batalji's paranoic fear of invasion, or coercion, from any source, but particularly from Russia. Only he knew that there were serious, and growing, domestic problems to be solved. His efforts to keep the peace within the CIS had only heightened his reputation.

While he remained a young, strong, virile man. However much he still valued Denise, or had grown to love Rosemary, the thought of taking Shallane to bed had to be stimulating, even if he could recognise that Batalji was appealing to all that was base in his character. He could relieve his conscience by telling himself, over and over again, that this was the hand Destiny had dealt him, and that he must play it to the end, and hope to return both the women, and perhaps even Shallane, to conventional morality in the end. And yet his heartbeat quickened as he thought of that tumultuous reincarnation of Selphine as a girl, waiting for him! But now... He cradled the babe. 'Have you chosen a name?'

'Well, I think Clive is appropriate for starters. I'll choose some others later. Now tell me what's on your mind. Or don't you really like your son?'

He restored the baby to her arms, kissed her forehead. 'I adore my son. It's this emigration problem. Over the past year nearly ten thousand of our people have upped and left Yakutistan.'

'I guess they don't like being drilled all the time.'

'I would say you're absolutely right. And Batalji won't do anything about it, even when I point out that it reflects very badly on his Government. Well, we've managed to keep it a private matter up till now. But the Ministry has just received an official complaint from the Krasnoyarskiy government – it's an autonomous state within Russia, you know, just as Yakutiya was before Batalji took over. Well, if that comes out into the open, it is going to be damned embarrassing for us all.'

'What are you going to do about it?'

He grinned. 'Not a lot for the next few weeks; I have been temporarily relieved of all duties to concentrate on my wedding.'

She stuck out her tongue at him.

Jagnuth instructed Clive in what he had to do. 'It is all playacting, of course,' the General said. 'But yet is it an age-old ceremony, and must be carried out properly.'

'I understand. But you are not happy about it.' Jagnuth raised his eyebrows. 'I have not seen you smile these past few months,' Clive said.

'I will smile at your wedding,' Jagnuth promised.

Clive knew that deception was part of a Mongol's stock in trade, that deception was always directed to his enemies. No Mongol would ever dream of deceiving a friend, much less a relative ... but Jagnuth was in possession of some knowledge, affecting him he was certain, which he was not prepared to divulge. 'Then I shall be your nephew-in-law,' he reminded him.

'I shall be pleased about that,' Jagnuth said, and left.

Clive was not altogether surprised to receive a visit from Selphine, on the morning before the day of his wedding, even if it was very unusual for the Princess to call on any of her son's subjects, rather than the other way around. Certainly she had never been in Clive's house before. She stalked through the downstairs rooms while the Yakut servants trembled, went out back to look at the garden and the river ... 'Shallane will make changes here,' she announced.

'I will decide what changes, if any, are to be made in my house, Highness,' Clive promised her.

She glanced at him. 'She will rule you, Stanton.'

'Batalji has told me that I need give the Princess no privileges not usually accorded a Mongol wife.'

'Ha!' She went down the steps, seated herself in the sun, her face turned up. Daschbog was one of her gods, and unlike her son, she believed in him. 'You are too confident, Stanton. You are arrogant.' She smiled. 'Perhaps that is what I like best about you. Sit beside me. Are you pleased with Rosemary, for giving you a son?'

'Of course.'

'Shallane is not pleased. When she heard the news she spat like the tiger cub she is.'

Clive grinned. 'She'll be happy when she has a son as well.'

'And you will never spare a thought for me again,' Selphine said.

'You will always be in my thoughts,' Clive assured her, and he was not lying.

'Then take me upstairs and fuck me in your own bed, Stanton.'

She lay in his arms, quiescent at last. 'Do you remember of what we spoke, Stanton?'

'We have spoken of many things, Highness.'

'Of my son's ambitions.'

Clive stroked her hair. 'I think Batalji is settling into contentment, Highness.'

'Because he is forty-three? Bah! He has not yet begun to live. Have you spoken to him about this emigration problem?'

Clive frowned; her head was on his shoulder, so he could not see her face. 'I have spoken with him, yes.'

'And what did he say?'

'He refuses to take it seriously. He says if his people want to go, then they should go. That is why I am suggesting he is losing his ambition.'

'You are a fool, Stanton. Do you not know that these people have been sent?'

Clive sat up, which meant that she had to as well, as her head bumped on his lap. 'Sent by whom?'

'Sent by my son.'

'I do not understand, Highness. Batalji is sending his people away? I cannot believe it.'

'It is true,' Selphine insisted. 'I do not understand it myself. I think you should ask him about it, Stanton.'

'When I resume my duties,' Clive promised. He did not wish to think about it right that minute.

THE THIRTEENTH CHRONICLE

Yakutistan, Spring 2005

Clive's stag party, organised and controlled by Batalji himself, lasted three days and nights and ended up with all the guests scattered about the Palace in a state of dishevelled, drunken unconsciousness, including the girls who had been brought in for the men's entertainment. Yet, as usual, Batalji was first up, driving people into the baths, making the corridors echo with his booming laughter. 'You have only a few hours,' he told Clive. 'Only a few hours.'

Clive staggered home, was bathed and shaved and dressed by his domestics. For the first time in his life he was to wear uniform. This had been Batalji's decision. 'The man who marries my daughter has to wear uniform,' he had insisted. Batalji had designed the uniform himself, as he had taken up designing all of his officers' uniforms. Clive wore a red jacket and green pants, with a white belt, and felt like a refugee from *The Chocolate Soldier*. He was acutely embarrassed when Denise arrived to take his photograph, several times.

'You look terrible,' she said. 'Did you enjoy your stag party?'

'I'm afraid I can't remember. Did we keep you awake?'

'I should think you kept all of Yakutsk awake. I know it was all Mortana could do to prevent Shallane from joining you. But I was awake anyway. I was filming it. I used the one-way mirrors.'

The ceremony took place in the great downstairs hall of the Presidential Palace; this was so that all the guests could be accommodated. There were several hundred guests, and the hall was filled with tables, at which they sat close together. Clive found himself seated between Almani and Jagnuth, opposite, at a distance of some six feet, Batalji and Mortana, who had Shallane between them. Selphine sat on Batalji's right, Barone on his mother's left. The two smaller boys, Tensan and Dorgat, sat beyond their grandmother and brother, respectively, and beyond them again there was another host of Borjigin and Serhat and Anhusat relatives. A place was set for Denise, but she was flitting around with her latest camcorder.

Shallane wore the traditional long white silk robe of a bride from the steppes. With her high-coned headdress and her braided hair she looked much older than fourteen – her fifteenth birthday was in fact the following week.

Vodka flowed, libations were poured on the floor. Foreign dignitaries and their wives got drunk. Denise filmed. Clive didn't have to get drunk, because one sip of vodka sent his head swimming again. He gazed at Shallane, and Shallane gazed back at him, and her pink tongue slipped between her teeth for a moment before being withdrawn again. 'It is time,' Jagnuth whispered.

Clive drank some more vodka, took a deep breath, and stood up. What he was about to do was so totally foreign to his nature that he felt a stranger to himself. But it was what everyone expected, because this was a traditional Mongol wedding. At the sight of him standing all the babbling conversation died, and the orchestra ceased playing. For a moment the only sound was the gentle whirring of Denise's camcorder, now focused on him. Clive stepped on to his chair and then on to the table, kicking crockery and cutlery to either side. 'Great Khan,' he announced, 'I claim my bride.'

He was not required to wait for an answer. He jumped down between the tables, ran forward, and leapt on to the second table. Shallane gave an impressive scream, Mortana and Selphine covered their eyes. Batalji stood up, but knocked over his chair as he backed away from the table; traditionally, the father of the bride played no part in the tableau. Barone also stood up, but he dragged his chair away with him to give Clive space.

Clive jumped down into the opening, stepped round Mortana, who now had her head cradled in her arms on the table, and grasped Shallane's hand. Shallane stood up quickly enough, and Barone grasped Clive's shoulder. Clive turned somewhat more violently than he was supposed to, and swung his fist. This was his own addition to the play-acting, and it was something he had been waiting to do for four years. His closed fist caught Barone on the chin and sent the young man tumbling over his brother and several more people. Shallane gave another dainty scream, this one far more genuine, as she saw her big brother spreadeagled on the floor, then she gasped as Clive drove his shoulder into her midriff and straightened. Her legs were in front, and these he grasped to stop her kicking him, but he could do nothing about her arms at the moment, and she added some play-acting of her own by thumping him on the back, and reaching down to pull up his tunic, drive her fingers into his pants, and scrape her nails over his buttocks. Batalji bellowed with laughter.

Clive hurried down the row of cheering guests, Shallane trying to kick in front and, frustrated there by his firm grasp on her thighs, punching and scratching behind, and out into the open. At the foot of the steps was a Mercedes convertible with the roof down, engine already running. Traditionally it should have been a horse, but Batalji knew that Clive was not a rider. Clive ran down the steps, puffing now, because even at fourteen Shallane was no lightweight, threw the girl into the back of the car in a flurry of legs and skirt, got behind the wheel, gunned the engine, and roared out of the drive and down The Avenue, before swinging off for the airport. All the roads had been cleared and the crowds were kept back by a row of policemen as the car raced down the street. People cheered as Shallane, having got her breath back, sat up and put both arms around Clive's neck, from behind, causing the car to sway dangerously from side to side. 'I could strangle you now,' she remarked into Clive's ear.

'You wouldn't make it before I stopped the car and ruined your complexion,' he retorted.

She gave a gurgle of laughter. 'We are going to have such *fun*, Stanton.' She kissed the back of his head, released him, and then climbed over the back of the seat to land beside him. 'Oof.'

The crowds cheered ever more loudly. Now the airport was in sight. Again, all traffic had been banned and all flights suspended. The Yak executive jet waited on the runway, its doors opened. Clive drove past the control tower and the airport building, on to the runway, and braked to a halt at the foot of the steps. Here there were several people waiting, but he ignored them, as he was required to do, opened the door, and dragged Shallane out. By now her headdress had come off and her hair was flying everywhere, despite the weight of the coins with which it was set. Clive was too exhausted to consider lifting her again, so he pushed her up the steps in front of him. She stumbled and fell, and he held her hips and thrust her through the doorway. There were two hostesses, wearing green uniforms and sidecaps and looking as uncurious as they could, as the bride entered the cabin on her hands and knees. The aircraft's interior had been redesigned for Batalji's comfort, and consisted of a galley immediately behind the flight deck, a lounge/diner with six comfortable armchairs and six more chairs around a dining table, and aft, a sleeping cabin with a double bed and a dressing table. This had its own bathroom right aft; the crews' toilet was forward, so that the

Khan and whichever woman he happened to have along were guaranteed complete privacy.

'Welcome aboard, Your Excellency,' the hostesses said. 'If you would like to fasten your seat belts . . .'

Their luggage was already stowed, and the aircraft engines were roaring. The door was closed. Clive helped Shallane to her feet, thrust her into one of the armchairs, sat opposite. The hostesses left the cabin and went forward. Shallane smiled at her husband. 'I scratched your ass all up.'

'I am not going to forget it.'

She stuck out her tongue at him. 'Papa says you fucked so many women during the last three days you won't be capable again until tomorrow.'

Clive couldn't remember how many women there had been. But he certainly meant to consummate this marriage just as soon as possible: he had waited too long to get his hands on this little she-cat – perhaps from the moment of their first meeting. The plane was airborne, and winging to the northwest. The seatbelt light went out, and Clive released himself. The forward door opened and one of the hostesses came in. 'Would you care for anything to eat or drink?'

'You have got to be joking,' Clive said. 'When do we land?'

'The flight will take three hours.'

'Right,' Clive said. 'Then take the rest of the afternoon off. No matter what happens, unless we are actually crashing, no one is to come through that door until we land.' The hostess looked from him to Shallane, then gave a brief smile and bowed. The door closed behind her.

'You are not capable,' Shallane said again. Clive bent over her to release her belt. For a moment she remained sitting quite still, then as he tried to close his hands on her arms to lift her up, she slid down the seat and past his legs, turning on to her hands and knees on the cabin floor. He turned as well, and as she surged away from him, wrapped his hands in the heavy folds of her skirt. She kept on going, and the dress ripped down the back. She staggered out of it, tripped, and landed on her hands and knees again, while he saw to his consternation that she was wearing absolutely nothing underneath, a marvellous slither of surprisingly well-developed femininity.

She looked over her shoulder. 'It was such a pretty dress. Mama will be very angry. She was married in that dress herself.' She was facing him now, ready for his next move, small breasts heaving as she panted, muscles flexing in her strong thighs. Clive gazed at her as he stripped himself; he knew he was not going to have the time later on. Her lip curled. 'You're the smallest man I have ever seen.'

'But growing bigger,' he pointed out, and ran at her. She attempted to duck under his arm again, but he caught her hair. She gave a shriek of mingled pain and rage, and fell over, hitting the cabin floor with a crash that made the plane tremble.

Still holding her hair, Clive caught a wrist as well and dragged her over the carpet towards the bedroom door. 'You shit!' she shouted. 'You bastard! You asshole.' She kicked her legs as she tried to regain her feet, and tried too to catch one of the chairs with her free hand. But Clive was pulling her too hard, and they arrived at the door in a heap. He released her hair to open it, and half threw her past him.

She landed on her knees at the foot of the bed, and before she could recover he had thrown both arms round her waist from behind to dump her on the bed. She lay on her face, panting, but he didn't trust her, and knelt beside her, one hand on each shoulder blade, pressing her into the mattress. 'Do I get five points for this?' he asked.

'Shit!' she moaned, kicking her feet, but unable to move her body beneath his weight.

'Now, let's see,' he said, 'I suppose you don't know about simple matters like lying on your back with your legs apart. Do you?'

'Let me go!' She heaved beneath his hands, to no avail.

'I could try buggering you,' he suggested.

'Bastard! Let me go.'

'The trouble is, I don't think I'm hard enough to make that. But if I let you go, I can't trust you to behave. And you've left me with a sore bum. So . . .' It was something he wanted to do in any event. He slid his hands down from her shoulders to hold her thighs, then lowered his head, and bit her right buttock, breaking the flesh. Shallane gave a scream of genuine pain and outrage, and twisted away from him. 'Now you have my mark,' Clive told her, watching the sheets stain with blood. 'You'll probably have that scar for life.'

'God, I am in agony!' Shallane shrieked. 'What are you, some kind of vampire?' She attempted to roll off the bed, but Clive caught her and brought her back. She struck at his face with her nails, and he held her wrists and forced her back on to the bed, throwing his leg across hers to keep her still, but now on her back. She spat at him, gasping for breath.

'What shall we do now?' Clive asked. 'I'm almost hard enough to batter down even your doors. I think my best bet is to beat you for a while. Your father suggested I should do that. And it's something I really want to do.' He lowered his head to put his lips against her ear. 'Will you scream, when I beat you, Shallane? Dear, dear Shallane.' Because suddenly he was lying on top of her, and kissing her mouth. Her response was immediate, her legs untwining themselves from his to wrap themselves around him, her hands going down to hold him. Then he was on his back and she was astride him, her face a mixture of pain and anticipation and delight and she sank on to him. Then she fell forward on to his chest to kiss him, while he exploded inside her. 'I really didn't expect to make that,' he said, when he got his breath back.

'You will always make me,' she promised him, sucking his chin. 'Until the day I kill you.'

'Won't be long now,' he agreed, reflecting that when he was sixty she would still be only thirty-three.

So what have you become, Clive Stanton? he wondered. Why, a Mongol, to be sure. In word and deed, now, as well as intent. He had even lived the life of a Mongol, for the past three weeks. The village to which Batalji had sent them was really nothing more than a large *ordu*, populated by a family of

Yakuts, but members of the Serhat clan, and therefore relatives of Shallane. Here they had been welcomed, and here he could see the simple, healthy, vigorous life of these people at first-hand, and indeed, take part in it, living off kumiss and millet, riding with the young men to tend the herds, while they laughed at the way he needed a saddle.

Shallane laughed as well, although she was anxious that he should do well in front of others, and spent some time teaching him how to sit properly and how to control his mount with his knees. Out here on the steppes, wearing loose pants and a baggy shirt, her hair trailing in the breeze, she was in her element, far removed from the hothouse harridan of the Presidential Palace. But equally she was the most tireless, consuming lover he had ever experienced. She swarmed over him in the warm seclusion of their yurt, taking pleasure in exhausting him, following which she would play with herself until she too was exhausted. And she was only just fifteen years old. Had he then achieved what every middle-aged heterosexual man dreamed of in his secret moments? He wished he could believe that, could convince himself that he was not really living a nightmare, from which he would suddenly awaken . . . to what?

It was not a situation he could ever expect any normal, civilised human being to understand. Yet he was aware of an utter contentment. This was partly because he was existing in a never-never world. The *ordu* to which they had been sent possessed no medium- or high-frequency radios, only an old battery VHF set, which was used for contacting other nearby clans, but which could not pick up any news bulletins from Yakutsk. The plane, having dropped them, had left immediately, and would not return for them until their month was up. So, for that month, they were completely cut off from the outside world, as far removed from affairs of state as if they had been on another planet. 'Would you not like to stay here with me, forever?' Shallane asked him, as they snuggled together on their bed of skins and blankets. But next morning the Yak was overhead, circling down to land on the grass strip beside the village. 'They are not due for another week,'

Shallane remarked, as they watched the steps being put down.

'Something has happened,' Clive muttered. He had, after all, been living in a fool's paradise. Which had now abruptly ended, for disembarking from the plane was Almani Serhat. Clive hurried forward to embrace his friend.

'Clive! Princess!' Almani saluted Shallane. 'I am sorry to interrupt your honeymoon, but I have been sent by the Khan to bring you back. He has found it necessary to invade Krasnoyarskiy.'

Clive was seated in the aircraft and it was taking off before he could properly digest what he had been told. 'You mean we are at war?' he demanded. 'With Russia?'

'Not as yet. That is why he wants you back, to *stop* a war.'

Clive scratched his head, and glanced at Shallane, who was looking from one to the other with great interest. 'If we have invaded another country, then we are at war,' he said.

'It is not as simple as that,' Almani argued.

'You had better tell me what has happened.'

'It is to do with the Yakut emigration to Krasnoyarskiy over the past year. There has been some resentment in Krasnoyarskiy.'

'I tried to warn Batalji about this.'

'Well, two weeks ago a band of Russians attacked some of our settlers. Apparently trouble had been simmering for some months, and the Russians were whipped up by a local agitator. Anyway, two houses belonging to our people were burned down. With our people inside.'

'My God!' Clive commented. 'And Batalji invaded because of that?'

'The Khan acted with great restraint. But he demanded compensation, and safeguards for the rest of our people. There was a great debate in the Krasnoyarsk Parliament. As you know, there has been virtual anarchy in Krasnoyarskiy for the past six months and a tremendous amount of unrest and dissatisfaction with the government. Now some members of their parliament sided with Batalji, and accused their own people of outlawry. There was uproar, and the result was that when the president adjourned the parliament, several members accused him of tyranny and seeking to make himself a dictator, and wrote to Batalji calling on him to intervene and save the country.'

Clive frowned. 'Batalji knew nothing of this beforehand? It wasn't his agents stirring up the unrest?'

'Of course not. And he was very reluctant to act. But then some more of our people were attacked by a mob, and stoned to death. Now there were demonstrations in Yakutsk, and calls for vengeance. And it so happened that our army was already mobilised on the Krasnoyarsk frontier, for the manoeuvres, so he ordered it across the border.'

'Just when did all this start to happen?'

'Three days after your wedding.'

'Then why was I not recalled immediately?'

'Batalji didn't think it was serious enough to call you back from your honeymoon, Clive.'

'So instead he invaded to protect his nationals. That has a very unfortunate historic ring about it, Almani. The first thing Batalji must do is call back his troops.'

'That is not so easily done,' Almani said.

'Why not? Even if he is engaged with Russian or Krasnoyarsk forces, it should be possible to arrange a cease-fire.'

'Our troops are already in Krasnoyarsk,' Almani said.

Shallane clapped her hands.

CHAPTER 13

New York, Summer 2005

Clive strode into Batalji's office, and paused in surprise. He had no experience of wars from the inside, as it were, but he would have expected ... something. Yet there had seemed nothing unusual on the streets of Yakutsk, and now, the warlord's office was empty, save for Batalji himself, seated at his desk smoking a cigar. 'Clive!' Batalji got up to embrace his son-in-law. 'I apologise most humbly for bringing you back from your honeymoon like this, but it is necessary. Tell me, how is Shallane? Did you beat her, as I advised you? Did she please you?'

Clive half fell into a chair before the desk. 'Batalji! What is going on? Almani tells me you have occupied Krasnoyarsk.'

'That is true. It is a great tribute to the fighting qualities of our troops.'

'Batalji, it is more than two thousand kilometres from Krasnoyarsk to Yakutsk. And this war has been going on for less than a fortnight. What you are saying is impossible, even if there was no opposition at all to our people.'

'Well, there wasn't much. But actually, Krasnoyarsk was occupied on the second day of the war, by our airborne *tuman*.

We softened it up a little first, by aerial bombardment, then we sent in the paras. The Commissars were taken entirely by surprise. Pirale was in command. He has accomplished a magnificent feat of arms.'

It was several seconds before Clive could speak, even as he realised that, to Batalji, the Russians were still the Soviets. Then he said, 'You sent in bombers and an airborne division, before any declaration of war?'

'There has still not been any declaration of war, yet. It has all happened so suddenly.'

'Were there many casualties?'

'You cannot have a bombardment, Clive, without casualties.'

'And what is the world doing about it?'

Batalji grinned. 'The Russians have mobilised, but there has been additional trouble along the Ukraine border, and they are afraid that if they attack us the Ukraine will attack them. President Obolonsky has said so.'

'I didn't know Obolonsky was a friend of yours. He has never appeared so in the past.'

'He and I have signed a pact of mutual support,' Batalji said.

'When did this happen?'

'About a year ago.'

'While I was negotiating a peace conference between Russia and the Ukraine.'

'Well, why do you suppose Obolonsky agreed to that conference?'

'Batalji, you did that behind my back.'

'I know how busy you were.'

'But you have never told me this until now. I am sorry, Batalji,' Clive said. 'But in the circumstances, I have no option but to resign as Foreign Minister.'

'My dear Clive, you cannot resign. What would you do?'

'I'll return to the West and resume my career as a TV journalist.'

'That is absurd. What about your wife? My daughter? And what about Rosemary? Your son? What about my mother?

What about me?' Clive realised he had never before stopped to consider how many hostages he had given to fortune over the past five years. 'Anyway,' Batalji said. 'I need you now, more than ever. The United Nations have demanded that I withdraw my troops from Krasnoyarskiy.'

'Well, that was obvious.'

'I am not going to withdraw them. There is no necessity to do so,' Batalji asserted. 'Indeed, there is every necessity to keep them there. The United Nations do not understand about these matters. But as I said, I was invited into Krasnoyarskiy by elements in the Government, and in the armed services, who wish to be ruled by me rather than by President Kutchuk. I am not surprised about this. Kutchuk is running a military dictatorship.'

'And you are not?'

Batalji grinned. 'My people like my form of dictatorship. Now the people of Krasnoyarskiy wish to enjoy it too. Don't worry, we intend to hold elections as soon as possible, and if a majority ask for my people to leave, then they will leave.'

'Only you know they won't. Not after you've had control of their media for a few months. Batalji, this is madness.'

'It is also necessary for our own safety,' Batalji went on as if Clive hadn't spoken. 'We have obtained documentation which proves that Russia is preparing to launch a pre-emptive strike against us, through Krasnoyarskiy, as soon as the Ukrainian question is definitely settled.'

'Is that true?'

'I will show you the documents. Now, what I want you to do, is go to the West, go to the United Nations, speak with the American Secretary of State – it is only he who really matters – and explain the situation to him. Explain that I am obeying the will of the inhabitants of Krasnoyarskiy, and at the same time protecting my own people. Make him understand that far from disturbing the peace of Asia, what I have done will maintain it.'

'You genuinely believe that, don't you?'

'What I believe is of no importance. It is what the world believes. What you make them believe.'

'You expect me to lie, and lie again. I'm sorry, Batalji, it's not my scene.'

Batalji leaned forward across his desk. His smile was as sleepy as ever, but his eyes were pools of brittle midnight. 'I am asking this of you, Clive, because you are my son-in-law, because Denise is precious to you, because Rosemary is your mistress, and because she is the mother of your son. Now, can you refuse me?'

Clive met his gaze. 'I had foolishly supposed we were friends. That together we were building something out here in the steppes. Something worthwhile.'

Batalji leaned back again. 'We *are* friends. That is why I can ask a favour of you. And we are building. What I am asking you to do is part of the process. I am sorry to rush you, but you must leave immediately.'

Clive stood up. 'As we are friends who ask favours of each other, Batalji, am I allowed to ask one of you?'

Batalji grinned. 'Anything you wish, and if it is possible, I will give it to you.'

'I would like your solemn word that everything that has happened is as you say, that it was not planned in any way.'

Batalji grinned. 'Then I give you my word. I give you my word that I seek peace and stability in Central Asia. Secure me that peace, and I will give you the stability.'

Clive barely had the time to kiss his baby on the forehead, hold Rosemary in his arms. Now he was home, what an obscene nightmare was his marriage. 'Have you seen the videos?' she asked.

'I'll look at them on the plane. Were they bad?'

'They were horrifying. Squadrons of Fulcrums and Rafales, and the new fighter-bombers, you know, the ones based on the European design, flying virtually at rooftop level, blasting away with their cannon. They cut a swathe across the countryside for their tanks to follow. They used their thousand-pound bombs on military targets, and they knew just where their targets were.'

'And on Krasnoyarsk, I gather.'

Rosemary nodded. 'What are you going to do?'

'Beg the UN to accept the situation.'

'They'll need their heads examined if they do. And so will you, if you try to persuade them. Clive, don't you see, in a fortnight Batalji has doubled the size of his country, quadrupled the size of his population, and gained possession of one of the richest areas in the world, as regards mineral wealth. And food supplies, as well.'

'I can see that.'

'But you're still going to help him.'

'I'm afraid he has given me a couple of very good reasons why I should.'

Rosemary glanced at the baby, then back at him. 'And you thought he was your friend! Clive, people are being killed out there.'

He nodded. 'Stopping that has got to be my first priority.' He kissed her. 'See you when I come back.'

She forced a smile. 'I forgot to ask you, how was your honeymoon?'

'Mustn't complain.'

'And now she's back to lord it over me.'

'I intend to have a word with her about that.' But when he went in search of Shallane, who, when last he saw her, had been making sure all her belongings and clothes had been moved across from the Palace, he found her waiting in the hall, with several servants and a pile of suitcases. 'Going home to Mother already?' he asked.

'Mongol wives do not go home to Mother, Stanton,' she informed him. 'Nor do they stay home while their husbands are out working. I am coming with you to New York.'

'You cannot. I'd be arrested for statutory rape.'

She stuck out her tongue at him. 'You have diplomatic immunity. Papa says so. And anyway, he has given me a passport. On it I am eighteen. So there.'

Clive directed his aircraft to make a stop at Krasnoyarsk, and had his pilot obtain permission to fly at well below the normal altitude: he wanted to see for himself.

Near the border there was considerable evidence of fighting, but further into the oblast or administrative area of Krasnoyarskiy life seemed to be proceeding as usual, if one excepted the columns of tanks and troops which could be made out, moving steadily to the west. Certainly there was no fighting to be seen, and as the Ilyushin dipped down to land at Krasnoyarsk International Airport Clive could also see that not a great deal of damage appeared to have been done to the capital, a huge modern city with a population of nearly a million. But there were rows of Rafales and fighter-bombers lined up on the tarmac, and the airport was surrounded by tanks, and there were also tanks on the streets as he drove to the building which had been appropriated as military headquarters. On the other hand, life in the city seemed to be continuing exactly as normal, with the streets crowded, and no one seemed unduly unhappy.

'My God, but it is hot,' Shallane commented. She had never been so far south before. 'I shall go shopping here.' She had brought with her a considerable amount of Yakutistan's newly earned hard currency.

'You will not,' Clive told her. 'There must be quite a few of these people would like to get their hands on the Khan's daughter. You can keep your shopping for New York.' He left her in an antechamber, under guard, while he visited Jagnuth.

'Resistance was minimal,' Jagnuth explained. 'I could have taken this city with a handful of men, much less four *tumans*. Of course, all the hard work had already been done, both by Pirale's paratroopers and our agents here.'

'You'll have to explain that to me,' Clive suggested.

'Well . . .' Jagnuth looked embarrassed at his slip. 'Batalji has anticipated this happening for well over a year. So he has had his agents preparing the ground, bribing sufficient MPs and government officials, so that they would support him when the time came.'

'And sending his emigrants across the border to stir things up,' Clive said.

Jagnuth grinned. 'It was how Genghis Khan worked. And he was very successful.'

Clive realised that Batalji had lied to him. Not, he supposed, for the first time. And there was nothing he could do about it, while Rosemary and Clive junior, not to mention Denise, were in Yakutsk. 'Is he going to stop here, Jagnuth?'

'Well, of course. He has accomplished everything he wished to do, and he has pre-empted the Russian threat.'

'Was there ever really a Russian threat?'

'You have seen the documentation.'

'Remarkably convenient documentation. Now, Jagnuth, if Batalji means to stop here, why are all your troops still moving to the west?'

'We need to protect our borders.'

'Your borders with Kazakhstan?'

'And with Russia.'

'All right. What will you do if you receive orders to invade Kazakhstan? I am assuming the Khan has agents there as well, stirring up trouble, bribing MPs.'

'I can assure you that the Khan has no intention of invading Kazakhstan, Clive.'

'I hope to God you are right, Jagnuth.'

'Just under a million square miles, nearly three million people...' Secretary of State Walter Ingraham snapped his fingers. 'Just like that! I'm sorry, Clive, but he's got to get out. And pay compensation.'

'Batalji is not going to go, Walter. He claims he acted not only to protect his nationals, but because he was invited in by a large minority of the Krasnoyarsk Parliament.'

'Do you think Russia is going to accept that?'

'Russia isn't important, Walter. Things are too volatile out there. The entire area of the old Soviet state is on a knife edge. Russia dare not act against Batalji without the agreement of all the other republics in the CIS, and she's not going to get it. Especially as she is not going to get any support from the Ukraine, and the Russians know they could find themselves in a shooting war there at any moment.'

'They're sure kicking up a stink at the UN.'

'Well, they would, wouldn't they? But the UN isn't going to do anything without a lead from you. So . . .?'

'And you feel pretty damned sure that after that Yugoslav business we are not going to commit any of our people over something that does not directly affect us.' Ingraham's shoulders hunched. 'We have a great dislike of being blackmailed.'

'In what way am I blackmailing you?'

'For Christ's sake, you know as well as I that there's not a goddamned thing we can do. It would take a mobilisation on a scale equal to that of World War Two to take back that territory if your friend Borjigin is determined to hold it, and the cost . . . I hope all those goddamned do-gooders who insisted we run down NATO and our own armed services now realise what short-sighted fools they were. Anyway, there's simply no way we can put any ground forces into Krasnoyarskiy without the agreement of the other CIS members.' He glared at Clive. 'As your boy well knows.'

'He knows he's holding all the high cards, yes,' Clive agreed. 'I happened to be on my honeymoon when this thing broke. I believe I could have stopped it happening. I certainly believe I can stop it spreading.'

'As long as Borjigin keeps Krasnoyarskiy. And you don't call that blackmail. When do you address the Security Council?'

'Tomorrow night.'

Ingraham brooded at the array of pens on the desk before him; he had a mania for pens, and there were at least a hundred, in every possible colour. 'His action has to be condemned,' he said at last. 'We will support a resolution condemning Yakutistan's action, and demanding an immediate withdrawal.'

'And when I defy the Security Council?'

'There'll be sanctions.'

Clive smiled. 'Such as?'

'Okay, you've got it all. You're self-sufficient in oil and natural gas, and if you hang on to Krasnoyarskiy you're self-sufficient in one hell of a lot of other things as well. But you won't be able to *sell* any oil, so bang goes your hard currency. And there'll be an embargo on any arms, or military knowledge, entering your country.'

'I see,' Clive said. 'But there will be no resolution for military action.'

'It'll be on the cards. But no, there'll be no resolution until we can work out how we do it.'

'Thank you, Mr Secretary.' Clive got up.

'So who're you going to lobby now?' Ingraham demanded. 'We'll make those sanctions stick, you know, Clive.'

Clive gave another smile. 'I'm having dinner at the Chinese Embassy. Mr Yuan is in New York, you know. He's come here specially for this debate.'

'Stanton,' Ingraham said. 'You are an asshole!'

'Just doing my job, Mr Secretary.'

An anxious manager met him in the foyer of the Plaza. 'Mr Stanton! Your wife . . .' His face was red.

'Oh, God!' Clive grunted. 'What has she done?'

'Well, sir, if you could have a word with her . . . There are certain proprieties which must be observed. Our other guests, you see . . .'

'What has she *done*?'

'Well, sir, it seems that after luncheon, when you went out, Mrs Stanton took a nap, and then she got up and rang Room Service. Unfortunately, she could not immediately get through – it was a very busy time of the afternoon – and, well, she had difficulty making herself understood because of the language problem . . . and she seems to be an impatient, ah, young lady. So she left your suite and went down to the kitchens herself.'

'Sounds like my wife,' Clive said. 'And it's against the rules for a guest to go down to the kitchens, is that it?'

'No, no, sir. Providing they are, ah, properly dressed.'

'Oh, shit!' Clive remarked. 'What did she have on?'

'Ah . . . nothing, sir.'

'Nothing at all?'

'She was not wearing anything, sir. However, she was carrying something. A revolver. The revolver was apparently loaded, sir. Because she fired it.'

'Did she hit anything?'

'She hit several things, Mr Stanton. Fortunately, nothing human.'

'And where is she now? Still holding up your kitchen staff?'

'No, sir. We managed to, ah, overpower the young lady and return her to her room. We also managed to secure the revolver. It is in my office.'

'I think it might be an idea to keep it there for the time being. You didn't call the police while all this was going on?'

'No, sir, I did not. We do not like policemen in the Plaza, and as no one was hurt ... but I will have to do so if there is a recurrence of this incident.'

'Hang on to the gun,' Clive recommended, and went to the elevators.

Shallane sat up in bed, drinking tea. 'This is absolute piss,' she remarked. 'And do you realise that I have been manhandled by half a dozen men? I shall complain to Papa if you do not do something about it.'

'The only thing I should do about it is tan your hide. Where the hell did you get that gun?'

'It was in one of the diplomatic pouches.'

'Why?'

Shallane looked genuinely surprised. 'I always have a gun.'

'You had a gun on our honeymoon?'

'Of course.' She grinned. 'And you never knew. I want my gun back.'

Clive knelt on the bed. 'Listen to me, you fifteen-year-old monster: we are here on a vital diplomatic mission, for your Papa. Can you imagine what would follow if a word of what happened here today got into the media? Now get up and get dressed. We're going out to dinner. And for God's sake behave yourself.'

It was at least amusing to watch Shallane attempt to cope with chopsticks ... until she threw them on the floor and started scooping the food from her plate with her fingers. Madame Yuan smiled indulgently, and Mr Yuan hastily engaged Clive in conversation. Yuan spoke good English. 'This business in Krasnoyarskiy,' he said. 'We in China sympathise, of course. It is a serious matter, to have trouble on one's borders. Until Yakutiya declared its independence of Moscow, there was always trouble along our borders with Russia. It is a great relief to us to feel that this anxious period of history is at an end.'

'You may rely upon it,' Clive assured him.

'Yet there are many people in China who remember the past, remember the name of Borjigin, remember the Genghis Khan, whose avowed aim in life was the destruction of China.'

'That is history,' Clive said. 'It can never happen again. Is not China the most populous nation on earth?'

'Nevertheless,' Yuan said. 'We have our problems, as I know you understand. Just as we understand your problems. Two nations with problems need to stand together.'

'We do.'

'Formally, and publicly, before the world,' Yuan said. 'We are thinking of an offensive-defensive pact with Yakutistan. I am not speaking of military assistance in coping with our private affairs. That is surely not necessary. But should the home territory of either of us be invaded by a third power, or combination of third powers, then each of us would pledge ourselves to support the other, as we will also pledge ourselves to support each other in public debates on matters of private policy.'

'May I take that to mean that China will agree to veto any United Nations resolution taken against Yakutistan?'

'Any resolution which is intended to restrict Yakutistan's understandable need to protect her borders and her people, or to punish her for taking steps towards such ends, would be viewed unfavourably by China ... once an alliance on the lines I have outlined was agreed.'

'I will have to contact Yakutsk, you understand,' Clive said. 'I am not sure I will have a reply by tomorrow afternoon.'

'Does not the Khan normally do what you advise him? We have heard this.'

'Normally,' Clive said cautiously.

'Then if you say that there will be an alliance, I am prepared to accept your word. It is widely known that you are a man of your word, Mr Stanton. Such an alliance, I am presuming, will include the return, to either participating country, of all dissidents who may have sought refuge.' Yuan smiled. 'You do not wish a lot of Chinese troublemakers causing disturbances in Yakutistan, a country so happily free of internal problems.'

'We would have to be assured that anyone returned to China will not be executed,' Clive said. I would have to be, anyway, he thought; he did not suppose Batalji would be the least concerned.

'Of course. They will merely undergo a period of rehabilitation. You have my word.' He held out his hand. 'You may count on our support tomorrow.'

Although it would have been nearly dawn in Yakutsk, Batalji was on the telephone to congratulate Clive when he returned from the UN building the following evening. 'That was a brilliant speech, Clive. Absolutely brilliant.'

'Not everyone agreed with it.'

'But Yuan vetoed the idea of sanctions. That is all that matters. Clive, you have my eternal gratitude. The draft alliance is being drawn up now, and will be faxed to you this morning. Now hurry back as soon as you can. How is Shallane?'

Clive looked across the table at his bride; tonight they were dining in their suite. 'Eating lobster and drinking champagne.'

'Ha, ha! You are corrupting her, Clive. Has she been enjoying New York?'

Clive looked at the pile of boxes stacked along the wall. 'She seems to have bought most of it.'

'Let me speak with him,' Shallane said. Clive handed over

the phone. 'Papa,' Shallane cried. 'This is a stupid place. They won't let me shoot at anyone. They took away my gun. Stanton let them do it.'

'Come back home,' Batalji told her. 'There is a great deal to shoot at here. And do not upset Stanton. I love that man.' He hung up.

Shallane smiled at Clive. 'Papa is pleased with you.'

'He should be. I've just given him the earth. Well, a million square miles of it.' He drank champagne and looked at her. She had not bothered to accompany him to the UN, preferring to watch it on TV. For a habitual TV watcher in any event, she found American television, with its ninety-odd satellite channels as well as its network programmes, an unending source of pleasure. Clive supposed that but for the equally great pleasure of buying everything she could see in Sachs she would never have bothered to leave their suite at all.

'Then I am pleased with you too. And now we can go home. Let's go to bed. We can watch TV and fuck.'

That seemed a sensible idea. Clive didn't want to think about what he had done. He had lied and cheated and hoodwinked for his master, while all the world said he was a man of his word. He had condemned a dozen Chinese radicals to at the very best a long term of unpleasant imprisonment. And he could no longer pretend that there was any prospect of Batalji calling a halt to his ambitions. So . . . let Batalji go on, until he overstepped the mark and was brought down in flames? Everyone who served him would also go down in flames. But there was no alternative; the thought of Rosemary or Denise impaled, or being confined in a chain-mail jacket while bits were sliced off them, was not acceptable, even if it was unbelievable that such things could be possible at the beginning of the twenty-first century.

That being so, of course, he had other alternatives, each wilder than the last. Top of the list was the idea of staying in New York and demanding the release of his women in exchange for Shallane. But that would simply not work. The outside world knew nothing of the savagery that lay deep in

Batalji's soul, nor would they believe a word of it if he tried to tell them. He would be condemned for using a fifteen-year-old girl as a pawn in some kind of internal power struggle in Yakutistan. He had sold his soul to the devil. Easy to say he had never really had a chance to opt out of the deal, once Batalji had got his hands on Denise. But Clive knew in his heart he had been bemused by the idea that he had been given the opportunity by Fate to make history rather than merely observe and record it, that he would be able to mould Batalji into a benevolent despot, and see Yakutistan grow into a rich and powerful, self-contained and influential state.

Now he could only lie back and enjoy moments like these, and wait to see what the devil would do next.

He slept heavily, and was awakened by Shallane digging him in the ribs. It was early in the morning, and the television was on. Perhaps it had been on all night: he had fallen asleep in the middle of a programme. Now he looked at columns of tanks and low-flying squadrons of attack aircraft, zooming across the screen. 'Isn't it exciting?' Shallane said. 'Papa has invaded Kazakhstan.'

THE FOURTEENTH CHRONICLE

New York, Summer 2005

Clive rolled across Shallane to reach the phone.

'I am sorry, sir,' said the switchboard operator. 'All lines to Yakutsk are jammed.'

'Get me a cab!' Clive snapped. He leapt out of bed and ran to the bathroom, returned in five minutes pulling on his clothes. He had not bothered to shave.

'What's all the fuss?' Shallane asked. 'It's just another war. You said we were going to the zoo today.'

'Stuff the bloody zoo. You had better get dressed,' Clive told her. 'But don't leave this room. Remember now. If you do I am going to break both your legs.'

She stuck out her tongue at him.

Clive reached the Yakut Embassy in fifteen minutes. It was still just dawn, but the staff were all at work, decoding messages. 'Get me the Khan,' Clive told the Ambassador, Batalji's old companion in arms, Maloun. 'And while you are doing that, tell me what the first reactions are.'

'We have actually had no reactions yet,' Maloun said. 'It is still early in the morning, and of course it is the weekend. I understand the American President left last night for a yachting holiday. Most people don't seem to believe the news, anyway. The reports are only now being confirmed from Kazakhstan.'

'Your call is through, Minister,' said a secretary.

'Batalji!' Clive shouted.

'This is Almani, Clive, not Batalji. Batalji is with the army.'

'Then what *happened*?'

'Have you not heard? I suppose you have been in bed. There has been a revolution in Alma-Ata, combined with a good deal of bloodshed and destruction of property. The group which carried out the *coup d'état* announced that they were putting an end to ten years of anarchy and misgovernment, and called upon their brothers of Yakutistan and Krasnoyarskiy to help them. Batalji left immediately for the front to take personal command of the army.' Clive felt physically sick. 'Are you there?' Almani asked. 'I have instructions for you from the Khan.'

'What instructions can he possibly give me? Almani, these people aren't fools. Don't you think they'll know that *coups d'état* in neighbouring republics in consecutive weeks, both culminating in an appeal to the Yakut army, have got to be a set-up?'

'It does not matter what they know, Clive,' Almani said. 'They cannot prove anything, right now. You will stick with your story, with what I have just told you. Tell the United Nations that Batalji wants only peace, and that he is being forced into these actions in order to *preserve* peace.'

'It won't matter a damn,' Clive said.

'Can we still count on China?'

'I don't know.'

'There is a fax draft of the proposed treaty on its way to you now,' Almani said. 'Have Yuan sign it. Make sure of that, Clive, and no one else matters a damn. Yuan will simply veto any United Nations resolution.'

'He'll want a quid pro quo.'

'Promise him anything you like. You have *carte blanche*.'

'You can't be serious.'

'Orders from Batalji. Whatever Yuan asks for, he is to be given, as long as he vetoes any resolutions against us.'

'Yuan can't stop the Russians, Almani. Their army is ten times that of Yakutistan. And they're already mobilised.'

'Forget the Russians, Clive. I guarantee there will be no trouble from them. When will you address the UN?' Almani asked.

'I imagine I will have to as soon as the Security Council can be convened. But that can't happen before tonight.'

'As soon as you are sure of Yuan,' Almani went on, 'make your speech. Until then, act at all times as if nothing out of the ordinary is happening at all. And then return home.' The phone went dead.

Yuan Shu-pi spread his hands. 'I understand exactly how you feel, how your president feels, Mr Stanton. He has been forced to act. His honour has called upon him to do this.' He looked at the fax document Clive had given to him. 'This seems eminently satisfactory.'

'Then we may count on your support?' Clive asked.

'Where China gives her word, you may be certain of it,' Yuan said. 'But of course, like you, the Chinese Government must take heed of ever-changing conditions.'

'Of course,' Clive agreed, muscles tensing as he waited.

'It appears to us that the entire situation in central Asia is changing. This is upsetting people, of course. We have heard that the governments of Iraq and Iran, Pakistan and India, have ordered partial mobilisation.'

'I can assure you, Mr Yuan, that my Government has no interest whatsoever in those countries.'

'I am sure of it,' Yuan agreed. 'But when armies are mobilised, who can say what will happen next? There is even a report that the Vietnamese are mobilising. This is intolerable. But then, the Vietnamese have always been an intolerable people. Time was when they were part of the Chinese Empire, you know.'

'Indeed, I do know,' Clive agreed, wondering if this benign gentleman recalled that forty years previously the Americans had burned their fingers very badly, interfering in Vietnamese politics. But if China *were* to become thoroughly embroiled in south-east Asia that could only be to the advantage of Yakutistan. 'I may say without reservation that the Government of Yakutistan will entirely understand any position the Government of China may take up in this matter.'

Yuan smiled, and picked up his pen.

Back at the Embassy, Maloun was very agitated. 'There are reactions enough now,' he said. 'An emergency session of the Security Council has been called for tonight. The President has abandoned his holiday and is returning to Washington. The Secretary of State has been on the line, and the Foreign Secretary of Great Britain, asking to speak with you personally, and also a Mr Crawford, and there is an invitation to appear on the Horace Latby chat show ... that's the number one in this country right now. And your wife has been calling; she says you were going to take her to the zoo today.'

'Accept Latby, and I will be at the UN immediately afterwards.'

'And the Secretary of State? The Foreign Secretary?'

'I'm taking my wife to the zoo, Maloun.'

They had to face a battery of cameras and microphones when they left the Plaza; it was obvious that the media did not intend to let Clive out of their sight. 'You don't seem to be taking this crisis very seriously, Mr Stanton?' someone asked.

'What crisis?' Clive riposted.

Shallane was delighted. 'I feel like a film star. I know, Stanton, when we're finished here, before going home, why don't we fly across to Hollywood and meet some film stars? We can get home just as quickly that way, can't we?'

'Relax,' Clive told her. 'In another twelve hours you're going to be up there with them.'

*

Horace Latby was a very large man, rotund as well as tall, with a totally bald head. His rise to fame as the successor to personalities like Sullivan and Carson was, Clive had always supposed, an indication of the way the media consumed essentially untalented people and spewed them out for public adoration or rejection. Horace was one of the lucky ones, thanks to his cultivation of an avuncular and slightly shocked manner when interviewing his guests. Clive had actually appeared on his show before, six years earlier, so he knew what to expect. He had supposed Shallane might be a trifle nervous, but of course she wasn't, and spent her time in the waiting room attempting to chat up her fellow guests, which, as she was only just learning English – as the staff at the Plaza had found out to their cost – and they spoke no Russian, was a difficult business; in fact, he realised, he was far more apprehensive: exposing an audience of thirty million Americans to Shallane promised to be embarrassing. On the other hand, there was no more certain way to distract both host and audience from what was happening in Kazakhstan.

'And now,' Horace cried at last, 'my special guests of this evening, the Foreign Minister of Yakutistan, and Mrs Stanton.' Clive led Shallane on to the stage, where Horace shook his hand, and kissed Shallane on both cheeks. They had, of course, had a brief chat with him before the show, and gone over one or two points, and Horace had decided that Shallane's name would make a good introductory gambit. 'What a lovely lady,' he remarked to the studio audience when the applause had died down. 'Now tell me, Shallane ...' he deliberately pronounced it Shallanne, 'have I got it right?'

'No,' Shallane said. 'Eet ees speak Shallain, you beeg sheet.'

There was a moment of silence, as her reply had *not* been rehearsed. Then Horace gave a loud laugh. 'I stand corrected. You come over here and sit next to me, young lady, and you, Clive, come and sit on the other side. I guess things are a little different now, in your new job, from the way they were when you were a correspondent.'

'Not really,' Clive said. 'I still spend my time rushing around the world, seeing people, trying to discover their point of view.'

'And lyeeng like a cheap vatch,' Shallane put in.

'Ha, ha, ha,' Horace uttered loudly. 'Your wife is quite a wit, Clive.' He rolled his eyes, off camera, as if in an attempt to say, Can't you control her? 'But I'm sure I'm asking a question which must have crossed the minds of a good many people, Clive: What made you emigrate to Yakutistan, and become their Foreign Minister?'

'My Papa told 'eem 'e 'ad to,' Shallane said.

Horace looked at Clive. 'Absolutely correct,' Clive said. 'We are old friends, President Borjigin and I, and when he wanted someone to do the job, well, I agreed.'

'Still, you must admit that it is unique for a country to have as its foreign minister, and perhaps its best-known citizen, internationally, someone who is not a citizen at all.'

''E ees a ceeteezeen,' Shallane pointed out. ''e ees married to me.'

'Ah. Yes, of course. Nothing like marrying the boss's daughter. Now, Clive, to be serious, your adopted country has been in the news quite a lot recently. Would you agree that a state of war exists between Yakutistan and Kazakhstan?'

'Certainly not,' Clive said. 'We are assisting the Kazakhs to restore order. At their invitation.'

'You can of course prove that contention?'

'Certainly. Ask any Kazakh minister.'

'Believe me, we'd do that if we could find one. But what I am sure the viewers are really interested in is where President Borjigin means to go next? He's absorbed Krasnoyarskiy, and now he's invading Kazakhstan, all in a matter of a few weeks...'

'My papa is no preseedent, like your preseedent,' Shallane interrupted. ''E ees Khan! Khan of Yakutistan! Zen Khan of all Russia!'

Horace looked uncertain: did he have the scoop of the century on his hands? 'Would you say that again, Mrs Stanton?'

'I am no Mrs Stanton,' Shallane declared. 'I am Princess Shallane. I am only daughter of zee Khan.' She pointed at Clive. ''E ees my 'usband.'

'I see. Well, I suppose they do things differently in Yakutistan...'

'My papa does theengs deeferently, yes,' Shallane agreed. 'From zee day I was born, 'e knew 'e would be Khan, and I would be Princess.'

'As long ago as that,' Horace remarked, and checked his prompt sheet. 'Back in 1987? But in 1987 your father was a soldier in the Red Army, Princess Shallane.'

Clive sat up straight as he realised what was about to happen. Then he relaxed again; a real distraction would get him entirely off the hook. 'I no born een 1987,' Shallane informed the audience, contemptuously. 'You zeenk I am old woman, eh?' The audience laughed politely. 'I born twelve May 1990,' Shallane announced.

'The twelfth of May 1990. Yes ... ah ...' The penny dropped. 'You're not serious?' Horace looked at Clive with a touch of desperation: a scoop was one thing – a case of statutory rape was another. 'My dear Princess, that would make you only fifteen years old. Just fifteen,' he added for good measure.

'Zat ees right,' Shallane agreed. 'Eet ees zee right age to get married.'

Horace looked at Clive again. Clive shrugged. 'As we agreed, Horace, they do things differently in Yakutistan.'

CHAPTER 14

Kazakhstan, Autumn 2005

Batalji Borjigin stood on a slight hillock and watched his army passing beneath him, flooding south-west out of the burning town of Ayaguz. The tank brigades roared past, followed by the APCs, leaving huge columns of dust behind them. Attack aircraft droned overhead, and between the motor infantry and the aircraft were swarms of helicopter gunships, the new Mongol cavalry. Behind them the town smoked, for there had been resistance, and Batalji had ordered its obliteration. Now, before him, lay the flat rolling hills of the Kazakhstan Desert; visibility was so clear that through his binoculars he could even make out the huge shimmer that was the waters of Lake Balkash.

But his attention remained on his men and women, who sang, and saluted him as they passed. Their morale was high. They were unstoppable. Beside the Khan, Denise, wearing green army fatigues, filmed with her invariable enthusiasm.

Jagnuth had been in the command caravan, awaiting word from the advance guard. Now he came to stand beside his brother-in-law. Although he was Chief of Staff, Jagnuth was still bemused by what he had been ordered to do, and even more by the success which had attended his arms. Invading Krasnoyarskiy had been frightening enough, but Krasnoyarskiy was hardly more heavily populated than Yakutistan. Kazakhstan had a population of fifteen million! Even before the crossing of the Kazakh border, however, Jagnuth had been concerned by the enormous distances across which he had been required to move his men in a fortnight. Everything he had learned in his years of studying military history had warned him that any army, and especially a modern army, strung out to that extent, was catastrophically vulnerable. They had commandeered the single railway track and all the rolling stock, and used that as their quickest line of advance, but of course there had been the inevitable breakdowns of their accompanying vehicles, APCs, and more important, tanks; even the modern monsters which could rumble along in excess of fifty kilometres an hour were susceptible to worn-out or damaged tracks.

Yet the army, constantly guarded by its air force and its gunships, had not suffered a setback, nor even a proper counterattack. Batalji had applied the tactics of the Afghan mountains to the Kazakh steppes, and found it a far more simple task. But he had also practised the terror, not only of the Red Army in Afghanistan, but of Genghis Khan in history. Immediate surrender and acceptance brought with it safety; any sign of resistance was met with obliterating force. Ayaguz was not the first town to be left a smouldering, corpse-ridden ruin in the wake of the Yakut army ... and the dead included women and children as well as men. Yet again Batalji seemed to have everything under control. The army which had occupied Krasnoyarsk had simply swept on towards the southwest. That in itself had been a traumatic experience to someone who took his soldiering seriously, like Jagnuth, for now his entire right flank had been exposed to a counter-thrust, by Russian forces, from places like Omsk or Sverdlovsk. But while the Russians had debated, and appealed to the UN, the Yakut army had occupied both Novosobirsk and Barnaul, and on receipt of the necessary message from Alma-Ata, it had occupied Semipalatinsk before the bewildered Kazakh border guards had realised what was happening.

Only since then, as they had followed the railway south, dashing now for the capital where it lay at the foot of the Tien Shan Mountains, had they encountered any real resistance. Batalji, taking personal command, had blasted his way through Ayaguz, but now...

'They have destroyed the railway track,' Jagnuth panted. 'At Aktogay. They are prepared to defend Aktogay to the death.'

'Then it will be their deaths. Get on the radio to the commanding officer and make sure he understands this. Tell him what happened at Ayaguz. Tell him the same applies to him: if he surrenders, the lives of him and his people will be spared. If he resists, I will destroy every man, woman and child in his town.'

'I will make sure he understands this. But the railway ... it is another four hundred kilometres to Alma-Ata.'

'Have the fuel wagons brought up. What is the news of Stanton?'

'He will be here this evening.'

Batalji nodded. 'Speak with the commander in Aktogay. If he still wishes to resist, tell him to speak with his superiors. Or die.'

The helicopter swooped in to land just before dusk. By then Batalji had already moved his headquarters to Tansyk, and had personally inspected the broken railway line, some twenty-five kilometres to the south, and a similar distance north of Aktogay. The camp itself was quiet. The aircraft, having bombed and strafed Aktogay, had returned to Semipalatinsk to refuel. Denise had gone with them to shoot some more footage of Ayaguz; she was having the time of her life. The tanks were parked in a huge laager, facing south-west; the infantry were encamped behind them. The gunships were clustered, like an immense swarm of grounded wasps. The Yakut army was awaiting the response of the Kazakh commander in Aktogay to their summons to surrender.

Batalji watched Clive and Nita disembark, clouded in dust as they ran for the APC in which he waited to welcome them. 'Clive! It is good to see you!' Batalji embraced him, and then Nita. 'You have no trouble in getting here?'

'We came back via the Pacific. And I refuelled at Semipalatinsk. Batalji, this is madness.'

'You are always telling me that,' Batalji said. 'Come and drink some vodka, and tell me about America. Madness? I shall be in Alma-Ata tomorrow night. And there will be cheering crowds to welcome me. Shallane is well?'

'Shallane is fine.' Clive clung to the door as the APC bounced over the desert. 'Batalji, the whole world is up in arms. Literally.'

Batalji shot him a glance. 'There has been a resolution? What about Yuan?'

'Yuan has not let us down. He vetoed the resolution. To do it, he required the right to invade Vietnam.'

'Then what is wrong?' The APC had reached the caravan, and Batalji led the way inside, where his secretaries stood to attention. 'Out!' They hurried off, accompanied by Nita, and Batalji uncorked a bottle of vodka, filled two glasses. 'To victory!'

Clive sipped. 'Batalji, Russia intends to ignore the United Nations, and declare war on you by herself. She has squared it with the US and Europe. They are all against you now. These tales of wholesale destruction, of entire towns liquidated ... they are screaming for your blood.'

'I am fighting as my ancestors fought.' Batalji sat down.

'That was eight hundred years ago!'

'You keep harping on these figures of times past. Time is always present, Clive. I am being successful because I am fighting like my ancestors. War is a matter of the shortest possible time between attack and victory. That way less people die than in a long-drawn-out campaign. You should know this.'

Clive sighed, drank some vodka, and also sat down. 'What are you going to do about Russia, Batalji? I was not fooling when I said they are out for your blood. There is an envoy on his way here now, demanding your instant withdrawal from both Kazakhstan and Krasnoyarskiy. If you will not withdraw, they intend to try you as a war criminal, and on all the old charges, as a deserter and a murderer and a rebel and an outlaw. And the world is going to applaud.'

Batalji grinned. 'They have to catch me first.'

'Batalji, they have an army of a million men, with all the modern weapons at their disposal. And your army is exposed, here in the desert . . .'

'I have told you, I shall be in Alma-Ata by tomorrow night. Anyway, Russia is not a threat. Believe me, Clive.' Batalji's voice took on that ring it could assume without warning.

'Very well, Mr President,' Clive said formally. 'I will believe you.' He took an envelope from his breast pocket. 'Here is my resignation. You have made me appear as a fool and a liar before the eyes of the world. While I have been solemnly assuring the United Nations that you seek only peace, you have been carrying out the most naked aggression. They have me on the wanted list as well, as a war criminal. I cannot continue in that role.'

'That is nonsense, Clive. No one is going to put you on trial for anything. You have my word.' Another grin. 'And that you can believe.' He tore the envelope in two, dropped it into his wastepaper basket, pointed a finger. 'Nothing has changed. Nothing at all. Besides, I want you at my side when the Russian envoy arrives.'

They flew in Batalji's personal helicopter to within ten miles of Aktogay. The town was only a few kilometres north-east of the shores of the lake, and the railway line actually bordered the water as it headed south for Alma-Ata. Beneath them, the strike force of the Yakut army was grouped: four tank brigades, several missile batteries, and three *tumans* of motor infantry – nearly forty thousand men, spread out in the usual semi-circle, across both the railway and the single road leading north-east to Ayaguz: Batalji had deliberately left the way to the south open, in case the garrison wished to run for their lives.

'They have refused to surrender or withdraw,' Jagnuth announced. 'They have said they will fight to the last man.'

Batalji shrugged. 'Call up the aircraft and the airborne division. How long will it take for them to get here?'

'They are on stand-by at Semipalatinsk. The planes should be here in half an hour. The airborne division will take a little longer.'

'Then have your artillery open fire in twenty minutes' time. Blanket coverage.'

Jagnuth saluted, and left. Clive followed him outside. 'There are civilians in that town.'

'It is their decision.'

'You mean it is Batalji's decision. Jagnuth, you cannot do this.'

'I am a soldier, and a soldier obeys orders.'

'You mean if Batalji commanded you to march into the gate of Hell, you would do it? Why?'

'He is the Khan,' Jagnuth said simply.

Denise dropped in, briefly; she had her own helicopter. 'Isn't it exciting? I've always wanted to film a war at first-hand.' She kissed both Batalji and Clive, and took off again.

'You realise she's risking her life?' Clive asked.

Batalji grinned. 'She is doing what she likes best.'

Clive watched the missiles booming into the doomed town, the fighter-bombers dropping their bombs, and then swooping low, cannon chattering. A squadron of Kazakh fighters appeared in response to the desperate appeals for help from the garrison commander, but these were out-dated MiGs, and were shot from the sky by their newer brothers. An hour later the airborne division was overhead, the gunships moving low to strafe the burning buildings before putting down their human cargoes. Aktogay became a huge pillar of smoke, visible for miles across the desert.

Batalji spoke into his radio. 'All the men will be shot,' he commanded. 'And the old women. Bring the young ones. My men need some sport.' He winked at Clive. 'So do we, eh?'

'You are a monster,' Clive told him. 'I want no part of it.'

'You will change your mind when you see some of these Kazakh girls. They are beauties.'

One of the secretaries came in. 'We have just been informed from Semipalatinsk that the Russian envoy has arrived there and demands to see you at once, great Khan.'

'Well, he will have to come here,' Batalji said. 'I cannot leave the battle front. But tell him he may fly down immediately.' He winked at Clive. 'This will be amusing.'

The Russian envoy arrived an hour later. By then it was dark, and Aktogay was visible for many miles across the desert, a huge bonfire. The Yakut army continued to ring the destroyed town, amusing themselves with the captured women. Batalji dined with Jagnuth and Clive, and three of the daughters of Aktogay's leading citizens, pretty Moslem girls who were forced to sit down naked, and shivered all the time. 'His Excellency, General Boris Simonoslov,' the secretary announced.

The Russian, a big, heavy-set man, entered the caravan and checked at the sight before him; he was in any event clearly shaken by what he had seen that day, the blackened scar that had been Ayaguz – over which his pilot had deliberately taken him, on orders from Batalji – and the funeral pyre that had been Aktogay: not even Hitler had waged war quite as ruthlessly as this. He was accompanied by a strikingly beautiful woman, tall and dark, with perfectly delineated features, and a wealth of black hair, upswept into a chignon and held in place with a magnificent large gilt pin. Clive glanced at Batalji, and saw that the warlord was as ever immediately interested in feminine beauty – Denise, still busily filming, had not yet returned from Aktogay.

'Come in, Boris, my dear fellow,' Batalji invited. 'How good to see you again. And this is . . .?'

'My secretary,' Simonoslov said.

'You are a very lucky man, Boris. Aren't you going to introduce us?'

'I am Alexandra Taychin,' the woman said.

Batalji frowned for a quick moment, then gave a bellow of laughter. 'Now I see the resemblance. But Boris and Ludmilla had no children?'

'I am a cousin, Your Excellency.'

'Ah! Out for revenge?'

'Should I not be?'

'Ha, ha!' Batalji shouted. 'You are at least an honest woman. I assume you were both searched, outside?'

Alexandra Taychin flushed. 'Very thoroughly.'

'It was an outrage,' Simonoslov complained.

'Well, if you are going to bring someone named Taychin to see me, what do you expect? Sit down, sit down. Here, beside me, Miss Taychin. And you, Boris. There is a place laid for you. You will forgive us starting without you, but in times like these a man must eat whenever he can, and fuck whenever he can, too. Sit down, sit down.' He smiled at Alexandra Taychin. 'The food will taste much better now. Boris, do you like any of these women? I don't think you do. Alexiev, fetch a woman for the General. Do you like them big or small, Boris? There is every variety available.'

Simonoslov looked about to explode. He had been selected for this task because he knew Batalji, and most of his officers, personally; he had accepted the assignment with reluctance – just because he did known them so well. Alexandra Taychin, Clive noted, did not seem the least put out by the presence of the other women. She sat beside Batalji, and made only the faintest *moue* with her lips as his hand immediately dropped to her knee; she was wearing a skirt. But Alexandra Taychin . . . Not for the first time in his acquaintance with Batalji, he wished he had not consumed quite so much vodka.

'I did not come here to dine with you, Your Excellency,' Simonoslov said, still standing. 'Or to . . .' He looked at the girls. 'Debauch with you. I came here to deliver this note.' He threw the paper on the table.

Batalji glanced at it. 'We will discuss it later. Sit down, man, sit down. Clive, give Boris a glass of vodka. You remember Boris?'

'Yes,' Clive said. He had met the General, briefly, just before the Russian garrison had been repatriated from Yakutsk, in the spring of 2001.

Simonoslov sat down, reluctantly accepted the glass. Batalji himself filled Alexandra Taychin's glass. 'Because for the moment there are more important things to discuss,' he said. 'The Ukrainian question.'

'That is not the issue here,' Simonoslov declared.

'Oh, but it should be, from your point of view. My army will resume its advance tomorrow morning, Boris. We Mongols do not stop to rest and regroup, eh? Alma-Ata will surrender tomorrow evening. It is arranged, but it will wish to do so, anyway, because it will not wish to suffer the fate of Aktogay or Ayaguz. I anticipate that the main part of the Kazakh army will also surrender, and then there will be nothing to stop me marching to the shores of the Caspian, which is what I intend to do.' Simonoslov looked even more ready to explode. 'However, the important point is that the moment news is received in Kiev that Alma-Ata has surrendered, the Ukrainian army and air force will invade Russia.' Simonoslov's head jerked. 'I know this is true,' Batalji said, 'because it is part of a treaty I signed with President Obolonsky, two months ago.'

It was the turn of Clive's head to jerk. 'It was the only way I could get him to agree to a peace conference,' Batalji explained, with his usual ingenuousness.

'That is outrageous!' Simonoslov shouted. Clive agreed with him.

'War is outrageous, to some people,' Batalji pointed out. 'What should matter to you, Boris, is that with your army, as I understand it, moving on Omsk to attack my flank, *your* flank is exposed to a Ukrainian attack. And were I to forget about the Caspian for the time being, and swing my armies up towards Omsk, why, you might find yourself in a very serious situation.' Simonoslov drank some vodka, inadvertently.

Jagnuth refilled his glass. 'I have always wanted to revisit Omsk,' Batalji said reflectively. 'I was at school there, you know, Alexandra.' He gave her a squeeze. 'Your cousin sent me there. Of course that was nearly thirty years ago. I wonder if any of my old tutors are still there? It would give me great pleasure to meet them again. Oh, to be able to renew my acquaintance with dear Vera Shackinarsky, if she is still around. She would find that I have learned quite a lot since I was at her beck and call. Why are you not drinking your vodka?' Alexandra took a small sip.

'I think you should know, Your Excellency,' Simonoslov was speaking as evenly as he could, 'that President Boroslov is quite prepared to use nuclear weapons if Russia is threatened by such a coalition as you suggest.'

'That would be sport. I think *you* should know, Boris, that there are six nuclear missiles, each armed with multi-warheads, situated on launch sites in the forests of Yakutistan. One of these is of course targeted on Moscow. The others are suitably directed.'

Simonoslov snorted. 'Do you expect me to believe that?'

Batalji smiled. 'I expect you to ask yourself what happened to those missiles which were unaccounted for when I handed over the site at Ugumun, four years ago. Then you may ask General Anhusat to tell you what he did with them.' Simonoslov looked at Jagnuth in consternation. So did Clive. Selphine had warned him of this, and he had refused to believe her. 'I think it will be a good exchange,' Batalji went on. 'Moscow for ... Yakutsk? Petersburg for ... Krasnoyarsk? I think you will run out of worthwhile targets before me, Boris.'

'You will plunge the world into war!' Simonoslov spluttered.

'I think the world at war would be rather a fine place to be,' Batalji said. 'War is man's natural state, is it not? It was my ancestors' natural state.'

'Millions will die!'

'The planet is over populated as it is. Unfortunately, Boris, I am afraid you are mistaken. The world is not going to go to war on behalf of anything that may be happening in Russia. All that will happen is that Russia will be smashed, defeated, crushed. And what is left will be divided between Ukraine and Yakutistan. That will change the maps around, eh?'

Simonoslov stood up. 'Have I your permission to withdraw, Your Excellency?'

'What, to hurry back to Moscow and warn them? No, no, Boris. Sit down. What I want you to do is send a message to Moscow, inviting President Boroslov to come down here to meet with me, personally. Tell him it is most urgent.'

'He will not come. Why should he come? To be made prisoner?'

'To save his neck. To save all of your necks. I have a solution to your problem.'

Simonoslov sat down again, slowly and suspiciously.

'I have given the matter much consideration,' Batalji said. 'And it seems to me that it would be vastly more to the advantage of Yakutistan were we to be firm friends and allies of Russia rather than Ukraine. I will be perfectly honest with you, Boris. Ukraine has the potential, with its oilfields and its immense food stocks, to become stronger and more dangerous than Russia, with its perennial bankruptcy . . . I mean, who is going to pay for this war? Well, I can afford to, you know. For both sides.'

Clive gasped as the magnitude of Batalji's plan, which had to have been determined several weeks – perhaps several years – earlier, became apparent. Simonoslov was obviously bemused.

'Thus it seems to me,' Batalji went on, 'that it would solve both our problems if, when Ukraine invades Russia in three days' time, I direct my forces, not at the Caspian, but not at Omsk either, and instead make for Saratov and Volvograd. After all, when the war is won, I can always visit Omsk, can I not?'

That there might be something slightly sinister in his last remark escaped the distressed Simonoslov. 'But you say you have a treaty with Ukraine,' he protested.

'Which I am prepared to replace with a treaty with Russia,' Batalji explained patiently. 'If you are interested.'

'Well, Your Excellency, of course...'

'Then get President Boroslov down here, tomorrow. One more day will be too late. But Boris, this must be done with absolute secrecy. No one must know of it, or at least the reason for it. If it leaks out our story will be that Boroslov is coming to see me to make a personal appeal to end the fighting. We will let the world make what it wishes of that. Now get on the radio, and then come back here, and we will find you a nice plump woman from amongst these captives.'

Simonoslov got up, beckoned Alexandra Taychin. She made to rise, and found Batalji's arm round her waist. 'No, no,' he said. 'Your charming secretary will stay and dine with me. I have never had the opportunity of entertaining a Taychin woman. I tried... but they would not let me.' Simonoslov hesitated, then left, escorted by Jagnuth to the communications centre. That left Batalji and Clive alone with the four women. Batalji grinned at Clive. 'Did I not tell you it would be all right?'

'You take my breath away,' Clive said. 'You have no need of me, any more.'

'I shall always have need of you, Clive, to tell the West what I have done, what I am doing, in language they can understand.'

'And you suppose I am going to do that?'

Batalji stroked the exposed neck of the woman beside him. 'Of course you are.'

Clive sighed. But he was, as ever, helpless while everyone that he loved was trapped in Yakutsk. 'So what is your plan now? To inform President Obolonsky of the change in the situation and tell him to call off his attack on Russia?'

'Oh, no,' Batalji said. 'He must go ahead with the attack. That is an essential part of my plan so that I can invade Ukraine, and take it, too. Besides, he must invade Russia. I do not believe the Russian army has the will to fight. I wish to find that out. Now, let us have done with politics. You may have all three of these girls, Clive. I wish only Alexandra.' He caressed her breasts through her blouse. 'Show me the most beautiful thing about you, Alexandra.' He kissed her.

'That would be my hair, Your Excellency.'

'Where?' He kissed her again, while Clive watched them, and slowly began to tense. He had heard how people had committed suicide for Batalji in the past, in order to save him for whatever destiny intended. Was it possible that someone would commit suicide in order to prevent that destiny being realised? But this woman had been strip-searched. Even if she was prepared to commit suicide, there was no way she could have hidden any Semtex on her body.

'Why, on my head, Your Excellency,' Alexandra said. 'Shall I not let it down for you?'

'Ha, ha!' Batalji shouted. 'All right. You let that hair down, and then we will look at your other hair, eh?'

Alexandra made another *moue*, and reached up. Batalji was still holding one of her breasts with one hand while he unbuttoned her blouse with the other. He was not looking at her hair at all. Clive watched Alexandra, slowly and carefully, withdraw the ornate pin which was holding the thick black hair on the top of her head. The hair tumbled past her shoulders, as she clasped the pin firmly between finger and thumb, and looked down at the warlord, whose head had sunk forward to kiss her breasts as he opened her blouse. Clive suddenly realised what was going to happen. He still held a half-full glass of vodka in his hand. This he now hurled, with all his force. The flying glass struck Alexandra Taychin full in the face, and she gave a little shriek and fell backwards, losing her balance and tumbling out of her chair.

Batalji also fell over, away from the assassin. The three Kazakh girls screamed, and cowered in a corner. While Clive stood above Batalji and the woman. 'Move away,' he snapped. For Alexandra Taychin was sitting up, and she still held the pin. She jabbed it at Batalji, but the warlord was already rolling, to come to rest on his knees, some feet away.

Batalji's tunic and belts were hanging from a hook on the door. Clive snatched the automatic pistol from its holster and levelled it at Alexandra Taychin. 'Just don't move.'

She gazed at him, then glanced at Batalji, slowly getting to his feet. Her face was expressionless. Then without warning she drove the pin into her own breast. There was a spurt of blood, a gasp, and she slumped to the floor. Batalji stood over her, watched her body contorting before stiffening. 'You saved my life,' he said. 'That pin was poisoned.'

Clive gazed at the girl. He wasn't at all sure why he had done it, certain, as he was, that it would be better for the world if Batalji *were* to die. But they had shared so much, and despite all, they were still friends.

Jagnuth ran in, Simonoslov at his shoulder. 'Moscow's present,' Batalji remarked.

Simonoslov made a choking sound. 'I swear to you, Your Excellency, that I did not know this was going to happen.'

'Do you know, Boris,' Batalji said. 'I believe you. You are a soldier, not an assassin. Tell me where you got her.'

'She was assigned to me by Ewfim Dolgorukov.'

'Ah,' Batalji said. 'The Minister of the Interior. And President Boroslov's right-hand man, Now we know where we stand. Well, Boris, I will give you a chance to prove that you are an honest man ... by saying not a word about this. Your leader is exposed by his methods. You are mine, now.' He grinned. 'But then, so is he.'

The people of Alma-Ata lined their streets to watch the Yakut army enter their city. 'Is it not strange,' Batalji mused, 'to think that there are more people in this city than in all of Yakutistan?'

But there was no resistance. President Taimanov had fled to the supposed safety of Georgia, and his successor, General Morodosky, had appeared on national television the previous day to appeal to his people to welcome the Yakuts as brothers come to save them from an impossible tyranny. The Kazakhs did not know what to believe, but they had firstly been overawed by the immense firepower of the Yakut air force as it had flown almost at rooftop level over the city, and now by the confident discipline of the Yakut troops. Stories had come in from the towns and villages to the north-east of how these men had scrupulously paid cash for everything they had found necessary to requisition on their march, of how they had been the soul of politeness to the Kazakh women, with not a single case of rape reported south of Lake Balkash. Equally there were reports that the towns of Ayaguz and Aktogay had been razed to the ground, their entire populations massacred in an orgy of rape and torture and murder. Again, the people of Alma-Ata did not know what to believe. But they could at least, certainly for the moment, believe the evidence of their own eyes, as they watched the disciplined Yakut soldiers, gazed at the smart T-84 tanks, and up at the gunships hovering overhead.

While the troops gazed at Alma-Ata with delight. The city had been renamed as recently as 1921, by the Soviets, the Kazakh words referring to the many apple trees in the district, and certainly, to the men from the northern steppes, it was a paradise of warmth and fruit and flowers and pleasant smells, and attractive people as well, who seemed happy to be 'rescued' from the tyranny of their previous rulers. 'In the old days,' Batalji remarked, dining in the Presidential Palace, 'it was known as Alamatay, and do you know, Clive, it was taken and sacked by Genghis Khan, eight hundred years ago? I am following in my ancestor's footsteps. I am proud of that. But you must admit that I am even more successful than he, for I have not found it necessary to sack the city. Is that not good, eh?'

Clive could think of no response. Though he had tied his fortunes to a tiger, and though he remained horrified at the destruction of the two previous towns, he could not deny that this tiger was a phenomenon, who continued to fascinate, continued to juggle with the lives of his people, and himself, who must surely at any moment come tumbling down in destruction, such as now, if this grotesquely grandiose plan did not succeed... A secretary stood in the doorway. 'The President of Russia has arrived, Your Excellency.'

The campaign that followed was over in a fortnight. On the news of the surrender of Alma-Ata, as agreed in the secret treaty, President Obolonsky of Ukraine ordered his troops to invade Russia. They swarmed across the border, encountering very little resistance, as the main Russian army had been withdrawn to the east to attack the Yakuts. At Belaya, the Ukrainian border was only four hundred and fifty miles from Moscow, and this was the objective of the main thrust. Bombers swarmed ahead of the tanks to attack the capital and paralyse the railway systems, while the Ukrainian armour smashed its way up a corridor towards Kaluga and Tula – and Moscow. Had Batalji, as agreed, hurled his forces north against the troop concentrations around Omsk and Sverdlovsk, Russia would have collapsed.

But instead Batalji sent his men to the north-west, crossing the Volga between Saratov and Volvograd, assaulting those two heavily defended but utterly surprised cities with their usual devastating ruthlessness, and driving on towards Kharkov and Kiev. Observers to the west, the south and the east were equally in a state of consternation. The media sent people in, who sent back to European and American television screens horrific videos of the carnage being caused. The United Nations Security Council held an emergency session that lasted three days. Both Russia and the Ukraine protested that their borders had been violated and that they were the innocent parties. There was no representative from Yakutistan at the meeting, and it was impossible to get hold of anyone. Even Foreign Minister Clive Stanton, a man with whom the West had felt it could do business, had disappeared. There were rumours that he had been shot for disagreeing with the Khan's plans, but soon it was learned that he was with the army.

His absence from the international diplomatic scene made no difference to the outcome of the debate, for China again vetoed all resolutions aimed at imposing sanctions in the hopes of bringing the fighting to a stop. 'What is happening in Russia is an internal affair,' Mr Yuan declared. 'It is an aberration of history that Russia has broken up into a dozen petty states. Now history is resuming its natural course. These matters are always attended by bloodshed.'

'And that,' remarked Secretary of State Walter Ingraham, 'is the last thing I had ever expected to hear a Chinese minister say. Yuan has been nobbled.'

'What do you reckon about Stanton?' asked the President. 'You know, I liked that guy.'

'He's either the biggest rat on the face of this earth, and the most successful rat I have ever known at concealing the truth,' Ingraham said. 'Or he's as disconcerted as all of us. I kind of go for the latter. As you say, he's always come across as pretty straight.'

'So tell me what we are seeing, Walter?'

'We are seeing either the end of Batalji Borjigin, or the resurgence of a unified Russian state. I wonder if he realises that there won't be any room for him in that set-up.'

Batalji surprised them again. As he had prophesied, the Russian army, ill-equipped, scattered, disorganised, short of fuel, largely unpaid and lacking in morale, hastening back from the east to defend its holy city, was beaten in two big battles south of Moscow and routed; Ukrainian troops were within sight of the capital when they were recalled, early in September, to combat the Mongols, who were at the gates of Kiev. Kiev was prepared to resist, and Batalji was prepared to raze it to the ground. Clive talked him out of that, but the threat, combined with the defeat of the Ukrainian army north of the city, brought President Obolonsky's Government to its knees.

Clive accompanied Batalji to Moscow, where a detachment of Mongol troops was taking part in the victory parade. Batalji was hailed with acclamation by the ecstatic crowds; they all knew that it was the Yakuts who had won the war for them, and saved them from disaster. Then he appeared before the Russian Parliament, and was again hailed with acclamation as the saviour of the state.

He grinned at them. 'I was but doing my duty,' he told them. 'My sacred duty, to the earth of Mother Russia. My friends, my *comrades*, we have been through a long and difficult period. For more than fifteen years we have been the laughing stock of the world, a colossus with feet of clay, visibly falling apart. This was the mistaken vision of men who could never understand where their misplaced liberalism was leading them, men who never understood what the morrow would bring. This will change. This must change. This *has* changed.' The applause rang out. 'Ladies and gentlemen,' Batalji said when he could make himself heard. 'We have now taken the first step towards the reunification of Holy Russia. I am in possession of Krasnoyarskiy, and Kazakhstan. The small republics south of Kazakhstan lie in the palm of my hand. I am also in possession of the Ukraine. But what are these vast territories to me? My people have all they wish, back in Yakutistan. I undertook this war because I had a dream. A dream of Holy Russia, rising from the depths, and again soaring above the world. Ladies and gentlemen, all I have, I offer to you, in unity. You have but to say the word, and Russia will again be united. It will be the Russia of the Tsars, the Russia of the Commissars, but more important, it will be the Russia of the Twenty-First Century!'

The applause was louder than ever. Batalji pointed at them. 'It is for you to choose, you to decide! Is our future to be one of small and impotent states, living in mutual misery? Or will Russia once again be great, and strong, and feared?'

He stepped down from the rostrum, and held out his hand to President Boroslov, who had listened to the speech with a grim expression. Now he gave the most perfunctory handshake before himself ascending the rostrum, and holding up his hands for silence. The noise slowly abated, and the President began to speak. 'President Borjigin has made a most inspiring speech,' he said. 'And like all of us, he is of course entitled to his dreams, his ambitions. Sadly, times have changed. Fifteen years ago we chose to go our separate ways. That decision cannot now be reversed...'

His voice was drowned in a huge roar of 'Out! Out! Boroslov out! Borjigin in! We want Borjigin! We want Borjigin!' The chorus was taken up by the huge crowds outside the building. More important, it was taken up by the soldiers gathered in Red Square, and by their generals, led by Boris Simonoslov.

'Oh, Clive, Clive.' Rosemary clung to him. 'To have you back ... is it all really true?'

'Yes.' He kissed her some more, then poured them both a drink. 'How's Baby Clive?'

'Sleeping. But Clive, what did happen in Moscow?'

'The Russian Parliament passed a unanimous vote of no confidence in Boroslov, and appointed Batalji provisional President pending elections.'

'But ... is he eligible?'

'Apparently he is still a Russian citizen. They have been so sure all these years that they would eventually bring him to book, they wanted him to remain Russian so that they would have more crimes to charge him with.'

Rosemary sat down, her glass held in both hands. 'Then Russia is reunited?'

'To all intents and purposes, yes. It will be, legally, by this time next year.' He looked out of the window at the rain clouding down. 'Nothing much is going to happen until then, except on the diplomatic front.'

'Does that mean you're off again?'

He nodded. 'I'm afraid so. I have a week.'

'Which you will have to share with Shallane, I presume.'

'Well ... some of it. How is she, anyway?'

'She doesn't come to my part of the house often, and she doesn't interfere in the running of it, either, thank God! Why don't you get her pregnant?'

'I have tried, once or twice.'

'I bet you have. Clive ... what's going to happen now?'

'Batalji has achieved his ambition. Do you know, I believe he had this in mind from the very beginning. Perhaps from when he was in that orphanage in Omsk.'

'And he is a man who makes dreams come true.'

'Yes,' Clive said, and held her hands. 'You know, my dearest girl, that I can never leave now.'

'You're Shallane's husband. But do you want to leave, Clive?'

He sighed. 'No. I want to stay. Of course I'm shocked and horrified by some of the things he's done, but then ... I was shocked and horrified at my first impalement. I should have known the way he would wage war. But he is right, you know. If you are going to go to war, it must be with total ruthlessness. That actually saves lives in the long run. As well as money.'

'Will the West accept it?'

He stood up. 'It's my business to make them do so. Anyway, at least Shallane will be out of your hair for a couple of months. She's coming with me.'

'To the States again? After the fiasco last time? We saw the video of her appearance on that chat show, you know.'

Clive grinned. 'She thought she was a great success. But this time she's getting off in Moscow. To be with her daddy.' He kissed her. 'When I get back, and have a little time to spare, you and I are going to get married.'

Selphine lay on her bed gazing at her six television sets, which were mounted in an echelon on the wall, the highest being placed on a bracket just beneath the ceiling. On each one there was a video of some different part of the war. 'I hate to say it,' she remarked. 'But that woman is a genius.'

Clive sat beside her. He hated to say it too, in this context. Perhaps the tragedy of Denise's life, before now, had been that she had never had a war to photograph. But here were distance shots of burning buildings, medium-range shots of men going into action, and close-up shots of people dying, every one held for just that length of time to make a horrifying impact. 'How I wish I had been there,' Selphine said. 'He should have let me be there. Do you know, Stanton, that had I not been there, five years ago, the coup would never have succeeded? It was I who drove them forward when Batalji was hit. It was I who executed Taychin. And his whores,' she added with satisfaction.

'Are you going to Moscow?'

'He has not sent for me.' Selphine's shoulders humped. 'He never sends for me any more.'

To his consternation, Clive saw that she was weeping. He took her in his arms. 'He is very busy. Is he not accomplishing all you could possibly wish of a son of yours?'

'He wishes to equal Genghis Khan,' Selphine muttered.

'Well, I would say he's not doing too badly at that. As a matter of fact, the Western press is calling him the new Genghis Khan.'

Selphine snorted. 'But he has not yet equalled him, has he, Stanton? Batalji has only conquered Russia!'

'Sit down, Clive.' Walter Ingraham gestured his friend to a chair, sat down himself. 'You're looking pretty fit.'

'Shouldn't I be?'

'You wouldn't agree that this summer has been the most traumatic since the end of World War Two? Christ, we thought the Gulf was bad, fifteen years ago, but this... You have any idea what's been happening with the stock market?'

'I'm afraid not. We don't have stock quotations in Yakutistan.'

'Pure as driven snow, eh? I suppose it impacted harder because no one had any inkling it was going to happen. Last April, there could not have been a more peaceful place than this planet. Now...' He pointed. 'And *you* knew it was going to happen, you son of a gun.'

'I can give you my word I didn't.'

Ingraham studied him for several seconds, then nodded. 'I'll accept your word. Yet you go on working for the bastard.'

'Let's say I believe in finishing a job.'

'Well, where's the bottom line, Clive? That's what we all want to know. This last summer we have witnessed warfare on a scale not seen for sixty years. In fact, that we have *never* seen. Not only the men and material involved, but the speed of movement, has left our military people gasping. So has the utter ruthlessness with which this campaign was fought, and again, I am not talking just about liquidating civilians because they happen to be in the way. What is most disconcerting is the way Borjigin changes sides, switches alliances, stabs people in the back ... It really means that his signature on a piece of paper isn't worth the price of the ink. So ...?'

'He's got Russia,' Clive said. 'That's what he always wanted. I'm pretty damned sure he can't hold it. He knows nothing of economics, nothing, indeed, of politics. He rules as what he is, a Mongol Khan. Right now he's a popular hero in Russia; they believe he saved them from the Ukrainians. He's a popular hero in Krasnoyarskiy and in Kazakhstan, because he's cut their taxes. The smaller republics in the south are all appealing to have the CIS abandoned, and once again to be taken under the Borjigin banner. I reckon he's even a hero to a good number of Ukrainians. You have to remember, Walter, that there is a very large proportion of the Russian population which has always been basically imperialist at heart, while of the remainder, the financial traumas and food shortages of the past fifteen years have made a lot of them dream back to the old days of Communist centralisation and controlled distribution. And there isn't a nation in the world which doesn't respond to military glory, to feeling that it is one of the big boys. Batalji has it made, at the moment. But ... it can't last. He doesn't see this. But even his oil can't bail Russia out of its economic mess, or finance sufficient growth. Anyway, it's the nature of the political beast that the more people are for you one day, the more they deride you the next. So ...'

'Come the election he's likely just to fade away? I hope to God you're right, Clive. I do sincerely hope that. I'd hate to think we've got another Cold War starting.'

*

Shallane sprawled across the foot of her father's bed in the Kremlin, watching a soap on television. 'Surely you have no more use for him now,' she said.

Batalji trickled his fingers down her naked back. As lord of all he surveyed, he made the rules, and he had promised his favourite woman this long ago. His bed, and other things. And now he owed Stanton his life: that was a dangerous debt. Once before he had owed someone his life, and the obligation to Homaira had all but cost him the future. 'I think the time is close,' Batalji agreed. 'When he returns from this mission. Which will mean that the West has accepted the present situation.'

'I want the bitch as well,' Shallane said. 'And that child of theirs.'

'I see no reason why not,' Batalji said. 'But it must be done in Yakutsk. Or better yet, on the steppes. Stanton and his entire family will take a holiday on the steppes, far away from anyone else, and there he will die, in an accident, with his wife. You cannot have the child. I gave Stanton my word that his son would be a prince, and so he shall be. Brought up by myself.'

'An accident?' Shallane sat up in dismay, hair flying.

'That will be the official story,' Batalji explained. 'They will simply not come back, and the world will mourn. What you do to them is your business, although perhaps you will tell me of it afterwards.'

'I shall have to think . . .' Shallane frowned. 'I will need assistance. People I can trust.'

'You may pick them yourself.'

Shallane was still frowning. 'But . . . it will soon be winter. We cannot go out on the steppes until next summer.'

Batalji grinned, and kissed her. 'What a hothouse flower you have become. Did you not spend the first ten years of your life on the steppes, summer and winter? But Stanton will be back in a fortnight. You will go on holiday then. It will only be the beginning of October. You can spend the next fortnight planning. Mind you do not let on *what* you are planning.'

Shallane giggled. 'I shan't do that.'

Batalji was not listening. He was looking at the screen. The soap had ended, and so had the commercials, and it was the beginning of a news programme. Hastily he turned up the sound.

'... deep into Vietnam,' said the newscaster. 'It is said that perhaps a million men are involved. The attack has come as a surprise to everyone, although it is known that there have been several acrimonious exchanges between Saigon and Peking during the past few months. Now it is supposed by observers that the Chinese are taking a leaf out of the book of the Russian President, Batalji Borjigin, and acting without reference to world opinion or possible repercussions.'

'Because there won't be any,' Batalji said.

'Is that serious, Papa?' Shallane asked.

Batalji hugged her, and rolled across the bed with her in his arms. 'It is the news I have been waiting for.'

He summoned a meeting of his generals, which now included Russians like Simonoslov, and gave them their orders. They were all aghast. 'You are starting World War Three, Your Excellency,' Jagnuth protested, formal in the presence of the other officers.

'That is nonsense,' Batalji said. 'America and Europe are not going to get involved in Asia. Have I not always been right? Do as I say.'

The telephone rang. 'Batalji,' Clive said. 'You've seen the news?'

'This morning. It is as we expected. But I wish you back here as soon as is possible. It is very important.'

Clive arrived in Moscow the following morning at dawn, and was shown straight to Batalji's office.

'What is the reaction in New York?' Batalji asked.

'They are very alarmed and upset. But...'

'There is nothing they can, or wish to do about it,' Batalji said. 'That again is as we expected. They are all fat cats, sleeping in the sun. Oh, they are willing to crush any small states, like Iraq or Yugoslavia, which get out of hand, but they dare not interfere with another superpower, eh, so long as they themselves do not feel threatened. Well, that is good.'

'What line do we take?' Clive asked.

Batalji gave one of his sleepy smiled. 'Oh, publicly we shall wave an admonitory finger, and privately, we will congratulate Mr Yuan and his colleagues, as we are obliged to do under the terms of our alliance. While secretly ... I am moving my armies to the east. Next spring we will invade China.'

THE FIFTEENTH CHRONICLE

Yakutsk, Autumn 2005

Clive knew he had to be very calm, and very rational. 'Batalji, no one has ever conquered China.'

'Now you know that is nonsense. Genghis Khan conquered China, and set his grandson on the Dragon Throne. China is a bubble. One quick thrust with a sword and it is no more. It will be a far more simple matter than conquering Russia, and I did that in three months. By next spring I will have concentrated forty *tumans* north of the Great Wall. They will be in Beijing in two days.'

'You don't think the Chinese will try to stop you?'

'Oh, they will try. But by next spring they will be totally committed in Vietnam. Now *there* is a country no one has ever conquered. The Chinese claimed suzerainty a thousand years ago, but they never actually managed to occupy it. The French tried for a hundred years, and the Americans for ten. Those jungles, and those people, will swallow up the Chinese armies.'

'They can still muster several million men.'

'So can I. But I have no intention of being drawn into some long struggle. I shall destroy Beijing in one night. These modern politicians do not know how to deal with situations like that. When they understand that they have to cope with several million dead, then they will beg for peace, on my terms.'

Clive's head seemed to be spinning, as he tried to think of every possible objection. 'You'll have an atomic war on your hands. China has a delivery system, you know.'

'So? I have a better one, now. As I have said before, the world is overpopulated as it is. Especially China.'

Clive finished his vodka. There did not seem to be much else to do. 'And I am to explain all of this to the world?'

Batalji smiled. 'In due course, perhaps. Right now, Clive, I am worried about you. You are not looking well.'

'I'm feeling bloody sick,' Clive told him.

'That is what I thought. You have been working too hard, for me. What I would like you to do is take a holiday. Go back to the steppes, where you honeymooned. Shallane has told me how happy you were there. Take her with you, and do nothing but relax, for the next month. And do you know what you should also do? Take Rosemary with you. And your son. I am sure they would like to leave Yakutsk for a while as well.'

'I can't see Shallane agreeing to that.'

'Oh, she will. I have already spoken with her. She is perfectly happy about it.'

'What you mean is, you want me right out of the way for the next month.'

'I want you to have a holiday,' Batalji said. 'And while you are away, I shall arrange your marriage to Rosemary.'

Clive went in search of Jagnuth, whom he regarded as the only totally sane member of Batalji's Government. 'You realise this is madness?'

Jagnuth's shoulders were hunched over his desk. 'He is the Khan.'

'And so you will obey him, blindly. You once told me you would lead his armies into the gates of Hell, if Batalji commanded you to. Well, I hope you realise he has just done so.'

'We can defeat the Chinese,' Jagnuth asserted.

'And do you think he will stop at China, even if you do beat them? Jagnuth, Batalji genuinely believes himself to be a reincarnation of Genghis Khan. Did Genghis Khan stop at China?'

'His sons got as far as the Danube.'

'And they only stopped there because of the death of the Khan, which recalled them to Karakorum. Batalji is not likely to die in the near future. He is only forty-three, and for all his drinking and whoring he is as healthy as a horse. That means he is not going to be stopped by the Danube. In any event, do you suppose the Western powers are going to just watch him march on them? I'm not sure they're going to stand by anyway, if he carries out his threat to use nuclear weapons on China.'

'We have nuclear weapons,' Jagnuth declared. 'We have sufficient to destroy all America.'

'While she is destroying you. For God's sake, Jagnuth you have a wife and family. Do you wish to see them caught up in a nuclear holocaust? The whole planet destroyed? Batalji is quite capable of causing that to happen. He does not care about what comes after him. He is the ultimate nihilist. Just as the old Assyrian kings died with their wives and concubines and faithful guards, after setting fire to their palaces rather than surrender, he would cheerfully go up in a huge bang, certain that he will be joined in the heavens with Pierroun. And probably with Genghis as well.'

Jagnuth's shoulders became even more hunched. 'What would you have me do?'

'You command the army.'

'You wish me to tell the army to turn on Batalji? They worship him like a god.' Jagnuth glanced at the door. 'Do you have any idea what would happen to us if Batalji learned of this conversation?'

'How can he, unless one of us tells him. Now listen, I am required to take a holiday, on the steppes, presumably to get me as far away from what's happening here as possible. I have been told to go for a month. I cannot disobey the Khan in that, or he would be suspicious. There is still time. When I come back it will only be November, and things will have settled down for the winter.'

'Batalji intends to use the winter to move his army.'

'But there will be no assault before next year, surely?'

'I do not believe so.'

'Then this may work out to our advantage. If he is concentrating sufficient forces to attack China, presumably the garrison in Yakutsk will be going as well? I am talking about the Seventh Tuman, commanded by Barone.'

Jagnuth nodded. 'They are on my list.'

'Then with them out of the way ... I am assuming Batalji will winter in Yakutsk, for at least some of the time.'

'Yes. But I shall be in the East, with the troops.'

'You have your own aircraft. You could come back, with a picked squad. Listen to me. As soon as I return from my holiday, I will set things moving. Our code word will be ... Atom. The moment I send you that word, Jagnuth, you must return to Yakutsk immediately, accompanied by a section of men who will obey you.'

'To arrest the Khan?'

'Yes. Until he rescinds the order for the attack on China.'

Jagnuth stroked his chin.

'Back to our old honeymoon *ordu*,' Shallane said, nestling against Clive as the aircraft flew east, carrying them from Moscow to Yakutsk. 'I am so looking forward to that.'

Clive had never known her so loving, even *on* their honeymoon. 'It is your father's wish that I take my whole family on this holiday,' he remarked, watchfully.

Shallane kissed him. 'I think that is a splendid idea. I have always wanted to get to know Rosemary better.'

Clive refrained from pointing out that she had had ample opportunities to do that in the past.

*

Yakutsk was still *en fête* in celebration of Batalji's victories. Every building wore bunting, in the distinctive Yakut colours of red crossed with yellow and black, and the people were in the highest of good humour: their Khan had proved himself the greatest man in the world. Needless to say there were summonses to the Palace awaiting Clive when he got home, and he had barely time to visit Rosemary. 'Thank God you're back,' she said. 'I have been so *worried*. But Clive . . . what's going to happen now?'

'I'll tell you all about it. Get packed. We're going on a holiday. You, me and little Clive. And Shallane.'

'That's a holiday?'

He kissed her. 'She wants to be friends.'

Of the two summonses, he answered the one to Mortana first. Not only was she technically superior in rank to her mother-in-law, but his interview with her was likely to be the less exhausting. He wished he could confide in her, but she was Batalji's wife more than Jagnuth's sister; he could only attempt to enlist her help through veiled warnings. 'Clive!' Mortana embraced him. 'Can it all be true? Oh, I have watched it all, and heard it all, but that Batalji should be ruler of Russia, just like that . . . it is unbelievable. Do you think he will send for me?' Her tone was wistful.

'You must realise that his new responsibilities keep him very busy.'

'I do understand that. But just to be with him for a few days, to share in his triumph . . . Do you think he will come back to Yakutsk this winter?'

'He always returns to Yakutsk for at least part of the winter.'

She smiled. 'Then I must be patient.'

Clive picked his words very carefully. 'I hope he does return here for the winter, Mortana. And that you may be able to persuade him to take life a little more slowly.'

She frowned. 'He's not ill?'

'No, no. But he has been under great stress this summer, as

you may well imagine. And now, well ... his mind as always is ranging ahead to new projects, new ideas ... It would be very good for him, and perhaps for all of us, if you could persuade him to devote the next few years entirely to the resuscitation of Russia, rather than any new political schemes.'

Mortana laughed. 'You are getting lazy, you mean, Clive, and wish to rest upon your laurels. I know that Batalji will never rest. He thrives upon hard work. You will be ready for work again when you return from your holiday.'

Clive went to Selphine. She was just as wistful as her daughter-in-law, just as anxious to have some share in her son's triumphs, and more than a little resentful, as usual. 'He has done it all, and left me behind,' she grumbled. 'I, who always rode at his side, in the old days, when the danger was greatest. Now there is nothing left to conquer, and I am ignored, thrown aside, discarded. How can a son be so careless of his mother's feelings? And *my* son!'

Clive was growing more desperate by the minute but Selphine had herself in the past expressed doubts about Batalji's ambitions. 'Highness, I would not say that there is nothing left to conquer, at least in Batalji's eyes.'

Selphine caught his hand. 'Tell me.'

'If I do, it must be in the strictest secrecy, or I could lose my head.'

She kissed him. 'I will protect you, Stanton. I could not live without you.'

He had to believe her. 'Batalji considers himself a reincarnation of Genghis Khan.'

'Well, so he is,' Selphine said. 'Everyone can see that.'

'Therefore,' Clive went on, 'he considers it his duty to carry out the same programme of conquest as did Genghis.'

Selphine's mouth slowly opened, then as slowly spread into a smile. 'You mean ... China?' She clapped her hands.

'It will mean millions of deaths. It will probably start the Third World War. And he means to use nuclear weapons, if he has to.'

Selphine bounced off the bed. 'It will be the greatest war in the history of the world. It will be stupendous. And my son will have fought it.'

'Selphine! You must stop him! Or he will be throwing away everything he has accomplished.'

Selphine snorted. 'What can a man accomplish that is greater than victory in battle? Victory against odds! That is the true mark of a man. Batalji has conquered Russia. Now he will conquer China. And this time I shall be at his side.' She laughed. 'So will you, Stanton. There is nothing to be afraid of. Batalji was born to conquer.'

There was but one last direction in which he could turn. Two days later, the afternoon before he and his family left for their holiday, Clive called on old Khalim Anhusat. Khalim was in his seventies now, and lived in retirement with his wives and children and grandchildren. As father-in-law of the Khan he had his own palace, and wanted for nothing, and as a Mongol chieftain he revelled in his latest wife, a girl of fifteen. Nadehzda was with him when Clive was shown in. 'Stanton!' Khalim's voice was as strong as ever. 'Are you not proud to serve such a man as Batalji?'

'Proud, indeed, Great Chief.' Clive glanced at the girl. 'Is it possible to speak with you alone?'

Khalim waved his hand, and Nadehzda ran from the room. 'There is something wrong?' Khalim asked. 'Batalji is not ill?'

'No, Highness. I wish to speak with you in the utmost secrecy.'

'Then speak.' Clive sat beside him. With every one of these people he was putting his neck on the line, and so far he had accomplished nothing. But he had to keep trying. Khalim stroked his beard as he listened. At least he did not clap his hands for joy. 'You say my son has agreed to act with you?' he asked, when Clive had finished.

'He has agreed.' Clive could only hope that was true.

'It is indeed a great undertaking.'

'In five years, Batalji has accomplished more than any man

before him in all recorded history,' Clive said. 'It would be a tragedy for him to throw it all away.'

'You do not believe he can conquer China?'

'He may well be able to defeat the Chinese armies, and destroy their government by the use of terror tactics, Highness. But the cost will be too great. China will retaliate before surrendering, and worse, such a war will turn all of Asia into a desert of dead animals, ruined crops, and starving people. That is if it does not kill all of us by atomic radiation. Highness, a nuclear war would mean the end of the world.'

Khalim continued to stroke his beard. 'You are speaking of a deposition? You would never depose Batalji. He would fight to the last breath in his body. And he would be supported by nearly all his people. Right this minute, by nearly all Russia. He could only be stopped by assassination.' He glanced at Clive. 'We are speaking of Mortana's husband, the father of my grandchildren.'

'And my father-in-law,' Clive said. 'But it is of Mortana and the children, including my wife, that I am thinking.'

'It is a great business, to kill the Kha Khan. It would earn us eternal opprobrium.'

'I think it would earn us the eternal gratitude of mankind, if it was the only way to stop this war.'

'Perhaps. I will see what can be done. As you say, there is time. Come to me again when you return from your holiday.'

Clive stood up. 'You understand, Highness, that were Batalji to learn of our discussion . . .'

Khalim's smile was grim. 'We would both deny that it had ever taken place. He must never learn of it, Stanton: I have no wish to feel a sharp stake being hammered into my ass. Visit me when you return.'

Clive wondered if he had actually accomplished anything, or merely endangered them all. But they could not be in greater danger than if he did nothing. Meanwhile . . . He smiled at Rosemary, seated beside him as the Yak soared into the sky, little Clive in her arms as the noise made him cry. Shallane was on the flight deck; she had announced that she wished to learn to fly. 'Happy?'

'Oh, yes. I wish you were.'

'Why do you think I'm not?'

'Your eyes.'

He decided not to pursue the matter. All manner of ideas were roaming through his mind. Unlike Shallane, he already held a pilot's licence. He could probably take over the Yak and fly ... where? There was the question. He might just have sufficient fuel to make Russia, but Russia was now in Batalji's hands. And even supposing he could reach Alaska, what would he accomplish? Even if the State Department believed what he had to say, they were not likely to start a preventive war to stop Batalji, nor would China accept a warning from them, in the present deteriorated state of relations between the two powers. He had mounted the back of this tiger, if not entirely voluntarily, certainly with growing enthusiasm. Now he had to see it through, and drive his knife into the tiger's heart. Or see that it was done.

'Wheee!!' Shallane galloped across the rolling grassland, hair flying in the wind. Clive had long abandoned any idea of keeping up with her, and Rosemary preferred to walk her horse well behind her; little Clive was back at the *ordu* with his Yakut nurse. Yet to his pleasure, the two woman had got on well on this holiday. If Shallane had been intent on showing off her innate ability as a horsewoman and huntress, Rosemary had done nothing but congratulate her, and Shallane had been forced to accept the compliments and make some effort to return them.

But now Shallane had turned her mount and was galloping past them, pointing at the sky. They had been a week at the northern *ordu*, and it was well into October. Winter was late, this year, but it was coming; the sky was black with the threat of snow. And out of the gloom could be seen the silver body of the Yak, swooping in to land. 'I thought we had a month,' Rosemary said.

'Something must have happened. Come on.' Clive preferred not to think what it might be as he kicked his horse into a gallop. Shallane surged past them, and Rosemary followed. There was no hope of catching Shallane, who reached the aircraft well before them, and leapt from the saddle. Clive arrived a few moments later, to watch the door open, and six young women emerge. They wore the uniforms of the Palace Guard, were armed, and clearly very fit and strong; one of them was the woman Yorcka, whom he remembered so well from his first meeting with Selphine. The women looked expectant, but at the same time clearly had no idea why they had been sent to the north. 'What's going on?' Clive demanded, dismounting.

Rosemary had by now reached them, and also dismounted. 'Are we to return to Yakutsk?'

'In due course,' Shallane said. 'Take them.' The women hesitated, and Shallane pulled a piece of paper from her pocket and thrust it at them. 'This is an order signed by the Khan.'

The women glanced at it, and before Clive could understand what was happening, he was faced with a row of machine-pistols, two of which were pointed at Rosemary, who gave a little gasp of dismay. 'Is this some kind of game?' Clive snapped.

'Oh, yes,' Shallane said. 'My game. I will tell you about it. Secure them,' she told her people. The women pulled Rosemary's arms behind her and handcuffed them, then did the same to Clive; Yorcka's eyes were apologetic, but she was obeying her master's written command. 'Into the *ordu*,' Shallane said.

The guards pushed Clive and Rosemary together, and marched them into the tent village, where the Yakuts stared at them in consternation. 'Clive,' Rosemary muttered. 'What is happening?'

'Hit her for speaking,' Shallane commanded, and one of the guards swung her arm to slash the edge of her hand into Rosemary's stomach. Rosemary doubled up and almost fell, gasping for breath; the guard seized her shoulder and thrust her forward.

'For God's sake, Shallane...' Clive said.

'Do you also wish to be beaten?' Shallane asked. Clive bit his lip, while his brain tumbled. They were pushed into their yurt, followed by the guards and Shallane. 'Sit down,' Shallane invited.

Rosemary was still panting from the blow in her belly. She sank to her knees and then sat; her face was wrinkled with pain and anxiety... about the possible mistreatment of little Clive. Clive sat beside her. 'You will scream when you die,' Shallane told them.

'Are you out of your mind?' Clive asked her. 'The Khan...'

'Has given me permission to do with you what I wish. That was my wedding present. Why else do you suppose I agreed to marry *you*.'

Clive was too stunned to think straight for the moment. 'Do you think you can get away with murdering me?' he asked. 'I am your country's Foreign Minister. All the world will know of it. What is more, your grandmother will know of it.'

Shallane smiled. 'My grandmother, and the world, will mourn the man who died with his mistress in an air crash. It is all arranged. When I have finished with you, you and her...' her tone was filled with contempt as she looked at Rosemary, 'will be taken up in the plane. When you have reached a suitable altitude, the pilot and co-pilot will jump with their parachutes, and you two will be in the plane when it crashes into the earth. You see? Your bodies will be so badly smashed up, and probably burned as well, that no one will have any idea what might have happened to you first. So, I can do what I like to you.'

'My baby...' Rosemary muttered.

'Oh, I am not going to kill *him*. Papa wants him. Let's eat,' she told her women. Food was brought, and Shallane chewed slowly and thoughtfully, while she gazed at her victims. 'I'm actually going to kill you myself,' she explained. 'I want to watch you die, Stanton. But before then, I'm going to enjoy myself. Is that hot?'

One of the girls brought a skillet from the fire, in which were several sizzling sausages. Shallane grinned as she took one of the sausages in a pair of tongs and pushed it against Clive's lips. He gasped as he was burned, and when his mouth opened, she thrust the meat in, causing him to choke. But she continued to force it in, while tears started from his eyes. It was such a childish way of hurting him. But then, he realised, Shallane was only a child. Certainly mentally. 'Aren't you hungry?' she asked. 'Let's give her one.' Rosemary had to undergo the same ordeal.

'Now strip them,' Shallane commanded. The women cut the clothes from their bodies with their knives. Rosemary stared at Clive, and he stared back, while he thought and thought and thought . . . with no possible solution. Save for Yorcka. Yorcka was unhappy about what she was being forced to do, and Yorcka had always been Selphine's woman rather than Batalji's – or Shallane's. But would she have the courage to go against a direct command from the Khan? And would he ever have the chance to find out? 'Heat those up again,' Shallane said.

The sausages were reheated, and Shallane used her tongs to thrust one at Rosemary's breasts. Rosemary grasped and could not restrain a whimper as the sizzling meat burned her flesh; she was still feeding little Clive and was even more sensitive than normal. Shallane stroked her for several seconds. 'Now you're all greasy,' she said.

'Shallane,' Clive said. 'It's me you hate, not her.'

'But I do hate her,' Shallane said. 'Besides, Papa wants to be rid of her too. But there is no hurry. You're not going to die for *days*. And first, I'm going to give you a treat. I'm going to tie you both up in a sack, so you can spend the whole night fucking. Then tomorrow I am going to put a rat in the sack with you. Then again you can spend the whole day, and the night, fucking. With the rat to help you. He'll get hungry, you know, as well as being afraid. And the day after, I will put a cat in the sack with you, and her, and the rat. Oh, it's going to be such sport. And the day after that, I'll take you out of the sack and castrate you, if the rat hasn't had it first. Then I'll put you back in the sack and take Rosemary out and impale her, what's left of her. Then on the sixth day it'll be your turn. That's the programme, Stanton. I wonder which part of you the rat will eat first? But I should think it'll start on her. She's softer. And her tits have been smeared in animal fat.'

'You are *sick*,' Clive told her.

She slapped his face. 'And you are going to scream,' she said. 'Eventually. Fetch the sack.'

'Clive,' Rosemary whispered, as she was thrust into the sack beside him. 'What are we going to do?'

'Pretend to fuck,' he told her.

Their wrists had been untied, but the sack was too thick to tear with their hands, and it had been secured around their necks; only their heads were exposed. While the women were watching their every move. Shallane clapped her hands in glee as their bodies writhed together, and to make sure they kept moving, she had her guards constantly poking them with sticks. 'Finished already?' she cried. 'You Westerners are weak vessels. You do not understand the art of love. I always knew this about you, Stanton. My grandmother must be a lonely old woman to value one such as you. Feed them,' she commanded. 'And give them vodka to drink.'

Clive and Rosemary were dragged into a sitting position, and food and drink was pushed into their sore mouths. Shallane sat opposite, herself eating and drinking, as did her women. 'Tomorrow, the rat,' she said happily. 'He will make you move your ass. Oh yes. Oh, you will scream.'

Rosemary shuddered. 'I'm going to scream now,' she muttered. 'Clive . . .'

'Go ahead,' he suggested. 'Let it rip.' Rosemary glanced at him, then threw back her head and uttered the loudest shriek he had ever heard: the very tent seemed to inflate.

Shallane clapped her hands. 'What a racket! But you will improve on that. Take them outside for the night. You can fuck some more, if you wish,' she suggested.

The sack was dragged outside into the open air, and they

were left on the ground. Inside the yurt they could hear the sounds of increasingly drunken laughter as Shallane and her companions consumed vast quantities of vodka. But the fact that they were getting drunk was not immediately hopeful: one of the women remained on guard, squatting cross-legged opposite them, staring at them. 'You keep still,' she warned.

She was armed with a machine-pistol, and while Clive did not suppose she would spoil her mistress's anticipated amusement by shooting them, she could certainly call for assistance if she wished. Several of the villagers came to look at them. These were people with whom Clive had ridden and dined, and laughed and joked. But they were Shallane's people, who stared at the man and woman in the sack, and went away again. Rosemary trembled against him. 'Clive...'

'Keep your nerve,' he whispered.

The night dragged on. Their guard was replaced after a couple of hours, and this new girl was definitely drunk. 'Why are you not fucking?' she demanded. 'It is the last time you will do so. Why are you not fucking?'

'We have been,' Clive assured her. 'Now we are exhausted.'

'You are fools to waste your time,' the girl said, and yawned and belched.

At midnight she was replaced, and this time it was Yorcka.

Yorcka had clearly not drunk as much as the others. She sat on the ground and stared at them. Clive returned her stare for several minutes, before he asked, 'Are you not afraid?'

Yorcka's head jerked. 'What have I to be afraid of?'

'Don't you remember how you held me, on the bed, on the day I first came to the Palace. You held my prick, so that Princess Selphine could shoot it off.' Yorcka blinked as she tried to concentrate. 'But she did not do it,' Clive said. 'Instead she sent you away, and released me, and took me into her. I became her man. I am still her man. Do you know what she is going to do to you, to all of you, if you are responsible for my death?'

Yorcka licked her lips. 'It is to be an accident.'

'Do you suppose Princess Selphine will believe that? Does she not know all things?'

Yorcka looked left and right, as if in search of inspiration, or a vodka bottle. 'Princess Shallane . . .'

'Do you suppose Princess Shallane can stand against Princess Selphine? Not even the Khan dares to oppose his mother. Princess Selphine is the most powerful person in Russia. And you would destroy her lover?'

Yorcka panted. 'There is nothing to be done. To oppose Princess Shallane would mean my death.'

'I am not asking you to oppose Princess Shallane. I am inviting you to save your life. Set us free. Then we will bind and gag you, and leave. No one will know how we escaped, and you were taken by surprise.'

'You must take me for a fool,' Yorcka said.

'I will take you for a fool if you do not save your own life,' Clive told her.

Yorcka licked her lips again. 'Princess Shallane will have me caned if you escape.'

'Is not a caning better than death?'

By now Yorcka was obviously in a state of total confusion, as well as being terrified. Indeed Clive was almost afraid he had overdone it, and that he might lose everything by a mental collapse on the part of the girl. 'I dare not,' she whispered.

'You must, Yorcka. Listen, when I get back to Yakutsk, I will tell Princess Selphine that it was you helped me, and she will protect you from Shallane.'

'Yes,' Yorcka said. 'Yes, you must do that. I will come with you. I cannot stay here. You must protect me.'

'All right,' Clive agreed. 'Just untie this sack.'

Yorcka crawled towards them, and checked, her knees against them, her face working. 'You will protect me?'

'You have my word.' A last lick of the lips, then she drew her knife and slit the cord securing the neck of the sack. Clive eased himself out, and Rosemary crawled beside him. 'Now give me your gun,' Clive said.

'My gun?'

'I will need it. If only to remind you not to change sides again.'

'You will take me to the Princess Selphine?'
'You, and Shallane,' Clive told her.

Yorcka was due to be relieved in another half-hour. Clive and Rosemary lay down again, beneath the sack but not inside it, while the woman continued to sit, cross-legged, staring at them. Clive thought it was the longest half-hour of his life, and he knew Rosemary felt the same; she was holding his hand, and her fingers kept biting into his. But at last a figure emerged from the yurt where Shallane was sleeping, and stumbled uncertainly towards them. 'What are they doing?' the woman asked. 'Still fucking?'

'They are asleep,' Yorcka told her.

'Lucky them. I have brought a bottle.' The woman held it out, and Yorcka took it as she got up. The woman went forward, to bend over the sack and peer at Clive's head. Clive released Rosemary, and thrust both hands up, to seize the woman's blouse and drag her down with all his strength, at the same time rolling to one side. She struck the ground with a force which knocked all the wind from her body, and before she could recover, Yorcka had broken the vodka bottle over her head. She slumped unconscious, surrounded by liquor. Rosemary and Yorcka hastily stripped off her blouse and pants, and Rosemary put them on; the boots were too small. They crammed the woman into the sack, head and all, and secured it. Rosemary now had her pistol.

The three of them crept towards the tents. There was no one to be seen, as even the Yakut spectators had gone off to bed. 'There is one woman in the tent with the babe,' Yorcka whispered. 'The other three are with the Princess.'

'Little Clive first,' Rosemary said.

Clive considered. He would have preferred to go after Shallane first, on the basis that once he had her the rest would fall into place. But he couldn't risk anything happening to his son, and that way meant another weapon. He nodded, and they crept towards the baby's tent. 'Get her outside,' Clive told Yorcka.

Yorcka opened the flap. 'Natalia?' she whispered. 'Natalia, are you awake?'

There was a moment before a sleepy voice answered, 'What is it?'

'There is something very peculiar in the sky,' Yorcka said. 'Come and see.'

There was a grunt, but a moment later Natalia emerged. As her head came through the opening Clive hit her with the butt of the pistol, and she fell without a sound. 'You've done this before,' Rosemary commented.

'First time ever,' Clive assured her. 'But I'm in the mood to do it a lot more often.'

Rosemary took little Clive to the parked aircraft – the grass strip was only a hundred yards from the *ordu*. Clive and Yorcka went to Shallane's tent. Here the braziers had burned down, but there was sufficient light to see. They threw open the flap. 'Up!' Clive snapped.

One of the girls reached for her gun, and Yorcka shot her. Then the second as she too moved violently – they had been her comrades! Clive shot the third as she tried to reach her feet. Shallane sat up and stared at them, then threw back her head and uttered a long, baying scream, which was cut abruptly short as Clive hit her across the side of the head with his pistol; he thought he might have been waiting five years to do that. 'Bring her,' Clive snapped, and ran outside. The pilots were just emerging from their tent, guns in their hands. Clive felt happier shooting at men, and he cut them both down in a single burst from his pistol.

By now the entire *ordu* was waking up, men running from their houses, most with guns of various descriptions in their hands. Yorcka emerged from Shallane's tent, dragging Shallane's naked body by the ankles, so that Shallane's head bumped in the dust. 'She is heavy,' she gasped.

'Get to the plane,' Clive told her, and threw Shallane over his shoulder, one arm round her thighs; her hair trailed on the ground behind him. By now the villagers were approaching, so he fired a burst into the air. 'Just stay where you are,' he called. 'We have been summoned back to Yakutsk.'

He retreated across the open space to the waiting aircraft. Yorcka was in the doorway; behind her, little Clive was wailing. Clive ran up the steps, threw Shallane into a seat. 'If they approach, shoot them,' he told Yorcka. 'And if she moves, hit her. I will tell you when to close the door.'

Five minutes later they were airborne.

CHAPTER 15

Yakutsk, October 2005

'There has been a great battle north of Hanoi,' Almani said, spreading the map on the desk before the Khan. 'The Chinese are fighting with total ruthlessness.' He grinned. 'I think they must have been studying your methods.'

'Are they winning?'

'It is very difficult to tell. But equally we know it is difficult to win against the Vietnamese, decisively. I think there is no doubt that the Chinese will seize Hanoi in a couple of days; or what's left of it after their bombers are finished. But the Vietnamese army is taking to the forests, as it did against the Americans, and the Chinese are going to have a hard time bringing it to battle.'

'Which is what we want,' Batalji said. 'World opinion?'

'The United Nations are calling for everything from sanctions to armed intervention. Of course there is absolutely no chance of armed intervention, even if China did not have a veto on any Security Council resolution. However ... there is an inquiry from the United States as to where Russia stands, as Maloun, as you instructed, did not attend the Security Council meeting. And the Chinese Ambassador has flown from Moscow to Yakutsk to see you. He wishes to discuss current affairs.'

'I take it he flew in one of our planes?' Batalji asked.

'Of course. He was allowed to see nothing that could possibly upset him.'

'And you have stopped all tourist activity and all civilian movement along the selected army routes?'

'Yes,' Almani said. 'The tourists are all going home now, anyway, with the approach of winter. But our action is in itself causing some comment. Especially in Moscow.'

'You will instruct Sartine as to what to say in Moscow, and I will see the Chinese Ambassador myself, tomorrow. Sartine will tell the Russian Parliament that to keep world opinion happy, we are moving certain units towards the Chinese border. The Chinese know we have our treaty of alliance, and I will assure Mr Ping that we have no intention of breaking it. But these movements are necessary to allay the alarm of our own people.'

'Do you think he will believe you?'

Batalji grinned. 'I do not think he has any choice, if his people are really embedded in the Indo-Chinese jungle.'

'Clive will be very angry when he learns of this.'

'By the time Clive learns of what is happening, it will be too late to stop.'

'Is that why you sent him away?'

'That, amongst other reasons.'

'He will resign,' Almani warned.

'Then he resigns. He has served his purpose, anyway. He has bought us all the time we need. Now, it is simply a matter of using that time. Is the Seventh Brigade ready to move out?'

'Yes.' Almani hesitated. 'You mean him no harm?'

'Who?'

'Clive, Batalji. He has served you faithfully and well. He has saved your life. And you have just agreed that you could not be where you are now without his help.'

'Of course,' Batalji said. 'His name will be honoured in our history for as long as there is a history. Now I will inspect my troops.'

The Seventh Tuman was drawn up on The Avenue, stretching past the gates to the Palace grounds. It consisted of ten thousand personnel, with a regiment of tanks, and four batteries of artillery; like all Batalji's divisions, it included a regiment of women, eight hundred strong. It was a strictly Mongol force, which formed the normal garrison of Yakutsk, and was regarded by Batalji as one of his elite units; it had spearheaded the advance through Krasnoyarskiy and into Kazakhstan and then the Ukraine. Now it was being sent against China.

The streets were crowded, because most of the Yakuts had relatives in this brigade. No one had any idea the troops were against being sent off to war, of course. They believed what their Khan told them, that because of the crisis in southern China, it was necessary to reinforce the Russian borders. Yet they were not entirely happy; the parade was fine, but their sons and daughters and sweethearts and husbands were being sent away at the onset of winter, after only having returned the previous month; it would be a hard winter, bivouacked along the line of the Amur. Despite their misgivings, however, they broke into huge cheers as Batalji emerged from the Palace gateway, on horseback as usual, with Almani at his shoulder and various other generals behind him. 'Batalji!' the crowd roared. 'The Khan!'

The soldiers came to attention, but they also shouted, 'Batalji!' and 'The Khan!'

Batalji dismounted to walk along the ranks of his devoted soldiers, accompanied by their *noyon*, or commander, Barone Borjigin. The inspection took a long time, for Batalji stopped to speak with several of the men and women, and to examine their weapons. But at last he was finished. He embraced Barone, remounted, and walked his horse to one side. Then he raised his hand. The soldiers gave another huge shout, the band commenced to play, and the parade marched off; they would cover the first several hundred miles on horseback and in their APCs, before joining the Trans-Siberian Railway. Batalji returned to the Palace, dismounted, and went inside. 'There should be a radio message from the Princess Shallane, some time soon,' he told one of his secretaries. 'Bring it to me the moment it is received.'

'A message from the Princess was received an hour ago, Your Excellency.'

'Give it to me.'

The secretary riffled through the various documents awaiting the Khan's attention, and handed over the slip of paper.

Batalji frowned at it. 'This is merely a request for the Princess's plane to land.'

'Yes, Your Excellency.'

'You mean her aircraft has returned? With her on board?'

'It would appear so, Your Excellency.'

'There is no mention of Mr Stanton. Why not?'

'I do not know, Your Excellency.'

Batalji glanced at the paper again, and then pointed. 'According to this, the plane landed forty-five minutes ago. Find out. Find the Princess and bring her to me. Quickly.' The secretary hurried from the room.

'Do you think there is something wrong?' Almani asked. 'She was not supposed to return for another fortnight.'

Batalji snorted.

Mortana reclined on the day bed in her apartment. She was alone. She was always alone, nowadays. Tensan and Dorgat might be only twelve and thirteen respectively, but they were already officers in the army, and seldom came home. Barone never came near her even though he was in command of the Yakutsk garrison, and neither did Shallane. Mortana accepted this, because they were princes and a princess of the royal household, and obviously they had enormous responsibilities. But she was lonely. She and her mother-in-law had little in common; Selphine kept suggesting that she take a lover. 'It is the only comfort,' she insisted. 'And Batalji will not mind, as long as you do not become pregnant.'

'He is my husband,' Mortana would insist.

'Only in name. You must know he has no more time for your body. He has no time for anyone's body, except that Frenchwoman's. I cannot understand why he has not grown tired of *her*. He has been bewitched. But he will grow tired of her, one day. And then . . .'

Mortana sometimes wished she could work up hatreds like that, but it was simply not in her nature. As for taking a lover . . . she loved only Batalji. He was her husband. And he was returning to Yakutsk for at least the first part of the winter. But he had not come near her apartment, either, although he was as charming and courteous as ever when they met.

Mortana felt she needed to discuss the matter with someone who might have less extreme views than Selphine. The question was who. Galina Anhusat, Jagnuth's wife, was a disciple of Selphine's, and so were Almani and his wife. Mortana felt that she would only obtain a totally sympathetic hearing, and any worthwhile advice, from Clive Stanton and Rosemary Leigh. She could hardly wait for their return from Clive's second honeymoon . . . She raised her head, because there they were.

THE SIXTEENTH CHRONICLE

Yakutsk, October 2005

Mortana gazed in consternation at the group who had just entered her apartment by its inner, private doorway. It consisted of Rosemary Leigh, who wore a bloodstained and ill-fitting woman's uniform and was bare footed, and held her baby in her arms; one of the palace guards, whose name Mortana could not immediately remember; and Clive Stanton and Shallane – but Clive was holding Shallane's arm, and was pressing a pistol to her head, and both of them were wearing a very odd assortment of clothes indeed. While Shallane . . . There was a bruise on her head, she was covered in dust, and she looked more vicious than even Mortana had ever seen her.

'What has happened?' Mortana asked, getting up as her mind roamed over every possibility, save the truth.

'These scum. . .' Shallane spat.

'Shut up,' Clive said, and pushed her away from him.

Shallane stumbled across the floor and into her mother's arms. 'He hit me, Mama,' she sobbed. 'With his gun!' Mortana looked at Clive, and saw that the woman guard had taken up her position by the outer door, pistol in her hand.

'I hit her, after she had outlined her plans to murder Rosemary and myself, slowly,' Clive said. 'And then fake our death in a plane crash. All an idea of the Khan's, apparently.'

Mortana stared at him, and then looked down at the girl. 'He is lying,' she said. 'Tell me he is lying, Shallane.'

'Of course he must die,' Shallane snarled, freeing herself and turning to face Clive. 'He is going to be impaled. That is what is going to happen to him now.'

'Your husband, Highness,' Clive said, 'is embarking upon a course which may well destroy the world. That is why he wants me dead. I tried to warn you of this. Now you must listen to me.'

'How did you get here?' Mortana asked.

'We flew back from the *ordu*, and Yorcka knew a secret way into the Palace.'

'And you expect me to believe this tale?'

'I expect you to believe the truth, Highness. Yorcka, take Princess Shallane into the next room, and keep her there.'

Yorcka hesitated. 'We were to go to Princess Selphine.'

'We shall, shortly. But I must speak with Princess Mortana first.'

Yorcka came across the room. Shallane clung to her mother. 'She is going to kill me, or beat me.'

Mortana looked at Clive.

'Nothing is going to happen to your daughter, Highness. But I must speak with you alone.'

Mortana looked down at Shallane. 'Go with the woman, Shallane.'

Shallane glared at her. 'I hate you. You are one of them. When Papa learns of this . . .'

'Go!' Mortana commanded. Yorcka was standing immediately behind Shallane, and now she held the girl's arm, the pistol presented at her head. Shallane gave her mother, then Clive, a last vituperative look, and allowed herself to be pushed from the room. 'Speak,' Mortana commanded.

Clive told her Batalji's plans.

'You expect me to believe that?' she asked.

'Did not the Seventh Tuman march off half an hour ago? Where do you suppose they are going, Highness? You may check with your father and your brother. They are my allies in this.'

'My brother? Jagnuth is Batalji's most faithful follower. He is in field command of the army.'

'He is Batalji's most *sensible* follower. He knows Batalji has lost his senses in this dream of recreating the empire of Genghis Khan. He knows what must follow. Listen to me, Highness. We had agreed to wait until I had returned from my holiday. But in the meantime, Batalji has decided to get rid of me. I do not believe he knows of the plot against him; certainly, Shallane does not. But the mere fact that he gave orders for my execution proves that he is bent on this course. He must be stopped.'

'I can see that you would wish him to be prevented from executing you, Stanton.' Mortana's voice was cold.

Clive took a long breath. But it was all or nothing now. 'Highness, may I beg that you send in secret to your brother? There is a password on which we have agreed. It is known only to your father, to Jagnuth, and to myself. The word is Atom. Send that word to your brother, and await his response. I beg this of you, not merely for myself and Rosemary and the child, but for yourself and all of your children, and for all the people of Yakutistan, and for all the people of the world. Send to your brother.' As Mortana gazed at him, the picture of indecision, the door opened, to admit Batalji.

Behind the Khan were several guards, and while four of these were the women normally to be found in the interior of the Palace, another four were men; all were heavily armed, and their weapons were pointed into the room. Yet Clive knew he had, for the first split second, the upper hand. Batalji had not really known what to expect, and now he paused in surprise, while Clive was standing next to Mortana. A single shot, much less a burst, from the machine-pistol would end Batalji's career there and then ... but Clive could not squeeze the trigger. Too many imponderables were flitting through his mind, that if the guard returned fire, not only himself, but Rosemary and baby Clive would die on the instant. No doubt they were all going to die anyway, but the hail of bullets might well also encompass Mortana, who was utterly innocent of any wrongdoing in her entire life. And there was still hope, in Jagnuth ... even in Selphine.

Batalji had recovered. 'Drop the gun, Clive,' he commanded. 'And you, Rosemary. Where is my daughter?'

'Papa!' Shallane burst from the inner room, where Yorcka, terrified at hearing the Khan's voice, had lowered her guard. Shallane hurled herself into her father's arms. 'Papa! He hit me, with his gun.'

'Disarm them,' Batalji said, and the guards moved forward to take the pistols from Clive and Rosemary, as well as Yorcka, standing stricken in the inner doorway. 'A fine executioner you turned out to be,' Batalji chided his daughter.

Shallane pouted. 'He seduced Yorcka. The bitch. I want to hear her scream.'

'You will hear them all scream,' Batalji promised. 'But it will have to be handled differently, now.'

'What is our crime, Your Excellency?' Clive asked. 'Apart from the attempt to save our own lives?'

'Your crime is that of disobeying me and returning to Yakutsk two weeks early,' Batalji said. 'And of harming my daughter.'

'You once promised me I could do what I liked to Shallane,' Clive reminded him. 'I could very easily have killed her, you know. As I could have killed you, just now.'

'But you did neither. You are not a killer, Clive. That is your misfortune, and my fortune. Take them to Miss Leigh's old apartment, and four of you stay with them at all times.'

'You *are* going to kill them, Papa?' Shallane was anxious. 'And make them scream?'

'All in good time,' Batalji promised.

Two guards seized Clive's arms; two more stood beside Rosemary, and two more were dragging Yorcka forward. Clive looked at Mortana. She caught his gaze, and turned to her husband. 'Batalji, did you really order Stanton's execution?'

'Do not interfere in matters you do not understand, woman,' Batalji told her.

Mortana's shoulders sagged, and she sat down. One reed broken, Clive thought. It was necessary to clutch at straws. 'I think you should speak with your mother before you do anything foolish, Batalji.'

'Be careful I do not present her with your prick as a keepsake,' Batalji said.

They were not bound or ill-treated in any way, but there were four men inside the apartment with them, their weapons drawn, and one of them was at the side of each of the prisoners all of the time, preventing the women from having the least privacy, preventing them from having even a whispered conversation. Rosemary tried to talk to Clive with her eyes, but she was close to a breakdown, he knew; the events of the past twenty-four hours had been quite traumatic, and she was overburdened with fear for the baby. Yorcka just sat and stared into space, and drank vodka; she already counted herself dead.

'What is happening?' Selphine demanded, standing before her son, hands on hips. 'I am told Stanton is under arrest. For what crime?'

'I am trying to find out.'

Selphine snorted. 'You have arrested a man before he has committed a crime?'

'Mother, these are matters of which you do not understand. Stanton is determined to oppose my plans. That is a crime in itself.'

'You mean your invasion of China?'

'Stanton told you that? Then he is guilty of at least one crime, betraying state secrets.'

'How can he betray a state secret to me? Am I not the state?'

'Ha!' Batalji commented. 'And how many people have *you* told?'

'I have told no one. Do you not suppose I can keep a secret? Batalji, I wish your word that no harm will befall Stanton. I do not care what you think he has done, or who you have married him to, he is my man. I will not have him harmed.'

Batalji looked at the doorway, and Almani. 'Are the Khans summoned?'

Almani nodded. 'But Batalji . . . Khalim has hanged himself.'

'Khalim?' Batalji could not believe his ears. Selphine was equally shattered. Since the death of Baltomar Borjigin, so many years ago, if Batalji had been universally recognised as the Prince, Khalim had been equally revered as the Prince's father-in-law, and Selphine had always honoured him for taking care of her when her son had been taken away from her.

'His new wife, Nadehzda, was hanging beside him.' Almani bit her lip. 'Mortana does not know, as yet. Then there is Jagnuth . . .'

Batalji was stroking his chin, thoughtfully. 'I will tell Mortana.'

'And Jagnuth?'

'There will be time to tell Jagnuth. I think there is more to this than is first indicated. I must have a talk with Stanton.'

Selphine's head rose. 'What has Stanton to do with Khalim's death?'

'You should ask, Mother, what has Khalim's death to do with Stanton, or at least, with Stanton's arrest. There is something going on. My instincts tell me this. Something which I do not know about. Now it is time to find out.'

'Your own father-in-law? Khalim loved you like a son.'

'Khalim has a son, and a daughter, and grandchildren. And he is an old man. Old men fear for the future.' Batalji got up.

'Batalji!' Selphine's voice was sharp. 'You promised me that Stanton would not be harmed.'

Batalji looked at her. 'No, Mother,' he said. 'You asked me to promise that. But I did not.'

The doors to Rosemary's apartment opened, and the three people inside sat up; the baby was fast asleep. Batalji entered, accompanied by several men. 'Your accomplice is dead,' he said. 'Do you not regret this?'

'I don't know what you are talking about,' Clive said.

'There is no escape for you,' Batalji told him. 'Khalim has committed suicide. He did this upon learning of your arrest. Tell me what you planned.'

Clive tried to think. What would Mortana do now? What would she be allowed to do?

'Listen to me, Clive,' Batalji said. 'I will have the truth. But because we have been friends, because we have shared so much, because you have helped me in so many ways, I will be as generous to you as I may. I know now that you and Khalim plotted against me. You must die. But admit this, and tell me who else was in the plot, and your women . . .' he glanced at Rosemary and Yorcka, obviously including the guard in his assumption, 'and your child, will be kept in captivity until after the war against China has been won, then they will be released, and sent to the West. I give you my sacred word on this. Defy me, and I shall torture them to death before your eyes, beginning with Rosemary. Now, decide.'

The room was still. Then Rosemary spoke. 'Batalji, I beg of you . . .'

'Be quiet, woman,' Batalji told her.

Clive took a long breath. He could only play for time, and hope. 'Very well, Batalji, I admit I went to see Khalim. I told him of your plan to go to war with China, and that I believed it would bring destruction upon us all. Thus we decided to act, when I returned from my holiday, and after most of the troops had left Yakutsk.'

'You intended to kill me?'

'We intended to put you under restraint, and countermand your orders.'

'Ha! You are mad. Both of you. Who else was in the plot?'

'No one.'

'Do you take me for a fool? You and Khalim? You have no following. And Khalim . . .'

'The Yakuts worship Khalim.'

'You planned this with other people besides Khalim. Tell me their names.'

It was every man, or woman, for himself, now. The one person he must keep out of it was Jagnuth. 'I talked with Selphine,' Clive said.

Batalji grinned. 'Selphine has told me this. Who else?'

'Who else could there be?'

'There is my wife,' Batalji said.

'That would have been absurd. Mortana worships you.'

'The fact that she worships me does not mean she would not work against me, to save me, as she would see it, from myself. That is how a woman's mind works.'

'Mortana is not involved,' Clive said.

'Always the gentleman,' Batalji said. 'Very well.'

'May I ask what is to happen to me?' Clive asked.

'As you will have gathered, I had planned your death to be an accident, after Shallane had amused herself with you. But now that you have publicly returned to Yakutsk . . . you will have to be publicly condemned. I am summoning my associates to sit in judgement over you. They will condemn you, and you will be executed.'

'The world will condemn *you*.'

'By the time the world learns of it, Clive, it will not matter. I am done dealing with the world. Now the world must deal with me. With Genghis Khan!'

'This place is so full of rumours,' Denise complained, assuming her favourite lotus position in the centre of the bed. 'Is it true that you have arrested Clive? That he is to be put on trial for treason?'

Batalji stretched, lazily. Even after five years, he would rather lie in his bed watching Denise than do anything else. 'Yes, it is true. And do not bother to start telling me how much he has helped me, or how we were such friends, or even how you and he were such lovers, once upon a time. He is guilty of plotting to overthrow me, and that is all that matters.'

Denise considered him from under drooping eyelashes. 'I suppose he is going to be impaled.'

'Some such thing. I am going to let Shallane decide.'

She crawled up the bed and lay down beside him. 'When?'

'As soon as my generals are assembled. They are on their way now. It will happen tomorrow.'

'Will I be allowed to film the execution?'

Batalji scratched her glossy head. 'If you wish. But ... you mean you do not mind?'

'Why should I mind what you do to Clive Stanton?' Denise asked, snuggling closer yet.

Batalji left her before dawn, went to his office and summoned Almani. Almani arrived still rubbing sleep from his eyes. 'Are my generals assembled?' Batalji asked.

'Pirale, Sartine and Carowan are here,' Almani said. 'Dalnuth will arrive this morning, and so should Barone, together with Tensan and Dorgat. As you instructed me, I have not recalled Jagnuth.'

Batalji nodded. 'The situation has got worse. It seems that my mother and Mortana are involved.'

Almani frowned. 'I find that difficult to believe. If Stanton told you that, it is an effort to shift some of the responsibility from himself.'

'That is it,' Batalji said. 'He did *not* try to implicate them. In fact he denied that they knew anything about a plot. But he could not deny that he had spoken with them, and neither of them told me about it, until yesterday ... after he had been arrested.'

Almani scratched the nape of his neck. 'You cannot place your own mother and wife on trial before the generals, including their own sons and grandsons.'

'No,' Batalji said. 'But neither can I leave them here in Yakutsk to plot against me when I go off to war. Nor am I prepared to leave the execution of my wife and my mother to some underling who may well insult their bodies.'

'You cannot execute Mortana without including Jagnuth,' Almani said. 'Our Chief of Staff. He is an essential part of our campaign against China.'

'An essential part of the *first* strike,' Batalji said. 'He will know nothing of what has happened here until after that strike. Then I will take command myself.' He got up. 'Are you with me?'

Almani also stood up. 'Of course I am with you, Batalji.'

Batalji nodded. 'It will be done now. Then this morning Stanton will be tried, and this afternoon he will be executed.'

'Barone and his brothers . . .'

'Barone and his brothers will condemn their mother when they know she is guilty of treason. The fact that she will already be dead will prove her guilt.'

'But what of Shallane?'

'Shallane will also support me. She will rule in Mortana's stead.'

Almani, who was not a doting father and was sufficiently intelligent to have correctly interpreted Shallane's character, looked unhappy about that. But he would never go against Batalji's wishes.

They went to Selphine's apartment. The woman guard was half asleep, but she snapped to attention at the sight of the Khan. 'Allow no one to enter,' Batalji told her, opened the door, and stepped into the darkness, Almani at his heels. The air was heavy with the clouds of perfume with which Selphine habitually coated herself. Batalji switched on the lights, crossed the living room and opened the bedroom door. Here too he switched on the lights.

Selphine was sprawled across the bed, naked, half on her face, snoring faintly. Batalji stood by the bed, looked at his mother for some seconds, then sat beside her. Selphine rolled on to her back, stretched, and opened her eyes. 'Batalji?' She smiled. 'Do you know what day this is?'

'It is the fifth anniversary of the coup, Mother.'

'That is it exactly. The fifth anniversary. Ah, Batalji, we rode together, then, you and I.'

'Indeed we did, Mother,' Batalji said, and signalled Almani.

Almani came up to the bed, and Selphine noticed him for the first time. 'Almani?' She reached for the covers, and Batalji wrapped his fingers round her throat. She stared at him in consternation, and Almani caught her wrists and held them, while she writhed and kicked. But under the pressure of Batalji's immense strength, she was dead in seconds.

'Do you wish to kill yourself?' Rosemary asked. She lay beside Clive on the bed. They had just woken up. After a fitful night baby Clive was at last sleeping heavily next to them; Yorcka was in the other room. 'If you wished to do so,' Rosemary said, 'I would join you. With Clive.'

'No,' Clive said vehemently. 'Never. You must live, to go home, and tell the story.'

'Do you think Batalji will keep his word about that? When he has broken his word about everything else?' She gave a wry smile. 'And you are supposing there is going to be a world to go to, when this is finished.'

Clive sighed, and gazed at their guard, who sat just inside the door, his AK-92 across his knees, watching them. The guards were changed every four hours, and so were always alert. Presumably he would fire if attacked, but Clive had to suppose he was sufficiently expert not to need to kill, and to be left with a broken leg or arm would merely make matters worse. In any event, he did not wish to take the risk that Rosemary might indeed follow him. Besides . . . 'While there's life there's hope,' he said.

There was always hope. Jagnuth! If only he knew what Mortana really thought about things, and whether she had sent the message to her brother. But even failing her, he could not believe that Selphine would allow him to be killed.

'I love you,' Rosemary said.

He looked down at her. 'I love you.'

She smiled. 'We had a pretty rocky beginning, I guess. So, what do you think of your little French friend now? Oh, shit!'

Because suddenly they heard Denise's voice. 'I am to

photograph them, asshole,' Denise was informing the guards in the outer room. 'It is the Khan's wish.' The bedroom door opened. 'Bring the woman in here as well,' Denise instructed.

Rosemary and Clive both sat up, to watch Denise enter. She was fully dressed, in ski pants and blouse, and carried her huge camera case over her shoulder. Behind her, Yorcka was pushed into the room, half asleep. 'All right,' Denise told the two guards who would also have followed her. 'Get out. I am not going to photograph *you*.'

The men exchanged glances, but Denise's position was well known, and it was equally well known that she was a law unto herself. They left the room, closing the door.

'Your pound of flesh?' Clive asked.

Denise made a face. 'I don't know why I am doing this,' she said. 'I must need my head examined.' She opened her bag, and took out her folding tripod. 'Go over there,' she told Yorcka. Carefully she set up the tripod, and then locked on her camcorder. This she now switched on; it made a surprisingly loud whirr in the confined space, and now she added a tape of music as well. 'Must get the mood right,' she said. Rosemary held Clive's hand. She had never liked Denise; now he could feel the hate seeping out of her fingers into his.

'Right,' Denise said, and from the recesses of the bag drew an automatic pistol, to which a silencer had already been fitted. Before anyone in the room realised what she was doing, she had levelled the gun at the remaining guard. 'Drop your weapon.' The guard stared at her with his mouth open for several seconds. 'No one will hear the sound of a shot above the music,' Denise told him. The guard brought up his gun, compulsively and Denise squeezed the trigger. As she had said, the silenced shot made no impression on the music; the guard's body hitting the floor was a far louder thump. 'Wouldn't you like to have that gun, Clive?' she asked.

Clive leapt out of bed and picked up the machine-pistol. 'Do you know that is the first time I have ever shot anyone?' Denise asked. 'There are still three in the other room. And I am not much good with guns.' Her hand was shaking.

'Give it to Yorcka,' Clive said, and looked up at the closed-circuit television camera. He could only hope there was no one monitoring it, this early in the morning, but just to be sure he swung his gun butt against the glass and shattered the tube.

'I don't know how to thank you,' Rosemary said to Denise. 'Even if I don't quite understand.'

'Clive is my old buddy,' Denise explained. 'But don't thank me yet. Do you think you can get out of here, Clive?'

'Can you take us out the way we came in, Yorcka?'

'Yes. But where will we go?'

'If we can get to the airport . . .' Rosemary said.

'We will never make it,' Yorcka said gloomily.

'Not without help, I agree,' Clive said. 'But I have an idea. Where is Batalji?'

'He left me before dawn,' Denise said. 'He thought I was asleep. I don't know where he went.'

'There's a pity. Getting hold of him is our only hope. What about you?'

'If you intend to kidnap Batalji, I had better come too,' Denise said. 'He is the only reason I have stayed in this dump. Anyway, I suppose he'd be quite nasty when he found out I'd turned you loose.'

'That is probably the understatement of the century.'

'He was beginning to bore me, anyway,' Denise said. 'And he couldn't get me pregnant and make me a princess. What a shit.'

'Right,' Clive said. 'We leave together. But you'd better leave the guards outside to Yorcka and me.' He put his arm round her, hugged her against him. 'I'm grateful too, you know.'

Almani threw one of the long curtain cords over the wall bracket of the highest-mounted of the six television sets. Batalji lifted Selphine's body across the room to beneath the set, and tied one end of the cord round her neck. Then between them they heaved on the other end until Selphine's heels hung several inches clear of the floor. Batalji closed her eyes.

'She had her days of glory,' Almani said.

'So did we all,' Batalji agreed sombrely as he looked at his mother. 'But you and I have some days of glory to come, Almani.' He opened the door. 'Remember,' he told the guard. 'No one is to enter that apartment until I say so. The Princess is unwell, and needs rest.'

He led Almani along the corridor to Mortana's apartment. Here again he instructed the guards to permit no one to enter, then opened the door and went inside, Almani at his shoulder. Mortana was up and fully dressed, eating her breakfast and looking out of her window at the Palace grounds. 'Batalji!' her delight at his visit was evident. 'Look! The first snow.'

The flakes were drifting past the glass.

'Today is the anniversary of the coup,' Batalji said.

'I know. That is exciting. What has happened to Stanton?'

'Nothing at all, yet. Mortana, I must tell you that your father is dead.'

He was now standing beside her, Almani at his shoulder. Mortana looked up, from one to the other, frowning. 'Papa? But . . . he was not ill. He was very well when last I saw him.'

'He hanged himself. He was involved in the plot against me,' Batalji said. 'With Stanton, and my mother . . . and you. My mother has just hanged herself as well. It is an admission of guilt.'

Mortana caught her breath, and tried to rise, but Batalji had already seized her throat. Almani stood behind her and caught her arms. Mortana kicked, while her eyes bulged, but Batalji easily avoided the flailing feet, and kept on squeezing. Then he and Almani laid Mortana on her bed. The door behind them opened. Batalji swung round, his lips drawn back from his teeth. 'I gave orders . . .'

'I countermanded those orders, Papa.' Shallane stared at her mother's body.

'She betrayed me,' Batalji said.

'I know. With Stanton. Papa! Stanton is escaping. I was watching them through the camera. It was the Frenchwoman. She entered their bedroom with a gun, and held up the guard. Stanton took the guard's gun. I could not see any more, because they blacked out the camera. So I came to you.'

'Denise!' Batalji breathed, his voice a whisper of concentrated venom. 'They will hear her scream in Paris.'

'What do you want done?' Almani asked.

'Find them. They will try to use the secret passage to escape; Denise knows of it. Block the exit. Turn out every man and woman in the guard, and find them. But I want them alive.'

Almani saluted, and ran from the room.

Shallane was still looking at Mortana's body. 'Now you have no wife,' she said, softly. 'And soon, no mistress, either.'

Batalji rumpled her hair.

CHAPTER 16

Yakutsk, October 2005

The Mongol warlords assembled in the main dining room of the Presidential Palace, having obeyed the summons from all over the empire. Sartine had come from Moscow, Dalnuth from Kazakhstan, Pirale and Carowan from the army in the east, together with the three princes, Barone, Dorgat and Tensan. All Yakutsk was rife with rumour, and the princes and generals were as bewildered as anyone. They were even more bewildered when they found themselves facing Batalji and Shallane, seated side by side in the centre of the huge table. Almani was seated beside Shallane.

'My friends,' Batalji said. 'My sons. I have the gravest news. At this most important moment in the history of Yakutistan, indeed, of Russia, when we are about to take that giant step forward we have planned for so long, I have learned of a plot to betray me, to betray us.' He looked from face to face. 'This plot, sadly, involves members of my own family, as well as some of my most trusted associates. My father-in-law, who was deeply involved, has committed suicide. My mother, and my wife, also deeply involved, have also killed themselves. This is a grave trial to me, and I know also to you, my sons. But government must continue, and so must the Course. I have called you here today to sit in judgement upon our associate Clive Stanton, whom I took to my heart, whom indeed we all took to our hearts, and who has repaid our friendship and our trust by heading the conspiracy against us. With him on trial will be two women who I also have come to like and trust over the years, and who, like Stanton, have now attempted to stab me in the back. Be seated.' The generals and the princes sat at the table, on the same side as Batalji, so they could look out at the rest of the room. 'Have the prisoners brought in,' Batalji commanded.

Almani signalled the waiting guards, and a moment later Clive, Rosemary, Denise and Yorcka were marched into the room. Their wrists were bound behind their backs, their clothes were torn, and they were all suffering from various cuts and bruises sustained when they had been rearrested as they attempted to find Batalji. But the Khan had given orders that no more force than was necessary should be used; little Clive had been removed to the custody of a nurse.

The four prisoners were made to stand before the table. Yorcka's head drooped; she was shivering with fear. Rosemary's head also drooped, but she was thinking only of her son. Denise stared at her judges with utter contempt. Clive also met their gazes, even if the absence of Mortana, or more important, Selphine, left him feeling sick with despair.

'You are brought to judgement before the tribunal of the Khan,' Almani said. 'You are accused of many crimes. You will answer as required. Yorcka Dorgun, you are accused of having attacked the Princess Shallane, daughter of the Khan, of murdering her guards, and of aiding and abetting the man Stanton in carrying out his treacherous plans. What do you say in answer to this charge?'

'I am guilty,' Yorcka mumbled.

'What is the sentence of the court?' Batalji asked.

'That she suffer the slow death,' Shallane said, eyes gleaming. Yorcka gave a great shudder and fell to her knees.

'Rosemary Leigh,' Almani said. 'You are accused of assisting Stanton in his crimes, of taking part in the assault upon the Princess Shallane, and of opposing the Khan in every way. How do you answer these charges?'

'I am guilty,' Rosemary said, her voice quiet.

'What is the sentence of the court?' Batalji asked.

'That the prisoner be impaled,' Shallane said. A slow ripple seemed to seep through Rosemary's body.

'Denise l'Auberon,' Almani said, 'you are accused of having committed treason by attempting to assist the Khan's enemies to escape their just fates. How do you answer this charge?'

'Piss off,' Denise told him.

'That is a plea of guilty,' Batalji said. 'What is the sentence of the court?'

'That she have her breasts, her nose, her fingers and her toes cut off, her tongue torn out, and that she be thrown to the dogs,' Shallane announced. Denise tossed her head, contemptuously.

'Clive Stanton,' Almani said, 'you are accused of having plotted the Khan's downfall, and of having worked against him, and also of having assaulted the Princess Shallane, your wife, and most grievously ill-treated her. How do you answer this charge?'

'I plead guilty,' Clive said, 'to having attempted to save Yakutistan from committing suicide.'

'What is the sentence of the court?' Batalji asked.

'That he be torn apart by four horses,' Shallane said, smiling.

'Let the sentences be carried out immediately,' Batalji said. 'Commence with the Frenchwoman.'

'You shit!' Denise told him.

The prisoners were turned by their guards to face the doorway . . . and Jagnuth.

Behind the Chief of Staff there were a dozen armed men.

'What is the meaning of this?' Batalji demanded. 'You have abandoned your post!'

'I was summoned by my sister, Batalji,' Jagnuth said.

'How did you get in?' Almani asked.

'I walked in,' Jagnuth said. 'With my people. Am I not Chief of Staff?'

'Yes,' Batalji said. 'Well, your sister has committed suicide. And you are under arrest for deserting your post.'

'My sister has been murdered, Batalji. By you.' An uneasy ripple went round the table.

'When I arrived in Yakutsk,' Jagnuth said. 'I went straight to my sister's apartment. The guard refused me admittance, although he acknowledged that Mortana was inside. I therefore removed him and entered ... and found my sister hanging from a beam in her bedroom.'

There was another rustle around the room. Shallane stared at her uncle as if she would strike him down with her gaze. Batalji glanced from right to left. 'We know this,' he said. 'I visited Mortana myself, to place her under arrest, as I had discovered that she was implicated in the plot against me, and found that she had hanged herself rather than face me. I am very upset.'

'You are lying,' Jagnuth said. 'My sister sent for me to come to her, using a secret code word. Having done that, she would never have killed herself.'

The two men stared at each other, while Clive held his breath ... and wished his hands were free.

'You are admitting your own implication in the plot, Jagnuth,' Batalji said. 'This grieves me. Arrest him!' He spoke at large, and all his generals, as well as his sons, stood up. But they found themselves covered by the assault rifles of Jagnuth's escort, as did the other guards in the room. 'Are you mad?' Batalji demanded.

'It is you who are under arrest,' Jagnuth said. 'All of you. Release these prisoners.' One of his men cut away Clive's bonds, then attended to the women.

'Mad,' Batalji said again. 'This is my palace, Jagnuth. My city.' He flung out his arm. 'My people.'

'Throw down your arms,' Jagnuth commanded. 'I have with me my own regiment, the Anhusat regiment. The Palace is occupied.' To confirm his words, the reports of several shots echoed from beyond the door.

Barone uttered a yell of defiance and drew his pistol. His brothers and the generals followed his example, while Batalji, with a great heave, threw the table on its side to make a barricade. But Jagnuth and his men had already opened fire with their assault rifles, while Clive hurled Rosemary to the floor, in almost the same movement grappling with the nearest of Batalji's guards to obtain a weapon for himself.

The huge volume of fire lasted only a few seconds. When it was done the room was a shambles. Pirale lay sprawled across the table, his pistol drooping from his dead fingers. Sartine had been hit in the middle of the forehead, and lay on his back, arms outflung. Dalnuth was a crumpled mass beneath the table. Carowan was writhing on the floor with a bullet in his belly. Barone was dead, struck by several shots, his body a blood-seeping riddled corpse. Tensan had also died in the first exchange. Dorgat was unhurt, but now stood against the wall, panting with fear; he had dropped his weapon.

Four of the Palace guards were also dead; the other six had their hands in the air.

On Jagnuth's side, several men had been killed and more wounded. Jagnuth himself was unhurt, as were Clive and Rosemary and Denise, but Yorcka was on her knees, coughing blood. 'Oh, hell,' Clive muttered. Because there was still so much to be done: concealed by the table, Batalji had got through the inner doorway, together with Shallane and Almani.

Jagnuth and his men went forward to make sure all the Borjigins were dead. Dorgat cowered against the wall as he looked into the barrel of Jagnuth's gun. 'It is a blood feud now,' Jagnuth said, and squeezed the trigger.

Rosemary, kneeling beside the dying Yorcka, gasped, and raised her head. 'Little Clive!'

'Find him,' Clive snapped. 'Jagnuth . . .'

'Take four of my men,' Jagnuth said. 'Don't worry, they are

in control of the Palace.' Rosemary ran from the room, her escort behind her.

'We must get Batalji before he can rally support,' Clive said.

'He won't escape,' Jagnuth asserted.

'Do you know the secret ways?'

'Yes. All their exits are in the grounds, and my men control the grounds as well.'

'Yet Batalji must be found, as quickly as possible,' Clive insisted. 'If he *were* somehow to escape, and join the army...'

'I will come with you,' Denise said. 'Give me a moment to fetch my camcorder.'

Clive's brain was in a turmoil. Part of him wanted to follow Rosemary and make sure little Clive was all right; part of him was still unable to believe this was really happening; and part of him was calling him to Selphine, hanging in her bedroom, murdered by her own son.

But the dominant call was the finding of Batalji, the settling of this business. The saving of the world.

The Palace was in an uproar, with disarmed guards and domestics running in every direction. But Jagnuth had disposed his men well, and every important corridor or hallway was guarded by an armed squad. None of them had seen the Khan. 'He knows this palace better than anyone,' Clive said. 'He could hide in here for days.'

'Then we will burn it down around his ears,' Jagnuth declared.

Denise panted up to them, having regained her camera. 'He will wish to escape,' she said. 'There is another secret route, of which you know nothing. He had it built himself, for just such an eventuality. Then he killed the workmen. It is known only to Batalji and Selphine.' She smiled. 'And myself. Batalji showed it to me. It exits where four trees grow close together.'

'My men control the grounds,' Jagnuth said again.

'This exits beyond the walls,' Denise told him. 'In the park.'

They stared at her in consternation, then Jagnuth thumbed his radio. 'Bellain,' he snapped. 'Take a dozen men to the park.'

He nodded at the acknowledgement. 'Bellain is at the gate. He will get there in time.'

'We must be there,' Clive said.

'Of course. But the inner entrance must be held as well.' Jagnuth looked at Denise. 'You know it. Take some of my people and stand guard, in case Batalji attempts to return.'

Denise pouted. 'I'd rather come with you.'

'Listen,' Clive told her. 'Getting him is more important than photographing him, right now. Do it. And listen, is the passage lit?'

'Well, of course.'

'Then kill the lights. Leave him in the dark.'

She nodded, and went off, followed by a sergeant and four men. Clive and Jagnuth left the Palace and ran round the perimeter wall to the little wooded park which led down to the river. Now it was snowing quite heavily. 'Over there.' Jagnuth pointed to where several trees appeared to grow together. 'In the centre.'

'If he has got out already...' Clive said.

Jagnuth summoned his lieutenant. 'Has anyone passed through here?'

'No, General.'

Jagnuth nodded. 'As I thought. He is wounded. Or perhaps Shallane. They are travelling slowly.' He waved Bellain's men to left and right, then moved forward himself, Clive beside him.

Shallane! Clive thought. He had almost forgotten Shallane. But he had even more to settle with her than with her father – and he did not doubt that she was quite as dangerous as Batalji.

It was very cold. But a few minutes later there was movement in the trees. 'He must die, now,' Clive said.

Jagnuth's face was the picture of indecision. Batalji had killed his sister, and could be held responsible for the death of his father. And now he had killed Batalji's sons. But they had fought together for so many years. He stood up. 'Batalji!' he shouted. 'You are surrounded. Throw out your weapons and come out.' There was a single shot in reply, and Jagnuth fell backwards.

'Open fire!' Clive shouted. The assault rifles chattered. Bark and leaves and even small branches flew from the trees. Clive bent over Jagnuth. The Mongol chieftain was hit in the shoulder, and his face was twisting in pain, but he would survive.

'Bind me up,' he told his men. 'You must get them, Clive.'

Clive nodded. 'Cease firing,' he shouted. The sounds died away, and the snow drifted down. 'You cannot go back, Batalji.'

There was no response. 'You must finish it,' Jagnuth said.

Clive waved his men forward, and they converged on the trees. There were no shots, and Clive led them into the bushes, gazed at Almani, dead, shot through the heart. He had served his Khan to the last. Before them gaped the tunnel exit. Batalji had retreated into the darkness, like the wild beast he was. Clive gave a quick consideration to calling Denise to restore the lights, then decided against it. Controlling the darkness was to his advantage. 'Lieutenant,' he said. 'I need some powerful torches, and six volunteers.'

He made sure the exit was covered by a dozen men, and then sat with Jagnuth. 'You should go to hospital,' he said.

'I must be present at the end,' Jagnuth said. His wound had been bound up, and he seemed comfortable enough, although clearly he was in a great deal of pain.

The lieutenant returned with flashlights. Clive took one, armed himself with an AK-92 and several spare magazines, and cautiously descended the steps into the tunnel; although the lieutenant himself was at his back, with five other volunteers, he could not ask any of these men to go where he was not prepared to lead. But he was conscious less of fear than of the pounding of the adrenaline in his arteries. As Jagnuth had said, this had to be finished. And as he had known for so long without being prepared to accept it, his was the responsibility to end this mad career of which he had hoped so much.

He did not switch on the light, reached the foot of the steps.

'Line the walls,' he whispered, and himself stood against the damp stone, then extended his right arm, and sent a beam of light racing along the passageway. It stretched up to the first bend, perhaps thirty feet away, and drew no response. But anyone in there would know where they were. Clive doused the light, and moved forward, still against the wall, so that he would know where the bend was. He could hear the lieutenant breathing immediately behind him. Once round the corner, he sent another beam of light probing the darkness, and again found nothing, except... He waved his men forward, knelt, touched the still-wet blood on the floor of the tunnel. One of their quarry had been hit.

The bloodstains were more numerous as they advanced, but they had covered a good distance and were, Clive estimated, well within the Palace grounds again, before, as he sent his beam round yet another bend, he was answered by a single shot, which ricocheted from side to side of the passageway. He switched off the light, and waited, listening. But there was no sound, until he thought he could make out some stertorous breathing. 'Batalji!' he called. 'There is no way out. I will give you ten seconds to come to us, without your weapon, and with your hands in the air. If you do not, we shall blast you out of existence.'

Again there was a short silence. Then Shallane said, 'Why don't you come and get me, Stanton?'

'Shallane! Where is Batalji? Is he with you?'

'Come and find out, Stanton.'

Clive could feel the tension behind him. His men were aware that Batalji had to die, if only to preserve their own lives, but they also only knew that Shallane was a very beautiful fifteen-year-old girl, who was also a princess of the house of Borjigin. They knew nothing of the horror that was her mind, of the necessity that she should die even more than Batalji. The ten seconds was up. 'Will you follow me?' he asked the lieutenant. 'It is possible that Batalji is there.'

'And the Princess?'

'She has made her decision,' Clive said. 'Now!' He stepped

round the bend, and fired into the darkness, emptying his entire clip. Had no idea whether anyone was behind him, but only a single shot was returned. The noise of the firing reverberated for several seconds, while Clive dropped his empty magazine and reloaded.

A single word penetrated the silence: 'Bastard!'

He went forward, several feet, then switched on his light. Shallane lay in a pool of blood, half propped against the wall, her empty pistol drooping from her fingers. Her clothes were torn and slashed by the bullets, and she was still bleeding heavily. Clive was relieved that he had not hit her face. Her lip curled as she looked at him. 'You will scream when you die, Stanton.'

Clive knelt beside his wife. 'Where is your father?' Shallane stuck out her tongue at him. 'He abandoned you,' Clive said. 'Can you still love him?'

'I made him leave me,' Shallane said, her voice now hoarse. 'I was hit anyway. But Batalji . . . you will never get Batalji. He knows another way out . . . he knows.' Her voice faded.

Clive looked up, at the men standing around him. While he tried to think. Batalji must know he was finished. Yet he had left the daughter he adored . . . Even if there was another way out, unknown to Denise, he could only be thinking of revenge, of going out in a blaze of savage fury which would please his god of war, Pierroun.

Clive started to run, behind the beam of his torch.

Exhausted by the excitement of the past few days, Baby Clive was fast asleep, in the care of a Yakut nurse. But the nurse was in a state of panic, as Rosemary's apartment, to which the baby had been returned, had been invaded by Jagnuth's men. In the ensuing gun-battle, three of Batalji's people had been killed; their bodies were still lying on the floor when Rosemary reached them. 'I meant no harm, Miss Leigh,' the woman stammered. 'I was obeying orders.'

'I understand that,' Rosemary said. 'Now you may go.' The woman ran from the room. Rosemary had no great wish to remain there herself, with the corpses, but she wasn't sure where she could go, and at least Clive would know where to find her. In addition, little Clive needed changing, and now he was waking up, and fretting... 'Hush, dearest,' she said, as she bathed him, and tore strips from the bedclothes to make an impromptu nappy. 'Everything is going to be all right.'

How she wished she could believe that, as she listened to all the sounds of the Palace, the occasional gunshot, the tramp of feet, screams and shouts of command... She was far more in the midst of this revolution than of the previous one, five years ago. And yet, it was swirling around her, without actually touching her, at the moment. It was just a matter of Clive returning, to tell her that Batalji was dead... She heard a sudden explosion of fire outside the door of the apartment, hastily laid little Clive down, and stood up, watched the bedroom door swing open, and gazed at Batalji.

His uniform was bloodstained and he moved hesitantly, but he carried a machine-pistol, and his yataghan hung from his belt; obviously he had surprised Jagnuth's people guarding the door. Rosemary moved away from the bed, still concerned mainly with her baby, but at the same time aware of a consuming hatred for this man who had so dominated and humiliated her for the past five years. Yet she knew she had to remain very calm, if she was going to survive. And bring him down.

Batalji leaned against the door, staring at her, drawing slow breaths. 'You're wounded,' Rosemary said. 'You should sit down.'

'My mother sent you to me,' Batalji said. 'Five years ago, she sent you to me. She thought you would bring me good fortune.' He grinned, a wolf's snarl. 'I thought so too.'

She had to keep him talking, until help came, or until he collapsed from loss of blood. 'Did I not bring you fortune?' she asked. 'You ascended the heights. It is your own ambition that has brought you down.'

'Bitch!' he said. 'They have killed Shallane. Did you know that? They have killed Shallane.' Tears rolled down his cheeks, and he slumped into a chair, head drooping.

Rosemary held her breath. His eyes were closed, and his breathing was more stertorous yet. If she could just get hold of his gun . . . She moved forward, slowly and carefully, watching him. He did not move as she rounded the bed. The pistol was lightly held, almost released. But if he dropped it he might wake up. She stood in front of him, slowly stooping. She reached out her right hand, and whipped the gun from his fingers, losing her balance and falling over as she did so, striking the floor heavily.

Batalji's head reared up, and he leapt to his feet. Rosemary hastily propelled herself across the floor, and came to rest against the wall; she still held the pistol. Batalji blinked at her. 'You wish to fight *me*?' he asked. 'You know you cannot do that. You admitted that, years ago.'

Rosemary got to her feet, back still pressed against the wall, pistol now held in both hands. 'You do not even know how to fire that,' Batalji said, contemptuously. 'But I know how to use this.' He drew his yataghan with a rasp of steel. 'I carried this,' he said, proudly, 'five years ago today, when I led my men into this palace. I carried this when we entered Alma-Ata, and Kiev, and Moscow. I am going to carry this when I enter Beijing. But first, I must destroy my enemies. You are my enemy.'

He moved towards her with terrifying speed, the sword carving the air. Rosemary leapt to one side. 'No, Batalji!' she shouted. 'Drop the sword.' Batalji had hit the wall. Now he turned towards her. 'Drop the sword, Batalji,' Rosemary said again.

Batalji grinned. 'You are playing games,' he said. 'Well, I can play games. But *he* cannot play games.' He leapt at the bed and the baby, his arm swinging above his head.

Rosemary squeezed the trigger.

'He will have a state burial.' Jagnuth was swathed in bandages, but he sat at Batalji's desk.

'And then?' Clive asked.

'I shall order a demobilisation, and hope to control events.'

'If you do as I recommend,' Clive said. 'And have it put out that there was a palace coup, in which the Khan was killed, but that you, his brother-in-law, suppressed the revolution and will now take over the Government, it should work. Even with the army, it should work.'

Jagnuth nodded. 'I agree. But Clive, you realise your part in this is too well known. No one knows you sent for me, through my sister. But everyone knows you were arrested by the Khan, for treason. You cannot remain in Russia.'

Clive nodded. 'I and mine will just fade away.'

'There is an aircraft waiting. But . . . what will you do?'

Clive shrugged. 'Denise will go back to filming, I imagine. Rosemary is going to try to be a wife and mother. As soon as we can be married.'

'Carrying the mental burden of what she did?'

'I think it is something she had wanted to do for damn near five years.'

Jagnuth nodded, solemnly. 'He treated her very badly. And you?'

'I haven't had a great success at making history,' Clive said. 'So I think I'll try to pick up the threads where I let go of them five years ago, and stick to reporting it.'

He looked into the camera. To his right Threlfall was like a cat on hot bricks, and Georges and Henri were trying to calm him down.

The red light glowed.

'Good evening,' Clive said. 'This is Clive Stanton, speaking on behalf of the Anglo-French Television Network, reporting tonight on the remarkable events which took place in Yakutsk last week. No doubt you have all heard the official communiqué issued by the Russian Government. Now I bring you a first-hand report of those dramatic hours . . . because I was there!'

Little, Brown now offers an exciting range of quality titles by both established and new authors. All of the books in this series are available by faxing, or posting your order to:

Little, Brown and Company (UK) Limited,
Mail order,
P.O. Box 11,
Falmouth,
Cornwall,
TR10 9EN
Fax: 0326-376423

Payments can be made as follows: Cheque, postal order (payable to Little, Brown Cash Sales) or by credit cards, Visa/Access/Mastercard. Do not send cash or currency. U.K. customers and B.F.P.O.; Allow £1.00 for postage and packing for the first book, plus 50p for the second book, plus 30p for each additional book up to a maximum charge of £3.00 (7 books plus). U.K. orders over £75 free postage and packing.

Overseas customers including Ireland, please allow £2.00 for postage and packing for the first book, plus £1.00 for the second book, plus 50p for each additional book.

NAME (Block Letters) ....
ADDRESS ....
....
....

☐ I enclose my remittance for ....

☐ I wish to pay by Visa/Access/Mastercard

Number ☐☐☐☐☐☐☐☐☐☐☐☐☐☐☐☐

Card Expiry Date ☐☐☐☐